DIRECT ACTION

DIRECT ACTION

AN SAS THRILLER

By Johnny "Two Combs" Howard

McBooks
Press
Guilford, Connecticut

An imprint of Globe Pequot, the trade division of
The Rowman & Littlefield Publishing Group, Inc.
4501 Forbes Blvd., Ste. 200
Lanham, MD 20706
www.rowman.com

Distributed by NATIONAL BOOK NETWORK

British Library Cataloguing in Publication Information available

Library of Congress Cataloging-in-Publication

Names: Howard, Johnny, author.
Title: Direct action : an SAS thriller / Johnny "Two Combs" Howard.
Description: Guilford, Connecticut : McBooks, [2022] | Summary: "When a
    US Embassy in South-East Asia is bombed by followers of terrorist Osama
    bin Laden, the US and UK decide it is time to act against the terrorist
    leader by striking at his stronghold in Afghanistan"— Provided by
    publisher.
Identifiers: LCCN 2022001943 (print) | LCCN 2022001944 (ebook) | ISBN
    9781493066353 (paperback ; alk. paper) | ISBN 9781493069033 (ebook)
Subjects: LCSH: War on Terrorism, 2001-2009—Fiction. | Bin Laden, Osama,
    1957-2011--Fiction. | LCGFT: War fiction. | Thrillers (Fiction). | Novels.
Classification: LCC PS3608.O9244 D57 2022 (print) | LCC PS3608.O9244
    (ebook) | DDC 813/.6--dc23/eng/20220114
LC record available at https://lccn.loc.gov/2022001943
LC ebook record available at https://lccn.loc.gov/2022001944

∞™ The paper used in this publication meets the minimum requirements of
American National Standard for Information Sciences—Permanence of Paper
for Printed Library Materials, ANSI/NISO Z39.48-1992.

Yang Xiao Yan

'Wo Ai Ni Zhi Dao Yong Yuan'

ACKNOWLEDGEMENTS

During my research for this book, I received help from several experts in their particular fields. In particular, I should like to thank Ranger Roach, Evan Pilling, Jerry the Blade, Mike Cox, Gene Austin, and Harry Sprague, the crazy American pilot.

A special thank you also to Dondeal who made this and all my books possible.

PROLOGUE

One of the very necessary parts of surveillance is that you quickly establish a pattern relating to those under observation. This gives the watchers a template to work on, one that highlights anything out of the ordinary. People, even terrorists have habits. They get up at certain times and go to bed likewise. They eat and talk, tell stories and air their worries. The very good ones never mention operations, nor use a name that can be attached either to anyone present or a member of their organization.

These guys had been exemplary. Their talk was all surface and no depth, so that the surveillance teams wondered if they knew they were being watched. They'd learned from past mistakes, taking up residence in an under-populated part of the United States close to an escape route on the Canadian border, a seemingly harmless group of co-religionists seeking a retreat from the mayhem of modern city life. The penetrating early February cold made the job of the FBI a misery. Icy cold when it wasn't actually snowing, the frequency of the latter made the job of planting listening devices sensitive enough to pick up the terrorist voices close to a nightmare. Sound had been successful, video less so, due to the need to get so close that tracks in the snow threatened to compromise the whole operation.

Eavesdropping produced good results. Muslims, they prayed rigorously five times each day, but discreetly, indoors, in a line on their mats, heads bent towards Mecca. The pair who went shopping locally for food spoke good English and dressed in western style. There were none of the halting phrases or flowing garments that would draw attention to them here in this backwoods setting. Just big puffa jackets with hoods.

The group had been targeted through electronic surveillance. The National Security Agency knew that Osama bin Laden used Internet connections to talk to his followers. With coded messages and constant

1

name changes, plus the use of non-active sympathizers to forward e-mails, they were a hard group to track. Internationally it was almost impossible; internally, with millions of e-mail messages flashing across the net on a daily basis, it still took an opposition mistake to pick out the ones that mattered.

Three half understood words on a regular sweep had been enough to alert the computers scanning the airwaves. With the assistance of the Internet server a domain address was isolated, its messages automatically passed to the NSA who got a fix on them, just before they changed both their telephone number and e-mail address. Nothing concrete, just enough to put the FBI on their tail. When the quartet left Albany and headed north, they were under routine surveillance.

The camera over the entry channel to the US at the Canadian border had picked up Ismail Luchayadev, though the time it took to identify him through computer screening meant that he nearly got clear. The alarm bells that mug shot set off rang all the way to Washington DC. The face of every biochemist or nuclear physicist who'd ever worked for the Soviet Union was on a computer file, bought from a senior KGB official in a secret, very lucrative deal.

That's when the FBI had a 'blue on blue', two friendly forces running smack into each other, each unaware of the other's presence. One group was tailing the Islamic militant cell going north, a second the Chechen biochemist on his way south. When Luchayadev met bin Laden's cell at a roadside diner the confusion was total, and very nearly terminal to both operations. Luck had sorted out the mess and had brought the surveillance teams here to the woods north of Lake Champlain.

They'd watched their quarry for two weeks now, followed them on their trips out of state, never more than two at a time, noting the purchase of certain chemicals plus the equipment necessary to set up a laboratory. The cell kept their communications to one single-word e-mail every day, never the same word, never the same destination, always the same time, midnight Eastern Standard Time.

The decision to go in had been discussed and put back several times, it seemed to those in charge worthwhile to wait in case a bigger haul could be caught in the net. Someone had to be running these guys. Who was he and where was he located? There might be another cell in operation whose job it was to take the produce of this farmhouse and deploy it. But as the list of chemical purchases grew pressure was applied from a government simply too terrified of what could happen to care about a clean sweep. The order came down for the assault to go ahead in the early hours of the morning.

'Confirm that all your seals are airtight and that no one has any leaks.'

Everyone did so. The weapons had already been fully checked: the shotgun to blast off the front-door hinges, the stun grenades that would incapacitate those inside, and the hand held firearms that would take them down if the stuns didn't work. The assault had been rehearsed time and again, the FBI agents using the original house plans and the voice intercepts to tell them the layout of the rooms, as well as the probable location of each member of the five-man cell.

The chemical alarm indicators went off as soon as the lead team went through the front door. Noise and smoke from gun blast and grenades slowed down the action. But as that cleared the panicky commands to evac could be heard over the comms. Through the minicams their agents were wearing, those overseeing the op could see the contorted faces of the terrorists, their racked faces twisted into strange shapes by the poison they were inhaling.

The biochemists found the fractured flask beside Ismail Luchayadev's body while their armed FBI colleagues were still in their suits. The first thing the FBI did was to seal the Chechen's glass flask inside a larger one of their own so they could examine safely the fracture which had allowed enough of the deadly VX gas to escape. The instant the assault was over the emergency mobile decontamination unit was called forward. The agents were dealt with as a priority then the teams moved on to decontaminate the whole area.

Before that happened the news came through about Jakarta and Lagos.

John 'JK' Kowalski loved being a Marine Security Guard, especially on a foreign-service assignment. Other guys in the corps might hanker after promotion, or prefer being nose to nose with the Cubans at

3

Guantanamo. They might sneer at some guy on an Embassy guard detail as having taken it soft. The schmucks didn't know what they were missing, especially on a posting like Indonesia. In Jakarta the beer was cheap, the dope first rate and the broads – well they weren't broads, they were delicate, fragrant women like the dark-skinned kitten curled up on the bed, girls who really knew how to take care of a guy. And the real plus was twofold: the sheer number of them, and the dream they had of catching and marrying someone like him – a tall, blond, good-looking hunk of raw Chicago male – and going Stateside.

JK was running a book on how many girls he could screw on his two-year assignment. Sure, he could never get it into the *Guinness Book of Records*, but he had a T-shirt with the motto above the Stars and Stripes that told anyone who wanted to know that 'JK screws for America'. He also had a calendar on the wall behind his bed that had a lot of days with one notch, and quite a few with more than one. The only blank days were those when he was on duty, either on the guard detail, or as a sentry, in dress blues, standing as a symbol of the might of his country on the steps of the embassy. And he was due on at six, which was very close to now.

'Come on, Kevin,' he barked into the phone. 'A couple of hours.'

'That's what you said last time,' Kevin replied, trying to sound angry, and failing. 'It ended up being four.'

'Hey, man, there were two broads. I needed time to recover to do the job. I have the reputation of the nation, man.'

'Shit, man, you are diseased. In the head. Do you know that?'

Kevin Imlach envied Kowalski. He was everything that he wanted to be but couldn't. A native of Alexandria Virginia, Kevin had got married at eighteen, and had his wife and two kids along on his posting. Sure the married quarters were nice, so were the neighbours, US personnel from all three services either attached to the embassy or part of the various military training units that kept the Indonesian army and airforce looking respectable. The schools were good, the weather pretty fine and the PX stocked everything a guy abroad could want to make him feel at home.

Only he didn't want to feel at home. Kevin Imlach wanted to be out there with the other jocks giving it to the local scene; smoking dope, snorting coke and taking on the youngest pussy he could find, in any number that cared to throw themselves his way. He wanted to do it, instead of listening to JK tell him how he did it. He wanted to live like he was in another country, not a soap opera part of his own.

'If that's JK, Kevin,' yelled Marge, his wife, 'you tell him to go to hell.'

'Honey, where do you think he's calling from. The heat's coming through the phone.'

'I'd have to be talking through my cock, ol' buddy,' said JK, safe in the knowledge that Marge couldn't hear him. The girl, whose name he was struggling to remember, had uncurled herself and leant towards him. JK, without force, entwined her black silky hair and pulled her head towards his crotch, his erection almost immediate as he saw her mouth open. 'Kevin, you just have to do this, man. Two hours and I'll be there, to take over and you can have off any shift you want.'

'You'll have to buy Marge a big present this time,' Kevin replied, smiling at a wife who was glaring at him. 'If I cover for you she's going to have to go shopping on her own.'

'I'll give her my charge card.' JK gasped. 'Now just say you'll do it.'

'Last time, OK?'

JK groaned. 'Last time, ol' buddy. Two hours max, I promise.'

'Shit, shit, shit!'

JK could see the embassy building, square and imposing in a landscape dotted with new high rise office blocks. His problem, apart from the time, was a solid block of traffic in front of him; Jakarta going to work, which to JK was figuring out a way to bilk Uncle Sam of development dollars.

'Hell you bastards,' JK yelled, hitting the horn. 'I'd like to get you cunts to a boot camp.'

Impassive faces stared back at this blue clad lunatic, a man stupid enough to have his window open in an air conditioned Cherokee, a man who had arms and expletives to spare, just to try and change what could not be changed, pushing through the traffic, horn blaring. JK was worried about Kevin, while his stand in was worried about Marge. JK's two hours were already a half-hour over, and he'd sworn to be back home. Standing rigid, as a sentry must, does not stop you moving your eyes.

Kevin Imlach saw JK's Cherokee almost barging its way through the traffic, which caused him to smile and curse at the same time. He also saw the truck that suddenly pulled out of the four-lane stream and headed for the concrete bollards, set at each side of the guard post at the entrance, designed to stop unauthorized entry. Two seconds were enough to turn the ceremonial weapon into what it was, an M-16, enough to see that the front fender was a piece of solid steel.

The bollards weren't thick enough. They were too tall and too thin, more decorative than effective, a fact attested to by everybody who worked in the building, not least the Regional Security Officer who had cabled Washington about a defensive deficit that the Security Assessment Team had chosen to pass as sufficient. They crumbled in front of that steel fender. Kevin Imlach was on one knee, firing off, in controlled regulation fashion, one and two shot bursts aimed right at the truck driver. He switched to the tyres as soon as he saw them bounce off the toughened glass windscreen.

JK had seen the truck as well, and had put his Cherokee off the road on to the grass lawn that fronted the embassy building. He was yelling his head off screaming words his friends couldn't hear as the truck slammed into the side of the Embassy. The flash was immediate, a blinding orange light that made JK cover his eyes. The blast almost stopped his Cherokee dead. He dropped his arm enough to see the front entrance of the embassy disintegrate, right at the point at which he should have been standing. In the midst of the cloud of dust that followed, the white marine cap that was all that remained of his friend and stand-in floated high above the billowing mass.

Then it started to come down on his jeep, eighty per cent of the place he was tasked to protect, lumps of concrete mixed with glass, metal and body parts, down on to a weeping US marine, who was sobbing sorry over and over again.

CHAPTER ONE

Time differences, just two hours between London and Lagos, at least meant that the British Prime Minister was informed of the Valentine's Day explosions at 10 a.m., during his normal waking hours. Not so the US President. When the bomb went off in Jakarta, blasting apart the US Embassy, it was 5 a.m., and he was in bed. He had to be woken from a deep sleep to be told the bad news.

Then the report came in telling him what they'd found at Lake Champlain. That too pointed to the likely involvement of America's number one international enemy, the Muslim terrorist Osama bin Laden. By the time he made the White House briefing room, at 7 a.m., all the members of the National Security Council were present and briefed. The live broadcast from CNN in Jakarta, showing the huge damage, was killed off as he entered.

'Good morning ladies and gentlemen,' he said, just before he sat down. 'This is, indeed, a sad day.'

It was. But for those round that table it was a sadness tinged with a touch of relief. Bombs striking at embassy personnel were awful, shattering lives for victims and relatives alike. In the past Washington had been guilty of ignoring warnings from those on the ground that they were vulnerable, a situation which that morning's events proved was still not resolved. It was not a day for showing a palpable sense of deliverance. Yet that very feeling existed. The one thing they all feared most hadn't happened. No weapon of mass destruction had been employed on US soil.

'What are the latest casualty figures from the embassy bomb?'

It was the National Security Advisor, Norland Jensen, who replied. White-haired, with pale blue eyes and translucent skin, he was the Chief Executive's right hand man in a crisis, something be rarely let the others at the table forget. Right now he cut across the State

Department, providing a response that should really have come from them.

'Over fifty dead already, Mister President, thirty of them our own people, but they fear at least thirty more buried in the rubble.'

'Lagos?'

'Nine confirmed, only two of them British nationals. The rest are local and unconnected to the legation.'

'They've been lucky,' the President mused.

'On balance, sir, so have we. I don't wish to minimize the loss, but without prompt action on our own soil we could have been dealing with a national emergency.'

Those words came from the Director of the FBI. He was eager to concentrate on the success at Lake Champlain, rather than the failure of the security measures in Jakarta.

The US Government had tried many things to prevent what had happened at the lake: bombing raids or chemical plants even in countries considered neutral; threats, arrests, comprehensive surveillance operations, some of questionable legality. But the threat persisted. That one lone bomber, armed only with a couple of innocent looking canisters, could get through with a weapon that would kill thousands.

'Have we talked to the Afghans?' the President asked.

'Yes, sir,' Jensen replied, again stealing the limelight from State. 'We have, as you requested, told them to meet us for talks.'

'Firmly, I trust.'

'The message stated in unequivocal terms that a refusal to do so would be seen as an act of aggression every bit as serious as bin Laden's bombs.'

'Good.'

The latest military intelligence briefing was in a folder on the table in front of his chair, and no one spoke as the President leafed through it. Legally trained, he had a very sharp mind and the lawyer's ability to rapidly absorb the main points of a case. The notes listed all the areas that could be designated as targets – places considered vulnerable, set alongside the names and organizations, world wide, that were being kept under close observation. The list was lengthy, and the explosions showed the extent of bin Laden's reach – that he had evaded the entire might of the western world's intelligence community, and got through with two massive bombs made of everyday fertilizer.

The folder also included a map showing the facilities that the Muslim terrorist had in his home base of Afghanistan: the camps outside Kabul, already subjected to an attack by cruise missiles; the new trio just outside Kandahar intended to replace them, with the Muslim leader's own private compound close by, inside the airport complex. There was the house in Jalalabad, as well as others, half a dozen in total, dotted around the country.

The last one, in the mountains to the north-west of Kandahar, near a lake and village called Zu ol Faqar, was the most interesting. Recently discovered, it consisted of two buildings that the intelligence watchers had concluded might be important. For what it was supposed to be the level of protection was excessive, and the mere fact that Osama bin Laden was a frequent visitor made it something to focus on. The man had been the objective at Kabul, and was still target number one.

'This Zu ol Faqar looks interesting,' said the President; words which had everybody at the table, except the Director of the CIA, leafing frantically through their briefing papers.

What they saw was a photograph of a ruined sandstone castle, plus the information that it purported to be a religious school. There was a second shot of a flat-topped one-storey building surrounded by trees. An attached memo pointed out that US satellites were, for obvious reasons, routed over Kandahar. Zu ol Faqar, over fifty miles away, close to a lake and with an elevated position in the mountains was at the edge of their range. The location also had the kind of microclimate that makes satellite intelligence difficult; frequent cloud cover with mist morning and evening.

But ground observation had been excellent, and the report they were reading had enough in it to have the whole table nodding at their boss's next words.

'If bin Laden is a visitor maybe as often as once or twice each week, that alone elevates Zu ol Faqar to a target of primary importance.'

Getting bin Laden had been an American policy objective ever since the first bomb. But it wasn't easy. Snatch raids had been planned, rehearsed and then scrapped. In Kabul he'd been surrounded by thousands of fighters, the only option a cruise missile attack launched more in hope than in any certainty that he would be a victim. That hail of Tomahawks had caused him to re-deploy hastily to Kandahar, a much more difficult facility to attack given its geographical location. The man knew he was a target so moved continually never, it was rumoured, spending two nights in the same bed.

After several minutes of further reading, the President put the report down. Invited to speak in turn, each member, privy to the same information that their boss had just studied, voiced their opinion. There was a familiar ring to the words; all had been here before, and most, though not all, were in favour of the strongest response. And each speaker was acutely aware of the limitations on what they could achieve, having hit bin Laden once and seen him survive. But all they could offer was advice. When it came to a decision the President was on his own.

The President listened, nodding at whoever was speaking, before adding his own conclusions. 'The options do now at least include the possibility of a ground assault. That stands a better chance of success than another air bombardment.'

The Secretary of Defense spoke again. 'I'm sure, sir, you are aware of the risks, even though the preliminary nature of the brief you have before you tends to cloud that aspect somewhat.'

'I am,' he replied. 'But it strikes me also that Lake Champlain is very significant. We must strike, and fast. Added to that the Lagos truck bomb alters the picture somewhat, guys. The US is no longer the sole target.'

'All it means, sir,' said Jensen, 'is that bin Laden has broadened his target base, not surprising after he extended the *fatwa* against us to include the United Kingdom. It does little to change the mindset we agreed on after the last outrage. Should we decide to strike we must do so with the utmost speed. Seeking to broaden the base of such an operation would not assist that.'

'Allow me to disagree.'

That produced the odd smile. The courtesy, from the incumbent, was common. It was also unnecessary. The President could do what he liked; yell, curse and scatter insults if he so chose. The right went with the office.

'Whatever we do, and I am minded to do a great deal on this occasion, opens the United States up to a high degree of international opprobrium.' A hand was raised to kill off the murmur of anger. 'It might not be justified, indeed we know it is not. But that's, unfortunately, the world we live in, folks. Even faced with the awful possibility that he might employ weapons of mass destruction which might even be targeted at their own citizens, most of our friends in the world fail to support us. It seems, faced with this, we have only one reliable ally.'

As he was speaking, the President looked at each face, trying to see if they'd got the point. US operations had always been hamstrung by the possibility of body bags coming home to the waiting TV cameras instead of live soldiers. It was a political leg iron that had hampered every occupant of the Oval Office since Vietnam. The Secretary of Defense was quite right to point out that what was being proposed could bring that very image into every US citizen's home.

But if the operation wasn't all-American, it not only halved the potential casualty list, it minimized vastly the opprobrium that could fall on a President's head. The taking of casualties, if the cost was shared with another country, an old and trusted ally, would make Americans proud instead of angry. Politically it was a master stroke.

'You wish to involve the British in whatever action we decide upon?' asked the NSA, proving that he at least was on the case.

'I wish to consult. I think it would be wise to put a call through to London.'

That took time, since the Prime Minister was not a man to be found sitting doing nothing. Meanwhile the President made contact with the Joint Special Operations Command to establish quite clearly that the notion he'd formed from reading the intelligence briefing was possible, and to secure from his military advisors what it was he needed to ask for.

JSOC, based at Fort Bragg, had convened at the same time as the men in the White House briefing room, ready to provide any military advice requested by the President. Comprising officers from all three services,

Army Intelligence, Delta Force and Navy Seals, it was formed as a direct result of the Desert One phase of Operation Rice Bowl.

That operation, to rescue American Embassy hostages held in Tehran by the late Ayatollah Khomeini, had gone badly wrong. A subsequent inquiry laid the blame fairly and squarely on two key elements: the insistence from the Joint Chiefs that all three services participate, combined with the *ad hoc* command structure, hurriedly put together to direct a complex set of military components. The rivalries and crossed lines of authority had led to a serious loss of life, as well as an embarrassing set of news stories which had described what had gone wrong without ever explaining why.

In the end it looked like an operation dogged by misfortune from the outset. Interference from the then President, seeing to put constraints on the mission, didn't help. But simple things, like helicopters prepared by navy mechanics who had no notion of how to ready them for a desert battle counted for just as much. Precious and very necessary assets were damaged by a sandstorm, rendering them ineffective. A final crash between a C-130 and a helicopter, a case of pilot inexperience that cost eight lives, caused the mission commander to abort the operation. The lesson learned was that for Special Operations everything had to come under one roof. So JSOC came into being, charged with overseeing any task that fell outside the normal US military role.

US forces had been waiting for a long time to prove that they could mount a major assault far from their home bases, one that would wipe the fiasco of the Rice Bowl op from the collective memory of the American public. Panama had been a plus, Grenada less so. They'd rehearsed snatch after snatch using small mobile teams, only to see them embargoed due to the risk of casualties. Could the mountains of Afghanistan provide them with what they so desperately wanted?

The first requirement for JSOC, should they be tasked to do any such job, would be to carry out a full mission analysis. That meant looking at all the available options and coming up with a plan that would achieve the operational objectives. Kandahar and Kabul and half a dozen other locations were already on file, though the first two were not considered viable due to the number of troops required.

The JSOC Target Board had been hard at work following the preliminary assessment on Zu ol Faqar. It was their job to identify and prioritize targets, to develop initial mission statements and mission concepts and to prepare a Mission Tasking Packet. That had to include a clear recognition of sensitivity and oversight requirements. Put simply, they had to look not only at an operation but also at the consequences.

Such Mission Tasking Packets were prepared for every foreseeable scenario and this operation was no different. As soon as the site had been identified as a potential target, the board had begun its work. Within days, the troops and equipment needed as well as the outline orders to move them, were on file. A rehearsal schedule was raised so that troops could be readied for that particular battle scenario. This sort of training went on all the time; the Target Board's efforts meant that, for the men involved, it had a hard and up to date edge to it.

But no situation is static, and no responsible commander would send troops into action without an up to the minute examination of all the factors pertaining to the operation. The most telling change in what was outlined as a solely US operation came with the President's call, alerting JSOC of his own feelings regarding possible targets, as well as his intention to request assistance from London.

CHAPTER TWO

'We are of one mind about the Kabul and Kandahar camps, Mister President. In that, nothing has changed. The troops and equipment required would render it more of a complete invasion than a surgical strike. We'd have to attack those sites in battalion strength.'

The speaker was the commander of JSOC, Brigadier-General Lucius B. Morton. The military part of the briefing the President had read on Zu ol Faqar he had compiled, so his agreement on that was automatic.

'But Zu ol Faqar is different. More isolated and with fewer of the enemy to contend with. There is also no indication of a camp follower element; wives, children and the like, which removes collateral casualties, a major obstacle to any attack. And it is my opinion that having the Brits along would not materially alter that scenario, sir.'

An ex-Delta Force CO, Morton was young for his rank, tanned and fit with hard blue eyes that rarely blinked. A man who had risen fast through a combination of ability and good connections, he was also an astute player of the political game, able to read the direction a conversation was going before it got there. He was no 'yes man', but he'd perfected the art of resisting an idea from a superior without in any way riling the person putting the proposal. Not that he was in that frame of mind now. Morton meant what he'd said.

Colonel John Franklin spoke next, taking the opposite view. That was his prerogative as the present commander of Delta Force, and no President asking for advice wants anything other than honest opinion. But Franklin had the reputation of being a tact-free zone, and as usual he managed not only to miss the point, but act in a more bellicose manner than was absolutely necessary.

'My boys would be exceedingly unhappy to be stood down, sir, especially in order that another force may be tasked to do what they see as their job. And might I add, they are accustomed to working together. We have, in part and very recently, put in place a training schedule for such a mission, which is not the case with an SAS squadron.'

'General?' the President asked.

'We have had a programme of joint training with the Brits for many years, Mister President,' said Morton. 'And I know from my own experience that it works better than OK, though I would have to concede that this particular target was confined in the original outline to Delta. That however, since they have yet to commence battle rehearsals, is easily rectifiable.'

Franklin responded again, his voice full of pique. Clearly he felt that Morton should be supporting him more fully, not fence-sitting.

'There are major equipment level differences between the two forces, both in comms and weaponry. We are up to speed on those, sir and that I think is going to be vital. The SAS are not.'

Morton sighed. Franklin was being stupid, seeing the whole scenario from the inside. If the operation went ahead, news of what happened and who was involved would leak out in the future. He was worrying about the effect on the morale of his men, which could be said to be admirable, if short sighted. Sure they'd be unhappy, especially having trained month in month out on snatch ops only to see them killed off.

But Franklin was ignoring the bigger picture, the one his Commander-in-Chief was concerned with: how zapping camps inside a foreign, sovereign state would look to the outside world. It would be big bad Uncle Sam again, throwing his weight around like a bully. Regardless of what success Delta achieved they would be vilified, even by some of their fellow citizens. An operation like this would result in a lot of spilt blood. But make it international and it might be possible to make it look like sensible world policing.

There wasn't a civilized country in the world now that failed to understand the dangers of international terrorism. If anything, most of them had woken up to that before the President's fellow-Americans. Oklahoma and the World Trade Center had concentrated minds in a big way. But, regardless of their real thinking, certain countries would use the United Nations to distance themselves from a purely American strike, even if it was against a person they actively feared. National interest would take precedence over everything. Involving the Special Air Service Regiment would stifle at least a portion of that.

And it was axiomatic that if the President put forward that kind of question, it wasn't speculative; he'd already thought it through. The only thing that would shift him from his present conclusion would be a strong and unanimous opinion against, based on purely military factors, which was not going to happen. Not for the first time, Morton wondered if Franklin had reached the pinnacle of his military career. As a field commander he was excellent, but he lacked the touch, the ability to view the world from a non-military standpoint that was a prerequisite of a move to higher command.

'The SAS train just as hard as your boys, John, and I wouldn't mind a small bet that somewhere in their files there's an action they rehearsed not too dissimilar to the one being proposed. I've known that to happen before.'

Morton's voice was deliberately pleasant, trying to give Franklin a way out. He was also seeking to remind him of the long and successful association the two forces had enjoyed, something Franklin himself had experienced on more than one occasion.

'And those guys are pretty good. You and I should know. We worked alongside them during Desert Storm. In fact, they were operational long before us and briefed our teams on everything they'd learned. Between us we took out a whole lot of Scuds.'

'I am aware of that, sir. I personally have nothing but praise for the Brits when it comes to Special Forces operations. But they are, in technology terms, a few years behind us. And by employing two separate forces we risk all the problems of divided command structures. I need hardly remind you, Mister President, what that can lead to. Operation Rice Bowl was destroyed by that very thing: oversight by non-military thinking and people who had no real knowledge of the task or how to pursue it, serving alongside those who did. This committee was brought into being to prevent a repetition of such an event.'

The non-military thinking jibe was particularly offensive to the man asking the questions. But the President didn't slap him down and remind him who was the boss, which was what Morton would have done. That caused the JSOC commander to speculate that he would no more make a politician than Franklin would make a general. The President's voice was as even as ever, with no hint of rebuke, yet it was in there for anyone listening.

'I'm sure you are aware, Colonel, that I have looked at that aspect. And I have come to you for military advice, speaking as I am from a room full of good people who can assess the political fallout. They agree with the position I have outlined.'

'Sir,' Franklin insisted. 'This is going to be a difficult job to see through and it is not without risk.'

'I know that, Colonel.'

'It is my contention that we stand to lose more than we will gain by a joint operation. I will be tasked to put my men in a battle, which is a responsibility I accept as their ground commander.'

'And it is one I accept as their Commander-in-Chief.'

Morton cut in, to stop Franklin from being a complete asshole. The man at the top must know that a serious loss of life was a real possibility. There was no need for the officer who commanded the soldiers to say so.

'I'd like to add one major factor, sir. You have looked at the targets, as well as the area they cover. I'm sure you have observed that there will be, tactically, no divided command. Colonel Franklin would have to assign two squadrons to the task, each one acting independently of the other, though offering mutual support.'

'Under my command,' Franklin insisted.

Morton finally realized what was bugging Franklin, and the thought, selfish and career enhancing, didn't please him. Aware that the President was still with them, his voice, when he spoke, was severe enough to make the rigid Delta Force officer sit up just that little bit straighter in his chair.

'You will command it as part of JSOC, Colonel. We will collectively oversee the operation. The tactical command does not lie with us. The Air Force Special Operations Command will deliver whosoever we decide to employ on to the target and extract them when it is

17

completed. On the ground, in the actual battle, the individual squadron commanders will exercize control.'

It was as good a way as any of telling Franklin that he wasn't actually going on the op, a position he might have finagled his way into with two of his squadrons engaged. If an attack on Zu ol Faqar worked, and bin Laden was put out of business, the fame to follow would be massive. None of the higher commanders would get even close in the celebrity stakes to the man who led the ground assault.

Franklin must have guessed he'd been rumbled and had the wit to stay silent while Morton did what the President required which was to seek objections from the other committee members. There were none. They could all see the political sense in what the President was asking for.

'So what should I request, Lucius?'

The first name, compared with the way Franklin had been addressed, was telling enough to make the Colonel frown.

'As I've already outlined, sir, it's a two-squadron operation. If you decide to proceed then one of those should be from the SAS.'

'Thank you, General Morton.'

Within the hour the British Prime Minister was in the Cabinet Office, on the secure line to a man who was more than just a political ally. The President commiserated first on the Lagos casualties, and accepted in turn the PM's words on the more serious situation in Jakarta. Then he outlined what had been discussed, and what he hoped for in the way of assistance, without admitting that a decision on the response had already been made.

'It seems to us that no other course has any chance of terminating this campaign. And the need to act before bin Laden ups the stakes to a biological conflict is paramount. We must take direct action.'

There was a pause to allow the emphasized expression 'direct action' to register in all its meanings: overt or covert action against an enemy force; seize damage or destroy a target; capture or recover personnel and or material in support of a strategic or operational objective. It was an expression rarely used because it was an option to be employed only in the most serious political situations.

18

'And before you point it out,' the President continued, 'we know here in Washington that this will not choke off Muslim terrorism or even end the *fatwas*. But we must send a message to say that we can get to you, that neither distance nor your God can protect you. What I am suggesting is a joint operation to get that message across.'

'Are the camps the target?'

'Yes. But bin Laden must be on site. We will strike at the chosen location only when and if he is present to be apprehended. We will, of course, try to inflict as much damage as possible on his support.'

There was no hesitation in London. It was made clear that the British Government was both willing and eager to come on board, with the single proviso that the Prime Minister would seek and be guided by his own military advisors.

'Tell me what you want.'

'The commander of the Joint Special Operations Command informs me that I should ask you for a full SAS squadron to participate. We will undertake to get them to where they will be able to do their job, and we will get them out again.'

'Then, subject to that one stated condition, you have them.'

'Do you wish to consult? There are bound to be members of your cabinet disinclined to agree.'

'I'll do that afterwards. In my experience, that's the best way.'

That engendered a laugh. Not much of one; the situation was too serious for prolonged humour. But the PM was telling him that he could carry his cabinet, and that was very important. He was also saying that he understood the reasoning behind the joint nature of the operation. London was just as much at risk as Washington from bin Laden now, and at a loss to know how to counter him. Though less hamstrung than his American counterpart, he too would shy away from too many deaths in a purely UK venture, even if, and this was a very doubtful prospect, they could find a way to carry one out. He was being offered a gift and he knew it. The fact that the benefit was mutual was a bonus.

'What will the operation be called?'

'Joint Strike,' the President replied, in a voice loud enough to elicit a nod from everyone in the White House briefing room.

19

'Bin Laden has to be expecting something,' said Rear Admiral Harry Shearsby, the naval representative on JSOC. With a Carrier Battle Group led by the USS *Carl Vinson* already in the Gulf on permanent stand by for this kind of operation, he probably had the least to do. Even the USS *Essex*, leading the Amphibious Ready Group, which might be required to participate, was attached to the CBG.

'He'll be expecting another dose of your Tomahawks, Harry,' said Morton, grinning. 'This time, we're going to give the bastard a mite more than that.'

Major-General Carter Radabee, a slow talking Georgian, spoke next. He represented the Air Force Special Operations command and had already stated his own force requirements. The 16th Special Operations Wing (Airforce), flying C-130s would be tasked to get the assault force to the Forward Operating Base. They would also provide Spectre gunships in a role that was yet to be finalized.

The helos – Chinooks and Black Hawks, flown by the pilots of 160th Special Operations Regiment (Airborne), the famous 'Night Stalkers' – were army and came under the command of General LeForgue 'Lee' Taylor. They were tasked to deliver the force on to the target.

'I take it, with the target where it is, we would be staging out of somewhere in the Persian Gulf?' asked General Taylor.

'Given the size of the operation,' said Admiral Shearsby. 'I cannot envisage a way in which it can be amphibious based.'

'That's what the target packet suggests,' Morton added.

'My helo pilots sure as hell want some training. I can't give my men realistic build up training and mission rehearsals in any of the bases in that area.'

'So?'

Morton was asking on behalf of the room, with each man well aware of the importance of what Taylor was saying. The Tehran hostage rescue had gone pear shaped as much through pilot error as any other factor. And lack of training had a lot to do with that. It was axiomatic that if you couldn't deliver the Special Forces safely, there was no point in going at all. And his words underlined that Taylor, like the good commander he was, had done his homework.

'We have facilities in Nevada that match the terrain around the proposed target area near Kandahar, from mountains to flat plain. I suggest that any rehearsals should take place at that location.'

'Time?'

'The President indicated that we have that, and Nevada is no more than a red-eye flight away from any of the bases you mentioned. Better a measured approach that gets it right than a hare-brained dash that repeats past errors.'

Morton looked around the room. John Franklin was so subdued he just nodded. Admiral Shearsby and Carter Radabee concurred, while the Army Intelligence representative always wanted more time to be sure that what he knew was accurate.

'OK, Lee,' Morton said finally. 'Nevada it is.'

Carter Radabee wasn't finished. He had one last point to raise.

'The outline plan may call for a Tactical Landing Strip inside the Afghan border, to act as a Forward Operating Base and a Forward Air Refuelling Point. We have two possible sites identified there, but there hasn't been a ground recce for some time.'

'CIA Special Operations have been alerted and are taking care of that.'

'Mister Director, I think we might have something, but I cannot yet be sure it is the real McCoy. Another couple of days and I might be able to give you a more precise answer.'

'I take it,' the FBI Director asked, sarcastically, 'you have a watch on?'

The best brains, as well as the most powerful software tools, had been put on to unscrambling the hard disc from the Lake Champlain portable computer. But the continuous running of programs to unlock what the field agents had presented them with took time. Hurrying it wouldn't help.

The Head of Computer Analysis answered with just as much sarcasm. 'I know the time.'

'But not the luxury of it. I need a percentage guess.'

'At sixty.'

'That's the best?'

'It is.'

'Go for it at midnight.'

'Your call, sir.'

'Damned right!' the Director snapped.

The Director of Special Forces, Brigadier Harry Millar, had direct access to the Prime Minister, and for security reasons received his orders from the Cabinet Office. The directive to activate a whole squadron, sent on the secure line to Hereford after the news of the Lagos bomb, induced no panic. The most experienced and longest serving Special Force group in the world was used to this. B Squadron was on standby, those not physically on the base on pagers that would bring them back within hours.

Once B Squadron had deployed, G Squadron, who were conducting training tasks, would step in to take the role of standby. A Squadron would remain on the Counter Terrorist team while D Squadron, although conducting overseas training could be called on to provide extra personnel if required.

Then the signal came though for the joint operation. A line was opened to JSOC within the hour, so that the CO would talk to his opposite number, as well as the command structure led by Lucius Morton that would oversee the operation. Signals flashed back and forth between Delta and B Squadron ensuring that both units had a full complement of compatible weapons and equipment, and outlining a joint build-up training programme to be undertaken in Nevada.

'Joint Strike,' said the CO of the 22nd Special Air Service Regiment. Julian Gibson-Hoare jabbed a finger at a point on the map, the Afghan City of Kandahar. 'About bloody time.'

CHAPTER THREE

I t is one of the oddities of British Government that the Prime Minister uses the cabinet room as an office, with anyone called in to see him occupying the other side of a very large table, in what is a cavernous room. Although he'd agreed wholeheartedly to the request from Washington, he was not the type to trust any other government or foreign agency blindly. He bore the responsibility for the troops he had committed, and he was obliged by his office to ensure that everything that could be done to ensure success was covered.

And he was fortunate to be in possession of many of the same intelligence briefs as the President, thanks to the close co-operation that existed in such areas as electronic surveillance. Right now he had in front of him his Cabinet Secretary, the head of the Indian Desk at SIS whose responsibilities included Afghanistan, and the Director of Special Forces, Harry Millar. Prompted by the PM, the DSF was discussing targets.

'Kabul will never figure in JSOC's plans,' said Millar. 'Lucius Morton and I have discussed the possibilities from time to time, and we both saw immediately that any operations they might undertake need a Tactical Landing Strip inside the country. To my mind Kabul as a target needs a landing strip mighty close to the Panshir Valley.'

'Where there is still fighting?' asked the PM.

'It's spasmodic, sir,' replied the SIS man, a fellow named Pierce who looked, to Harry Millar's way of thinking, like a bit of a poof. The hair was just too neat; the lips thin and compressed. And the hands, flopping about, well they were a dead give away. 'The Taliban push Masood's men back to the Tajikistan border, but they can't finish them off. And after a while, re-supplied with old Soviet tanks and equipment, they're back down the valley threatening Kabul.'

'As you will see, sir,' the DSF continued. 'He's constructed a trio of camps on the plain outside Kandahar, duplicating everything he had outside Kabul. And I must tell you, even if I haven't looked at it in much detail, my own gut feeling is that it's not on either.'

'Why?' asked the PM.

'Too large an area, too close to Kandahar and support, and frankly sir, too many bloody fighters. It's also a hell of a trip to get in and out. Mid-air refuelling. And for safety's sake, probably a Tactical Landing Strip.'

Pierce, who had already been in the room when Millar arrived, used his long fingers to push another map across the gleaming table.

'There's a satellite camp they've picked up fairly recently – in the mountains some eighty-five kilometres from Kandahar – and the prelim assessment is that it presents a tempting target.'

'Have they indeed?'

Harry Millar looked at the map, as much to cover his anger at the SIS man as to read it. What he wanted to do was to say sarcastically, 'Thank you for making me look like a right arse.' Not that he would. Why give the bastard the satisfaction. It was just another pinprick in the endless turf war between two departments that were supposed to work hand in hand, but rarely did. The only people in the intelligence community from which Harry Millar could expect true co-operation were ex-SAS officers.

'You're sure of this?'

'Oh, yes,' Pierce replied, smugly. 'The Americans have done their homework. Much easier to get to and not nearly so many of the enemy to contend with when you do. Washington also has intelligence that bin Laden is quite often to be found spending the night there, which gives a large time window.'

Harry Millar could read a map, and there was one glaringly obvious point that had been missed. 'This is still long range. I can't see how they will get to this location, either, without the use of a Tactical Landing Strip.'

'I am right in thinking, am I not,' said the PM, 'that this Tactical Landing Strip you speak of is the point from where the operation will be launched?'

'Yes. Given the distances and the time over target, they must, for safety's sake, have a FARP.'

'No jargon, please, Brigadier.'

'Sorry. Forward Air-Refuelling point.'

The PM pulled a face, and looked at his Cabinet Secretary. 'Which is what they had when it all went wrong on the Tehran rescue?'

'I'm sure they're better prepared now,' said the DSF, with just a trace of haste. The last thing he wanted, having just discovered that his previous reservations might be groundless was the PM getting cold feet about committing his men.

'I'm sure you're right. But you know the extent of my responsibilities. How will the site be chosen?'

'It's already identified, sir. But the Americans will certainly send in a team to take an actual look at the location and report back.'

The PM addressed his next question to the SIS man. 'Can we do that?'

'We could,' Pierce replied, with an overly glum expression. 'But I doubt if our cousins would be delirious about handing the entire responsibility for such a vital part of the mission over to us.'

'No more happy than I am to entrust it entirely to them,' snapped the PM. He looked at the Cabinet Secretary again. 'I think this should be a joint responsibility, to go with the joint nature of the whole operation.'

'One of each?' asked Pierce.

'That is feasible?'

'Yes. But it would require to be arranged very speedily.'

'Then I suggest you do it now.'

'Am I to insist, sir?'

'I doubt you'll have to,' the PM replied, noticing as he did so how unhappy that made Millar. So he addressed his next remark to the DSF. 'But if you must, I think you should. That, for me, is a precaution against a repeat of what happened before. It is a fact, Brigadier, that soldiers have to accept casualties. Unfortunately politicians are the people who are required to explain them to the public.'

Jake Steel's pager beeped about two seconds before Blue Harding's phone rang. He killed the sound on the TV, leaving just the image of the second shattered building. It had been twenty-four hours since the two embassies had been hit. The British Legation in Lagos had been lucky, the car bomb exploding seconds before it actually arrived at its target. The building had been badly damaged and the casualties were serious. But that was nothing compared to what had happened to the Americans in Jakarta.

There, the terrorists had blasted their way in through the outer defences, and got their van close to a wall in a narrow alley that served to double the effect of the blast. That was where the news was coming from now: the grim face of the reporter, behind him the silent anguish of those trying to cope with the tragedy of broken bones and the knowledge that over two hundred people, half of them embassy personnel, had been killed.

The pager was in Jake's jacket hanging in the hallway, so he had to retrieve it. Returning to the kitchen, he read the message calling him back to Hereford.

Jake also heard his father say, loudly and clearly, 'Shit!'

Blue was listening intently, nodding silently as the information was imparted, lips pressed hard together. But the eyes flicked sideways as Yan Yan appeared from the bedroom, hastily tying her short dressing gown, and somehow managing at the same time to run her fingers through her long, jet black hair to take out the tangles of a night's sleep. Jake couldn't help looking either. Yan Yan was Dad's latest floozie; long legged, elfin like and Sichuan Chinese. She was lithe, young and capable of oozing sexuality through a labourer's donkey jacket. Yan Yan was also the same age as him and that dressing gown was just short enough to make you wonder if, underneath, she was wearing any knickers.

When Jake looked back to his dad, the lips had parted into a thin smile. He was still listening to the voice on the phone, but half his mind was on the way his son had looked at Yan Yan. There would be no anger, Jake knew that, just amusement. Since they'd got to know each other he had learned a lot of things about his Dad. The first was that he was non-judgemental, never presuming a paternal right to criticize. And he didn't have a jealous bone in his body. He expected other men to admire his women, and that included his own flesh and blood.

'Coffee?' asked Yan Yan.

'When you've got things sorted ring me back,' said Blue, his face now unhappy.

'Already made,' Jake replied. He wasn't listening to Blue, but looking at Yan Yan, who'd made a better job of straightening her hair than her dressing gown.

Jake held up the pager as Blue put the phone down. 'Hereford.'

'One of these days, eh?' Blue responded, glaring at the phone.

He'd known that Jake, along with the rest of B Squadron, was on standby. It was a risk he'd accepted when he'd arranged for the three of them to go to an Arsenal-Aston Villa match, with full VIP treatment thrown in: Director's box, smoked salmon and Champagne, plus a chance to meet some of the players after the match. The Arsenal chairman was a Charter Security client: Blue had been used several times by Dave Heffer at Charter to give him close protection on short trips abroad.

In the five years since Sierra Leone Blue had gone from being an unemployed ex-SAS trooper to being a highly sought after operative. When Jake walked into his life he'd realized, very quickly, that Blue Harding was now connected, back on the firm. There was money around, with no known source, trips taken suddenly that Blue never talked about. Language CDs and books, Spanish, French and Arabic, surrounded his computer. And he worked out as if he was still in the regiment, running a regular five miles a day with a weekly ten-miler thrown in for good measure. He'd looked fit when Jake first met him. Now he looked sleek as well.

'Dave Heffer might go to the match instead,' he called into the kitchen. 'Do you want to go with Dave if I can get him, Yan Yan?'

'Don't tell me you can't go either?' said Jake.

'Two oil pipeline guys have been lifted near Grozny. There was a shoot out apparently. One of them might be hurt. The insurance assessor needs a bodyguard.'

Jake couldn't be certain, but he reckoned his dad was lying. There was just a hint of glibness in the voice. And it had been said loudly, so that Yan Yan could hear. Besides, a story like that would have made the news big time. Not as big as the embassy car bombs maybe, but certainly second or third on the bulletin.

'You gotta job?' Yan Yan asked from the kitchen doorway, her face unhappy.

Blue shrugged. 'Got to make a crust somehow.'

'Can you not go after the match?'

'It's first flight out, sweetheart,' Blue replied. 'I'm just waiting for the call.'

'I'd better split,' Jake said, heading towards the door that led to the spare bedroom.

Blue stood looking at his back, feeling that surge of pride that came over him every time he calculated his luck. Three marriages and countless live in lovers had failed to produce any kids. The lack of complications had been a source of quiet joy. Yet here was Jake, product of a one-night stand when he'd been no more than a green army squaddie.

A lot of things had happened to improve his life in the last five years. Blue had gained a lot of brownie points in West Africa, not only for the way he'd carried out his tasks for Charter Security but also for his part in taking the heat out of a potentially hot hostage scenario. He'd done excellent work for Charters' client, and left in place as protection a well-armed mercenary force and a training programme that had stayed intact throughout the upheavals that followed. Whatever happened in the rest of the country, the client kept on mining, and Charter kept on being paid.

And word got round in what was, and still is, a tight incestuous business. People come and people go. The guys who'd had a down on Blue Harding had moved on, to be replaced by men who cared only for his skills and reputation, not for the way he'd departed the regiment. Sierra Leone had raised Blue's profile, and several other successful jobs had caused his name to be mooted as a potential operative in the right quarters. The approach, given his record, was only a matter of time. Every government needed men for 'black ops', work too secret for any formal agency to undertake, and HMG was no different.

There were various establishments where the spook community drank, and one of these was an obvious place in which to make the initial contact. Such select spots acted as a magnet for those who'd served in all the branches of special operations: SAS troopers, some still in some retired, including grey-haired OAPs who went all the way back to those who'd started with David Stirling: Det.14 intelligence staff from Ulster; Scotland Yard S10 negotiators and Special Branch officers. The latter tended to use such places to get away from their fellow coppers. On top of that you would, if you were in the know, run into operatives from both branches of the security services, MI5 and MI6.

Sitting in any of these places, watching the clientele, you could never be absolutely sure who was what. That ancient guy on the two sticks, who could hardly walk from the wounds he'd received in the Western Desert, could be a real mover and shaker, just as the loudmouth at the bar, busy hinting to everybody how important he was, could be a total nobody. And, intertwined with all of these, ran the nexus of the security companies, all staffed by ex-players, men who recruited mercenary and body-guarding teams, or provided highly trained consultants who could create a degree of safety in the world's danger zones.

Francis Christiansen, his old troop commander, had invited Blue to this particular club, one of the most frequented haunts on the circuit. And he also made the introduction, trying but failing to make it look as though the thing had not been pre-arranged, greeting Tom Bowers as though he hadn't seen him for months.

'Tom, this is Blue Harding. Do you know each other?'

'Only by reputation,' Bowers replied, holding his hand out.

'What'll you have, Tom?' asked Francis, moving away.

'Laphroaig, please, old boy,' Bowers replied, before sitting down, his eyes fixed on Blue. 'And that's some reputation. Dave Heffer at Charter can't stop singing your praises.'

'He can't stop pissing either,' said Blue.

'The old pancreas, I believe,' Bowers responded, deliberately ignoring Blue's remark. 'Quite gone to hell. Poor bastard did like a drink too.'

'And now he just lives for his work,' Blue replied, lifting his glass of wine.

He was being Bolshie and both men knew it, and if he'd been asked Blue could not have said precisely why. Bowers was a Rupert, an ex-SAS squadron commander, but Blue had never served under him so there was little enough cause for the cold shoulder, especially in a place like this where it was an unwritten rule that all grudges were supposed to be left at the door. Perhaps it was his bearing, that air of total superiority; public school, black-button regiment, private income and a job waiting when he retired – the bloody old boys network that would keep Bowers

29

in clover regardless of whether he fucked up or not, the same network that had in the past condemned Blue to scratching a living.

'What really matters,' said Bowers, 'is Heffer's judgement, and I won't hesitate to say that I trust it absolutely.'

'Good show,' Blue responded, in a perfect upper class drawl.

'Drinks,' called Francis as he left the bar and headed for their table, his still youthful face wearing the keen look it had carried the first day they'd met.

Blue hid his smile with the rim of his wineglass as another was laid in front of him. If Francis had wanted to alert him to some kind of approach, he couldn't have done it better. That call, from such a distance, was unnecessary unless they were discussing something that needed to be kept discreet. What was said next only confirmed that.

'Bit of business at the bar, Tom. Don't mind if I leave you with Blue for a trice?'

'No prob, Francis. You carry on, old boy. In fact, while you're over there, do me a favour and get the barman to chuck up another round.' He turned to Blue as Christiansen moved away. 'Lovely fella, Francis, don't you think. Right out of the top drawer.'

'I like him,' said Blue.

There was no sarcasm this time, he did like Francis Christiansen. There were few ex-Ruperts he would ever term a friend; Blue had spent all his life keeping them at arm's length when he wasn't cursing them. But that didn't apply to Francis, Blue's first troop commander in the regiment: he was, quite simply, the best officer he'd ever served with. The man had no side and was honest to the point of embarrassment. Moreover, the fact that he was heir to a massive fortune had no effect on him whatsoever. He was that rare creature, somebody who could treat everyone the same, general or squaddie, without ever giving offence.

'He's also wont to sing your praises, though God alone knows how along ago you two served together.'

'It's over fifteen years,' Blue replied, in a tone deliberately wistful, designed to draw Bowers out.

Blue Harding was all for subtlety in the right quarter, but he hated people who wanted something from him to beat around the bush. He was more inclined to respond positively to a direct request.

'You sound as if you still miss it,' Bowers said, his own tone sad. What followed proved he'd fallen for Blue's stratagem. 'Can't say I'm any different. Once you've been in the regiment, nothing quite seems to measure up. One keeps in touch, of course, but it's not like actually being a part of things.'

The look was in the eye, inviting Blue to speak. But he stayed silent, happy to let Bowers do the work. The man was no mug. He knew what Blue was doing and how he had to respond. The voice dropped to a level that excluded everyone but the man he was talking to.

'I have contact with certain people who occasionally require the services of someone trained in the right skills. Of necessity the jobs they wish carried out are highly sensitive. Given your recent activities, and the discretion with which you have undertaken them, we feel that you could be very useful to us.'

It was lovely, the way he avoided committing himself. 'Having contact' made him a player. The 'right skills' covered everything from a simple money drop for a working agent to assassination. 'Sensitive' quite simply meant, 'get caught and we don't even know you'. And 'we' was the Secret Intelligence Service.

'Naturally,' Bowers continued, 'should you agree, you would be retained, paid monthly, though there would be no written contract. Provided notice was given, you would be free to top that up with other short-term commitments. And there are, of course, bonuses.'

Bowers was right about that. The biggest bonus was to be back on the inside track, a player again. Then there was money. When it came to black ops the British government, normally as tight as a duck's arse, threw away the purse strings. And when you came back, usually by a route and time chosen at your own discretion, nobody asked for receipts or insisted on change. But despite all the things that had gone right in the last few years, nothing compared to that day when the deep voice on the phone, a man's voice had said, 'I'm your son, and I'd like to actually meet you.'

31

CHAPTER FOUR

Packing was no big deal. Jake had permanent access to Blue's place, so he could leave clothes there. He was back in the kitchen before his dad had time to console Yan Yan. She tended to get a bit weepy if she ceased to be the centre of attention. She was at it now, sniffling and pouting because her man was on a fastball. Much as he fancied her, Jake knew she'd be no use as a serving trooper's wife. Blue was rarely absent for more than a week or two, but for Jake Steel it was different; he could be away for weeks or even months. The SAS was busier than ever. That tended to make a lot of his carnal arrangements affairs of short duration.

Yan Yan's tears bored Blue; that was obvious. He might cuddle her and mouth platitudes, but he'd also manoeuvred her round so that he could look at the TV over her shoulder, which was reporting the latest release of IRA prisoners. That brought on a flood of memories; the hypertension he'd experienced walking alone and armed into a bar in bandit country; high-speed car chases mingled with stake outs that had gone on for months only to come to nought; the occasional ops that suddenly went from total silence to ear-splitting action in the space of a split second.

And the kills! Not many – there couldn't be for an organization that prided itself on being unseen. But there had been a couple of occasions where he'd downed his enemies, taking them out in a cold professional manner before they could do the same to him. One, maybe more, in a roadside ambush; two more on a hard arrest in a terrorist hideout, operating in the dark with no time for shouted warnings or the reading of rights, no time for anything but instantaneous reactions. That brought back a feeling tinged with sorrow. Blue Harding would kill if he had to, but it was not something he enjoyed.

He sensed rather than saw that Jake was ready to leave, so he detached himself from the clutching arms and came towards him, his thumb jerking over his shoulder to the faces on the screen.

'Christ. I spent half my life lifting those IRA bastards. Ever since the peace deal they're letting them out and giving the fuckers pensions. Do you know some of them are getting as much as ten grand?'

'The sign of a wasted youth.'

'Take care of yourself, Jake.' The arms wrapping round the shoulders, and the grasping of the body were hard, genuine and brief. 'Don't do anything I wouldn't do.'

'Are you kidding?' Jake scoffed, as the gap between them opened. 'I wouldn't do half the things you did. How you old buggers survived I'll never know.'

'We were hard in the old days, mate. Old and very bold, not like it is now.'

'Yeah!' Jake responded, tapping his head. 'Solid from ear to ear.'

The crack doesn't change, thought Blue, just the people. When he'd been badged he'd wound up the old timers too, scoffing at their assertion that they could still get through selection. But that had only been a wind up to mask the truth: those old bastards had been really tough, had worked the street when the only kit they had to aid them was a map and a compass plus total trust in their mates; that and their inability to admit pain.

They'd set the marker by which later generations operated, guys who'd come in after a life of decent food, better education and adequate housing. And the technology the regiment now had at its disposal, as well as the back up, was truly awesome.

'It might be that embassy shit,' said Blue.

'More likely the CO needs his car washed.'

'Well, if you want a job done properly, call in the experts.'

'Grozny?' asked Jake, with the merest hint of doubt in his voice.

His dad paid him the ultimate compliment by winking. He might not say where he was going, but he wouldn't lie to him about a non-existent job in Chechnya.

'Bring me back some caviar,' Jake said.

'And what am I to do,' demanded Yan Yan, glaring at Blue, adding a loud sniff and a bit of Chinese word displacement, 'with you away God knows how long, only?'

'I know one thing you'll do,' said Blue, grasping Yan Yan and shaking her with mock anger. 'You'll be on that phone to Chengdu every day.'

Yan Yan smiled, a sweet secret expression that hinted at her sense of mischief. 'Maybe not every day.'

'That's what she does when I'm not here, Jake, she phones home.'

'Never mind, gorgeous.' Jake grinned. 'I can always nip back to cheer you up.'

'You're not man enough, Jake.'

'Viagra has done nothing for a young guy's chances. All the old dogs are rigid now.'

'Who needs pills. The juice improves with age, my son, like good red wine.'

'When did you ever drink good red wine?'

'Every time somebody else pays.'

'See you, Dad,' Jake said, turning away, still grinning.

The crisp morning air was wonderful. So was the view, high snow capped mountains rising like steps all the way to the north. Aidan McGurk had been getting up at dawn ever since, as a boy, he had started his first newspaper delivery round. It was a habit that had, many times, paid dividends, even in the years he'd spent incarcerated on the edge of Belfast in the Maze prison. Early mornings had been a time of peace in the H blocks, before his fellow-IRA inmates woke and began that endless, nonsensical chatter which never strayed far from politics – repetitious conversations which, because they bored him, he tended to avoid.

It was a favourite time of day here as well, a time when you could actually pretend that this Afghan camp, a sprawl six kilometres square of mud-huts and half-constructed buildings in a near desert, was a place you wanted to be. That fantasy would die as the morning wore on. The heat would increase and the men training here would begin to move around, creating choking clouds of dust that would cut off that stunning mountain view. The labourers building the mud dwellings intended to house the fighters would jabber and shout. And he would spend another day – sniffing the smell of shit from poor latrines mingled with spice in the air from men bent cooking over small charcoal fires – waiting for a summons that seemed as if it would never come.

Osama bin Laden would see Aidan McGurk in his own good time. The terrorist leader wasn't sure he needed the Irishman; that much was obvious. The location in which he'd been accommodated seemed to underline his standing – at the very furthest edge of the camp, the spot reserved for the newest recruits to the cause of Islamic fundamentalism. Some of the men and boys here had never seen a Western face, and so treated him with deep suspicion, as if avoiding him was some test of their faith.

McGurk had no doubts; he needed the Muslim badly. You cannot wage a guerrilla war without money. Fighters, especially in an urban environment, need a lot of cash. They require money to buy arms and explosives, the wherewithal to live without working, to move wherever they want and to rent properties or buy cars, even to engage the services of prostitutes so that sexual frustration, on the long slow build before an operation, can't grow to a dangerous level.

Aidan McGurk had to go all the way back to his student days at Queen's University to remember a time when he'd been without money. You walked tall as a member of the Provos. Funds had been plentiful; the fruits of bank robberies, protection rackets, or from sympathizers everywhere from America to Libya, not to mention tins rattled every Friday night in the pubs of Irish-dominated North London. For the likes of him that had now dried up, choked off from those still willing to fight by the men dedicated to surrender, the very men who'd arranged his early release from the Maze. Thinking about it now, it seemed like another life.

Brendan O'Dowd was the man selected to visit him at the prison, not surprising given that they'd known each other since their primary school years. They had been part of a gang that played football in the cobbled streets, fought for firewood at bonfire time and stuck together in the face of Protestant prejudice. All those games had gone by the board when the Troubles started, to be replaced by the thrill of throwing lumps of paving at the RUC, soon followed by the British Army.

It was easy still to picture Brendan as he was then, with his dirty face, blond spiky hair and bright blue eyes. Always the mad bastard of the group, he'd been the most daring – a breaker of windows, the best at shoplifting, the boy who would stand high and visible atop the slide in the park, before sending, with noisy glee, a stream of hot piss down the shiny silver metal.

There had never been rivalry, Brendan acknowledging that Aidan was a brainbox while he was good with his hands. They'd kept in touch later when Brendan was fighting institutionalized anti-Catholicism in the Belfast shipyards, his old schoolmate studying at university. Aidan McGurk had recruited Brendan O'Dowd, still fiery and loud, then watched him fit into the Provos in a way that he never could, rising in time to lead an active brigade.

He came to the Maze prison in his capacity as a Sinn Fein local councillor, well dressed, hair thinning but neat, the eyes now guarded no longer twinkling. The suit and tie, allied to the smooth vote-winning smile might fool the electors, and the media cameras that had elevated every Ulster politician to international prominence; but it was no secret either to Aidan McGurk or the Brits that Brendan O'Dowd was also the chief intelligence officer of the Provisional IRA.

'Jesus, Brendan. You're looking as smooth as a pint of stout.'

'The new image, Aidan boy,' O'Dowd replied, pulling carefully at his trouser creases before he sat down. 'Christ, when I think of the shite we used to put up with, scrabbling around in the bloody hedgerows like a bunch of fecking cowboys. We all have clean fingernails now.'

'I can't see why you need them if you're not handling.'

O'Dowd grinned. It had been a joke in the past, Aidan McGurk's fetish about cleanliness. Brendan had been a messier individual altogether. But Aidan's natural sense of order came in handy when making a bomb. It cut out the chance of fatal mistakes.

'I hear you keep yourself to yourself, Aidan. The other lads here reckon it's fair hard to get two words in a row out of you.'

O'Dowd wouldn't see him react to that. McGurk was too good in the poker stakes to let on, even to someone he knew very well, how his mind was working. But if his long-time friend was sensitive to atmosphere,

36

he'd pick up the sudden charge that the seemingly innocent observation created. The truth was, as both men knew, there were no innocent questions. It was a time of danger for everyone connected with Republicanism. Those who rejected the moves towards peace had their old colleagues to fear. Should the peace process fail or the spirit of compromise go too far, the shoe would be on the other foot.

'You know me Brendan, I was never one for shooting off at the mouth.'

'True.'

'Mind, you can get words by the hundred thousand out of them eejits in here, Prods as well as our own. And to tell the truth they're the same fucking words every living day. Verbal diarrhoea ain't in it.'

'A little bit of the old verbal has its uses, Aidan. It lets us know how the lads are thinking.'

'Thinking, is it? Let me tell you, Brendan, that's the one thing they don't do.'

'But you think, don't you Aidan?'

Again he had to be guarded, had to cover his true feelings. And he knew he had spoken sometimes, choosing his words and the recipient carefully, so that people like the man sitting opposite him would hear what they wanted to hear.

'What else is there to do in this hole, apart from burying your nose in a book?'

'I hear you've been studying the old computers, programming and the like.'

'With a Prod screw at me back while I do it.'

'There's a lot going on outside.'

'I know that, Brendan. And you will be at the centre of it, no doubt. You were always a fella to busy yerself.'

'For the cause.'

Aidan McGurk wanted to scream, 'What cause!' All the talk, inside and outside the Maze, was of compromise, of how a whole and united Ireland could be achieved by democratic means. That it was intellectually right made little difference to him. A purely military victory had never been on the cards, it had always been the aim to force the Brits to the table. But he was convinced in his own mind that the concessions being made were too great; that the ultimate aim of subsuming the six counties into a United Ireland was being thrown away for half a crust of recognition.

'You know why I'm here?' asked O'Dowd.

It was hard to sound as calm as he did, almost disinterested, but Aidan McGurk desperately wanted out of this prison, and that had nothing to do with any Republican cause.

'Word gets round, Brendan. I know you're advising on early releases.'

'You have a sound case, Aidan, and there's going to be a big discharge at Christmas. It's only the fact that you broke out of here once that's kept you locked up. The rest is of no account. Christ, nowadays, for possession of a gun you get community service.'

'So I've heard.'

'Bein' as quiet as you are leaves questions in the air, though, Aidan. There are those that say you're still brooding over the twins. That it's warped you.'

'And what did you say?'

O'Dowd made a pretence of laughing, because it wasn't really a joke: 'Christ, Aidan, I told them you were always warped.'

Aidan McGurk wouldn't have disagreed with that at any time in his career as a freedom fighter. He'd always been hard and uncompromising, but time and events had deepened that. His anger was personal as well as political. How could it be otherwise? He'd seen the two people he held most precious in life gunned down before his very eyes, murdered by a trained killer from the SAS.

'Sometimes I wish I'd gone down with them, Brendan. It would ease the bad dreams. If I'm morose it's the thought of them that makes me like that.'

O'Dowd reached across the table to pat the back of Aidan's hand, which produced the faintest of reactions from the warder set to watch them. His voice too, was full of sympathy.

'Sure that's thought enough to warp any man. But life is better than death, Aidan. And in the end an honourable peace is better than a never ending war.'

'It's hard to believe that sometimes, Brendan, even though I know you're right.'

'You got away, Aidan. There's no shame in it.'

His own escape from that ambush had been accomplished more by luck than judgement: luck that got him out through the coal flap in the cellar, slithering, sometimes staggering through hedgerows, fields and dense copses to avoid the pursuit in what had become an area so well sealed off it was like a large cage. Everywhere he'd looked he'd seen the Streamlite torches, zeroed on to the weapons the Brits were carrying. Once let a torch beam touch him and a hail of bullets would follow in a split second.

The need to survive had kept him from self-reproach, but only till he had reached a point of relative safety. Once secure and less fearful, he was able to replay in his mind what had happened. Aidan McGurk prided himself on many things, not least on his ability to think clearly. As the leader of the cell he should have known, should have had the men in place to spot an enemy presence long before he and his group were bounced.

'That doesn't make it any less my fault.'

Brendan O'Dowd shrugged. 'The only ones who don't fail are those that don't try.'

His failure was spectacular. The SAS must have had the safe house under surveillance for a long time. How had it been done? A hide that gave them sight of the house? Not possible, since he'd chosen the location himself with that very possibility in mind, making sure the few neighbours who existed, good South Armagh Republicans, were the sound types who would never willingly let Brits occupy their properties.

How had they known where to look? That didn't matter now. The RUC had their informers, but, regardless of the quality of the material, they wouldn't do anything else without checking. That meant they had to eyeball the place, using walk- and drive-pasts. Someone had been careless perhaps; caught looking out of a window without the net curtain closed, spotted on the concealed camera worn by that innocent looking passer by, run through the computers and identified.

He'd endured his turn watching, though never taken a chance on being compromised. In his mind he ran through the faces he'd seen, trying to match those to the ones he'd observed when he did the recces to select the place. It wasn't the milkman or the postman. But there were possibilities, like the man who walked his dog morning and evening, letting it stop to sniff at the numerous trees and few lamp-posts. But these were no more than possibilities: men dressed to fit into the background of a small town, a real rural backwater.

Once they suspected a Provo cell was in occupation, with modern technology, the rest was easy. Fibre optic cameras, even miniature listening devices, would, during the hours of darkness, be inserted into the walls. Every word spoken must have been overheard. How, otherwise, could the Brits have timed their attack to the precise moment they were about to depart to carry out the job?

It was bad enough to have failed. But to have lost what he had lost was unbearable. The twins were barely out of their teens, the only family he had left. They idolized their big brother, and he returned that in full measure. Drink killed his father and worry was enough to take his mother to an early grave. But not before she'd extracted, or her deathbed, a promise from her eldest son; that he would look after his little brothers, keep them out of the war, and let them live normal lives. The SAS had made sure his promise was broken. Hard, uncompromising and intolerant before, Aidan McGurk became even more so, to the point of recklessness.

None of his fellow fighters, from that day on, were entirely happy in his company. Not that he'd ever been a comfortable companion. He was too aloof, too brainy and inclined to show it to make many friends. Some must have guessed that he was engaged in a private campaign as well as a political one, determined to find the man responsible for the murder of his loved ones.

The soldiers who captured him only lived because he wanted to live. They were regular army, a patrol that caught him because he had been careless. They were not the people he sought, so he had to stay alive because revenge was more important than Republican glory.

'Have you had any luck in yer searching?' asked O'Dowd, breaking the chain of memory. 'Christ. Rumour has it you went at it hard enough.'

McGurk wasn't surprised that he knew. There were few secrets in the Maze, which was one of the reasons he had been so close-mouthed. But the way he'd chased down, in the early days of his sentence, every source he knew, inside and out, was not a thing he could keep to himself. Single-mindedly he pursued the one goal, trying to find the name of the murdering bastard who'd led that SAS patrol, the man who'd given the order to fire almost in the same breath he'd used to warn of arrest.

The legendary secrecy of the regiment wasn't foolproof. Some of the troopers came from Irish backgrounds, though their personal caution was exemplary. Sometimes the troopers got drunk and talked too loud, especially if they were trying to impress some girl. But if they had an Achilles heel it was the fact that they got married, and, given the nature of the job, they also frequently got divorced. The information that came to McGurk proved to him that if you tried hard enough all things were possible; that luck would often provide where skill failed.

Through an abandoned wife, who was totally unaware of divulging a secret, and had not the faintest notion that her Limerick cousin was also related to a Belfast Provo supporter, he got a name. Her marriage had only lasted for four years, and she still cherished the memory of the wedding: the church, the white dress, the Rolls Royce, the meal and the speeches – not least the witty one given by her husband's best man, John 'Blue' Harding. He'd only just made it to the ceremony, having been held up commanding a patrol on a job in Ireland, in which, according to her new spouse drunk and boastful on his wedding night, several IRA men had been blown away.

That was not a regular occurrence, and the simple matching of the dates told Aidan McGurk who his man was. The request from a close relative for a copy of one of her cousin's wedding photographs seemed the most innocent thing on God's earth for a woman who considered the ceremony the highlight of her life. That photograph was sitting on a Limerick mantelpiece waiting for him.

All he needed now was the means to find and eliminate him. But first he had to have his freedom, and O'Dowd was waiting for an answer. It was a moment of truth, a situation rehearsed time and again in his mind. The information he'd received had come to him from outside the structures of the Provos. Could his cousin have passed on the same information, the same name, to the leadership?

Slowly he shook his head, but his eyes never left O'Dowd's face. 'I'm not sure I want to any more. Sitting brooding in this place makes you wonder if any of the killing was worth it, ever.'

'It was, Aidan, never doubt it. We wouldn't be where we are today without it had happened.' O'Dowd took a deep breath before continuing. 'You know why I'm asking, don't you?'

'I do.'

'It's not a job I would have wanted, this one, and I have to be careful, even if we are old friends. We've got no end of refuseniks out there as it is. It's my job to help see we don't let out any more.'

'I take it you were at the conference.'

'On the platform, Aidan, taking all the shite that was flying, and Christ, there were sackfulls of that.'

The meeting, to get the Provo membership to put a stamp of approval on the political process, had been stormy to say the least. Every word of the meeting had been reported to the men still inside the Maze, the prisoners whose opinions had done so much to move the IRA from war to peace. The majority of the inmates wanted out, craved a normal existence after the years of conflict and imprisonment. They had no time for the groups that had broken away to form the Real and Continuity IRAs. And then they had the Omagh bomb, which, apart from killing a lot of people, had nearly blown everything Brendan and his kind were working towards out of the water.

Aidan McGurk had looked with some interest on his fellow inmates, men who had killed to get themselves put in the Maze. He railed internally at their hypocrisy and the crocodile tears shed over the 'innocent' victims of Omagh. But he also watched the way the wind was blowing, saw that with American help the peace process would continue. And so, when he chose to speak at all, he mouthed the same platitudes as his reformed cell-mates. That would have got back to O'Dowd as well.

42

'Am I on the list, Brendan?' McGurk asked, his heart near stopped with apprehension.

'You are, Aidan, you are. Mind there's those that don't agree, who say you're still up for the fight. So watch yourself, and more than that watch who you talk to, in here, and on the outside.'

Fuck them, was the only thought that Aidan McGurk had. He was getting out and that was all that mattered.

CHAPTER FIVE

The £10,000 McGurk had taken off the UK government, intended to ease his passage back to normal life, was never going to last, just as it was never going to be enough to fund what he needed to do. The idea of work was a joke. A twenty-year-old degree in chemistry wasn't much use in the job market, and to put on his CV that he was an expert bomb maker and a handy man with an Armalite would not be wise. The idea of buying some poxy corner shop to sell newspapers and fags was not in the least appealing.

McGurk needed help, not least with money. To stalk this ex-SAS trooper, John 'Blue' Harding, would not be simple, or cheap. Was the bastard still with the regiment? Or was he retired, doing the only kind of work shite like that could get, working as mercenaries or jumped up security guards. It could take time – months, even years – and even then you'd need to be lucky, with only one pair of eyes in your head. The only answer lay with those still prepared to carry on the fight.

The feelers he'd received from old comrades, O'Dowd's refuseniks, had been so tentative as to be near non-existent, and he had been cautious in return wanting to make sure he wasn't being tested by those who'd got him released. But contact had eventually been established, carried out with care by men who'd lived all their lives in the twilight world of the freedom fighter. The Real IRA didn't appeal, being too close to the Provos and too riddled with potential informers, so he played the peace lover with them. The Continuity IRA seemed a tighter organization altogether. His past successes as a bomber and a Maze escapee gave him a high profile, an almost automatic right to a position in the only cell that had the personnel to get active.

It didn't' take long for McGurk to realize the parlous state of the group, despite their tight security. They had hardly more than twenty active members, some of them novices, few guns and little money – a difficult situation to manage with the added need to be secretive even in their own previously safe environments. To arrange a meeting took a whole week, with cut outs and anti-surveillance drills. Not that there was much to discuss.

The job was simple: to keep the war going and to scupper the peace process. The mass of Republicans were fence sitting, prepared to go along with the process but uneasy. Action would get some of them back on board; enough to build the same kind of organization that had been created at the beginning of the troubles. Easy to say, much harder to achieve!

'No more bombs on Irish soil,' said Malachy Keegan, the man elected as Chief of Staff. 'Omagh was a blunder for us as well as the RIRA. We must hit the mainland. That got those traitorous bastards to the table, and it will get them away from it again.'

That got the other three men nodding, all aware that Keegan was right on two accounts. A bomb on Irish soil might drive recruits away; one in a mainland city would do the opposite. Besides, even with the kind of surveillance the Brits had, as well as the suspicions of the Provos, it was easier to operate abroad than here in Ulster. You knew who the enemy was for a start.

'And it'll have to be done quick, as well as on the cheap.'

'You're asking for trouble, Malachy,' said McGurk. 'You can't rush these things and you can't do them without a decent amount of funds. You're just asking to be lifted.'

Eamon Gilhooley spoke up next. 'Perhaps, considering what we're after, getting caught at it isn't such a bad notion.'

Aidan McGurk was the only one to give that idea some thought instead of reacting with anger. Gilhooley was young and had never been inside, so he had no prison experience. The other three present had, and it was not something they wanted to risk if it could be avoided. But to McGurk it proved that young Gilhooley had a brain. The British Government might be working flat out to get peace in Ulster. But the security services, who'd grown fat and self important because of the Troubles, were less enamoured of the idea. A nice capture, the roping in of a Continuity IRA cell, might just suit their book, and give both parties the public reaction they sought.

'We might as well pack up now, Eamon.'

That protest came from Connor Boyle, the fourth member of the cell, another bomb maker, a man who'd been on the big island with Aidan McGurk, part of a cell that had enjoyed great success.

'We need to make a noise, and a fucking big one at that,' Connor added.

'Before they get anywhere near sitting down together at Stormont,' Malachy Keegan insisted.

'My preference is for London,' Boyle added. 'And no prior warnings, either.'

As ex-Provos they had certain advantages, like a list of targets already studied, personal knowledge of the methods of entry to the mainland and how to set up a safe hide. But most of all they were ruthless, wholly committed to their cause, prepared to contemplate massive casualties. Every bomb planted by the Provos had come with a warning, usually in time, occasionally not. It was Con Boyle's contention that the mistakes had done more for the cause than when the warnings had been successful. He persisted in his argument until it was accepted.

'That's in the short term, lads,' said Malachy Keegan. 'But there has to be a long term too.'

Eamon Gilhooley spat out the word. 'Money!'

'Lots of it,' added McGurk.

One blast would not blow the peacemakers away, but it would bring recruits, all of them eager and wanting something to do. That means guns, ammo and a stock of explosives. Avenues to funds were discussed and discarded, until only a few possibilities were left. Eamon had contacts in Holland, in the drug trade, outside those he'd known and used on behalf of the Provos. Aidan McGurk, with his history, had a degree of fame in Republican circles. Both men would seek funds, while Keegan and Connor Boyle made for London, to set up a safe house and gather materials that the two travellers could come back to.

Malachy Keegan would set up a mail drop, an e-mail contact using a less active sympathizer, so that the four could stay in touch.

'Right,' Keegan said. 'We know where we're goin'. All we have to do is find a way to get there.'

'Fuck you!'

Brendan O'Dowd spat those words out loud, so hard they bounced off the walls, even though he was alone. He was so angry he nearly spat out the name. Only years of keeping his mouth shut stopped him. The Brits and the RUC were so adept at surveillance that even here, in this windowless cellar room, he suspected that he was being watched and listened to.

The report he had, of Aidan McGurk's meeting with Keegan, Gilhooley and that mad bastard Boyle, made uncomfortable reading. They had been careful, but not careful enough. And he knew he'd have to take it to the Army Council at the next meeting. What to recommend?

The options were there: a verbal threat, maybe even a punishment beating; the final sanction was a bullet in the brain and a grave that would only ever be found by some future archaeologist. Beatings by their nature became public, execution was more secret, but set the rumour mill alight. But a verbal warning might not be enough – all it would do was warn them and make them more careful. There was no sentiment in O'Dowd's appreciation, no consideration like old friend-ship would cloud his judgement. He was well versed in the arts of *realpolitik*. He didn't just have to keep the refuseniks in line, part of his job was to avoid giving the Brits and the Unionists a stick with which to beat the Provos.

As yet McGurk and the Continuity IRA had done nothing but talk. They had few guns and, as far as O'Dowd knew, no explosives. He could keep them under observation and make sure it stayed that way. The aim, agreed after much bitter dispute, was to keep the lid on, to avoid violent acts that would look like Provo bad faith. Slowly, he reached for his lighter and set the note ablaze, letting the bits fall into an ashtray. When it was burnt to a cinder he mashed it up with his fingers, before taking the ashtray to the toilet and flushing the contents through a Saniflow system designed to pulverise human waste.

'Just you stay quiet lads,' he whispered to himself, even that non-committal remark covered by the noise of the flushing toilet. 'Stay quiet and you'll stay alive.'

The raid the following day, on a sub-post office, certainly changed his mind. But worse was to follow when he discovered that they had dropped out of sight, probably to somewhere down south in the Republic. No one knew where they were. It had to go to the Provo Army Council and the decision was unanimous. The word went out, with no equivocation.

'Find them and take them out!'

Given the amounts needed by the travellers, when the four totted up their resources there was scant money left for the London end, especially since Keegan and Boyle needed to buy a car. Stealing such things was all very well if you were going to be quick. But it was asking for trouble to drive around in a stolen vehicle for any length of time. Better to purchase something clean, which is what they did not long after they'd landed – even filling in the paperwork – for a second hand low mileage Ford Mondeo.

Aidan McGurk set about organizing a false identity, growing a beard to match the photograph on the unused Irish passport given to him by the man who'd once provided them for the Provos. His first stop was Boston, home to plenty of Irishmen who shared his views, men who'd helped before, but the story they told him was bleak.

America had gone to sleep on the six counties, convinced that the peace process was the only game worth playing. And it was dangerous to be open. A country that had always turned a blind eye to IRA fund-raising now threatened arrest and deportation. Americans, after what had happened in their own country, no longer thought of people like McGurk as romantic freedom fighters. They were plain terrorists, outlaws to be hunted down and killed.

In a life that had included bombings, shoot-outs and assassinations, plus a high profile escape and re-capture, he had one card left to play. As a young man, fresh from university and good with languages, he'd been part of a delegation to Libya, seeking arms and money from Colonel Gaddafi. The smattering of Arabic he'd crammed into his head during the journey had given him a higher profile in Tripoli than his actual status justified. Young Aidan McGurk found himself taking almost a lead part, often engaged, much to the annoyance of his older, fellow Provos, in stilted conversations with Gaddafi himself.

He never claimed that he'd tipped the balance, but his contribution had been positive. So much so that, in any further dealings with the Libyans, he'd been called in to help, brushing up on his Arabic to do so and establishing a strong bond with the Libyan intelligence community in the process. Just before his arrest he'd become the main IRA man on the computer link that had been set up between them. The help they gave had never been as significant as the Brits had been led to believe. But help there had been, and the chain of communication, through the intelligence officers of various Libyan legations in Europe, was still there. It was a long shot but worth a try. Contact was slow and cautious, but eventually a secure channel was opened.

That, too, proved a disappointment. The Great Leader, as Gaddafi styled himself, might still mouth the old anti-imperialist rant, but the messages that came back told Aidan McGurk that he was much chastened, aware that the slightest contact with an act of terrorism led to a visit by the American airforce, showering his capital with bombs. Since the Colonel was convinced that the prime aim was his demise, he was extra cautious. But help could be had from another source: there was one man who carried on the fight, one man who had the funds to aid good men like Aidan McGurk. Libya, indeed Gaddafi himself, would gladly sponsor a visit to that man.

That had landed him here, on this godforsaken Afghan plateau outside Kandahar, where he sat, seemingly ignored, while the other great leader, Osama bin Laden, mused on the proposal put to him by Libyan Intelligence: that this Irishman could be useful; that he was experienced; he could get closer to the target in a Western city than any Islamic militant; that America, with its policy of helping Britain to broker peace in Ulster, was now as much an enemy to a true Irish Republican as it was to the followers of Mohammed. Here was a man who had spoken with the Colonel, a man who, even if he was an infidel, could be trusted.

Aidan McGurk knew he had a rebellious streak that manifested itself as arrogance. He'd fought all his life to control it, not so that he could gain the trust and respect of others, but so that he could mask his own passions and never let those he worked with see how he despized their narrow minds. He had to fight it now; the temptation to just up sticks and leave. But he suppressed the thought, telling himself he must stick rigidly to his plan. Besides it was too late today. The camp was stirring, the fighters rising to say their morning prayers to Allah, facing Mecca on their brightly woven prayer mats, asking that he intercede and help them destroy the filthy Mushrikeen.

They paid no attention to the bright red Toyota Hi-Line that wove its way between tents and half-built barracks. Highly decorated with Islamic messages and symbols the Hi-Line was the vehicle of choice for the young bloods of the Taliban. McGurk, however, had spotted the car and could see the bearded face of the driver, one of bin Laden's most senior lieutenants, the man who had acted as his go-between, Mohammed al Kadar.

He suppressed his rising excitement when he realized that the Hi-Line was heading towards him. In a life full of disappointments that had almost become a habit, he would not let his imagination act positively now. Al Kadar spun the vehicle round so that he could talk to McGurk out of the fantastically decorated window.

'Our leader has sent me to fetch you.'

McGurk didn't hesitate. He was round and in the passenger door in double quick time. As he pulled away, Kadar turned to grin at him.

'You will find out when you see our leader that his fighters have achieved a great success. Bombs delivered by the good sons of Allah destroyed two infidel embassies, one in Lagos and one in Jakarta, Allah be praised. It would be as well, when you gain his presence, to congratulate him.'

'I will, I will.' McGurk took a deep breath before adding, to himself 'Ye can bet your mother's life on it, I will.'

'Zu ol Faqar, Lucius,' said Harry Millar, consulting the fax on the desk in front of him, one which he'd like to have read before seeing the PM and that SIS poof. 'Tell us about it.'

The Headshed at Hereford and JSOC were on a video linked

50

conference facility, covering points about the proposed op before anybody physically moved a muscle so as to ensure that everyone was singing from the same sheet by the time the SAS squadron crossed the pond. As well as Harry Millar, Julian Gibson-Hoare and his 'Green Slime' intelligence chief were in the room. Lucius Morton was prepared to be open, in a way that would probably have freaked out the spooks of the CIA, who hated to see any intelligence they gathered disseminated by anyone but themselves.

'We picked it up in a routine way, Harry. A happy accident with a local agent passing back a suspicion that made Langley put it under the microscope.'

A series of photo images followed, with Morton doing a voice over and the guy from intelligence taking notes.

'The main building, the ruined sandstone castle, is tagged as a religious school. You will be aware of how numerous these schools are in that part of the world, now that the Taliban are in power?'

The image changed to a photograph of a flat-topped one-storey building surrounded by trees.

'The CIA thought this was part of the school too, then changed their mind when bin Laden began to be mentioned in the local bazaar. They reckoned that it might be another residence.'

'And?' Millar asked.

Lucius Morton wore an unhappy face as he came back on screen.

'Seems the product of that was limited. Our satellites are, for obvious reasons, routed over Kandahar. Zu ol Faqar is over fifty miles away, close to a lake and high in the mountains. The location has the kind of microclimate that negates a lot of satellite intelligence.'

The CIA had explained that along with morning and evening mists, being in the mountains added the problem of extra cloud cover. That, and the orbit limitations, cut down substantially on the amount of time the area could be eyeballed. Angles of view, given the high castle walls and the surrounding mountains, further reduced the flow of information. Likewise, the road leading to it was only visible at the points where the mountains parted to give a clear view.

'Thankfully,' Morton continued, 'this local guy we had in place, ex-

Mujahideen, had seen some of the men who occupied the place, and assessed that, with their fitness, the guns they carried and their confident bearing, they were unlikely to be religious students. He also calculated that the supplies bought locally in the bazaar at Zu ol Faqar suggested a high number of occupants, as many as three hundred personnel. Yet, even after several sweeps, no more than one hundred had been identified by satellite intelligence, and there was no indication of the kind of training programmes going on around the facility to back up the local agent's interpretation. No rifle, grenade or demolition ranges like those that existed in the other camps.'

'But,' Lucius Morton added after a short pause, 'look at this.'

The following images showed a guarded entrance, with sandbagged positions to protect it, and a barrier across the road.

'Not nice,' said Harry Millar.

'One other activity gave cause for suspicion, picked up by a re-routed satellite, operating after dark, using thermal imaging. We think we caught them out for a couple of days, before they realized they were being observed after dark. On both days trucks departed the facility during darkness. The dedicated satellite, given a clear morning, picked up the same number of vehicles arriving at Kandahar. We'd seen them before, of course, but we never knew where they were coming from.'

'You think,' asked Julian Gibson-Hoare, who'd hitherto remained silent, 'they're doing the noisy stuff away from that site?'

'We do.'

'Because that would attract attention to the place?'

'What bugged our watchers in the end was that the site is so inactive when it is in view, because they know the routes and timings for our satellite tracking systems. Maybe some friendly government somewhere is helping them out. That would certainly explain the way those trucks stopped running. Langley took the decision to seek more intelligence on the ground and it was this that paid the dividends. Equipment was sent in to beef up the local guy's ability to assess the facility. They provided him with the kind of intelligence-gathering tools necessary to carry out a thorough assessment of what was going on at the site. A digital camera, operating at ground level, once the images had been computer enhanced, highlighted certain things that the overhead cameras could not pick up. The results are coming up.'

The screen showed a pair of anti-aircraft batteries on the site, the guns hauled back below overhanging cliffs to keep them out of sight, with a firing position to the fore on to which they could be rapidly deployed. The sandstone castle had what looked like a trio of sentry positions on the battlements, covered overhead, surrounded by camouflage netting, again to mask them from satellite view. They appeared to be manned permanently and the best guess was they were deploying heavy armament: 12.7mm heavy machine guns, one at each position, useful against ground assault or air attack.

Nor was the one storey building half a mile from the old castle a mere residence. Ground observation got under the trees, and showed the reception dishes and aerials that identified it as a communications centre. British intelligence knew that bin Laden had several of these already, places from which, via the Internet and satellite communications he sought both funds and recruits. Electronic surveillance routed through GCHQ had also indicated that these were the sites from which he issued his *fatwas* and orders to strike at his enemies.

'Langley and Cheltenham beefed up electronic surveillance,' Morton continued, 'and that showed a lot of traffic. The messages are the same as he's used for some time, re-routed e-mails encrypted in one-time codes, hard to crack without the base document. But it did show that on the few occasions we could say with some certainty that bin Laden was present, traffic increased ten-fold. The conclusion was that these facilities, for that reason alone, represented a high value target. Forgive me if I'm stating the obvious, Harry, but the protection, in terms of weaponry, is only justified if the buildings house something of significance. The steps taken to avoid overhead surveillance point to the same conclusion. The fact that the number of personnel cannot positively be established only demonstrates the success of the terrorists' counter-measures.'

'The conclusion being, Lucius,' said Millar, 'that it's a command and specialist training centre, as well as a major communications facility. In fact, it might be the only one.'

'On the button, Harry. Bin Laden is a visitor maybe as often as once or twice each week. Given the heavier traffic, we think he even spends the night there occasionally. Confirmation of that is what we are now waiting for.'

CHAPTER SIX

He could have had a better car. Blue, he knew, would have offered to help him out if he had wanted to buy one. But Jake Steel was happy with his three-year old Cavalier. A more pricey motor would only attract attention, and Jake had learned very early the value of being a grey man. Likewise, to anyone in the regiment, he rarely mentioned that Blue Harding was his father. Nor did he discuss his private life. A couple of his close mates had stayed at the house, and taken full advantage of the hospitality, but they knew how to stay shtum.

It was no secret, the way that Blue had left the regiment. He'd been good, maybe one of the best, but John Harding had gone up against the brotherhood of Ruperts and lost. Some of the officers he'd served with would have been really sorry, but the bonds of commissioned free-masonry exerted a greater pull. That and personal ambition. Failure to support a fellow Rupert was a good way to kiss an army career goodbye.

Jake wondered if his attitude was a genetic inheritance. Basically, when it came to Ruperts, he would tell them Jack shit, and that applied in spades about his relations with Blue. Since his Mum had died, it had become the central relationship in his life. He was on speaking terms with his stepdad, and got on well with his two half brothers, but he saw them rarely. Since the day they'd met, and after those few first awkward hours, he and his real father had become like mates.

Trust was not an emotion that Jake threw around. Yet he trusted Blue Harding because he'd done what Jake was attempting to achieve. He'd been a man his fellow troopers knew they could rely on, a patrol commander in some very tight scenarios. Even the Ruperts had respected him, though nobody gave a fuck what they thought. The only opinions that mattered were those of the guys you worked with. If they had faith in you, that was the best mark of respect you could get.

As he hit the M4, Jake put his lights on and his foot down, till he was tailgating slow coaches or doing over a hundred miles an hour. The Old Bill might clock him and pursue, which would be fun. And if they pulled him over he would make no attempt to ruin their day. He would take the ticket and the bollocking and look contrite. And when he got to Stirling Lines he'd just hand the ticket over to Admin, who would glare at him for sure. But they'd also pay it.

Blue was out of his front door twenty minutes and one more phone call after his son. He had a smallish bag permanently packed with all the essentials for a fast take off. The car was waiting, engine running, Bowers inside, briefcase on his lap and lips pursed with what Blue liked to call professional impatience. It was an attitude that he personally could never be bothered with. Time and events had their own characteristics; trying to push either physically or emotionally, was pissing into the wind, likely to damage the ability to operate, not enhance it.

'Maps!' snapped Bower, lifting the briefcase lid to produce a heap. 'Baluchistan including Quetta, and Ordnance Surveys of southern and central Afghanistan.'

'Alone?'

'No. You're going in with a Yank. He's a local operative, and will have everything you need both for cover and to do the job.'

'Which is?'

'We need to eyeball a potential landing,' Bowers continued. 'Big enough to take C-130s and a helicopter-borne assault force.'

'What numbers are we talking here?'

'Speculative, but it could be up to six C-130s and twelve helicopters.'

'Fucking hell. You're not asking for much, are you? You want a covert Tactical Landing Strip and you're going to bring in half the airforce.'

Bowers' nostrils dilated, making him look more of a prat than ever.

'Don't worry, Harding. We're not sending you off into never-never land. The site has been identified and has also been under satellite surveillance for some time. You're just going in to have a look on the ground. You'll see the Green Slime have indicated the area most likely to provide what's required on this other map.'

Blue looked at the smaller scale map, and saw the flagged area tinged yellow by a marker. He made a mental note of the map reference, knowing that the marked map would not be going with him. The area, surrounded by mountains, was at the eastern edge of a flat plain, called the Dash-I-Margo, between two rivers. The script that came with the map described the proposed landing site as a salt lake in a barren location. The route to it through the well irrigated and pastoral Dash-I-Margo meant it would be crawling with ragheads. It was poppy-raising country, the home of Afghan heroin. But the crop had already bloomed and been harvested, so it might be relatively quiet.

Questions filled his mind, triggered by the obvious thrust of such a job. With what had been on the news, no genius was required to deduce the target for such a force in such a location. An assault group of that size, going into that kind of area, was not going to be British. It was too big and too long-range an op for the UK to mount, yet there had to be a Brit element or he wouldn't be going. And the area he was tasked to operate in was small, which was just as well for a two-man team.

'I take it we're not alone?'

Bowers hesitated before replying, another bit of nonsense designed to show his superiority. But it was information Blue and his Yank had to have. You couldn't have teams of guys wandering around unaware of each other's presence. You didn't need to know who they were, or in which area they were operating. You just needed to know they existed.

'We are tasking two teams. Both areas have been surveyed before, and are, as I have already said, under constant satellite observation. But obviously no one is going to send in an assault force this size without undertaking an up to date ground appreciation.'

That only confirmed the target to Blue. But he didn't say so, nor did he ask questions that had nothing to do with his mission. There was no point, anyway. Bowers wouldn't answer. And he'd been chosen because he'd been there once before, for a month when the Mujahideen had taken on the Ivans. It didn't make him an expert, but it did give him some advantage over any guy totally new to the place.

'Passport and ID.' As Blue took them, Bowers gave him a rundown. 'You're Irish, he's Canadian, so you're neutrals. You'll see on the docs, cards and the bio that you're geologists, freelancers with your own company, and that you work as subcontractors, sending in survey reports to some of the big Yank mining concerns.'

'There's no shortage of rocks,' said Blue, with feeling, remembering the hard tab it had been to get in and out on foot over rough mountainous terrain. 'The bloody place is full of them.'

Bowers ignored this attempt to be conversational, sticking rigidly to his briefing. 'Langley has informed us that your opposite number has been in-country before as well.'

'How are we getting on with the locals these days?'

'Officially, they're neutral,' said Bowers, with a raise of the eyebrows designed to show just how much he trusted that opinion.

'The crossing?'

Bowers bent over the large-scale map, and pointed his finger at a point where pink met grey. 'The CIA have people in place all along that border. It's their job to get you into Afghanistan.'

'The Pakistani side must be crawling with Taliban informers. That's where the bastards came from in the first place.'

'It is,' Bowers replied, as if to say, that's your problem. But he countered the impression with the words that followed. 'You've got a viable cover story that will see you through, and I'm told your other half is a top notch chap.'

'Bloody good show,' said Blue sarcastically.

Proof against piss taking, Bowers ignored him and carried on. 'Once you've eyeballed the site, send in your report and wait for instructions. If it's decided that yours is the most viable, you will be tasked to sponsor the landing and be pulled out by the departing air assets. Either that or your mission is complete, in which case you must exit the area.'

'Fast?'

'Could be very fast.'

'And God help us if we don't.'

'Quite. You'll have every tribesman on the border just dying to hand you over if you don't make it.'

The way Bowers spoke made it sound as if that outcome would be welcome. It wasn't, of course, but his natural supercilious manner made it seem that way. But it was a reminder that they were on their own; that if things went pear shaped HMG didn't know him. There would be no appeals for release or even clemency. That was part of the deal on black ops, the reason they were so handsomely rewarded.

'I want a promise you'll bury the bits, and get me a space on the regimental clock. I don't care if it's where the dogs piss.'

Bowers didn't appreciate the joke. A plaque on the clock at Stirling Lines was for serving troopers only, killed while on duty. Blue had as much chance of getting on that as of being invited to lunch in Bowers' St James's Street club.

But he also knew that Blue had the right to refuse. So did the Yank, probably being briefed at this very moment by another senior spook from the CIA. Blue wasn't worried about working with a stranger. The kind of guys who signed up for this sort of work loved risk. That's what made them tick. But they also had to have a brain, and the sense to stay out of trouble.

'This is likely to get you out of any tight corners.'

Bowers passed over the briefcase. Blue flipped the lid open and looked at the most significant part of the contents, neat bundles of dollar bills. Both men knew that this was window dressing, a fee for the job. The idea that you could, if you got stuck, bribe your way out of a place like Afghanistan, given what was probably going down, was a joke. Offer any of those bastards money and they'd suss out not only the connection, but also the fact that you had to be carrying. Once they'd done that, they'd cut your throat, take all the money, then hand your carcass over to the Taliban.

'Where are we going?' asked Blue, as the car pulled out and accelerated on a road that was now motorway.

'Mildenhall. We couldn't find a commercial flight that would get you there in the time window we're working in. So the Yanks have laid on a flight for you. Now, I suggest you study what you have before we get there.'

Along with the money and the maps, Blue had been given the whole shooting match on Afghanistan: books, magazines, press cuttings, Internet files in English, Arabic and the main local lingo Pushtu. He tried to study them as the car raced north, turning off the M11 to head for the main USAF airbase. But he couldn't keep from speculating about what was going down: embassy bombs, his sudden call but most of all Jake's pager summoning him back to Stirling Lines.

He'd had that kind of recall himself. Sometimes it meant nothing. On other occasions he'd found himself rushed over to Ulster to take over the duties of one of his mates, either wounded or wasted by the IRA. When serving, Blue had never been a worrier; you signed up and took what was coming your way. But the thought that whatever was being planned might involve his own son certainly had him troubled now.

'Mildenhall,' said Bowers, softly.

When they arrived, they were whisked through what looked like a small airport terminal – complete with a crowd of unfit looking people standing around, some in airforce or army uniform, others in everything from suits to gaudy holiday attire, suitcases piled up around their legs.

They were waiting for TAC flights. The US forces had planes flying all round the world, all the time. If there was space on them, any American serviceman, or veteran, could fly on them with their family for free. It was strictly first come, first served. That applied to transport aircraft of any kind, including a general's private jet if it was flying empty. It was one of the privileges of being a citizen of the most powerful military nation on earth. What they'd laid on for Blue was a Boeing 727 jet all to himself, with seats that reclined into beds.

He buried his concerns for Jake and worked hard on the stuff Bowers had given him, absorbing information like a sponge. But you can only do so much before you go boss-eyed. Once the airforce steward had fed him, Blue eased the seat back and slept most of the way to Bahrain. The steward woke him in time for a wash and a shave, plus a change into something more suited to the warmer climate.

There was an unmarked car waiting to take him to the civilian airport, where he boarded a flight for Karachi. Looking down from the clear blue sky to the distant sea below, criss-crossed with the wakes of dozens of ships, it was hard to imagine the Persian Gulf as a war zone. But it was, and one in which civilian airliners had to be careful to stay on their designated routes and keep their recognition code broadcasting. Some of those wakes down there had been left by guided missile cruisers of the US Navy, one of which had already blasted a passenger jet out of the sky.

Once through customs, he made for the domestic terminal, and took an internal flight to Quetta, where he had been told his contact would be waiting.

'John Manganelli,' said the American, pocketing the photograph he'd used for ID and holding out his hand to greet Blue. He had an oft-broken, craggy nose, dark skin and brown eyes under floppy, greying hair.

'Most people call me Gino. I've got one of the vehicles we're using outside.'

'Lead on.'

It was a Nissan Patrol, the rear packed with kit. They talked as Gino drove, exchanging enough information about each other's past to engender a feeling of trust. Gino was older than Blue by some eight years, an ex-player in the last throws of the Vietnam War, a man who'd actually majored at his home state university as a geologist. If asked awkward questions, he could answer without bluffing.

'And me?'

'I'll give you a crash course, old buddy. But don't worry about it. Stick to English and bad Arabic.'

'You don't know just how bad that is.'

'Hell, that's no problem. The Afghans are such ignorant bastards, they wouldn't understand you if you were fluent.'

The men on sentry duty could see the butter carrier quite clearly, but his passage across the hillside on the opposite shore of the lake excited no attention. They'd seen him too often before at this early hour of day, either herding his fat-tailed sheep to new pasture or leading the donkey that carried his weekly load of butter down to the market in Zu ol Faqar.

And he was such a creature of habit. Just as he did each time he passed by, he would stop by the lake, relieve the donkey of its burden of muslin wrapped butter, the packages laid carefully on the ground so that no filth should penetrate to his product. Then, after allowing the creature to drink, he would remove his sandals, made of old truck tyres, to bathe his hot feet in the cooling water that came down from the surrounding

61

mountains. The path he took, on the uninhabited side of the Zu ol Faqar lake, was little used, so while his donkey grazed he could rest as he wished without being disturbed.

The sentries' binoculars swung round quickly as they heard the first beat of a rotor blade. The butter carrier had heard it too, and he shaded his eyes from the sun to watch the old Soviet Hip helicopter as it swung round the far end of the lake to make its final approach. Skimming across the flat surface, it turned and gained altitude to land on the pad that lay between the old sandstone castle and the long low building, hidden by a mass of trees, which lay several hundred metres away. The butter carrier saw the bearded face of the man sitting beside the pilot, and spoke out loud in clear if heavily accented English.

'There he is.'

In the CIA building at Langley, it was just like watching TV, only the sound and the pictures were better. Deftly, their operative turned the digital camera to follow the flight of the Hip, the images it took conveyed in near real time through the TACSAT link disguised inside the seemingly innocent muslin butter packs that lay at his side. Fed in encrypted form to a satellite, unreadable to anyone who picked up the signal, it was then passed on to its decoding station at the speed of light. The heads of American intelligence were seeing what the camera was seeing, and that was being patched through to where JSOC sat, in the sparse briefing room at Fort Bragg.

'That's our man,' said Lucius Morton, as the slight figure, bent to avoid the blast of air from the slowing blades, scurried to a point where he felt it safe to stand upright. 'No doubt about it.'

Two black clad guards had preceded him and two more followed, to join a small escort that had rushed up from the house. Soon, bin Laden was surrounded, hidden by tall men, as if his escort believed that there might be a sniper hidden in the hills, ready to take him out. That wouldn't be surprising. The US Government had put a price of five million dollars on his head.

'So what else can you tell us?' asked Morton.

The voice from Langley had no name, just a crisp clear method of delivery. 'We have to work on the assumption that, having confirmed his presence, if the Hip is there, he is there. He plays a cat and mouse game with us, General, and that includes not always being aboard, either on the way in, or the way out. The guy is no fool and he knows just how much surveillance he's under.'

'How much observation do we have on the site?'

'With satellites around seventy per cent if you include the hours of darkness and if the weather is good.'

'What's the reality?' asked Carter Radabee.

'It has gone as low as forty when cloud cover and mist are heavy.'

'Frequency?' said Morton, posing the next question.

'There's no pattern. It does happen sometimes that he's there for the night, we think because this is his most un-compromised comms set up, which he uses to communicate with his most important followers. Keeping it secure takes time, since he has to re-route even his coded messages to make it hard for us to pick up their ultimate destination. We're pretty sure that once he goes past a certain hour, night flying is not an option. That could be because the ship is old and the avionics are unreliable. On the other hand it could be his pilot isn't happy flying in the dark in that kind of terrain. What we have observed is that when it's there at sunset, it's also there at dawn.'

'There's no way of being one hundred per cent sure though? He could depart by vehicle, for instance.'

'None. But in those parts it's an even more shitty drive in the dark than flying. Our best guess is he sticks with the Hip.'

'OK. We need you to be able to tell us if the helo stays there after dark,' Morton insisted. 'We are looking at a first light attack option.'

'That's no problem. We can activate the thermal imager on the passing night satellite. There is always a certain amount of residual heat left behind from the engine parts, and once we have pinpointed the Hip position, we can tell if it hasn't moved.'

'Thank you, Langley.'

'Pleasure, General.'

The voice ceased, but the image stayed on the screen, the Hip still now, with just the pilot and co-pilot chatting beside it. Then the screen went blank as the transmission ceased.

The sentries saw the butter seller pick up his packages, reload his donkey and carry on down the sloping path towards the market where he would sell his produce.

'Gentlemen,' said Morton, addressing the other members of JSOC, 'that is our target.'

Had they stayed visual for half an hour longer they would have seen the Hip, with bin Laden, depart again. But they had to wait for the daytime satellite to begin its pass to learn that. What had seemed a reasonably rosy picture just got a little murkier.

CHAPTER SEVEN

Aidan McGurk might have had a short fuse on his temper, as well as a dogged personality that made it hard to attract friends, but he had never been a fool. He'd been a member of an active service unit of the Belfast brigade of the Provos since his college days. You needed sharp wits and a cool head to walk the well-patrolled streets of Ulster with a gun in your jacket. An extra sense was necessary when approaching an arms dump, the kind of tingling nerves that told you the place was under surveillance long before you got close.

A steady nerve was a prerequisite when making a bomb, and it took balls to press the lever on a command wire knowing that the British Army lorry crossing the viaduct would be blown to hell by the charge you'd laid in the culvert, littering the countryside with body parts. And the first time you put a gun to a man's head and pull the trigger marks you for life.

Did Mohammed al Kadar need to go through Kandahar? It didn't seem so by his route, which zigzagged like a tourist trail. And he talked non-stop, pointing out, when they got to the centre, the various places that might have been of interest to a less single-minded passenger. The young man's English was clear and rather upper class, hardly surprising for someone who'd taken a degree in Political Science at Cambridge, not that he told the Irishman his educational background.

McGurk knew nothing about al Kadar but his name and had no idea what these people knew about him. What had the Libyans told them? He didn't know, and was very cautious about what he himself disclosed. He had made a point since arriving, outside basic greetings and asking for food, never to use what Arabic he had – the long remembered residue of all those years of contact with Libya. But he listened a lot, pleased that he understood more and more of what was being said in his presence.

'Here, Mister McGurk,' said al Kadar, gesturing towards a substantial wall, 'is the house that Osama bin Laden built for himself.'

The youngster took his eyes off the busy road ahead to see if this Irishman was impressed. McGurk pulled a face, and nodded, but it wasn't very convincing.

'The inscriptions on those pink and green pinnacles that line the walls are a message, commanding the faithful to remember Allah at all times. Do you know that he gave the whole complex as a gift to Mullah Omar, the leader of the Taliban? They are great friends and allies. You will hear, if you listen to Western lies, that Mullah Mohammed Omar wishes our leader to leave Afghanistan. Do not believe such falsehoods.'

'Sure, it looks a nice enough place to live,' McGurk replied, not out of any real interest, but to break al Kadar's flow of praise for his leader.

'Mullah Omar does not choose to do that. He has used it to accommodate his wives and children.'

'Christ, how many has he got?'

'Two wives, many children. The Mullah himself resides in the palace that lies just ahead.'

McGurk followed the finger and picked out the high white walls and the massive arched gate, as well as the crowd of people lining the walls, part of a snake of a queue that disappeared into the shaded interior.

'Many people come each day to seek his guidance or money. It is from here that he controls the armies that fight in Allah's name. He is a great leader of men, a true believer. To think that the palace was built for a godless leader of the country, a man owned by the British. And yet he looked out every day to gaze on the shrine that contains a relic of the Prophet's cloak. How could it not inspire him to expel the infidel, as it has for Mullah Omar and his holy warriors?'

Al Kadar babbled on about Omar: how he gave cars away to soldiers who had shown conspicuous bravery; the way he gave money to petitioners from a large chest that he kept at his side, like some medieval king. He urged McGurk to visit Sinsegar, the mosque school close by, where the Mullah studied and where he laid the foundations for his religious and seemingly unbeatable armies.

'It is a place of pilgrimage now. Fighters come from far and wide to see the mud house where their great leader studied. On the wall there is

66

preserved a bloody palm-print. That is the spot where Mullah Omar wiped his hand after pulling out his wounded right eye.'

That led to a seething tirade against the Russians, who had fired the shell that wounded the great man. The next item on the itinerary turned out to be the infamous Foreign Ministry. There the religious councils called Sharia Courts ruled, staffed by men who were so strict in their observance of the Koran, they would not even allow themselves to look at a woman, let alone touch one.

The Irishman had to look away, to mask his disapproval, as bin Laden's lieutenant rabbited on, listing as achievements things that McGurk found disagreeable: the imposition of the *fatwas* that had brought an end to a mass of former pleasure.

Television and video recorders were banned, so was photography and music. The prohibition on alcohol he could understand, given the fanatical Islamic nature of the regime, but what the hell was wrong with kite flying, chess, homing pigeons and fighting partridges escaped him. The bastards had even banned brown paper bags and white socks for women. In an open square, he was shown the spot where stoning took place, the ritual killing of adulterers. On the perimeter, pederasts were buried under the walls, in unknown graves that no relative could visit to mourn.

Aidan McGurk wanted to make a joke, to say, 'You people certainly know how to enjoy yourselves,' but al Kadar was a very serious guy. He wouldn't appreciate it, any more than his passenger appreciated the way they were now going. It was at a right angle to the direction they had first taken, and, leaving the centre of Kandahar, had to be the route that led to bin Laden's residence. The visit to the sites had been unnecessary, just an attempt to impress, perhaps even to convert him.

The compound was isolated from the other homes that had been put up along the side of the road, a ribbon development of breeze-block dwellings and small workshops on the route to Kandahar airport. It had been built inside the airport complex, which, being military as well as civilian, meant that it had security gates and a regularly controlled perimeter. Osama bin Laden guarded himself well on what was a substantial site. McGurk lost count of the buildings, which included the minaret of a mosque – looking incongruous with an old battered helicopter parked next to it – and a set of well-built stables with a fenced off paddock.

High walls surrounded the compound and trees were interspersed with strong fencing, the gates manned by well-armed fighters who looked, in their dress and manner, like proper soldiers. Certainly the search they gave him was coolly professional and thorough. And there were a lot of them judging by the size of the barracks that stood across the route to the inner set of buildings. The men responsible for guarding the actual villa in which their leader lived wore different uniforms, black instead of khaki, and were obviously an elite personal bodyguard.

As a man who'd always had to watch out for betrayal, Aidan McGurk could appreciate the precautions. Fellow Muslim fanatics might surround Osama bin Laden but he had the sense to know that security was not a thing that could be guaranteed. The Taliban, and old one-eyed Mullah Omar, could switch allegiances in double quick time. A fleet of black Land Cruisers with heavily tinted windows stood parked on the road, drivers at the wheel. There would be a fuelled plane always on the runway of Kandahar airport, plus another place of safety already set up to receive the man who had built all this.

Bin Laden had made his money in the boom years of Saudi Arabia, some people putting it as high as $200 million, yet even he could not have afforded, personally, the cost of his operation. Contributions poured into his coffers from around the Islamic world. He was as rich as Croesus, and the Irishman wanted him for that alone. The religious bollocks, which al Kadar had been bashing his ear about all the way here, he could poke up his Muslim arse.

It was the right code word, but on the wrong day. Osama bin Laden had gnawed over that on the trip back from Zu ol Faqar. He stared at the printout of the e-mail from the cabin near the Canadian border, and checked it for the tenth time against the dated list in his other hand. Was it just a mistake or was it a way of telling him there was something wrong? He had to know, regardless of the risk. The last thing he wanted to do was to initiate a threat that had no force behind it.

That meant activating another follower to go and take a look, someone known to his people. That was the arrangement. His nerve gas cell had strict instructions to ignore any incoming messages on their computer, in case they were a trap designed to locate them by the mere act of downloading.

Mohammed al Kadar entered, speaking from the doorway. 'I have the Irishman.'

'Good. Bring him to me.'

Malachy Keegan and Connor Boyle discovered quite quickly that they were under surveillance, though how they'd been picked up was anybody's guess. Not that it mattered; it was just a fact. It would have been as early as their point of entry into the UK, or at any time since they'd rented the North London accommodation. It had looked a good place to hide up, a two bedroom flat in a small enclosed block above a row of small shops, with the entrance at the rear. That meant that any observation point had to be close, and that was risky for the people who manned it: being distant, with long lens cameras was, for them, a better option. Even the parking for the car was within the confines of the block and private, and at the front was a busy road, with slow moving traffic and double yellow lines which precluded long-term waiting. So, once they'd sussed out the neighbours and put a reasonable watch on the roads, it was hard for the security services to tag them using anything mobile.

But cars they had to have. If the target is moving the watchers have to be moving too, and the two Irishmen were professionals, with nothing to do but suss out targets, wait for a message and look out for the enemy. Two days every week, when the midday traffic was heavy, Connor Boyle sat by the front window while his comrade took the car out. From his vantage point he could jot down the numbers of the first hundred cars to follow Malachy. If the same number came up twice, that was possibly coincidence. If it came up three times they could be in trouble. When the same two numbers already clocked twice came up on the same day there were no doubts left.

Both men were too experienced to panic. They didn't run, or search the flat, looking for the microphones and hidden fibre optic cameras which could be anywhere, pushed through the wood of the window sills, or up through the floor from the shop below into the skirting boards. They just assumed that every word they said, as well as every action they made, was being filmed and recorded.

Only when they were out together in the car did they seek to avoid their pursuers. London, like any major city with too much traffic, is very hard for surveillance teams. The followers can't get too close, and there are a finite number of cars. Helicopter observation was possible but unlikely, and even then there are places where they cannot see, like underground car parks.

Once inside the car park, on the very lowest level and surrounded by other parked cars, Malachy Keegan went to work while Boyle kept watch. It took him twenty minutes to find the radio signalling device, flat and button-sized, shoved under the gap in the dashboard where the wiring was at its heaviest. He didn't move it, and replaced everything with as much care as the operative who'd planted the bug. As soon as he was finished, they drove out of the car park and straight back to the flat. Neither on the way out nor back did either man speak, since there was the possibility of a voice bug somewhere as well.

The voice on the phone, to the Vauxhall HQ of the security services, had the right code word, which was more important than his Northern Irish accent. So did the desk operative taking the call, which would, as a matter of routine, be taped.

'We have found number three, Gilhooley. He is in Amsterdam talking to drug dealers, but the way he's behaving makes us think he has no funds to buy. The address is Rillenstaat 28.'

'So he's waiting too?'

The pause was long, the answer considered. 'It would appear that way.'

'For McGurk?'

Another long pause, another gap so that very word used could be weighed. 'Likely, but that can't be confirmed.'

'Anything else?'

'No.'

The line went dead.

Jake Steel, with his kit, was on the bus for Pontrillas ten minutes after making it through the gates at Stirling Lines. The SAS PATA camp, some nine miles from Hereford, doubled up as a training facility and as a secure location where men going into action could be isolated. No phones for that last minute call home to say goodbye to the wife and kids. Security was a must, and even there they'd probably be told Jack shit, though the rumour mill would be working overtime.

There would be no need to get equipment ready, since it was always ready, for whatever task the regiment faced. He'd refused to indulge in speculation on the way up, keeping the radio off and the new Oasis double CD on. Speculation was a waste of time; you ended up worrying about things you could do nothing about. But that rush to the bus got the blood moving a bit quicker, so that by the time he got to Pontrillas he was eager to hear what was going down. Four of the guys were already there, including his best mate, Tony 'Parsnips' Parsons. They hardly got a chance to greet each other before the squadron CO, Major John Lancing, whipped them off for a quick brief.

'Where we goin' boss?' asked one bold soul.

'Need to know,' Johnny Lancing replied. 'You'll require warm weather and desert kit. There will be no lift-off before sixteen hundred hours so you have ample time.'

Every trooper's kit contained all they needed to fight anywhere in the world, and quite a lot of it had to be unpacked – no point having Arctic clothing in a hot climate. But certain things were all weather, all terrain and there were individual items that no trooper felt comfortable without. They sifted through, each man packing his Bergen with the necessaries, putting what he didn't need in a kit bag which would be taken back to Stirling Lines: Arctic hat, heavy wool Norwegian jersey and shirt.

'I'm taking my thermals,' said Parsnips. 'If we're going to be in the desert it gets fucking cold.'

'Better take your Gortex as well,' said Jake, 'cos in the middle of the night I'm likely to piss all over you.'

71

A combat boot, surplus to requirements, was thrown at Jake's head, to be fielded by the SAS windproof smock and trousers he'd just taken out of his Bergen.

'Temper!'

Each man checked what was left. They made sure they had their desert boots, equipment for operating in hot climates, belt kit and Ops waistcoat. The SAS kit list was a long one, running to over fifty items, and each man went through it, checking on things like Leatherman tools, torches, knives and compasses and GPS, pilot gloves and the heavier duty ones for fast roping. Anything on the official list that was missing was supplied by the SQMS, one of the few people who did know something about their destination. That stood to reason. You couldn't fuck off to the four corners without telling the squadron quartermaster sergeant. But he was as tight-lipped as any Rupert, and wouldn't respond to Tony Parsons' badgering questions.

'My guess is we're going after bin Laden,' said Parsnips, a new set of lightweight desert fatigues under his arm. 'Even if he hasn't put up his hand to the Lagos embassy job, or Jakarta, his prints are all over them.'

'He's in fuckin' Afghanistan, right!' said Jake.

'So they say,' Parsnips replied, with a smug air.

'And how many guys is he supposed to have in his training camps?'

'Two, maybe three thousand.'

'Is that all? Piece of piss for B Squadron. What are we, fifty strong at best? Probably tab in and out too with hundred and twenty pound Bergens because we're such hard case fuckwits. The other squadrons will be queuing up to get us up to full complement. I can just see it. Have you figured out, by the way, how far we are from friendly territory?'

'Nobody's saying it would be easy.'

'Fucking right, Tony. I'll tell you what: you go and slot the bastard, and I'll wait for you.'

'Probably turn out to be a training exercise anyway.'

Neither Parsnips nor Jake had ever been to Afghanistan, but they'd heard enough about it: hard country with hard-nosed tribesmen, Muslim fanatics who would, if they thought you might betray them, remove your cock with a knife just before they gouged your eyes out with their thumbs. The Regiment had been in the place in the eighties, helping the rebels when the Russians were shooting the shit out of them.

The two governments, UK and US, had even set up a training camp in Scotland, and shipped some Mujahideen over to show them how to fuck Ivan. Now it was 'out of bounds country'. You couldn't operate in that kind of place without local support, and that had disappeared long before the Mujahideen had fallen foul of the Taliban. As soon as Ivan said goodbye, all the outside assistance was politely asked to do the same.

'We must have time to get some scoff before somebody comes and gives us the good news.'

Jake nodded. Four hours on the road had left him hungry. Not that he would ever eat like Parsnips. If his mate could be said to have a hobby it was food, not cooking it or discussing it, just eating it. Tony Parsons filled himself up at every opportunity, on the grounds that you never knew where the next meal was coming from. Yet on a hard routine op he could go for days on chocolate and water, living as he put it, 'off the fat'. That was a joke too; Tony, strong and tenacious, was like a string bean.

His other hobby was electronic surveillance, the placing and operation of listening devices, information about which he consumed at the same rate as food. He'd claimed once to have a recording of a fart from every Rupert in Stirling Lines, as well as all the things they said, sung or did to themselves in the privacy of their *en suite* bogs. He let it be known that a copy existed and had been played to a private audience in the B Squadron interest room. It was a great wind up, and led to some serious latrine searching by everyone from the CO down. The fact that they never found anything didn't reassure them. Parsnips was so good he practically had them searching up their own arse.

'Did you know,' Tony said, as they made their way to the cookhouse, 'that there's an old Pathan love song that starts with the line, "The boy across the river has a bottom like a peach"? Did you know that?'

'What's the second line?' asked Tommy 'Bull' Bisset, his round face already prepared to laugh.

'"But the swiftly flowing water means such pleasure's out of reach."'

'Don't show them your arse, Tony,' said Jake. 'It won't be peaches they'll be on about. More like two prunes and an olive.'

'There's a lot of it about up in them thar hills. Might take off for the old sex tourism, one day, the Hindu Kush. Must be some good skiing up there. Maybe it'll even rival Bangkok.'

'Only for lurkers who like goats, mate.'

'Richard Burton wrote a paper about the boy brothels of Kashmir,' added Mike Hutton, egghead number one in B Squadron.

'What, the actor?' asked Bull.

'Naw, you berk, the explorer. Sir Richard Burton. Tried to find the source of the Nile and all that.'

'Well, if he was looking in Kashmir, old mate,' Parsnips hooted, 'he was a fucking awful map-reader.'

The cramped cookhouse was busy when they entered. A lot of the guys were getting some scoff down their faces, a good idea when you were waiting, not really knowing what was going down. Service was slow, and they'd just got served when they heard the distant thud of the Chinooks. The call went out to bus up before their wheels hit the deck. Parsnips was finished before he got to the clockhouse door, with Jake still trying to make a sandwich out of sausage, egg and chips.

'Where we going?' Tony asked one of the troop seniors.

'How the fuck would I know?'

'Right, I bags that I organize the sweep.'

Tony loved this, a list of places with each trooper betting a quid on the destination, the whole kitty going to whoever was right. He loved it because he reckoned he was the best in the regiment at sniffing out where they would land up. Most of his oppos thought he loved it because, as the organizer, he could cheat.

'Bollocks, I don't trust you,' said Bull.

'Besides,' added Mike Hutton, 'the whole squadron's going on this one.'

'So?'

'I don't reckon you've got the brains to come up with over sixty places we might end up in.'

'They're all shit, wherever they are.'

'Then pick your shit, Parsnips,' said Jake.

'Before everybody else!'

The 'too fucking right' came from at least a dozen throats.

'It's simple, arseholes. We're going to Cyprus. Which is about halfway to where we're going to next.'

'Where's that smart arse?' demanded a lone voice.

'That, old son, is for the next sweepstake.'

CHAPTER EIGHT

Delta Force resides at Fort Bragg, not that you can tell from the outside. They have a compound within the main compound, shut off from all the other units on the base. Made up, like the SAS, of four squadrons they are at the sharp end of American military force, separate from the other Special Forces groups and Ranger battalions. Given the global responsibilities of the United States, each squadron has an area of primary responsibility, with soldiers trained in the languages and cultures of the countries that fall within their remit. For this operation, A Squadron had been ordered to move to Nevada. Lieutenant-Colonel Stanford Jay Fuller, 'Stan the Man' to his troopers, had been the last to board the Starlifter that would take them there.

His blood was racing at the prospect of real action, yet throughout the flight he'd worked hard to look calm on the exterior. Jay Fuller was determined to maintain in front of his men the fiction that this trip was just another training mission, not even part of the general Gulf build up that had been announced on the network news bulletins. Only he knew what they were to train for in Nevada; knew that at last his country might commit ground troops to do a job that not even the most sophisticated cruise missile could accomplish.

A West Pointer, Class of 79, this was what he'd trained for all his life. Stan the Man was a career soldier, with his eye on the prize. The best job in any organization was the one occupied by the boss, and that was his ambition: Chairman of the Joint Chiefs. He'd done his infantry training with that in mind, taken course after course in languages, communications and even politics – not something to ignore in the American Army. Delta Force had been a good move, first as a captain commanding a troop, next, on a second tour, taking over a squadron.

Somalia had seen the shots fired in anger that were so necessary for future advancement. He'd been on the fringe of the op to lift warlord General Aideed and several of his lieutenants, been on the net when the Black Hawk went down, listening to the commentary on death and mutilation that followed. Worse was to come, as the ground team sent in to undertake the hard arrest came under fire. Jay Fuller had led in a hastily put together back up team, and, even though that itself had been an imperfect operation – taking casualties and coming close to further disaster – it had raised his profile. When the shit got handed out later, his head was safe as a man who had taken impromptu action which had helped redeem a terrible situation.

Desert Storm was even better; Scud hunting and reconnaissance missions well forward of the ground assault, head down stuff where the real plus was to remain unseen by the enemy and in position to back up all that techno stuff with the good old human eye. He'd pulled back from a forward OP just minutes before the main attack went in, able to tell the ground commanders coming forward that the Iraqis were real shitty in the soldiering line. When Stanford Jay Fuller wore his medals, there wasn't too much free space on his chest.

Stan the Man could picture the whole forthcoming op in his head, each frame as detailed as a photograph. He had always trusted his luck to help him fulfil his ambitions, and it hadn't let him down now. Another month and he would have left Delta, slated for another more mundane assignment – the kind of Pentagon desk job that was just as necessary for career enhancement. Joint Strike had come just in time. Get this one right and his rise in the service would be meteoric.

'If you wouldn't mind strapping in, Colonel Fuller,' said one of the flight crew, interrupting his thoughts. 'We are coming in to land.'

Before he complied, Stan the Man looked out of the small front windows towards the long runway they were approaching. To the right, on the hardstanding areas he could see some of the other components that his men would train with, the aircraft of the Special Operations Command of the US Airforce – Combat Talons for deep insertion, Combat Shadows for mid-air re-fuelling or for missions with limited numbers.

Behind them stood the AC-130H Spectres, nicknamed 'Spookys',

77

surely the deadliest aircraft ever to take to the skies, if you excluded the nuclear delivery fleet.

'Man,' Fuller whispered to himself, an image of bin Laden now filling his mind. He was enemy number one to every serving American, so it wasn't hard to conjure up the face. 'Are we going to shit all over you.'

The English was good, almost faultless in fact, though he tended to talk in that lyrical Arab way that took an age to get to the point. In the flesh, bin Laden was not impressive, a slight figure with an almost sad face made to look even more sallow by the fullness of his black beard. The eyebrows looked heavy against the white of his turban. Aidan McGurk had seen photographs of him before, carrying a rifle, scowling but failing to appear warlike. He looked what he was, a thinker and scholar, not a fighter. Yet he had half the world hunting for him.

He now walked with the aid of a stick, making McGurk wonder if he had sustained some kind of wound. He was certainly at risk of one, not just from the Americans and their missiles, but from the conspiracies of his fellow Muslims. One Saudi Prince had sent in a mercenary hit squad to get him. They had failed, the price of that a painful death, but that didn't mean there hadn't been others.

The face might be scholarly but the eyes had real power, the ability to hold those of the man he was addressing. Aidan McGurk knew he had to be careful. To return a strong and calm look was essential. Any attempt to either avoid the stare, or to react with defiance, would be fatal.

'You will sit, Mister McGurk,' bin Laden said, closing the lid on a laptop computer so that the message on the screen would remain hidden.

He indicated a low couch, half-bowing to acknowledge the congratulations that his visitor offered, fruit of al Kadar's prompting. The Irishman did as he was bidden, then waited for his host to speak, noticing that the black clad guards moved away from the pair to a point where they could not overhear the conversation. After ten minutes, he wished he'd started first. The Great Leader went through the entire card of Muslim fury without even a hint of brevity, nor much sign of breathing: the US occupation of the Holy Places, as well as the entire

Arabian Peninsula; the plundering of its riches and the humiliation of its rulers and people; the turning of its bases into a spearhead to gain hegemony over the neighbouring Muslim peoples.

And the reason? To further the cause of the rogue-state Israel! The Jews were castigated for their occupation of Jerusalem, for the daily murder of Palestinians, even for their very existence. The Americans had, to serve their greed, declared war on God and His Prophet – the price to be paid by true believers in all lands that had the good fortune to be blessed by the hand of Allah.

'Nothing is more sacred than belief, except the repulsing of an enemy who is attacking religion and life.'

McGurk took a chance, and interrupted bin Laden. In the Maze he'd read endlessly – it was the only way to stay sane – books on everything including biographies on several dictators. And, having met Gaddafi, he knew that what was implied in those books was right. Dictators all had one thing in common as far as he could see; the ability to talk their listeners into the ground. The Irishman reckoned that if he didn't speak, the Muslim leader would never stop. He would use up all the time he'd allotted to this interview lecturing and hectoring, and would then have no time to listen to the proposal McGurk wanted to put.

'That is exactly the situation in my own home country.'

Bin Laden stopped. Clearly he was surprised to be interrupted, but also thrown by the claim.

'And we have the added curse that it is some of our own who are doing the most damage.'

'We too have people who betray the trust of Allah, who bow to the Western imperialists. You need look no further than those who support what the west does to our brothers in Iraq.'

'America has turned its back on us,' said McGurk, swiftly, taking back the conversation before bin Laden could get going again. 'It has become a friend to our enemies.'

The Irishman didn't believe this to be wholly true, but it was a shrewd way to engage bin Laden's attention. It was the US government, and especially the President, who had changed their attitude to hard line republicanism. The people, including the Irish exiles, had been brainwashed into believing that peace was possible.

'The Great Satan never shone its face on the followers of the true faith.'

'Which is why you and your followers strike so hard against the enemies of Islam.'

'Yes, Mister McGurk.'

'But only at the edges, sir.'

The 'sir' sounded strange to him. Apart from Gaddafi, he'd never called anyone by that title since his last days at school. Judging by the hard look in those fanatical eyes, bin Laden was unused to people implying that his efforts were peripheral.

'Would it not be better to strike at the heart of your enemy?'

Bin Laden didn't say anything. But he stopped pacing and, without any show of haste sat down, which was as good a way as any of indicating that McGurk's point had got home to him. Blowing up embassies was all very well, but it would never get bin Laden what he wanted. It was time to give him a history lesson about the Provisional IRA, and what it had achieved. As well as that, he needed to include a little bit of boasting of his own. His chronicle of the struggle had to be given in précis, but it also had to be passionate, that being an emotion that Osama bin Laden would comprehend.

And history was important to a man who probably thought in thousand year cycles, so the names of kings, Norman through to Tudor, rolled off the Irishman's tongue. There was no harm either in describing it as a religious war, the same kind of conflict in which bin Laden was engaged. McGurk concluded by bringing events right up to the start of the present troubles, and what had been achieved.

'The people I fought with enjoyed success. Look how close we got to Thatcher at Brighton. We mortared the Major cabinet while they sat in Downing Street. The whole of the City of London was turned into an armed enclave by one single bomb.' McGurk pushed his palms forward. 'I made that with these hands, the device that destroyed the Baltic Exchange.'

'London is not the heartland of our greatest enemy, Mister McGurk. Washington is.'

'Yet you issue a *fatwa* and the man who brought me here, Mohammed al Kadar, tells me that I am to congratulate you for bombing the British Legation in Lagos.'

'They aid the Great Satan, and praise every act of aggression made against a Muslim country. Without Britain, the US would be isolated in the world, less free to act in their imperial way. Therefore they, the British, must pay the price of being a lackey. They, too, must see their nationals die, as I have seen the sons of Allah perish.'

'A higher prize would be to make them think twice about backing America.'

'That may not be of interest to me.'

That was a stupid thing to say, and bin Laden knew it, judging by the way he grabbed at his stick, suddenly got to his feet and began pacing up and down again.

'I think you would dearly love to harm London in the same way you wish to harm America. With our experience, perhaps we can be of use.'

'Your leaders have made peace.'

'I haven't!'

'Just you, Mister McGurk.'

'There are others, men like me, people for whom half a victory is not enough. The majority don't know which way to turn. With the means to inflict harm we can gather them to us.'

The narrowed eyes almost stopped McGurk breathing. This was the nub of both his offer as well and his problem. He had to convince this man that there was a force ready to be activated, just waiting for sufficient funds, waiting to restart the war with the old enemy both on Irish and British soil.

McGurk had the floor now, not bin Laden, and he was as gifted as most of his race when it came to laying on the blarney. The picture he painted to the Muslim terrorist was one in which his aims would be realized by proxy. To make it sound as easy as he did was bollocks, but the Irishman was working on another premise he'd picked up from meeting Gaddafi: dictators, or fanatical operators like bin Laden, tended to believe their own propaganda.

The endless stream of half-true shit they fed themselves soon became the only reality, leading them to believe what they wanted to believe rather than the truth. He dropped Gaddafi's name into the conversation at every opportunity, trying to demonstrate how the money and arms he had given to the Provos had provided the Libyan leader with the Holy Grail of the terrorist: a damaged target with no blame attached to the person who'd helped initiate the action.

Yet, for all the confidence of his spiel, McGurk sensed he wasn't getting through, that this man was not falling for the line he was proposing. The unblinking eyes rarely left his face, and in the stare there was no sense of a man convinced. McGurk felt his confidence ebb away, to be replaced by a feeling of potential failure. Worse than the thought, he sensed that the change in emotion was reflected in his voice and manner. He knew he was now speaking too quickly, gesturing too much, that he was beginning to sound like a liar.

Bin Laden held up a hand, which forced him to stop. 'You have given me many things to think about, Mister McGurk. A man in my position has to listen to many submissions, and yours has been most interesting. Mohammed al Kadar will take you back to the camp, once you have had some refreshments.'

'And then?'

Bin Laden gestured to one of his black-clad guards, who came over to lead McGurk away. His host gave him the Arab form of farewell as he replied.

'And then, if Allah so desires it, we may talk again.'

'You have observed this Irishman, brother. Tell me, what do you make of him?'

Al Kadar paused before replying to bin Laden's question. The others in the room, two key aides to his leader, pretended they were uninterested. But they couldn't be or they wouldn't be here now. Osama bin Laden had seen McGurk alone, but he must have briefed Sheikh Tassir

Abdullah, his military commander. The same would be true of the Egyptian leader of Al Jihad, Ayman al Zawari.

'He is watchful, a careful man, self-sufficient, who does not suffer from being seen as an infidel by our newest recruits. There is a streak in him that speaks of defiance, and deep anger in his eyes. But he is dangerous, and, I would say, ruthless.'

'And our cause?'

'Is not his cause, and never will be.'

'He has just sought to persuade me that they could be one and the same.'

'Did he succeed?' al Kadar asked.

Osama bin Laden smiled, which did a lot to soften the slightly fanatical look in his eyes.

'No, Mohammed my brother, he did not. And he knew he had not.'

'Good.'

'Not so. I would rather he believed he had convinced me. It may be possible to make use of him. The best way to achieve that is to have him feel that he is in control of matters, even if he is not.'

'I would kill him.'

There was a growl of assent from the other two, proof that they were listening closely. Bin laden shot them a quick glance before replying to al Kadar.

'I cannot, even if I thought it was the right thing to do. He has seen much, and could harm us. But we need to remember who it was who sent him to us.'

'Gaddafi?' demanded al Kadar, unable to keep the scoffing tone out of his voice. 'That flatulent madman.'

The eyes hardened again, though the voice remained friendly, even if it was much louder. 'Never say that in public! Never say it even to me. What we think often must be just that. Thoughts! Only Allah knows what the future holds.'

Al Kadar's head dropped at the mention of God. He clearly felt admonished. The import of his leader's words was clear: for all the warm words in the past, relations between Osama bin Laden and Mullah Omar had soured.

The Taliban government was not viewed with much approval in the West but needed its help. For all the teachings of Islam, isolation from outside influence could never be more than a dream. Afghanistan needed to trade with the world, needed loans to repair its war-ravaged infrastructure, needed something to convince the ordinary citizen that life under Taliban rule would be an improvement on what had gone before.

The same government asking for help was harbouring a man wanted most by those who had the money: the oil-rich Gulf States and the Western Powers. The planting of bombs and the blowing up of embassies, as well as the news conference announcing that biological and nuclear weapons might in future be employed, did little to aid the Mullah Omar's efforts. The Taliban leader, a secretive and subtle man, had made his displeasure felt at the end of Ramadan by his failure to invite bin Laden to celebrate Eid. One day, bin Laden might need Gaddafi for more than mere funds. One day, he might need to set up home in the Libyan Desert.

Bin Laden moved to reassure al Kadar, laying a gentle fatherly arm on his shoulder. 'You and I are merely his servants.'

'Allah be praised.'

'Allah be praised indeed, brother.' Bin Laden took al Kadar by the arm, moving him away from the others, speaking softly so they would not hear him. 'He has sent this Irishman at a time when our presence in Britain has been severely damaged.'

'Am I allowed to know?'

'You are, but it is not for others to know. Our brothers in London have been under tight surveillance. Policemen watch their every move. Even when they leave the country they are followed. They have not been arrested but they are unable to function as they would wish, as the sword arm of the Prophet.'

'Can this Irishman be His servant?' al Kadar demanded, his voice soft but insistent.

'He is desperate. He seeks to convince me that things are not as they are. He wishes me to believe he represents many when everything about him leads me to suspect that he speaks for but a few. He talks of an army waiting to rise, the harder crust of one that has made peace.'

'You are sure of this?'

'Why else would he be here?'

'For money.'

'That desire for money may be turned to our advantage.'

'How?'

Bin Laden's face suddenly became animated, as though a great weight had been lifted from his shoulders. His voice became louder, almost a shout.

'I have arranged to go fishing with my children, brother. Perhaps looking into a river will provide me with an answer to that question. Take McGurk back to his dwelling and leave him to brood. Yet I would want you to hint that I am favourably disposed. A short period of silence should follow. Let us make him so desperate, that he will do our bidding.'

'Praise be to Allah,' al Kadar replied.

The young Muslim was thinking about that interview, ignoring McGurk completely, as they drove back through the gates that shut off the airport. Mostly his mind was on the way his leader had seemed to confide in him, cutting out his key aides from the conversation by leading him away and speaking in such soft tones. Did that mean he didn't trust them? Did that mean he was speaking the truth? Had he moved him away so he could lie without them reacting? Would he ever know?

The full headlights on the lead vehicle of the oncoming convey made him slow and pull well to the right hand side of the road. A column of trucks, six in number, went by full of khaki clad soldiers. In the middle came a blacked out Mercedes limousine that he recognized as being the property of Mullah Omar. In his mirror he saw them slow and turn into the airport.

Aware that McGurk was watching him, al Kadar shrugged and accelerated. But he was no actor, and it was clear that he was worried.

'Social call is it?' the Irishman asked.

'What?'

'That was some big cheese going to see your boss, was it not?'

'Or taking a flight out.'

'Big escort for that, I think, son,' McGurk replied. 'Unless this place is even more dangerous than I think.'

CHAPTER NINE

Parsnips knew he'd lost his sweepstake almost as soon as they lifted off from Brize Norton, just by the direction of the sun. And the time they were in the air, most of it was blue endless water beneath them, didn't leave much room for doubt, which made him quiz the winner, his troop senior, Lance Price.

'How did you know we were going Stateside?'

'Who says?'

'The flight steward.'

'I didn't, you miserable bastard. If you remember I was the last one to get a pick.'

'I bet you knobbled the fucking Quartermaster.'

'Why shouldn't I, arsehole? You tried.'

They only found out the actual destination when they landed and debussed in the baking heat of the Nevada desert. The place was crawling with Yanks and awash with planes. Almost the first thing they saw were the shoulder flashes of Delta Force, along with those of the three Night Stalker airforce squadrons. The barracks were spotless and air-conditioned, and that extended to the cookhouse which served American portions.

'Look at that,' Parsnips slavered, as he surveyed a plate heaped with eggs, strips of bacon, hash browns, toast and beans, 'Now that's what I call scoff.'

'Best get it down you, mate. We're due at the briefing theatre in five minutes.'

'That's the second time this has happened,' Parsnips moaned. The rest of his indignation was muffled by the food in his mouth. 'Some bastard is trying to give me indigestion.'

The walls behind Gibson-Hoare were covered with aerial photographs, clear shots of the valley and the hills surrounding bin Laden's various camps, all of which were severely eyeballed before the squadron sat down. There were maps as well, which meant that some crazy bastard had gone in and recce'd the ground.

Based deep in Afghanistan, his men spread out over a dozen bases, bin Laden was entitled to think he had a degree of security. And, despite the endless Taliban promises to rein him in, he was free to train his men and send them out on operations with near impunity. There was no way a political organization made up of fanatical Muslims was going to stop one of their own taking on the godless heathens in the West, especially when they suspected, with good cause, that those same powers were arming and helping their opponents.

Gibson-Hoare pressed a button on the lectern, and the image came up behind him, on a screen big enough for a Hollywood movie, of the destruction wrought on the American Embassy in Jakarta. It was a neat way of enforcing silence.

'The latest embassy attacks have made some form of reprisal essential, and this time it has to be more precise than cruise missiles. This time we are tasked to assist Delta Force in a major assault to take bin Laden, and his organization, out. Thus the initial briefing will be given by Colonel John Franklin. Many of you will have met Colonel Franklin on his visits to Stirling Lines.'

'I recorded his fart once,' said Parsnips, just loud enough for Gibson-Hoare to hear. The CO ignored the laughter that ensued, but the look on his face left no doubt of what he thought of both the notion and the man who had voiced it.

Tony Parsons mouthed his response, hoping that the CO could lip read. 'I've got yours too, boss.'

Gibson-Hoare looked right over his head, to talk to the whole room.

'As of this moment we are operational and we will train alongside Delta Force. And, though this is a joint operation, we will not, repeat not, assault the same target. We will be assigned our own and take it out as a separate unit from Delta.'

'Thank Christ for that.'

The speaker this time was Bull Bisset, a man with a well-known aversion to all things American. In that he was unlike most of his fellow troopers, who envied the Yanks their superior kit, plus the membership of a much larger army. Winding up Bull Bisset was a doddle: just praise Delta and he was away. Doing it while standing too close could be put under the heading of suicidal, given that Bull was a real hard case.

He had a round, jolly face but there was no doubting how he'd got his nickname. His shoulders were massive, as befitted a man who played prop for the regiment and that face had as many scars from active service as it did from rugby. He had been in some hairy places, Bull, always in the thick of whatever action was going down, and it was a commonplace in his chosen sport that props from opposing sides exchanged the odd swipe of the handbag. That went in spades for the 22nd SAS team. Everybody else in whatever side they played saw it as their bounden duty to try and punch the lights out of men they thought of as a bunch of fucking prima donnas.

Bull's remark was unnecessary and everyone knew it. The Headshed were prats, but they weren't that daft. To try and mount a joint operation with both Special Forces groups assaulting the same target would lead to mayhem. And that was nothing to do with ability, more to do with method, command systems and a general understanding of each unit's mode of operation. The Delta guys were just as well trained, though probably less experienced, than their SAS counterparts.

'Our task will be to take out what we suspect is a command and specialist training school, Delta will take out bin Laden's HQ – fitting since it is their operation. It may be that Delta will come across bin Laden. Maybe it will be us. Whatever, he is not to escape, and neither, if possible, are any of his fighters. We will be in a position to take and extract a certain number of prisoners. We will, in any case, as a part of our task, try to gather intelligence on any operations these people might have planned.'

Lieutenant-Colonel Julian Gibson-Hoare paused to let that sink in. Not that there would be any dissent; to the men crammed into the command tent a hard slap on a terrorist organization was worth ten tons of diplomacy. Bin Laden had blown up two more American diplomatic missions since his first hits in Nairobi and Dar es Salaam. Now he'd included a British embassy as well, using a truckload of fertilizer, that only made it more immediate to the men in the room.

International trading nations had legations all over the world. You could never spend enough money to make them absolutely secure against a determined, and quite possibly suicidal, bomber. The best way was an operation at source, and that meant surgery of the lethal kind. All that talk about prisoners was bollocks, in there so that when the orders were looked over by any subsequent reader or researcher, it could never be said that the regiment went out to kill its opponents. But that's what you did; not because of a pathological murderous streak, but because in a firefight there was no way to do anything else.

Gibson-Hoare continued. 'This operation, as I'm sure you will realize when you are fully briefed, is not one that the United Kingdom could undertake alone. It is thanks to our cousins that we are going to get a chance to spoil bin Laden's party. The first thing they are going to do is upgrade our equipment so it's compatible with theirs. Then they will get us on to our chosen target and bring us home. They will exercise overall command. When we are on target, we will repay this kindness by doing an exemplary job. And in the meantime, until the off, both in training and here in barracks, we will be suitably grateful for all that we receive. Each and every one of you will be the perfect guest. Any departure from that will be viewed very seriously indeed.'

The sixty odd faces before him were blank, a picture of collective child like innocence. The CO was warning them that there would be no wind-ups, no trying to take the piss out of their hosts. Every man present knew how good Delta Force could be. But they also knew that the Yanks took their soldiering really seriously, and had some trouble understanding the way British soldiers debunked all and sundry, especially their officers and their own skills. Taking the piss, in the American Armed Forces, was considered bad conduct. Not in the British Army; there was a strong school of thought that reckoned it was the only thing that kept it together.

'We'll be sweetness and light, boss, as long as we're not walking,' said the Squadron Sergeant Major, Tommy Baker, nicknamed Dr Who for obvious reasons. The remark produced a slight, amused murmuring.

It was an old joke from the days of the British Army on the Rhine. If a party of soldiers were marching, they had to be British. Everyone else in NATO went around in trucks, sneering over the tailgate at the foot-slogging Brits for being too poor to afford the petrol. The Falklands War wiped the smile off their faces, when the only army in the world that could tab for days on end across peat bogs and mountains in atrocious weather, beat a force five times their number.

'So to summarize: we will be mounting a joint operation with Delta Force. Aims: this operation is a direct action against bin Laden himself with the specific task of neutralising bin Laden and destroying his ability to operate. So, gentlemen, you now know why we are here. Troop commanders have been issued with planning packs and, as of now, you are on standby to move to a US operational mounting base either at Diego Garcia, Bahrain or Saudi Arabia.'

The air was cold and crisp, the night sky clear and a mass of stars. Blue Harding was driving the Nissan Patrol, while Gino Manganelli took care of the navigation, not that it was hard on this side of the Pakistan-Afghanistan border. There were roads and signposts, so he had time to go through some of the kit they'd be using. Naturally it was bang up to date, state of the art, and Gino was keen to show it off.

'For the border crossing, and operations in bandit country, we have this GPS: it's the latest, the US forces AN/PSN-11 Precision Lightweight Ground Positioning Receiver.'

'Nice and easy to say.'

'PLGR for short, so it's called a Plugger.'

'I could have used something like that in some of my private jobs. I've had to use a civilian Mark One Garmin.'

'Bows and arrows,' said Gino, with a dismissive wave of his hand. 'Christ, they fit that kind of shit in your car these days.'

'Not my car.'

Blue actually had a Garmin G3 in his pocket, the latest model from that manufacturer, a GPS the size of a small mobile phone. There was no point using it when Gino had a much more accurate piece of gear. The US leased the use of its military satellites to private companies like

91

Garmin and Magellan, but only at a certain level of accuracy. Though never admitted by the manufacturers, the latest hand held civilian jobs could be fifty to a hundred metres out. The military Plugger that Gino had was much more accurate.

Both were, to a man who'd been weaned on a map and compass, just amazing. Switch one on and it would search and select three orbiting satellites. Next it would tell you your present location on an integral map beamed down from space, including your elevation off the ground. Plot in any destination in the world and the GPS would tell you how far it was and how to get there. As you moved, it would calculate your speed of travel and count down the time you would take to get there at that pace. Turn off your route for whatever reason and an arrow would indicate the precise direction you should then take as a heading.

For a fighting soldier it had everything, be he in deep jungle or open pitch-dark desert. All that it needed was a patch of sky and it would operate. The Plugger was much bigger than Blue's Garmin, more than twice the size, and was four times heavier. That was mostly padding though, absolutely necessary as it was used by soldiers. But it was nothing like the first one Blue had used, which had been the size of a suitcase.

'I remember those bastards too, old buddy,' said Gino, scowling. 'I also remember how often they went wrong.'

Blue nodded at the other piece of kit that Gino had on his lap. 'That TACSAT's the same. Weighs bugger all now. I can remember the first one I used. It was in the Falklands, which was no place to lug the fucker around in a Bergen.'

'Bad country?'

'Very. Wet, boggy and cold.'

'I guess you were young and fit then, huh?'

'What has it got?'

'Digital motion video or still imagery, voice and data – as long as you have a Sunburst computer interface.'

'Which, I take it, we have.'

'Damned right. We're on a dedicated up link. There's a twenty four-hour operation room just for us.'

'Aren't we just the business, Gino?'

Both the tactical satellite phone and the Plugger were encrypted for secure transmission, the TACSAT to send via the Defence Satellite Communication System, the GPS to receive its information from NAVSTAR. Dedicated frequencies ensured that none of their messages would get mixed up with other traffic. Added to the IBM notebook they had an Iridium hand held commercial satellite telephone. It was all stuff a modern geologist would be expected to have in his equipment. There was nothing they were carrying that would draw suspicion on to them, and that included the weapons for personal protection. No one went into the country they were entering, to work, without a gun and an armed escort.

The weapons they had were Russian. In a search it would lower their profile, since old Ivan gear was the weaponry most often found in Afghanistan. On black ops it was standard practice. Both had AKSU-74 5.45mm sub machine guns, a modified version of the AK-47 with a much shorter barrel length, 207 as against the standard 413 millimetres, with a folding butt and conical flash suppressor instead of a muzzle brake. The pistols were Marakov 9mms, another weapon that Blue was familiar with from his SAS days.

Both men were tense, with that degree of concentration that comes from operating at the edge. But they talked of old times; Blue of being here before, crossing into Afghanistan during the years when the Mujahideen had fought the Russians. The country was the Ivans' Vietnam, the place where their huge military machine had been fought to a standstill by a committed guerrilla army. Not that the Mujahideen had gone into battle without a lot of help!

They'd been armed, supplied and trained – both inside and outside the country – by the USA and Britain, happy to see the Russians getting a good hiding. The Brits had delivered intelligence gathering skills, training in small arms and anti-tank weaponry, and, when asked, the Scottish training camp. The Yanks had come up with proportionately more, best of all the Stinger missile, so accurate and easy to transport and use that it had almost wholly negated Russian dominance in the air, keeping the helos under control and forcing the MIGs to fly high.

It had been good then, a place where the locals welcomed a Western face with joy. Not any more! Afghanistan, except for a small bit in the far north, was real bandit country, peopled by the very same guys who'd been so friendly before. Now, they'd murder you just for your boots if they could get away with it. And they still had Stingers. The CIA had sent in operatives to steal what were left or buy them back, not with much success. The locals wouldn't part with them, and any contemplated air operation in this part of the world had to take cognisance of the fact that they might be used against once friendly air assets.

The mindset they'd need over the border was already in place. Pakistan was not entirely safe for an infidel either, especially here in the north. It was the home from which the Taliban had sprung, the product of the numerous religious schools that lined the border. Supposedly, the country was neutral, but if you'd served in the SAS you knew it was fatal to take chances. All Special Forces training was designed so that you would keep yourself alert at all times, ready to react to whatever threat materialized, and that was a habit you never lost, even long after leaving the service.

Blue Harding had been hyped up since the flight landed at Karachi; the slow formalities of immigration and customs a more difficult thing to cope with than a hot contact. You have to work very hard to look relaxed and weary, to yawn and appear bored, especially when every nerve in your body is screaming for movement, the full money belt round your waist itches like hell and your arse muscles are twitching.

Blue and Gino Manganelli had gelled like men who'd known each other all their lives, two pros who quickly learned to respect one another. The American, married with two grown up kids, was from a small place called Port Reading, a dormitory town about an hour's drive from Manhattan and the bright lights of New York. Tall and thin, he smiled easily and enjoyed the way Blue ribbed him about the supposed 'history of his locale'. A two hundred-year-old church was not likely to impress someone who'd lived close to Hereford Cathedral.

And though he didn't elaborate, it was obvious this was Gino's patch, which made him the boss as far as Blue was concerned. Stain him with tea and put him in a red and white check keffiyeh and Blue reckoned he could pass for an Arab, even if someone stopped him for a chat. And, as an old

SAS mate of his had once pointed out, Arab dress was best, because underneath the flowing robes, you could hide so much firepower.

This was what Blue had trained for through a long stretch of his life. He'd been in situations like this in the past, out ahead of the pack, laying the ground, doing the recces for the guys who would come after. You cursed when you were working and moaned when you were unoccupied. And the bottom line was simple: it was good to be back in the fold!

It's tempting, when you know you're being watched, to tease the surveillance teams, to do things that run them ragged. But that must be avoided, since they will suss out that you've twigged them, which will make them very twitchy. Keegan and Boyle knew they had to do something, but what? was the question. Using a notepad they discussed it, while seemingly engaged in idle chatter. The first written question was a return to Ireland, posed by Boyle, killed off by Keegan. To stay in the UK was not really an option either, which only left the idea of joining Gilhooley in Amsterdam.

'The car?' Boyle wrote saying. 'Do you want an Indian tonight?'

'Money?' replied Keegan by pen. 'Christ, I'm fed up with spicy food, Con. Let's just get a fry up.'

The discussion went on, a seeming argument about food, in reality a written discussion of the options. It took time, and must have bored the listeners rigid, but it ended up with the outlines of an escape plan that just might throw their pursuers.

'Well, if it's bacon egg and chips you're after having, I'll have to do some shopping.'

'We'll both do it,' Keegan replied.

The watchers saw their two targets come into the hall and take their coats off the pegs. Only one watcher spoke, alerting the mobile teams to stand by, and to get someone in place at the local supermarket to tail them down the aisles.

'Shall we get a video as well?' asked Keegan. 'There's nothing but shite on the box tonight.'

The video store was no problem. Small, glass fronted and open, it only had the one entrance and exit.

CHAPTER TEN

Encrypted to connect with the US Military NAVSTAR system, the Plugger was accurate to within eight metres, which, as Gino pointed out, was enough to take the unwary over a precipice on the kind of roads they'd be using. He also had a Silva compass just in case the whole GPS thing broke down.

Saindak, their destination, was in a small range of mountains called the Küh-a-Sultan. Small that is, for this part of the world. They were high enough to make the Brecon Beacons look like pimples.

The back of the Nissan Patrol was full of canned food, five-gallon plastic jerrycans of water, a medical kit and enough spare batteries to light up a small town. Gino and Blue were wearing personal locator beacons – the same as worn by Gulf War pilots and Special Forces – so that they could be lifted out in an emergency, the beacons backed up by a Sarbe ground to air emergency radio. The night vision equipment was state of the art – the Litton M944, interchangeable between naked eye and digital video camera. The same supplier provided the IRM-K infra-red marker kit specifically designed for marking out helo landing zones and fixed wing TLSs. That was backed up by infra-red Cylums, flares that could operate without a power source. There were two infra-red strobes for the pilots to visually lock on to on approach.

There were boxes for rock samples, picks, shovels, two compasses, Bergens, sleeping bags, knives, rope, karabiners and a small pup tent, in fact everything a geologist would want on the job including the notebook computer. Gino had also added extra jerry cans of petrol as well as two spare tyres.

The conversation was spasmodic, punctuated by long silences in which Blue was left to his own imaginings. Often these took the form of selective memories, ops he'd been on where a real threat existed – only he interposed Jake in his imagination instead of himself. The

96

physical resemblance made it easy. Both were of the same compact build, with an air of alertness that tended to animate the features. And Jake had a slow smile that Blue recognized as similar to his own.

Inevitably he recalled the thoughts that had surfaced on the way to Mildenhall. To a mind as well trained as his own and in such a location, figuring out active scenarios for an SAS squadron was simple. Even easier to see were the places where those mentally plotted operations could go pear-shaped, leaving the troopers tasked to do the job up shit creek with leaking water wings. He could see in his mind's eye, hear in his head, some dimwit Rupert giving the go ahead for a flawed plan, the kind that got people killed, people like Jake.

'Bastards.'

'What?' asked Gino.

'Nothing,' Blue replied. 'Thinking aloud.'

Fifty kilometres after a town called Noh Kundi they turned left off the main drag. The road to Saindak, which had not been paid for by misspent foreign aid and had little military value, was rough and full of potholes, winding through mud hut villages built on steep hillsides, dark and seemingly deserted. But there would be eyes to see them – both men knew that – some just curious, others wondering if they should contact relatives up ahead to set up an ambush for the two white travellers mad enough to move during the hours of darkness. Gino had a way of dealing with that, switching on the map reading light as they drove by. One hand would hold up the edge of the map. It also supported, quite conspicuously, the conical muzzle of his machine gun.

That had to be put away when they passed through an army checkpoint, their papers examined by illiterates whose education extended to a recognition of the face of George Washington on the quickly palmed one dollar bills. The officer who could read, and might have questioned them more closely, was either in his own bed, or somebody else's. He would have required a higher-denomination bribe to let them pass without unnecessary fuss, but it was a fair bet his troopers wouldn't even mention their existence, lest he demand they hand over the money they'd taken.

Dawn was breaking about ten kilometres from Saindak, the sky that dull grey tone it holds before sunrise, when Gino flicked open the phone and made a call. It was answered immediately. He could imagine it at the other end, a group of guys staring at the phones waiting for them to ring. They would have little more idea than Gino or Blue Harding what was going down, but with the effort being allocated to it, they'd sure know it was important.

The company name was the call sign for the listeners, the conversation actually innocent in that it merely informed the people supposedly employing them that the work they were undertaking was going well. GCHQ monitored radio traffic all over the world, and picking up a signal from Baluchistan, especially when waiting for it, was child's play. It would be their job to tell Bowers, when the information was processed, that his man was in place. That they would try to do before the Yanks told JSOC.

'That's the Northwest Frontier for you,' said Gino, in his heavy New Jersey accent, when he finished the call. 'They're short of water, medicine and food round here, but there's no shortage of fuckin' mobile phones.'

Their contacts, four armed tribesmen, were waiting on the other side of the town in another Patrol. Spray from the river beneath set up rainbows in the low morning sun, and in the background the hills rose to an imposing range, one or two of the peaks high enough to be topped by snow. Yet, for all the beauty, the landscape was arid, a dry pale brown at best with the odd stunted tree, but mostly grey and barren both in rock and soil.

'Do they grow anything round here?' asked Blue.

'Heroin by the ton,' the CIA man replied.

'What's our route across the border?'

'Rough,' said Gino. 'We could get in at a main crossing point, but bin Laden's antics have made the Afghan border guards just that bit more attentive. So we've cleared it with the local smugglers to use one of their routes.'

'Geologists are no threat,' said Blue.

'Agreed. But it's not unknown for perfectly legit people, even UN aid workers, to be held up for a day or two just because some border guard is having haemorrhoid trouble. There are to be no delays in getting over. So our papers, properly stamped, will show that we crossed into Afghanistan, with our escorts, a week ago.'

'Our friends,' asked Blue, nodding towards the quartet of armed tribesmen, 'are they smugglers?'

'Probably, in their spare time.'

Gino gestured towards the Patrol, and one of the tribesmen climbed out, cradling his standard AK-47 in his arms as he slowly walked towards them. The CIA man kept talking as Blue watched the Afghan approach.

'Ever heard of a guy named Mohammed Panah?'

'Yes,' Blue replied. 'But don't ask me where.'

Gino gestured in a vaguely northerly direction. 'Here. He was a famous Mujahideen commander. The Taliban wasted him, along with every other leader they found. This guy was one of his fighters.'

'Nice,' Blue said softly, as the tribesman stopped before Gino, who turned to make the introduction.

'Abdul Siygas, the leader of our escort. Abdul, this is Mister O'Leary from Ireland.'

Abdul, of medium height, very thin and with a full beard, gave them the ritual Islamic greeting, followed by a greeting in halting English. Looking into his eyes, Blue was struck by the lack of expression. It wasn't just Abdul, he remembered that as commonplace in a country that never experienced any peace. Until a man knew you, and was prepared to trust you, he would shield every inner thought he harboured.

Blue smiled, shaking Abdul's hand, thanking him for his attention and generally going out of his way to make him feel good. Then he insisted on being taken over to meet the other three – Milaad, Badar and Gullam – all Abdul's nephews, all younger than him, all bearded, and all obviously in the pay of the CIA. Each had his AK-47, the weapon of choice in these parts, and handled it with an ease that underlined the fact that he well knew how to use it.

'How far can we take these guys?' asked Blue as they returned to their Patrol.

'All the way if we want to,' Gino replied, confirming that they were on the payroll. 'They're ours.'

'We're airlifted. Can they get out on their own?'

'Piece of cake.'

'What's it like over there?'

'Bloody!' said Gino, using the word in an American, not an English sense. 'A lot of the Muslims on this side of Afghanistan are Shiite. That applies to Abdul and his cousins. The Taliban are Sunni, and inclined to indulge in the odd massacre of folks they consider heretics. The flip side is that the Shiite are not too crazy about the Mullah Omar and his fighters. The smuggling routes are therefore very secure, which is why we can trust them as a way to get in.'

Maps were spread out on the bonnet, held down with some difficulty in the strong southerly wind while Gino plotted the map references into the Plugger. Blue made a mental note of them; he'd seen technical kit go down too often to wholly rely on it.

'At the top of the pass, we'll be able to see this big lake, the Gowd-a-Zirreh. During daylight it's visible from any elevated point on the flat country, so it will give us a fix that will allow us to move fast while avoiding the lakeside villages.'

The finger moved on. 'At the head of the lake we follow the Hamur River due east until it turns sharp south. We stay on the road till we get to the Helmand. There we choose a point to cross, not hard since the rivers are wide, low and slow at this time of year. We then turn north and cross some hill country and join up to the road from Rudbas to Landay, well away from any populated parts.'

'That's two roads?'

'No choice, Blue. Time!'

Blue didn't argue, it was Gino's call. Instead he pointed to the Plugger. 'You'd better give me a quick noddy guide on that thing, since I need to know which buttons to press. I take it our destination is already in there.'

'It is, as well as all the way stations on the route. And you were always going to get a operating crash course on this baby as we head for the border.'

100

The two men exchanged a glance. Both must have speculated about where they were going and why, but it was sure as hell that Gino knew more than Blue. If he'd wanted to pass more information on he would have done so by now. That meant there was no point in discussing it.

'How busy is that first road?' asked Blue, pointing to the line between two sizeable Afghan towns.

'It's a main route for freight, but in terms of trouble it's quiet. But you never can tell. Two months ago the Taliban were all over it, trying to convert the Sunnis in the towns and villages along the way, not too hard a job when the other option is a bullet.'

'The border itself?'

'Patrolled, but it's wild country where smuggling is a way of life. Most of the officials have been in place for years. There's the odd fanatic, but they tend to be rare. If we do come across a customs type we don't shoot him, we pretend we're buying dope and bribe him accordingly. If he hesitates to accept it, he's Taliban, so then we kill him.'

Gino rummaged in the back of the Patrol and emerged with a couple of long flowing garments, clean but not new, followed by a pair of flat round hats, the kind the locals wore.

'Time to go native, pal.'

That was logical too. Even if they were passing themselves off as geologists, it was best to dress and look like a local. In a place like Afghanistan it wasn't just officials you had to worry about, especially when you got away from the main population centres. Every man and boy, in every tribe – Pathan, Hazara, Uzbek or Nuristani – was a born bandit. Western dress was just an invitation to indulge in the national sport of larceny.

The same went for an armed escort. Even the most officious bastard of a bureaucrat would understand the need for self-defence in the mountains, where the writ of officialdom had never run. Not even the Taliban could control the tribesmen in their own natural habitat, nor would Blue and Gino be the first pair of Westerners to just disappear.

'Time to be off, I think.'

The road to Saindak had been bad. But it was tarmac heaven compared to the tracks, dropping down off the mountains, they went on to. They bucked along, half the time on slippery shale, along tracks with a sheer cliff face on one side and a precipitous drop on the other, the huge lake of the Gowd-a-Zirreh shimmering in the distance. Gino and Blue, once the lesson on the Plugger was over, played a game of spot the raghead with no success whatsoever.

They were there of course, in the hills, watching, making sure that the Westerners stuck to their side of whatever bargain had been struck. The route over the border would have been chosen for them by the very smugglers eyeballing them now, keeping them well away from any other stuff that might be going down.

Whatever tale Gino had spun them, and it was for sure he hadn't told them the truth, both he and the CIA would come out of it well. And that applied even if Blue's supposition proved correct – that a heavy assault was going in on either bin Laden or the Taliban. Lying was a way of life in these parts, the bigger and more successful the falsification the more juice garnered by the man who produced it. Provided nothing was done directly to affect their ability to operate, the local smugglers would appreciate the way they'd been suckered. A sum of money would change hands just for the sake of face, and it would be a good-humoured exchange, with much ritual tea drinking to accompany it. And the locals would keep their mouths shut. Being turned over was one thing, broadcasting it quite another.

'The Plugger puts us over the border,' said Gino. 'D'you know what happened the first time your guys crossed into this shithole?'

Gino Manganelli was, along with all his other pursuits, an antiquity buff, full of the history of his native New Jersey – one of the original colonies in America – happy reeling off the names of places that were direct copies of English towns. He wasn't talking about home now, but Afghanistan, and Blue had a fair idea what he was on about. Given that it reflected badly on his country, he was damned if he was going to admit it.

'All I can remember, mate, is that it was a fucking long tab, and that my Bergen straps were killing me, cos of all the shit I was bringing in for the ragheads.'

'I'm talking about a bit further back, pal, like over a hundred years. And I'm talking about the British Army.'

'Please don't, Gino. Thinking about the British Army gives me nightmares.'

'It did more than that for them, buddy. Ten thousand came in, if you include the camp followers, and only one guy came out alive.'

'The lone doctor.'

'You know?'

'You're not the only one who reads books, Gino. Every serious sod in the regiment was telling that tale from the first day we were tasked to tab in here, especially the bastards who were staying at home. Throats cut, bollocks chopped off, women and children raped and mutilated, and that doctor staggering over the border, kept alive just so he could tell the folks back home what happened.'

'It wasn't only the women who were raped, old buddy.'

'Then you've got something to look forward to.'

'Make a good movie, that lone doctor bit,' said Gino, punching another reference point into the GPS. 'I can just see Tom Cruise in the part.'

'No way. Ewan McGregor or maybe Liam Neeson.'

'They're all probably too good-looking. The local faggots would never let them go.'

'Just as long as we don't have to do it, mate. I want to fly out of here, not walk.'

At Gino's command Blue braked on a flat open space beside a hill, the crest of the route, but cut off from view both to the north and the south. The ground around the base of the hillside was littered with fallen boulders, some of them as big as a house, which had Blue looking up to see if any more were on their way down. Up in these hills rock falls were common. In fact, every so often you could hear one in the distance.

'How secure are we up ahead?'

'Should be plain sailing,' Gino replied. 'Otherwise there would be a messenger here to tell us what to avoid. That's part of the deal with the guys who cleared us to use this route.'

'They're that certain?'

'Yep!'

'They don't often get caught, do they, these smugglers?'

'Not quite accurate, Blue, old buddy; they never get caught.'

Gino signalled to Abdul, driving the escort Nissan, to follow in their wake. Blue gunned the engine, and then made Gino Manganelli laugh when he cried, in a perfect plummy, upper class tone. 'Tally Ho! What.'

CHAPTER ELEVEN

Tiers of planning went into an operation like Joint Strike. At the very top the political direction was handled by the two defence departments, with the White House and Downing Street in constant touch. There was no way of getting to the target without compromising neutral airspace, both over Pakistan and Afghanistan, and quite possibly Iran as well. That was a situation that had to be dealt with.

Iran, regularly overflown, and in a non-sensitive area, presented not much of a problem – there was every chance it wouldn't happen anyway. Pakistan, even with all the recent spats about nuclear testing, was still a US client state, so would be informed of the operation at a time that would do nothing to compromise the security of the mission. Afghanistan was a different case. It would not take kindly to what the joint operation intended, and so prior warning of any kind was out of the question. Yet, much as they might disapprove of their way of governance, the last thing the Western political leaders wanted to do was to involve the Taliban in any way. Plans had to be included to neutralize them, as much for their own good as for the good of the mission.

Likewise, the options of staging from Bahrain or Saudi Arabia had been abandoned by JSOC; they were simply not secure enough. Diego Garcia, just a dot in the Indian Ocean, had been selected as the FOB. Yet the distance from that base was too great for a straight flight that would meet the mission requirements. A forward staging area was essential to avoid having planes return all the way to Diego Garcia if the mission got an abort signal.

So it was decided to utilize the barely used airfield at Marisah, a small island off the coast of Oman. It was discreet and isolated enough for a stopover, though not suitable as a full Forward Operations Base for something of this magnitude. JSOC knew that from experience. It was the spot from which the US had carried out Operation Rice Bowl, which might make some of the more superstitious a bit flaky. For JSOC it was just a chance to lay a ghost.

By the time Brigadier Harry Millar, the UK Director of Special Forces, and his staff landed at Fort Bragg to join the Joint Special Operations Command, the choice of targets, as well as the outline plan, had been finalized. The two sites in the mountains some eighty-five kilometres north east of Kandahar were perfect. It only remained for JSOC to give an outline of the forces to be deployed to infill and back up the two squadrons.

The reception committee, when the DSF landed, was headed by the Commander of JSOC in person. Having met and co-operated during Desert Storm, Millar and General Lucius B. Morton greeted each other warmly. Good manners demanded that Morton inform Millar of the decisions already taken and ask for his comments. They were positive, because the decisions seemed to be sound.

Not that a contrary view would have counted for much; Millar was very well aware of the limits of his influence. He was very much the guest at the party, and that included planning. He would have to disagree violently to even get a polite hearing, though he did have the authority from Downing Street to object. But only a PM to President call would effect any changes that the Brits thought necessary.

By the standards of the British Army, Millar was a bit exceptional. An old Etonian, with the brains and connections to pursue whatever career he wanted, he opted for the army by choice. Most officers from his kind of background chose service life for the very sound reason that they lacked the intelligence for anything else, and had the private means to exist comfortably on the low pay in the more expensive regiments. That they tended then to favour each other, imposing a glass ceiling on the brighter middle class intake, accounted for the oft repeated observation that the British Army was still a force of 'lions led by donkeys'.

The DSF was no donkey, nor was he overly polite to his superiors. In fact his brain was as sharp as his tongue. He was often heard to remark that whatever appeared on a senior officer's shoulder stood in direct correlation to the number of dead brain cells in their head. He also held the view that should a war break out, every officer of staff rank should be immediately retired, to be replaced by juniors less hidebound and in closer contact with the men they led.

When questioned on this, he would point to the opening campaigns of every British war for the last two to three hundred years, all the way back to Marlborough; to the inevitable debacles that the soldiers had faced under moribund leadership, to be followed by their success once the dead wood had been chopped. It was a credit to him that opinion had not been changed by his own elevation.

Busy as they were at JSOC, there was time for a small reception to welcome and introduce him to the other members of the command set-up. It was a very American affair, strictly teetotal. Amongst the greetings and the positive statements about the plan lay the residue of the arguments. Even in an area where total agreement on aims existed, disputes on the means employed existed. It was nothing new to a man like Harry Millar who had been a long time in the army; it was the old story of the differing aims of competing services.

The US Navy had wanted to deploy its latest weaponry, in this case the new MV-22 Osprey vertical take-off and landing plane. With the present cost running at $50 million a throw Millar could see their point. International sales of the VTOL would bring that cost down for the US Marines, and they'd been presented with an opportunity for the plane to show off its paces in the hardest sales pitch it was possible to create: a real-life battle scenario.

It was a development programme that he had taken a real interest in. As far as Special Operations were concerned, the multi-role Osprey was designed to take over from most of the present Night Stalker fleet, replacing the present eighty aircraft with a mere fifty. It was a lulu of a plane, perfect for Special Forces. It could take off either from a proper airfield or a forest clearing because, when its wings were tipped and the rotor blades activated, the Osprey behaved exactly like a helicopter. Capable of a 230-knot cruising speed it could fly eighteen combat ready troops 2100 nautical miles, with one in flight refuelling, and go into action using terrain guidance as low as one hundred feet.

Added to that, as a new development it had the most advanced

107

avionics available: forward looking infra-red sensors; a digital map display; a mission computer capable of storing hundreds of navigation waypoints; and an integrated electronic warfare suite, with everything the four man crew needed to know on head up display. Harry Millar wanted them for the SAS, but was pretty sure that, at thirty million quid each, he'd have a fight on his hands to get the funds.

'Christ!' said Harry Shearsby softly, having got Harry Millar into a corner. 'It was practically designed for this mission: a direct flight from Diego Garcia on to target, with air refuelling outside any hostile radar window; and no need for a Tactical Landing Site, with all the inherent problems that can stem from the use of imperfect terrain. Adverse weather or not, the MV-22 can fly as low as any plane in the present air fleet. The avionics are state of the art, and its in-air defence capabilities are second to none.'

'It does sound perfect,' Millar replied. He knew, without being told, that the decision had already been taken, so being polite cost him nothing. 'Why was it turned down?'

'Catch 22,' sighed Shearsby. 'It's not combat tested. But we managed to squeeze one in for casevac.'

Rear Admiral Shearsby had been forced to settle for casualty evacuation. He had, it transpired, encountered a real problem in that one of Lucius Morton's nephews was a MV-22 pilot, and he had crashed his plane on a rotor blade approach. Morton had no hesitation in telling the navy representative how the scenario would look if anything like that occurred on the mission. Millar, as he listened, could not help feeling slightly disappointed. While not one to risk his men in untested equipment, he would have liked to have seen the Osprey in action. If it performed well it would have aided his own sales pitch at the MOD.

Another conversation with Lucius Morton got Millar the other side of the argument. Morton hadn't been unsympathetic to Shearsby's concerns, having been in the same bind himself many times, sometimes left to feel as if he was more of a salesman for some arms manufacturer than a career soldier. It had been real bad after Desert Storm, where every senior officer in the American armed forces who'd served in the Gulf was roped in to spread the good news about the fine performance of Uncle Sam's technology.

Skilled in the art of avoiding outright confrontation, with Shearsby, Morton had taken refuge in the safest place he knew, someone else's worries.

'I told the Admiral we had to take cognisance of what the tactical commanders want.' Morton and Millar exchanged a knowing glance, then a smile, before Morton continued. 'Time to give you a full briefing, Harry.'

A major from US Army Intelligence gave the briefing in its initial stages. He was typical Green Slime to Millar, a real indoor type, wearing a set of crisp camouflage fatigues the paler sections of which somehow matched his complexion.

The actual presentation, compiled on PowerPoint, would have done credit to any sales conference given by a big corporation. It was colourful, with lots of dashes and flashes, flow charts and grids showing forces to be employed, methods of infiltration and exfill, equipment available, plus satellite and ground images of bin Laden's camp. It had everything, to Harry Millar's way of thinking that smacked of puffery; the man at the head of the table was selling an operation to people who intended to do it anyway. The one thing he had failed to put in his presentation was blood.

The two governments were proposing to commit close to 120 men to take on a force that could be as much as treble that number, in prepared positions – on paper a mad idea. Given the importance of the sites and their presumed functions, these would be the best-trained fighters bin Laden had. They would also be fanatics, prepared to die for their cause. Certainly they would have suffered casualties from the hail of cruise missiles planned to impact just before the assault, and they would certainly be disorientated after the Spookys had given them a pasting. But if enough of them survived the air bombardment, they would still outnumber the attacking force.

Harry Millar could choose to be diplomatic when he wanted, and he had been so throughout the PowerPoint presentation, content to sit there and absorb the beauty of the colourful technology. And in truth he had little to argue about with the overall plan; it was as sound as it was going to be. The whey faced major, trying hard to look like a real soldier, had identified the landing sites inside Afghanistan – one to be confirmed – that would take the C-130s carrying the assault troops. There was no doubt the helicopters – MH-47E Chinooks and M60Ks – should make the Tactical Landing Site undetected, and be able to refuel in the security that location provided. They were perfect for the insertion, being armour plated and able to withstand small arms ground fire. The rest of the air defence – the M60K Black Hawks, and the Air Support AC-130U Spectres, gunships all – was designed to ensure they faced no more than that. But that couldn't be guaranteed. There could be some kid in a bunker cuddling a Stinger that he got for his birthday, and luck might just get it past the electronic counter-measures. You just couldn't tell. And it was an SAS maxim never to underestimate your enemy.

'Do we have an appreciation of potential casualties?'

He saw how uncomfortable that remark made the other JSOC members. The spectacle of body bags coming home haunted the US military, right up to and especially including the Commander-in-Chief himself. Presidents hated the sight, seeing it translated into lost votes even as they shed genuine tears. There was not a man at this table who thought a direct action operation of this magnitude could be carried out without casualties. But they didn't want to be the one to allude to it. To Harry Millar that was a failing.

'We expect a minimum ten per cent,' Morton replied.

'Very wise, Lucius,' Millar replied, smoothly. 'Let's hope it's no more than that.'

It was the one area where he could speak with a voice as powerful as everyone else at the table. The plan was American, the insertion was the same. But when the shit started flying it would take out SAS soldiers just as quickly as Delta Force.

'That's the role given to the Osprey,' said Shearsby, making little attempt to disguise his continuing pique at such meagre use. 'It can make a direct flight from the battle area to a proper hospital. We have thought it advisable, for the same purpose, to have a medical team on board.'

'Do we have any provision for the dead? I know there's not a lot we can do for them. And I expect the usual rules will apply, of course, this being a Special Forces operation.'

That meant no identifying equipment or possessions other than the dog tags and syrette of morphine each man would wear around his neck. Any trooper sure that a comrade was dead, would remove those and make him anonymous.

'I was thinking about the propaganda angle,' said Millar. 'We don't want to see the bodies of our soldiers dragged through the streets, with the local Afghanis claiming a victory.'

That brought back an unpleasant image of Somalia to every mind at the table. The sight of despoiled American bodies had had a huge effect at home, making the continued presence of US troops in the country impossible. Millar knew that certain people at the table thought he was being deliberately rude, reminding them of what was an operational failure. In some senses he was, but that was hard luck for those so sensitive. He merely felt the need to remind everyone in this air-conditioned room that they were talking about a real battle with real blood, not a PowerPoint computer game.

There were men sitting at this table who'd reached their elevated rank without ever seeing a shot fired in anger. They were about to commit men to a situation they themselves had no experience of. Harry Millar wanted them to think about it now, and think about it all the time, and if that meant being a little rude, so be it. That didn't apply to Lucius Morton of course, who was the least phased by Harry Millar's allusion to the subject.

'I think you'll find we have thought of that, Harry. The orders to both squadrons will be the same, that is if you don't object. All bodies to be brought out, regardless of condition.'

'Good!'

Morton then made a big play of looking at his watch.

'Dinner, I think, guys, and an hour's thinking time. That will give you a chance to have a nap, Harry. Reconvene at nineteen hundred hours.'

'Just a thought,' said Millar, as they made to stand up. 'This "Tiltrotor" thing. You'll be using one in Nevada?'

'Of course.'

'I take it some assessment will be made of how it performs.'

It was Shearsby who replied. 'Damned right it will.'

'These assessments. Could you include the MOD in London? Strikes me they might be quite interested. That would go for the post-operation report as well, if you don't mind.'

Being American it was quite possible that they would be classified, and if unflattering, they could be doctored before being released. Millar was taking advantage of the present liaison to extract a future favour.

'I don't see why not,' replied Shearsby, cautiously.

'Thank you, Admiral,' replied Millar loudly, as though in receipt of a promise. 'I shall hold you to that.'

Morton, as they left the room, dropped his voice to a whisper, so that only Millar could hear. 'Just how many of those mothers do you want to buy, you cunning bastard?'

Millar whispered back, 'As many as I can get my hands on, Lucius. And as to my being a cunning bastard, is that not a very necessary attribute for high rank, in both your army and mine?'

'You must speak to those in the nearby camps,' said bin Laden, addressing his military commander, Sheikh Tassir Abdullah. 'Tell them that the Taliban are still our brothers.'

'Will they believe us?' asked Mohammed al Kadar. He'd got back to the camps with McGurk, only to find Mullah Omar's men at the command centre disabling the communications. 'There was a near battle from our fighters. All it needed was a word from you and they would have thrown the interlopers out.'

There was a degree of weariness in bin Laden's response, a measure of the strain he was under. 'We cannot fight the Taliban, Mohammed.'

'Nor can we just lie down,' said Tassir Abdullah.

'Better to die fighting.'

Al Kadar was young; those words showed he was still full of all the passion that went with his age and inexperience. It was with a weak smile that bin Laden recalled his own youthful ardour. He too, at one time, would have fought the Taliban, and dared them to do their worst. But he was older now, wiser, with a task to perform: he had to keep his loose knit organization in place. He led the only people in the world who had the ability to strike back at the enemies of Islam.

Mullah Omar had deep religious convictions and recognized bin

Laden's abilities, but he was also cunning and ruthless. For him the Taliban was everything: to stand against him was to invite complete destruction. The move against bin Laden's communications was a compromise that took account of Omar's needs as well as the concerns of the clerical council that ran the Afghan government. There was no way to calculate the hatred these men felt for the West. And when it came to killing, anyone who did not believe as they did was entitled to only one thing, a painful death. Yet all around them they saw the effect of standing up to a world that didn't share their faith: a lack of food, a worthless currency, children dying from disease and malnutrition, a war against the last of the Mujahideen they could not win for lack of resources.

It was their faith and their hatred which made them shy away from the ultimate sanction, the one act which would please the Americans the most: the news that Osama bin Laden was no longer welcome in Afghanistan, that he had been kicked out. Instead, when they met with the Americans, they would say that he had disappeared; that he could not be found. They would not be believed, but that mattered little. What did matter was to keep the aid agencies in the country; to be allowed the small amount of exports they could manage, but most of all, to stop the United States from arming their enemies!

Thus they must emasculate him, stop him using his weapons and communications. Not all at once, but the breach had been made in the wall of their support that now could only weaken. Bin Laden could see no way that the status he'd enjoyed so far could be restored. They would reduce him slice by slice; as if they were carving a succulent lamb, each cut small enough to assuage their beliefs.

'Go, Abdullah,' he said to Tassir. 'Speak to them, tell them this is a minor setback, a play to fool the Americans. Tell them the camps are safe, that our brothers in the Panshir Valley still fight shoulder to shoulder with the Taliban.'

'They would rather hear that from you.'

'They shall, and in a very short time. We have struck hard, which has caused those who govern Afghanistan many problems. But they are with us.'

'I think we shall die by degrees,' al Kadar said as Tassir Abdullah left.

'No, Mohammed. We shall not.'

The youngster looked at him keenly, but bin Laden was not about to reveal his thoughts: those same thoughts which had sustained him in Mullah Omar's council chamber – a long narrow room, lined on both sides with comfortable seating, each chair occupied by men of some importance in the Taliban movement. The orotund way the one-eyed Mullah had spoken caused no confusion. All were too well versed in the ways of the world they lived in to demand direct points. Like Osama bin Laden, sat at the far end away from Mullah Omar on his raised dais, they listened for the arguments buried in the folds of Islamic rhetoric.

Osama bin Laden had barely blinked as he'd watched his old friend and helper manoeuvre himself away from outright support for the *fatwas* he'd helped to declare. How different were these words to the ones he had used before he came to power, railing as he had at the way the Mujahideen took assistance from the West. Not for the first time in his life, bin Laden was left to wonder if he was the only one who could be entrusted with the task of dealing with the infidel?

But how to do it? Would it be better to move to Iraq, where Saddam Hussein would welcome his support? Iran might take him in as well, though they seemed at the moment to be more keen on a *rapprochement* with the West. Besides they were Shiite, barely to be trusted. In truth, given the number of his followers and the sheer scale of his operations, the logistics of a move were horrendous. He knew he needed to stay here in Afghanistan.

It was tempting to speak, to explain, but he knew he must remain silent until he had firm news from America. He was outside the Pale as far as the West and most other Arab States were concerned, and he'd deduced a long time ago that the way to stay in Afghanistan was to have a lever that would put the Taliban outside with him. The lever was to threaten an act so compelling that these sons of Allah would be forced to join his cause, forced to help raise the crescent flag of Islam. It had the added advantage that at a time of his choosing he could initiate a conflict which, though it might engulf the world in war, would also see the word of the Prophet triumph.

CHAPTER TWELVE

Planning for Special Operations differs greatly from the same task undertaken for normal green army units. In a major conflict involving large bodies of troops, the only information that the Headshed wants from below is numbers and combat readiness, both in weapons and men. Decisions are handed down from on high, objectives set out, forces nominated and deployed, and a set of orders issued.

Joint Strike required a different set of criteria. The men going in had a big say in what they could and could not achieve. The tactical command headed by Colonel John Franklin and Julian Gibson-Hoare set the tasks of the various units all the way down to troop level. The troop seniors broke these down into components and assigned groups, either one or two men patrols, to carry out a section of the overall task. These men then worked out themselves a way to execute that assignment before passing it back up to their ground commanders. Their job was to pass each plan or reject it, and from the information provided create an assault that would work.

Then there was the timing; an incursion of this size into hostile territory had a strict time limit. For all their formidable skills, Special Forces are lightly armed infantry designed for a quick and devastating blow, not a prolonged battle. In this case their job was to get in, do the job and get out, with a maximum time on target of thirty minutes. The job was simple to describe: stay within your allocated area, kill anything hostile that moves, conduct a fast search of all buildings and/or tents to collect anything that might be useful, then get out.

At least the guys knew they were going to be well equipped. Delta opened its storeroom to the SAS and invited them to help themselves on the very good ground that compatibility of equipment could only be to the good. The first item the Brits got was the new Special Forces modular 5.56mm M4A1 Carbine.

They were issued with the Camelback water system, a thermal-lined container that would be integrated into a variety of load-bearing equipment ranging from op waistcoats to different sized backpacks, day sack or Bergen. The fluid, kept cold, was fed forward by tube over the shoulder of choice through a one way bite valve so that the man fighting could take a drink on the move without recourse to a water bottle, or taking his hands off his weapon. That was a good thing, since the first thing that went in hot contact was the fluid in your mouth.

The Delta op waistcoats they declined, on the good grounds that they were used to their own and could find everything they wanted in the pitch dark; a new waistcoat would only cause confusion. But the minicams they did take, miniature video cameras pointing in front of them that gave the commanders all the way back to the USA a clear view of what was happening on the ground. Parsnips, true to form, helped himself to enough rations to feed the five thousand.

The briefing theatre was more crowded the second time Jake and his mates were ordered in. This time the Delta guys were there too, and it was their boss man on the podium, in front of the big screen, Gibson-Hoare sitting to one side, taking no part.

'Right,' Franklin called, commanding instant silence, 'let's talk about Osama bin Laden. Because gentlemen, that is why we are all here in Nevada. We are going to give the bastard a taste of his own medicine.'

He nodded to an intelligence major, operating the slide projector. The screen immediately filled with a series of slides, showing air reconnaissance images of destroyed buildings and cratered hillsides.

'That was, and still is, Kili Zawa al Badar, bin Laden's camp near Kabul. You will see from those damage-assessment photographs that we didn't actually destroy it. Even though the walls of the main buildings are single thickness breeze-block, some of them survived our best efforts to blast them apart.'

The Colonel was using a laser pointer to show each crater in turn, each point at which a Tomahawk had impacted with the ground, its bomb exploding on a proximity setting just before contact. Every eye in the room was following the tip of the beam.

'I'm showing you this because when we go in, we will hit the sites

116

within two minutes of the cruise attack, so that the target will have sustained the kind of collateral damage you see here. The Tomahawk Land Attack Missile is a good weapon, with eighty per cent of all ship-launched ordnance impacting within eight metres of the assigned target. There are spectacular misses, as you all know, missiles that go off target before they even hit the coast. The US military command accepts that as legitimate. As you all know, Saddam Hussein does not.'

There was a ripple of polite laughter around the briefing theatre.

'Whatever damage we inflicted, it sure scared the shit out of bin Laden. He upped sticks and ran off to get a mite closer to his pal Mullah Omar. Why? Two reasons. He suspects that with the possibility of Tomahawks going off target, we will be reluctant to launch them against a site so close to a major Afghan conurbation containing thousands of civilians. In that assumption, bin Laden is correct.'

The Colonel paused to let that sink in.

'Secondly, the flat desert terrain on the western side of Kandahar is intrinsically less susceptible even to air exploded ordnance. The soft ground will absorb much of the blast and cut down on the level of damage both to buildings and to his human assets. Having suffered one cruise attack he thinks he knows what to expect the next time. Again he has made a wise choice.'

The screen came up again with overhead shots of another trio of camps, very different in layout, and set on flat ground. 'But then we come to his most basic error. He underestimated how good our intelligence is. Osama bin Laden wanted us to think he shifted his communications centre and his specialist training school from Kabul to these new camps outside Kandahar.'

With a series of clicks the image was enlarged, the laser beam moving over various items on each picture.

'You will see here satellite dishes. Here we have a firing range and a grenade range. We have also observed various objects being blown up by other forms of explosives. A comms centre and training school we're meant to think, if we weren't fooled that he'd left them behind in what looked like the ruins of the old Kabul camps.'

The screen went blank. 'Without boring you with too much detail, the logistics of a ground attack on the Kabul camps were discussed and discounted. The idea of trying to get ground troops in over that distance, with any kind of useable Forward Operations Base were close to being insurmountable. The Kandahar camps hold close to three thousand people. Not all of them are fighters, but we would be hard put even with all the technology we can muster to give an exact number of the fighters we would face.'

Franklin smiled as pictures of a well-fenced complex, including a house, barrack blocks, stables and even a minaret, came up on the screen.

'Question? Is he tempting us to try? We think he might be. This is his private compound, inside the airport complex and not too far away from the city. This, too, looks like it might at least be a comms centre, a tempting target. He's no fool our man. He's figured out that the problems around Kabul limit us. So what has Osama bin Laden done? Why, he's gone and moved his camps to where we think we can get at them. Now I don't know about you boys, but I take that right kindly.'

This time the laughter was louder, but quietened when Franklin began to go into detail. To the side sat Gibson-Hoare, sitting forward eagerly, seeming to drink in his words, keeping buttoned up within himself his pique at not being included in the briefing. He was absolutely convinced that, had the situations been reversed, he would have extended the courtesy of taking over a part of it to Franklin. But then John Franklin had made little secret of his dislike of the SAS being there at all. To the Delta Force commander's way of thinking, they were a bunch of unnecessary guys piggybacking on superior American know-how. Harry Millar had ensured he didn't respond, by underlining that Franklin, as far as the JSOC command was concerned, was in a minority of one.

'Except it is not meant kindly. If we attack with cruise missiles, the risk of killing civilians is high. That makes the political cost high, maybe too high. Ground troops? That's a lot of opposition to take out without the target being softened up. But who knows? When Uncle Sam gets real mad there's no telling what he'll do. So, old bin Laden, being shrewd, makes sure that the bits of his empire that really matter are not in either of the places he would have us believe. They are, to be precise, quite a way off, some eighty-five Ks from Kandahar. And he thinks we don't know about them. But we do. And now I require your undivided attention gentlemen. I am about to show you where we are going.'

He got it and nodded again to the member of his intelligence staff who was operating the slides. What came up first was a picture of a half ruined red sandstone castle, battlements and all – more like something out of a tourist brochure than a Special Forces briefing.

'Christ, they're going to give us a Spanish holiday first,' said Jake.

'Can you still do the *Macarena*?' whispered Parsnips.

The image changed immediately to show a modern flat structure made of brick, shaded by trees, with a tarmac road running from a set of wrought-iron gates. It looked like something that Frank Lloyd Wright might have designed for spacious desert living, right down to the satellite dishes that littered the grounds. Then the screen split to show both images.

'These, gentlemen, are your targets.' Franklin placed his pointer on the red sandstone castle. 'This is bin Laden's top training centre. The only people who get to see and work in this place are the best people he has. They are as competent as everyone in this room at combat skills and the making, planting and detonation of explosive devices. They are good at training other terrorists, and are likely to be sent around the world to do that very thing.'

The pointer moved to the flat roofed building. 'This is the very nerve centre of bin Laden's operation. It is six hundred metres from the specialist training centre so that they can offer each other mutual support. It looks like a house and it is, with everything you'd expect: bedrooms, bathroom, even a TV lounge, I guess. But we suspect there's more underneath than we can see, quite possibly a deep bunker built into the hillside. From here he sends out his message to the world, both via the Internet and satellites. He has phones manned at all hours of the day and night, and his people are in constant touch with the elements of his world-wide terrorist organization.'

'Osama bin Laden himself is a constant visitor to both sites, either to watch his fighters become experts, or to communicate with his followers. You will see, two hundred yards from the comms centre, the helipad he uses to land and depart. The next time he is there, we are going to drop in as well.'

The sandstone castle filled the screen again, this time the photographs taken from various angles to show new brick built structures that had been added to the original, each one cunningly hidden by the walls of the castle so that no spy satellite could pick it up.

'The number we believe to be accommodated in this facility cannot be below two hundred. This has been calculated on the level of supply, which remains a constant. And this will be the target for the Twenty-second Special Air Service Regiment of the British Army.'

No sound came from the floor. The SAS contingent just nodded to each other, or looked at the ground in silence. Franklin was used to Delta, who would have raised the roof, and was slightly thrown by the silent controlled response of B Squadron.

'This is just a general briefing. Your own commanders will go through the tasks with you.'

The image changed again, back to the Frank Lloyd Wright type dwelling. Again it was shown from various angles, revealing under the trees a tent city hidden from observation by the leafy canopy.

'The guard force, some two hundred fighters, who have one task only – to make sure that Osama bin Laden stays alive, and continues to speak to the outside world. Well, let me tell you, Delta Force is going to spoil their day. This is the target for Delta Force.'

This time the reaction wouldn't have disgraced a film star; foot stamping, high-pitched whoops and whistling.

'We have to take both camps and neutralize both ordnance and human assets. The overall plan is to destroy bin Laden's HQ and specialist training camp, and to arrest bin Laden. We have no idea what he has in place already, just waiting for an activating signal. And, gentlemen, we intend the attack to go in when our number one target is present.'

No one asked how Franklin could be so sure of bin Laden's movements, but it had to be a man in place, someone who could pinpoint bin Laden and get the information out. Technically gained intelligence could never provide such information accurately, and neither, after dark, could satellites, even using infra red filters.

The Delta guys had exchanged significant glances and the odd nudge at the word 'arrest'. That was just another one for the file.

'Now, to the way in and the way out.'

Franklin talked on, giving the basic outline of what they would use, the timings. But, like that which had preceded it, the information was general. The exact briefings would be handled by the individual commands.

'The helos will take us in using NVGs and terrain mapping, with Spectres and Black Hawk gunships neutralizing the perimeter. There will be no time to assess damage. You gentlemen will fast rope down to carry through the assault regardless. Every building, even a tent if you find one, has to be searched. Anyone that looks important, search him before arresting him, anyone that doesn't should just be constrained. Time on target, thirty minutes. I now hand you over to your individual unit commanders, so that you can go into the final details of your tasks.'

The Chinooks and Black Hawks arrived in Nevada the same day as B Squadron, half assigned to the SAS, the rest to Delta. They were expected, but the arrival of the Osprey Tiltrotor came as a real surprise, and it attracted a lot of attention as it buzzed over the field, showing its paces as it turned from plane to helo and back again.

They could show off as much as they liked, but the guys on the ground had only one thing in mind, and several voiced it: given that this was slated for the Special Forces, could you fast-rope out of the fucker without getting hurt?

Jumping out of a hovering helo and sliding down a rope sounds easy. But it's not. The ropes come in thirty – sixty and ninety foot lengths, but the height of the drop matters little. Any distance from a non-static airframe, even the minimum thirty feet had to be controlled. Lose that and you could lose anything from an ankle to a neck. But it was something the Delta and SAS guys did all the time, so that required no practice.

All the pilots, fixed wing and helo, were taking turns on the Orbital Science Mission Mapping Simulator. The latest battle simulator to be put into service, it allowed each pilot to fly the mission on a computer screen several times before the real op. It showed the terrain as a three-dimensional image, and at the flick of a switch, it allowed the flyers to alter and practise under differing weather conditions or moon states. Enemy counter measures, radar, and ground fire from both AA guns and missiles could be programmed in with ease, so that when the mission took place the pilots would be flying over a landscape they knew as well as their own backyard.

Out in the Nevada desert, American Army engineers were erecting mock buildings: a single storey replica of the layout of the red sandstone castle, another of the flat building, the sentry positions and, up in the hills, the triple A batteries. While they waited, the various patrols, both Delta and SAS, sat round portable computers working out their own plans.

Before them was a program containing all the information that the US intelligence systems could collate regarding the area around bin Laden's training camp. And that amounted to a great deal. The standing joke was that you could lay out an open newspaper anywhere in the world and, as long as it was daylight and the sky was clear, the spy satellites could read it.

And the computers could, with limited information, build up a pretty good image of what lay inside solid walls. Gone were the days of bits of cardboard and matchsticks. Now, when they wanted to look at the sector to which they had been assigned they simply zoomed into a three-dimensional coloured presentation of their own personal target area. Some people loved the technology, others, like Parsnips, hated it.

'Why?' Tony Parsons exclaimed when asked, spitting out bits of sandwich, while pointing the remainder at his best friend and glaring at the others. 'You tell em, Jake.'

Jake Steel shrugged before speaking. He shared to some degree Parsnip's view, but he wasn't as passionate about it.

'Cos there's no way of knowing if that's still going to be there that's why. You heard them at the briefing. The target may already have sustained collateral damage from air bombardment.'

'Too bloody right,' said Parsnips.

'They're going to time our landing to take place while there's still shit in the air,' insisted Bull Bisset.

'My point,' added Parsnips, pointing a finger at the computer screen, which showed their target. 'Look at them castle walls. They were put up to stop bows and arrows. If a cruise goes off anywhere near them the fuckers will collapse.'

'It's got to be better than leaving them standing,' insisted Jake. 'Sometimes, Tony, you sound paranoid.'

'I'd rather fight in buildings than shit,' Parsnips replied.

Jake Steel gave him a heavy shove. Parsnips was a heavy reader of all books military. He hated fiction and loved facts, but they did tend to stick with him.

'He's never been the same since he read that doorstop about Stalingrad. He's shitting himself about fighting in rubble.'

'You could have practised in my kitchen, Parsnips,' groaned Mike Hutton. 'I was in the middle of doing the bastard when the call came. My missus was well pissed off.'

The finger jabbed at the screen again. 'What I'm saying is be careful of that. Don't get that image fixed in your mind, 'cos when we hit the ground it could be very different.'

'The visit is fortuitous, Mister President,' said Norland Jensen, the National Security Advisor. 'And with the Vice-chairman of the Joint Chiefs in Pakistan, it makes sense for us to bypass the State Department.'

The President was silent for a moment, aware that the constant turf war between the NSA and State could be a factor in the suggestion that was being made. There was, he'd been advised, no way of executing the plan for Joint Strike without invading Pakistani airspace. Even with the rumbles still echoing from the nuclear tests and other difficulties with aircraft orders, Pakistan was still a friendly country. They used US equipment, took US advice and formed part of a chain of alliances that

America relied on to maintain stability in the area. But they would not take kindly to Uncle Sam just wafting through.

'The trouble is, sir, as you know, that if we involve State it follows we have to use the ambassador to Pakistan. That means either a signal or a personal message telling him what to do. In turn, that requires us to inform the Secretary of State. He cannot be expected to pass on this information himself, so security is further compromised by the way he will have to route things through his subordinates. I return to the ambassador himself. He was appointed by the previous administration. We can issue as many orders as we like but we cannot, I repeat cannot be sure he won't, to cover his own back, consult his professional diplomats.'

'How long is General Bronowski there?'

'Until ten days from tomorrow, sir. The chances are, from what we are receiving from the CIA, that we will have a go in that window.'

'What about the men tasked to carry out the mission.'

'They are training, sir. But JSOC assures me that if they were slated to go tomorrow, they'd be on their way.'

'That's not an order I would issue. I will only give the green light to this when I'm sure everyone is fully prepared.'

'I know that, sir,' said the NSA, backtracking.

'The timing of the mission means our boys will be airborne for quite some time. That will allow me to contact the Secretary of State. Instruct General Bronowski that he will receive a coded signal to inform, in Pakistan, the most senior person he can find.'

'Might I also suggest that we give them something to sweeten the pill.'

'Not the F-16s.'

'I was thinking of the Orions, sir. They are more of a defence-related weapon than the F-16s. With India and its nuclear capability next door, it could be seen as a move to assist in keeping the peace. Orions would give them electronic oversight of the whole sub-continent.'

'I'll think about it.'

The side door to the Oval Office opened and an aide entered carrying a slip of paper. This was passed to the President who read it and looked up at the man sitting opposite.

'A message from the Taliban Government. They have important representatives attending a regional Islamic conference in Hyderabad. They have requested that we send a delegation to meet them.'

'Do they say what they are prepared to offer?'

'Nope!'

'Then it will not interfere with Joint Strike?'

The President replied emphatically. 'Nothing short of bin Laden's head on a platter is going to interfere with that operation.'

'I suggest that such a meeting would be a job for the ambassador.'

'Which will just happen to keep him out of the way?'

'Neat, to my way of thinking.'

CHAPTER THIRTEEN

The roads across the Afghan border weren't good, but at least they existed, potholed remnants of the Soviet Army's construction programme to move their troops and tanks around the country. They were busy but there was little alternative to using them, regardless of the risks. Time was not on their side: Gino and Blue must get to the site ASAP and they just had to hope that the quantity of traffic made the kind of proper roadblocks or checkpoints that might hold them up an impossibility.

Gino was sure that this part of the country was fairly peaceful. Certainly it was free from anything approaching a war. The last remnants of the Taliban's Mujahideen predecessors and enemies had been pushed out of this area two years previously. Any fighting at this time of year was taking place way north, confined to an enclave at the head of the Panshir valley. And he had good intelligence that the forced conversions of Shiites had come to a halt, partly because the Iranians had threatened to intervene and invade the country if the killing of their co-religionists didn't stop. Mullah Omar had huffed and puffed, but in the end he knew, faced with a vastly superior enemy, he had to comply.

They bucketed along, with Abdul on their tail, often behind lorries so overladen with freight listing precipitously, that it seemed wise to keep a distance. Buses were worse, crowded inside like Japanese commuter trains, with people clinging to the roof or hanging off the side. The extra coating of dust they threw up was welcome, cutting down on the view that those on the road had of the occupants of the two Nissans.

This was typical Asia, a multitude of people moving this way and that, either carrying goods themselves or urging tired donkeys to take that extra vital step, all looking as though they were going nowhere. Every so often they would encounter a group who'd stopped to say prayers, a line of believers bowing in the direction from which they'd come.

'Does it say anything in the Koran about road repairs?' asked Blue, retrieving the map from the floor. He then waved his Russian sub-machine gun. 'If I hadn't had the safety on I could have blown my bollocks off.'

'It can't do, pal,' Gino replied. 'Otherwise we'd be driving on a pool table. We're in amongst the strict adherence to the word of Mohammed tribe. The true believers.'

'You've studied them deep?'

'I have at that. Kinda like my life's work, now that I look back at it. Christ, I know the Koran as well as my Bible.'

'Have you ever thought of converting? Let's face it, you can have group sex with multiple wives.'

'I don't know that's allowed.'

'OK, so they can't all have a headache.'

Gino grinned. 'I thought about converting for about two seconds, and that was between Martinis. Not that it's a bad religion if you're inclined that way. Supposed to commit you to the good life. Trouble is the bastards that run this place take it too far. Ban this, ban that, grow a beard or I'll waste you. And the way they treat their women is like the dark ages.'

'Hard to chat up a bird with a *burka* on, that's for certain. You'd have no idea if you were getting the mother or the daughter.'

'There are ways of telling.'

'You'd better fill me in.'

'No way. You strike me as the kind of guy that gets into enough trouble with women as it is. And so will the Taliban. It'll blow up in their face one day.'

'Not today, please.'

'My guess is the Iranians will sort them out eventually. The Sunnis can only go so far with the Shiites.'

'You said it, mate.'

Gino talked on, steering round as many hazards as he could, over-taking through what Blue thought was impenetrable dust, always making sure Abdul was on his tail, talking, without lecturing, about the split in the Muslim world, the way that played into the hands of the

West. It was his opinion that if they ever healed it, ever got together in one cohesive whole, we'd all be in deep shit.

Blue lapsed into silence, half-listening, his mind running over the problems they might face and the possible solutions. Their job, even if they were armed, was to stay out of trouble, get to their destination and send in their conclusions about the suitability of the site for a landing. He hated being on this road and desperately wanted to get off it so that they wouldn't forever be in the dust cloud of a truck or bus, unable to see or prepare for an upcoming threat. Even when they could overtake they couldn't see much; there was always some vehicle on their side of the road.

'What's up ahead?' asked Gino suddenly, easing his foot slightly off the accelerator.

Blue traced the route on the map. 'No obstacles, that I can see.'

Gino slowed even more, forced to by the traffic in front doing likewise. 'Pray for a pile up.'

'What's the oncoming like?'

'Shit. I should have spotted that. The traffic's been spaced out. That's why I'm able to overtake so much. I think we're in for a checkpoint.'

'Got to happen some time.'

The traffic was slowing to a crawl, then it finally came to a halt. Gino kept a good distance between himself and the lorry in front, enough to pull out fast if he had to. At best this was no more than an inconvenience – they had proper papers and a legit reason to be in the country – but Afghanistan was too volatile a place to take any chances. Any threat was unlikely, but the last moment was no time to find out if they were wrong.

'We need to eyeball this, Gino. See what we're up against.'

'Yep.'

Gino slid out the door, grinning as he spoke, with Blue easing himself over to take the wheel. It had to be that way, Gino had the language skills.

'Anyone tries to talk to you, Blue, just glare at them.'

Then he covered the lower part of his face, nodded to the other Patrol and slithered down into the opposite ditch. Two of their escorts, a pair of nephews, Blue wasn't sure which, immediately jumped out of Abdul's vehicle and took up station behind him, their eyes ranging round on craned necks to spot any threat.

Looking ahead Gino saw that the line of vehicles stretched for about 300 yards: mostly lorries, the odd bus, with only one or two private vehicles sandwiched in between. He moved forward slightly to stay level with the creeping Nissan Patrol, trying to see what lay ahead. But there was no way to assess the situation from this distance. Giving Blue a wave he started forward, head down.

It took him ten minutes to get close enough to the checkpoint, Abdul's two nephews a few feet to his rear, weapons now pointing non-threateningly at the ground. The guys who'd set it up had stuck a pole on two oil drums across the road on either side of a culvert bridge, one each way. Gino counted half a dozen fighters in all, none in anything approaching a complete uniform, two heavily bearded guys wearing long black garments and white turbans were engaged in talking to the drivers, examining papers. The other four scruffy bastards standing back, guns at the ready, were like something out of a bad movie, darting threatening looks at non-existent dangers, AK-47s raised and aimed at no target Gino could see.

They were young, with the air of the seriously untrained about them, and that had nothing to do with their clothes – baggy trousers, embroidered but dirty shirts, and the standard round hat on their head. It was their general air of jumpiness that marked them out as useless. Only one had managed a full growth of beard, the rest seemed to be in various stages of sprouting tufts of wispy hair and growing spots – which made them look younger instead of older. Taliban cannon fodder was the assessment he made.

That was until one turned to look at him, a guy with practically no forehead and piggy, stupid looking eyes. His head jerked dramatically and a sharp cry came from his lips. The gun was up too, the muzzle pointing right at Gino's eyes, seeming a lot larger to the American than it was in reality. Like with an animal, it was dangerous to stare so he slowly turned his head away, keeping his body as still and non-threatening as possible. Out of the corner of his eye he could see that

Abdul's nephews had not responded either, well aware that any gesture on their part, any movement of their own weapons, would only see the man they were there to protect get a bullet in the head. The fact that they would immediately kill the perpetrator and all of his companions was no comfort at all.

Though the threat only existed for a matter of twenty seconds, it felt like a lifetime. Finally, the guy got bored. The game of scaring people only entertained with a constant supply of fresh victims, and eventually he swung away and dropped the barrel and began to look for another thing to excite his pea-sized uneducated brain. Gino slowly turned back to his observation of the checkpoint. Without looking at his watch, he counted through several of the vehicles, timing the exchanges which seemed to be short and cursory.

The sudden commotion on the other side of the road made him edge up the bank to get a better view. Some poor bastard was being hauled out of the cab of his high-sided panel van and slapped around.

The pea-brains were in their element, rushing forward, guns up, to surround the unfortunate, who was forced to his knees and beaten around the head by swinging blows. One turbaned bastard pulled the victim's head back so that he had to look up, and point to one of the youngsters, tugging at one of his partly grown tufts, screaming as he slapped the clean-shaven victim around the chin. The words he heard, clear because they were so loud, made Gino rub his own three day growth, a heavy stubble that was a long way from being a beard. Then he turned round, indicated that his escort should do likewise and made his way back to rejoin Blue.

'So?'

'Religious police or some such, checking for beards.'

'You're taking the piss, right?'

'No. It won't be just beards. They'll go apeshit if they find a woman who's face is uncovered. I wouldn't put it past the bastards to shoot her.'

'They've set up a fucking roadblock for that?'

'Six up and four armed, though they're only kids.'

'Kids kill.'

'Tell me about it,' Gino replied with feeling. 'There's a couple of guys doing the checking who look like mullahs. It's bound to be their idea. Anybody can do it if they want.'

'What, just close the road?'

'I told you they were crazy in this place.'

It was now Blue's turn to rub his chin. He asked in a jokey voice. 'So, what do we do, Gino, since we ain't got no beards.'

'Have you been circumcised?'

'Why?'

'Just in case they want to look at your cock.' The look on Blue's face made Gino laugh. 'Just kidding, pal.'

'Great timing.'

'Just remember, we ain't Muslims.'

All Blue did for the next half hour was creep forward every time the lorry in front moved, always doing as his partner had done and leaving enough room. Finally they got close enough to see the two mullahs doing the inspections, and in another few minutes were being subjected to a long suspicious look from a pair of dark brown eyes, under a grubby white turban, set in a face the colour and texture of unbaked bread.

Gino had their papers out, but held on to them as the mullah tried to take them out of his hand. He would show them but not pass them over, which led to a high pitched tirade that had the youngsters with the AK-47s moving forward again. Blue had his sub-machine gun by his feet, stock up, ready to haul up and fire, but with the mullah halfway through the window jabbing at Gino, it was no time to be grabbing for it.

Abdul's three young cousins, Milaad, Badar and Gullam, were suddenly there, voices raised, arguing with such passion that the mullah was forced to haul his head out and confront them. Blue could vaguely see that their AKs were shouldered and that the faces were more hurt than angry, something replicated in the tone of their voices. Gino was grinning.

'What are they saying?' demanded Blue, easing the sub-machine gun up so it was covered on his lap by the large-scale map.

'They're pleading poverty, telling that turbaned bastard they are poor tribesmen who are depending on us to give them enough to live for the rest of the year.'

Milaad's hand came through the window, jabbing at the papers Gino was still holding.

'Now Gullam is saying they're insulting Mullah Omar himself, the sainted leader who has given permission for these two men who are well-disposed to the country to search for that which will make them all rich. He's quite an actor.'

'What about Abdul?'

'He's like you, Blue, only ahead. He's probably got his gun trained on those kids at the back, ready to waste them the second things look like going wrong.'

'Will they?'

'Not the way it's sounding. I think mentioning Mullah Omar has made the guy think he might need his left hand very badly.'

Blue grinned. Afghans used their left hands to wipe their arses; which is why they never used them to eat, nor accepted gifts from anyone who offered with anything other than the right.

The noise of the argument had subsided a bit, and it fell even further as the trio of escorts kept up the pressure. Suddenly the pudding-faced mullah was at the window again, but this time less aggressively asking to look at the papers. Gino held them up, flicking through the various sheets one by one. The brown button eyes checked the signatures and official stamps. Finally, with a sharp gesture designed to show that he'd lost patience, the mullah indicated they could go on.

'Could that bastard read?' asked Blue.

'Don't know, Blue, don't know.'

'I think we're going to have to give those boys a bonus.'

'Give it to Abdul, it was his idea.'

The car and van auction at Brentford was totally surrounded by high buildings, many of them glossy new HQ offices for major corporations, sited off the busy A4 that led out to Heathrow Airport and points west. The auction premises, by comparison, looked like a throw back to the Industrial Revolution, a scruffy brick built structure and a open field full of cars of varying ages, the whole surrounded by a fence. There was only one way in and one way out, which is why the watchers stopped their vehicles in one of the office car parks, and didn't follow their quarry right in to a place where their presence might be spotted.

The two Irishmen would attract attention – strange faces at car auctions always do – and if they started bidding for cars the regulars would bump up the price by false bidding so that they wouldn't get as good a bargain. Malachy and Connor Boyle weren't bothered, since they weren't buying. But it was a good place to avoid surveillance, especially in the room where the low-mileage good condition cars were sold, a compact place dotted with poker-face buyers, a place where those who didn't bid for the cars stood out like a sore thumb.

Keegan showed the paperwork for the two-year-old Ford Mondeo they'd bought in Bristol to the guy in charge of entering cars. They'd phoned in the details, registration, chassis number, engine number and mileage earlier in the week from a public phone, so that they could be checked against the stolen vehicle register. That was kept updated daily. Provided their car wasn't on it and the documents were sound, the car could be sold.

'I'll just do a finance check,' said the clerk responsible, after he'd lifted the bonnet and compared the numbers on the registration document to those on the plates attached to both chassis and engine.

'No problem,' replied Keegan.

That was another dodge that had to be covered – selling a car that had an outstanding finance loan, pocketing the whole price and failing to pay the loan company back. That too was on computer.

'Clean. Stick it over in the car park.'

The bug showed the car as stationary for a long time, which made the MI5 controller twitchy. Two operatives were sent in on foot, but they were very exposed and said so. They also said that both their targets and the vehicle were static, so they were hauled out. With only one road in and out, the place was reasonably secure.

'But watch out for vans. That's what they might be there for, to buy a van.'

The speed at which cars move through an auction would shock the uninitiated. Most are sold in seconds rather than minutes, to dealers who care only that they look right and don't have too many miles on the clock. The dark green Mondeo was in very good nick. The watchers had seen Connor Boyle clean and polish it several times with a pride in its appearance that surprised them. And the Irishmen had put no reserve on it, so that it was a bargain to the purchaser. Since he had an account with the auction, the pay out was there and then, in cash.

The two Irishmen moved to the lot for van sales. Then, having clocked the people present for a whole hour, and agreed they were genuine, they slipped out and headed for the fence behind the parking lot. The only thing that Malachy Keegan had taken out of that canvas bag in the boot of the Mondeo was a pair of wire cutters. The fence was not a real problem, nor was the wall that ran along Boston Manor Road. The walk to the tube station took no more than ten minutes, and as soon as the Piccadilly Line train came in, on an empty platform, they knew they were as free as birds.

'Missing?' the President asked, his eyebrows raised in disbelief.

'That's what those important representatives of the Taliban said.' Norland Jensen paused for a second, before adding, 'They also said that they have destroyed his communications equipment. That may be why he has gone AWOL, perhaps even out of the country.'

'Shit!'

'That only applies if we believe them.'

'You don't.'

'They came to the table mighty quick when we asked.'

They had too. Since such talks could only be about one thing the speed with which they claimed to have neutered bin Laden rang just a little hollow.

'We have to read the way their minds work. If they had cruise missiles, and a target to take out, the notion of collateral civilian casualties wouldn't even enter their heads. They'd just go ahead and fire them off, then blame the opposition for endangering human life. They think, after being on the receiving end of the Valentine's Day bombs, we might work to the same criteria.'

'Sometimes democracy is hell.'

'Only sometimes?' the National Security Advisor replied, a wide grin on his face. 'I had it down as a permanent pain in the ass.'

'Keep the pressure on them, Norland. Don't ever let those bastards think we might back off.'

'I won't.'

CHAPTER FOURTEEN

The first rehearsals were carried out in broad daylight, very basic stuff without any air assets. It was a walk through talk through, the idea being that the troopers would get to know the layout of the target and their position in relation to the other callsigns, something that is vital for mutual support. When it came to input it was open season. Even the newest trooper was invited to and did give his opinion. All over the rehearsal area these Chinese Parliaments were in progress, both for Delta Force and the SAS. B Squadron 6 Troop had been given the north-west anti-aircraft position, dangerous if it survived because of the helos still in the air. Moreover AA guns could be used in both an air and ground role, so could give the assault teams a serious and very bloody nose if they survived the air attack.

The lucky thing for 6 Troop was that they were a Rupert-free zone. Lance Price was the troop senior and would be leading. The rest of the troop comprised Jake Steel, Pete Harris, Mike Hutton, Parsnips, Bull Bisset, Tommy 'Whacker' Simpson and the kid of the outfit, Gaz Mowlem.

Parsnips worried about relying too much on technology, while Jake prayed that the place would be totally mullahed before their feet touched the ground. That was, as Mike Hutton pointed out in his studious way, a sterile argument.

'Sterile?' said Pete 'Chemo' Harris.

Chemo was generally held to be the most single-minded guy on the troop. Some said he wasn't that, just thick. He'd had his head shaved once, on the way to a jungle trip, for a bet. It was some shock to the rest of the squadron to see a fully hirsute man go into the toilet, and come out five minutes later with his head shaved, a man who then loudly called to one of his mates, 'Jocky, you cunt, you can pay me that fifty quid, now.'

Later he went round the plane collecting for the driver, which severely pissed off the DSF who was flying out to Malaya with them as Trooper Harris insisted that the contributions match the rank – which cost each trooper a pound and the Brigadier a tenner.

Growing his hair back had made him look like he was on chemotherapy, hence the moniker. His great and only love was Premiership football and the yo-yo progress of his team Bolton Wanderers, which occupied his every waking leisure hour. That, and winding up Mike Hutton every time he used what Harris called a posh word.

'Would you talk in bloody English?'

'It is English, mate, it's just not stuck on a football shirt.'

'It's not even long, Chemo,' added Bull Bisset, laughing. 'It's about the same as Adidas.'

'OK,' Chemo responded, 'the argument is Adidas. That I can live with.'

'All I mean is, we could speculate endlessly . . .'

'There you go again, Mike,' hooted Chemo.

'Somebody take this arse away and give him a brain implant.'

'Arse. That is a word I know.'

'Can it, fellas,' called Lance Price. 'Let's get serious.'

They'd never really been anything else. Under all that banter each man was assessing the job the team had to perform and his role in it, eyes moving constantly to see which directions trouble could come from. And at the same time they were aware that any plan, even the beauty they had been presented with, could go to total rat-shit the second they hit the ground. In a perfect world they would fast rope down on to a neutralized target strewn with dead bodies, their sole task being to check pulses and pockets. But you have to work on the assumption that you'll be taking on live ones, and they'll all be trying to kill you. They spent a lot of time working out their arcs of fire and direction of approach.

The next stage was dry drills. No ammunition, using helos to fast-rope on to the target and assessing the impact of every member of the squadron being in their primary battle position, again with the proviso that some would, for various reasons, not be. Then they did another dry drill, again fast-roping out of the helos, hitting the deck hard and going into action. That was a rehearsal that could be done time and time again, but it had one flaw, it was not taking place at the intended attack time, which was, for the moment, first light.

The following day everyone, Delta and SAS, were up and kitted out in darkness. A detachment from the 10th Special Forces Group had been helo'd in from Fort Carson to represent the enemy, and both forces would work on the principle that there would be survivors from the Tomahawk and Spectre attacks to put up a fight. No conversation, apart from that required for the rehearsal, was to be allowed with the guys from the 10th SFG. They looked hard and you could feel the curiosity, but they went away disappointed, shipped out after the rehearsal to another camp, on standby to do it again if required.

The Chinooks and Black Hawks were already whirring their blades, ready to go. The troopers had their weapons loaded with blank ammunition, each SAS man who'd been given the new M4s stroking it like a favourite cat. That had been a bonus, the issue of a weapon that until now only the US Forces had acquired. The M4A1 carbine is a shortened variant of the M16A2 rifle and came in its own case, with a complete accessory kit specifically designed for the Special Forces instead of the bits and pieces that made up its predecessors. Fitted neatly into the padded box, each man had the weapon, laser and night sights, a grenade launcher and a collapsible butt so that the weapon was more useful in close quarters combat.

The whole air packet lifted off as per op, gunships ahead, troop carriers echeloned behind in two groups. They stood off, playing it like everything else for real. At this point there was little activity on the communications net. At a given time the whole helo packet suddenly rose to a higher altitude and separated, then, after two minutes the order to attack was given.

The gunships, simulating their attack role, swept in ahead of the troop carriers before swooping sideways to allow access. The troop carriers vectored in to their drop height, and suddenly the air was full of thick green ropes immediately occupied by a stream of descending troopers. That was when the first thing went wrong. It's a well-known fact to all

Special Forces that more men sustain injuries in rehearsals than they do in combat. The reason for this is quite simple: mission rehearsals are carried out time and time again, but the mission is only carried out once. Train hard, fight easy.

It wasn't really the helo pilot's fault either. Air pockets can happen at any altitude, especially when each airframe is surrounded by other whirring rotor blades. The Black Hawk didn't drop far, no more than ten feet, but it took down with it Kenny Collins, from 7 Troop, who was the last man on the rope. To those in his troop just deploying, the crack of his leg bone going was inaudible, but to the victim it was like a gun going off. The noises he made after that certainly got some attention.

Everyone carried on with the rehearsal, the man nearest Kenny pausing for a moment to check it wasn't serious. A thumbs-down gesture told him that he was out of the game. With B at near full strength for this op, made up with men drawn in from the other squadrons, there were ample reserves, one of whom would be brought in to take Kenny's place.

The net was like a speeded-up football commentary as each callsign reported its progress. There was a brief pause while each carried out its primary task. Lancing, Zero Bravo, took stock, then directed each callsign onto its secondary targets; and the net was alive again with a cacophony of sound that would have confused those not trained to interpret it.

'Shit,' shouted Gaz Mowlem as he tripped, skewering the muzzle of his weapon into a patch of soft ground. Bull Bisset, right behind him, went head over tit, his magazine dropping off from the base of his M4. Bull didn't curse, even though it must have hurt, but immediately got on to one knee and carried out the standard stoppage drill, clearing and reloading his weapon before rejoining the attack. They didn't stay on the target for long, there was no point. It was better to practise the exfil, then set the choppers down so that everyone from Officer Commanding down to lowest trooper could assess what had happened.

'You fucking arsehole, Gaz,' said Chemo, looking at the M4's earth filled muzzle. 'That was a real bone thing to do. If there'd been any shit flying around we would have been bollocks't.'

'Don't you start winding me up Chemo.'

Which was precisely what Harris was doing, taking on the newest badge and ensuring that when he fucked up, he suffered. Mowlem had a hurt expression on his ridiculously young face that gave Chemo terrific satisfaction.

'Talk about fucking Tom and Jerry,' Harris added, including Bull Bisset in the criticism.

'Don't you start, Chemo,' said Bull, 'You have trouble walking and talking at the same time.'

'What about tripping over some cunt.'

He aimed a pretend punch at Gaz Mowlem's head, before stepping back smartly to avoid the sweeping fist that came in return, his voice filled with mocking laughter.

'Fuck me. You're as wet as half a pound of smacked twat.'

Seven troop members had the chance to tell Gaz Mowlem it could happen to anyone. No one did; they just got ready for the next rehearsal. But Gaz Mowlem, even though he realized it was a wind up, knew it had a serious side. He had fucked up big style.

Again, the four Black Hawk gunships led in the eight troop carrying helos, cutting away to take up positions for their support role, allowing the following helos to hover into position so that both Special Forces Groups could fast rope on to the hard rock surface of the Nevada mountains. The sound around them was deafening in its intensity, the thud of rotor blades mixed with half-heard shouts.

The rehearsals were backed up by filming, which when transferred to the computers allowed for a constant re-appraisal of the now digital imagery. This was combined with the original satellite photography that had gone into making the computer training packs.

There was no way the facilities in Nevada could entirely replicate 6 Troop's actual primary target, the ground surrounding the two ZU2 40mm quick firing anti-aircraft guns. They were sited about one hundred metres outside the confines of the main base at Zu ol Faqar on the rising ground to the north-west, overlooking both the helipad and the lake. The troop would land on what was expected to be a destroyed target, their task to ensure that was true, while at the same time covering the arcs of fire from their position, which, added to the others, created a solid perimeter.

Their secondary task was to take on opportunity targets within the visible parts of the castle itself, given that they had an elevated position. The entrance to the facility was protected by sentry positions, twin turrets each mounting a 12.7mm heavy machine gun well able to take out a helicopter. These were matched on the west elevation by another pair, all four permanently manned. Two more positions were set on the ramparts to the rear of the base facing the high ground, able to give covering fire from their elevation to all the other posts, including the triple A positions. They would be target number one for the Tomahawks, given the threat they posed to the entire air packet. They had to be a primary target for the Spectre gunships as well.

Dawn the next day was slated for the first live firing rehearsal. 6 Troop had their M4s loaded, with six spare mags each and their M203 40mm grenade launchers attached; two Minimi light machine guns, and two M72 LAWs, a lightweight 66mm anti-tank weapon that could be used in a bunker-busting or anti-personnel role. Everything else was for real too: the light, the time and the nature of the attack.

The main assault party in each group, tasked to take on either the sandstone castle or the comms centre, was the fulcrum of each attack. They came in on the Special Operations Chinooks. Twenty-four strong, their task was to suppress any defence of the buildings and then engage any of the enemy who took refuge inside the ruins. Three Black Hawks would each deliver eight troopers who would take their targets after fast rope descents, employing assault drills using fire and manoeuvre. The DAPs, Black Hawk gunships, would stand off to avoid presenting themselves as targets, but were on call to provide close air support.

Having done it half a dozen times, and having spent every waking hour left on the simulators, the helo pilots had refined their techniques to speed up the process. But there was no compromise on good procedures. They were only too aware of the dangers that were inherent in having a dozen aircraft operating in what was a confined space, all of them exposed to the threat of ground fire and needing room to manoeuvre. At the same time the Spectres were on the edge of the scene, circling around like huge grey vultures, ready to provide massive firepower if required to do so. The MV-22 Osprey Tiltrotor was up there too, on call for dust off.

Delta and SAS were operating on two separate communications nets to cut down the amount of traffic on any one net. However, each unit had the ability to switch to the other's channel, if required. Likewise the command element, Zero Bravo, with one signaller on each net, had access so that joint actions could be co-ordinated should the need arise.

The US Navy provided fighter top cover, the planes that would move to dominate hostile air space as soon as the need for secrecy evaporated, and they played a full part in rehearsals. That meant the air controller had as much experience of the actual event as the troopers on the ground. When you practise, it makes sense to practise everything.

Lance Price led his eight man team each time, fast roping down, the heat from the friction felt every time through the heavy gloves they wore to protect their hands. The drills were becoming instinctive, each trooper knowing exactly where every member of his callsign would be if the shit hit the fan. As previously, the operational commander hovered above the rehearsals, directing the ground troops while listening to the mass of traffic on the net, refining his ability to control the battle as much as the men on the ground sought to fight it.

The castle, or what remained of it, was 6 Troop's secondary target. Intelligence only gave them the exterior structure of the buildings. The interior layouts could be guessed at by computer analysis, but in no way could they be established. Besides, as Parsnips had so forcibly pointed out, not all of them would be intact.

Additional to the two targets, the Yank engineers had been busying themselves building a FIBUA range. Each callsign thus had the opportunity to rehearse the very different conditions that existed when fighting in built up areas. The structure also provided the facility to practise house clearing and room combat skills.

No Ruperts issued any orders to work at it. None were necessary. The images of the embassy bombings were still fresh in everyone's mind, and these combined with the sheer competitiveness natural to every trooper and callsign, and the presence of Delta Force were enough. These were the very best men in the British Army, and one of their traits is self-motivation.

One telephone call on a mobile would be enough to initiate a message that could be picked up by the listening stations. NSA and GCHQ, the twin communications monitoring facilities for both NATO and their own security, work on a simple system. With millions of calls being made each day all over the world, listening into every one is impossible. But the computers are programmed to scan the airwaves for key words. Few were more key than bin Laden. Every call that mentioned his name was put on a trace.

Then there were the sightings. Some came from previously reliable sources, others through the listeners picking up a casual reference. The problem was that, combined, they put Osama bin Laden in about twenty different places at the same time: Iran, Iraq, Libya, the Yemen, Jalalabad, the Afghan province of Helmand, over the Pakistan border and even in Moscow. The one place they didn't put him was Zu ol Faqar, which induced no end of jitters in the intelligence community tasked to feed information to JSOC.

Though he had no idea of the effect of this confusion, bin Laden was happy to keep it going. It gave him time to gather what he needed, and get it to where it needed to be. The codes from America were still coming in, correct except for the day. About that he could do nothing but wait. Yet fortune, the hand of Allah, had given him another option to pursue. He had the material to hand, held back because he could not deliver it safely. There was only one component missing, and Mohammed al Kadar was tasked to take care of that.

'Fetch your Irishman, McGurk, and take him to Zu ol Faqar.'

'Is there anything I need to tell him?'

'No!'

CHAPTER FIFTEEN

In the admiration stakes few people garnered more respect than the helo pilots. To SAS troopers, they were mother, father, uncle and aunt, the guys who got you into a fight, looked after you while you were there and then got you out, regardless of how much shit was coming their way. When it came to balls, they were in a class of their own.

That went for the Tiltrotor pilot as well. Simulated casualties and fatalities were his to evacuate. But, just as would happen in a battle, some of them had to be placed on to the nearest available airframe regardless of the seriousness of their injuries. And as usual, on any rehearsal, there were a few genuine cases.

In Special Forces operations the crew of a Black Hawk consisted of a pilot, a co-pilot and two men designated crew chiefs. The last pair had a dual responsibility: first to assist with dispatching the troops, second to man the 7.62mm six-barrel minigun mounted on each door. Capable of firing off 6000 rounds per minute, they could suppress opposition in the immediate area around the landing zone.

All sectors got to know each other. 6 Troop's four-man crew became their friends in the few days they all spent together. The Pilot in Charge was a guy called Brian Bewley, who because of his love of all things spicy was nicknamed Biryani. Bewley was a compact guy, from Wyoming, always chewing a Cuban cigar. When not flying and eating hot Thai food he rode a Harley-Davidson, drank too much malt whisky and talked endlessly aboaut 'scrogging' women.

The co-pilot was John Dandeneau, known to his buddies as Dirty Dick. DD hailed from Miami and was another Harley freak, but his great desire was to race Formula One. He travelled with an F1 simulator, to be set up wherever he was called upon to lay his head. Dandeneau, when at the controls, flew the Black Hawk like he was one hand driving his big road bike. The super-cool bit hid a passionate care about the way the bird performed.

Due to them both suffering from serious hair loss, they were, as a pair affectionately known as the Bald Brothers. Because of that they'd named the ship Grover, after the hairy monster that occupied a dustbin in Sesame Street.

Mike Hutton, with his endless questions about the way the bird flew, its instrumentation, avionics and electronic counter-measures kit, drove them mad. But they were shrewd enough to find a solution, which was to tell Mike that if he thought this bird was interesting, he should go see the Spectres and Combat Talons. To a man like Hutton, the temptation was irresistible. He was off like a shot. The only problem was that he came back and tried to pass on everything he'd learned to the rest of the troop.

The lead crew chief, the man designated as the Fast Rope Master, was a black guy of Jamaican descent called Winston Graham. Chemo and Parsnips took the piss out of him endlessly, asking if he was interested in a job as a cricketer, or maybe even an ITN newsreader. It was a good thing Winston took it in good part. He was a big strong bastard, built like a brick shithouse, with a laugh that could shake the helo at full throttle.

Winston was as important to the guys as the pilots. As the Fast Rope Master they had to rely on him for the state of the equipment, from the rope itself to the fast rope bar they'd be using as they exited out of the helo. He was the man who inspected it and rigged it. Winston also worked out the cycle of counting warnings to the pilot, and gave him the final position adjustments on the target.

At the point of descent he had more control over their survival than either of the Bald Brothers and he was treated accordingly. The fact that he was game for a laugh made him an easy man to get on with.

The last and final rehearsal was as close to the real thing as ingenuity could get, and, like the real thing it had its share of pain. The Tomahawk missile strikes were simulated by explosive charges that had been placed on all the targets. The charges, coupled with the amount of fire then applied by the Spectre gunships had reduced the area to something resembling the aftermath of an earthquake.

'Two minutes,' called Winston into his comms headset, the timing info passed to the troopers by the agreed hand signal.

'Fuck,' said Bull Bisset, searching around as they lined up to rope out, right over the target. 'I've lost one of my gloves.'

'Just favour one hand,' shouted Jake, busy checking his own kit.

'The pilot glove was inside.'

It was a statement, and not one that any of the others could do much about. Each man was wearing thin pilot gloves, which they would use in combat. But over that they needed the heavy working gloves that protected their hands from the serious risk of rope burn. What Bull did next was up to him. He could stay aboard if he wanted and not risk injury, or rope out with one bare hand, which would certainly lead to serious burns that might mean no go on the mission. No one asked or ordered. Lance Price, on the brink of leading his troop out, was too busy thinking about himself to care about Bull, who was standing right behind him.

'Bollocks!' Bull shouted, venting his frustration as well as any fear he had. Then, in a moment of inspiration, he hauled off the sweatband he was wearing on his head and wrapped it round his palm to minimise rope burn. It wouldn't protect his hand completely, only a thick glove could do that. But it might save him from too serious an injury, and allow him to carry out his part of the mission.

The rope went out the side door with Winston calling endlessly on the intercom to Biryani Bewley regarding the helo height from the ground. As soon as it hit dirt he gave the command to the fast ropers to go.

Lance was gone and Bull went after him, trying to keep his ungloved hand at minimum contact with the rope. It only partially worked and he could feel the sweatband disintegrating and the heat burning with his skin beginning to blister. That made him let go a fraction too early and he was lucky to land on flat ground. But it was hard, sending a jarring thud through his body that took a second off his pace. That meant he nearly got Jake Steel number three on that rope, round his earhole.

'Move, fucker,' Jake yelled as he hit the deck.

All around them bullets were flying, the ground throwing up spurts as they made contact. Lance and Mike Hutton were already firing off bursts from their M4s, each carrying out with his battle partner their fire and manoeuvre drills. One foot on the ground at all times, pepper-potting forward, one man firing one man moving, an action replicated by every member of the troop. Then they were on their feet, moving to assist on their seconday target, which was the mocked up FIBUA range that the engineers had constructed.

There wasn't a lot left of it now, the blast from the explosions on all the other targets ripping through the single breeze block walls. But there was just enough left to rehearse one more drill; a grenade in, a split second after it went off followed by the trooper throwing it.

It seemed only seconds before they heard in their earpieces the order to exfil, 'Zero Bravo to all call signs, Red Dragon, I repeat, Red Dragon, out.'

That was the exfil code and the troopers rushed for the helos, now down on the ground, their rotors kicking up great clouds of choking dust. They didn't climb aboard so much as jump. Each airframe lifted off as soon as they were loaded, moving forward instead of up to avoid collisions, then forming up under the air controller's command into an exfil formation, behind the command Black Hawk.

Within fifteen minutes the final rehearsal was over. The next time they did this it would be the real thing. But, again, as in every rehearsal they'd undertaken, there had been blood. Bull's blistered palm counted for nothing when they heard that one Delta guy had a broken back, the result of an M4 slipping off a descending trooper's shoulder, taking the guy below on the head, and dropping him twenty feet on to a boulder. Another had been wounded by a ricochet that had rebounded off a rock, not seriously but enough to put him out of the op, so providing an opportunity for one of those standing by to replace him.

Three days and nights of intense training brought everybody – Delta, SAS, fixed wing and rotor blade pilots – to a peak that was unlikely to be surpassed. Information from the rehearsals had been fed in to beef up the computer simulation programmes, so that every man or flyer could over the following days, run a visual display of the whole battle. John Franklin did the final briefing, this time with Gibson-Hoare assisting, before the order was given to enplane for Diego Garcia. Once there, they would get their final confirmatory orders, and go on immediate standby for an operational go.

Troopers and flyers reacted in various ways to that. Some were cock-a-hoop and loud, others silent and introspective, and there was every shade in between. Fighting men go into battle in many different ways. It was nothing to do with willingness, just attitude. Everyone was ready, and all were prepared.

'Please bring your things with you, Mister McGurk. Our leader wishes to see you once more, and he has assured me that, following your meeting, you will not be coming back to this place.'

The words had enough of a chilling quality to make Aidan McGurk look hard into Mohammed al Kadar's eyes. But all he saw in those dark brown pools was the same look of innocence that had been there the first day he'd met him. It was difficult for a hardened freedom fighter like himself to believe that this youngster with the long soft eyelashes could be as ruthless as him. But that must be the case; bin Laden didn't strike the Irishman as the type to keep anyone around just for their good looks.

There wasn't much to pack; one large grip contained almost every-thing he owned. Al Kadar stood watching him as he gathered up all the scraps of rubbish he'd accumulated. These included bits of paper with a list of potential targets, as well as the names of people he might be able to use in both Britain and the US, the whole bundle shoved into the very furthest recesses of his grip. A careful man, McGurk normally would have made sure he destroyed them, but time was too short with al Kadar waiting, clearly impatient to take him to bin Laden.

'I won't be sorry to see the back of this,' he said to al Kadar as they emerged. 'In Ireland you don't normally have to check for snakes and scorpions before putting your boots on of a morning.'

The young Muslim smiled. 'Yet to the people who come here, it is something of a paradise. To be fed and have a roof over your head is

148

special. That, Mister McGurk, will give you some notion of the quality of their previous lives.'

'Sure, Ireland used to be like that, son,' McGurk replied, climbing into the passenger seat of the Toyota Hi-Line. 'But they've got fat the last few years, so fat they've forgotten there's still a war to fight.'

'Maybe, one day, our people will be fat,' said al Kadar wistfully.

'And maybe you too will forget.'

'How can we, Mister McGurk, when we have Allah.'

'Are you planning to take me through Kandahar again?' demanded McGurk. As soon as they set off he'd noticed that al Kadar was following the same route as before.

'I must,' al Kadar said firmly. 'To get to where we are going.'

'Your leader's compound is that way.'

'I know that, Mister McGurk.'

Again the Irishman felt the chill of fear. Then it subsided. If bin Laden had wanted him out, he would have sent more than this boy to carry out such a task.

'Then may I ask where we are going?'

'To the most secret of places, one that only those close to Osama bin Laden are allowed to see.'

'Another camp?'

'A very special camp.'

'That'll do me then.' McGurk said, sitting back in the passenger seat and relaxing.

Driving out for the last time, weaving through the camps to the nearby city, the Irishman seemed to be able to look at them with fresh eyes. There were really three camps, spread out over some six miles. The satellite camp he'd been in, a place for the new recruits to go through assessment and some training in the most basic of skills, lay furthest from Kandahar.

The base camp, the place where the fully-fledged fighters lived and trained was in the centre. Within it, fenced off by double barbed wire, lay the headquarters compound, with the now disabled comms, the radar and the intelligence centre, guarded by a pair of ex-Russian tanks as well as anti-aircraft weaponry.

Also within the base camp was a parade ground where the recruits could show off for the leaders. On the perimeter lay the rifle, grenade and demolition ranges and explosives dugouts, as well as the assault courses on which the fighters rehearsed killing *Mushrikeen*. He could hear the familiar rat-a-tat of machine gun fire, the odd crump of a grenade. The whole thing was satisfactory to his ear since it meant that bin Laden could afford to use live ammunition for training, confirming that he had money to spare.

But was this the nerve centre of the operation? McGurk knew from his own experience that bin Laden was rarely present. Though he hadn't said so, on the first visit al Kadar had hinted at a residence in Kandahar itself. Osama bin Laden probably had ten to a dozen places to lay his head and work from, none of them used two nights running. He knew if he stayed still too long he'd get a flight of cruise missiles up his arse, and that he was keen to avoid.

The third camp lay on the eastern side, close to the city. It was a place for wives and children, along with all the people and facilities necessary to service the life of an Afghan freedom fighter: the mosque, the medical centre, the commissary; repair and manufacturing shops where guns and explosives, as well as uniforms, were manufactured or mended. Meals were prepared there to be trucked over to the long low huts in the base camp where the fighting men ate and slept.

Impressive as it all was, McGurk was clever enough to figure out the point. The whole thing had no bearing on the kind of international terrorism bin Laden was famous for. All these fighters were of no use whatsoever when it came to blowing up embassies and the like. Sure, a few of the better ones could be brought on to train as bomb makers. Perhaps, too, there were people here capable of the coolness needed for delivery, fanatical enough not to care if they survived the actual blast. Such men were the real cutting edge of bin Laden's operation, and could have been accommodated and trained in a camp a hundredth of the size of this place.

Yet all these thousands of followers did have a number of purposes, the primary one being to make bin Laden look good in the eyes of the Arab world. To the credulous masses of Islam, he wanted to look like a real power. That brought in the contributions he needed to fund his campaigns. The secondary reason was almost as important: a stake in the Taliban's war against the Sunni heretics and the remnants of the Mujahideen, the chance to sit close to and influence his friend Mullah Omar. Self-preservation was the final motive: a warning to anyone thinking of giving him grief that there would be a price to pay. With three thousand men, a couple of tanks, and artillery, no one could take him on unless they were really serious.

'He's not daft, your leader, is he?' said McGurk, as they left the last part of the support camp.

The way al Kadar looked at him told the Irishman that the remark, intended as a compliment, had not been taken that way.

The ferry to the Hook of Holland was a good way out of the UK, especially since the security services would be looking the other way, at the exits, both sea and air, that led back to Ireland. Besides all the surveillance was for people coming in, not going out. And it was a service with cabins, so they could stay out of sight. MI5 or Special Branch wouldn't be on board necessarily, but there were always nosy customs men pretending to be travellers, trying to ferret out smugglers.

Malachy Keegan and Connor Boyle made sure that they exited down the gangway in a crowd. Not that they had much to fear from the Dutch, even if their faces were picked up on a video camera. A bus to Amsterdam was the best. You could see who got on and off, and also get a good chance to memorise the faces of the passengers, to recognize them if you saw them again. The whole thing looked sound, and after casing out the area around the house in which Eamon Gilhooley was staying, they made their approach.

'Mobile two up,' said the head of the MI6 surveillance team.

CHAPTER SIXTEEN

The risk of compromising in-country agents had to be taken. This operation had such a high priority that the hazard just had to be accepted, as the intelligence, both satellite and monitoring, was not as precise as it needed to be. Fortunately, the CIA wasn't short of people and an organization like the Taliban, with its deep intolerance of any opposing views, was almost bound to create enemies. Given the way they'd massacred the leaders of the Mujahideen as soon as they achieved power, they had, in that respect, excelled themselves.

Everyone that could be activated was, and the message was simple, find and confirm bin Laden.

In a country like Afghanistan, you could not become a Mujahideen commander unless you possessed great presence and skills, allied to a superior social standing. Men like Mohammed Panah had been revered by their fighters, often assuming an almost god-like status, not least because of their acts of personal bravery. And many of the Mujahideen commanders had agreed to send their men abroad to train, away from the threat of interdiction by the massive force the Soviets had deployed in the country. Some had gone to America, more to the remote MOD camp in the Scottish Borders. There they'd learned not only guerrilla combat skills, but also how to gather and collate intelligence on their enemies.

When the Taliban took over, many of these trained operatives were back in Afghanistan, the only people who knew they'd been abroad massacred by the new rulers. Recruitment, which should have been near impossible for the CIA, was ridiculously easy. The motive was simple, a desire to exact revenge on the men who had murdered those revered commanders.

Ahmal was one such man. A native of the plateau above Kandahar, he'd fought for ten years against his enemies – first the Soviet-backed puppet government, then against the Russian Army itself. A shepherd, he had no need to explain his presence in any part of the area around the lake, either herding his fat-tailed sheep in search of pasture, or taking a stick to the flanks of the donkey that carried his load of muslin-wrapped butter down to the town of Zu ol Faqar. This stood no more than a kilometre from the fenced off camps at the top of the hill by the old Emir's castle.

Taking tea, eating mulberries and apricots, or haggling over the money he was owed for his butter, he could gather a mass of information that seemed so innocent to those imparting it. The quartermasters from the camps shopped in the local bazaar, ordering food in quantities too great to be carried away. Occasionally, men from the hill would walk through the town, conspicuous in their red and white checked keffiyehs, the badge that marked them out as fighters for the cause of Osama bin Laden. Silent and deeply religious, they said little to any one person. But, to someone trained in intelligence gathering, a word to a weaver of prayer mats added to an overheard conversation in a teashop amounted to a whole which was more than the sum of its parts.

Ahmal tried never to show outright curiosity, which was a dangerous thing to display in such a small town. There was a Taliban presence even here: fanatical young men who had been brainwashed at some Pakistani seminary during the war years, idiots with nothing in their heads – an empty space filled by the teachings of the most strict of the mullahs. He didn't have to, anyway. In this obscure, depopulated part of the country, where little of interest happened, the camps and what they were doing was a constant source of gossip.

And, to add to all his garnered knowledge, he had the equipment he had been trained to use by the Americans. The TACSAT phone and the digital video camera, recently given to him so that he could relay information, were in a secure hiding place outside town, waiting to be picked up on his way back up the mountain. He augmented these tools with his knowledge of the area as well as his ubiquitous presence. His forays in Zu ol Faqar, his constant stops on the way to and from his mountain hut, or the sight of his driving his sheep towards a patch of grass, excited no comment from anyone.

But intelligence gathering wasn't something he undertook daily, and the instruction to do so, and to report on the arrivals and departures of that old Russian helicopter, was bound to involve a certain amount of risk. His questions about the helicopter produced an alarmed reaction in the eyes of those he asked, and no answer. That helicopter, and whosoever it transported to and fro, was a subject about which people were cautious. Ahmal reckoned that no one really knew who it was, and that was what made them so fearful.

He wasn't a stupid man. He could not have survived if he had been. Nor was he blindly obedient to the instructions he received over the same phone that carried the images back to his distant contacts. He knew that if he changed his routine it would be noticed, so he disobeyed his orders and set up a hide made of rocks and brushwood for the digital camera, with the lens fixed on the helipad. Each night he went down the mountain to change the TACSAT and video batteries, taking the used ones back up to recharge from the old car engine he used to provide heat and light for his house.

Back in Langley they weren't angry at what he was doing, they were impressed. To them the guy was a real star. With a constant watch, they could build up an analytical picture of bin Laden's movements to see if there was a pattern. And Ahmal was determined to stick to his own pattern, herding his sheep and taking his weekly pack of butter to Zu ol Faqar, drinking his tea, eating his mulberries and talking to people who had known him for years.

Since the road between the flat topped house and the castle ran behind the helipad, and the air was, for once, totally clear, the camera picked up the arrival of Mohammed al Kadar and his passenger. Even through the Islamic totems that decorated the windows they could identify al Kadar in Langley, simply by blowing up the image and coupling it to the computer that held identifying software on every known member of Osama bin Laden's group. But the passenger in the cab of the Toyota Hi-line, with only his sunglasses showing, was hidden by the driver. So all that the record showed was that two fighters, one of them a senior lieutenant of bin Laden had arrived in the camp.

McGurk was a trained fighter, and al Kadar had opened up enough on the drive to tell him where they were going. So he was alert from the moment he spotted the barrier across the road. He'd clocked the outer defences, easy to see from ground level, as they passed them: an anti-aircraft gun position dug deep into the hillside, plus various covered and camouflaged sentry positions. The locations and weaponry looked good, so did the alert way the fighters manning them behaved. Yet, outside that, the nature of the place made him curious. Apart from the sentries it seemed sleepy; there were none of the facilities he'd seen in Kandahar, no rifle range or demolition area.

Up at this height the air was naturally much cooler, even though there was a constant and strong southerly wind. And the air was clear in that way it can only be in mountains. Aidan McGurk liked this much more than the hot and dusty plain, and, judging from the attitude of al Kadar, he was sure he could relax. Yet he felt the tension that had occasionally assailed him return as they drove up to the forbidding gate of the half-ruined castle. The tower that had probably once held heavy wooden gates was intact, and the change from sharp sunlight to a near pitch dark as they entered its shadow could not help but conjure up images of dungeons.

Mohammed al Kadar was out of the door almost before the Hi-Line had stopped. McGurk grabbed his bag and followed, heading for a small arched gap in the castle wall by the main gate. In Langley the brief glimpse this afforded of the two men was showing on another screen, the back view picked up on satellite. Later, an operative would recall the image to his screen, and using computer generated image intensifying would enhance it enough to identify the Jaguar logo on the green grip in McGurk's hand. There was also the stub of an airline baggage ticket, but that defeated all attempts to identify it. What physical characteristics they could make out on the short walk between the van and the doorway were fed into the computers, and it was logged that no match came up for this individual in the Muslim terrorism programme.

The air inside the castle had that slightly foetid quality that goes with a place that never sees daylight. The walls were several feet thick, stronger at the base than at the battlements, and it had been built to withstand not only assault but also the heat of the fierce Afghan summer. For winter; huge fireplaces stood in every chamber. The place was a warren, with small heavily doored chambers off each side of a corridor – more like the sort of thing to be seen in a monastery. That, to McGurk's way of thinking, was fitting. If these fighters of bin Laden were like anything, they were like warrior monks.

Al Kadar threw open a door at the far end of the corridor, and gestured with his hand.

'This is for you, Mister McGurk. Please rest here until our leader arrives.'

It was a tiny room, eight feet by five, flagstone-floored, with a wooden bed base in one corner below a narrow embrasure that looked as though it had once been used to fire arrows in defence. The ceiling was arched and mossy from damp. On one wall, facing west, a previous occupant had marked the direction of Mecca, so that he could face the right way when saying his prayers.

'And when will that be?' McGurk asked, throwing his grip on to the bed.

'I have no idea. Our leader does not tell anyone where he is going to be at any time.'

'It could be days.'

'Yes,' al Kadar replied.

'I don't suppose you have any books I can read.'

'Only the Koran, Mister McGurk.'

There was a look in al Kadar's eye, almost begging him to request it, and, tactically, that would be a shrewd thing to do since it was bound to get back to bin Laden's ears. But that rebellious streak of his wouldn't let him say yes. He had to let this kid know he was his own man, and had to hope that message got back to his leader.

'I'll pass, if you don't mind.'

Al Kadar left abruptly, leaving the door open, before McGurk could ask him simple things like where he could go for a piss, or if there was going to be any food.

'Fuck him,' he said to himself, walking over to look out of the embrasure. He couldn't see much right to left, but straight ahead the slope fell away to the gleaming lake he'd seen on the way in. 'Christ, it's like being back in jail.'

The whole strike force left in three groups. The troopers of Delta and the SAS flew in the comfort of a C-141 Starlifter. The rest of the fixed wing formed a second packet; the Combat Talons, the Spectre gunships flying escort and the Combat Shadows along to provide mid-air refuelling. Because of the time element, the original helos, including Grover – the third group – had been shipped to Bahrain after two rehearsal days while the designated mission pilots had transferred to back up machines. The maintenance crews flew out with the mission crews to service the ships they were tasked to keep flying. None of the flyers would be happy unless they had their own ground crew.

The flight to Diego Garcia was non-stop. Everyone aboard got as much sleep as they could, knowing that as soon as they touched down they were on standby for the op. That could mean ten days or ten minutes. With the distances involved and the timing of the attack for first light, it was always possible that they would get well on their way to the target only to receive an order to abort that would take them back to Diego Garcia. All the briefings had emphasized that bin Laden was the target, and that was a variable. JSOC could only pray for a quick solution, aware that the strain on the aircrew and men would tell if it went on too long.

Unless it's on a real fastball, there's always a gap between the rehearsals for and the execution of any mission. And while no one could quite put it out of his mind, every trooper had a way of putting it on the back burner. Some people just slept – like hibernating bears storing up energy for an active summer. Nostalgia helped others, the telling of anecdotes that had been heard before but were still funny – because for some they were personal experiences, and for others part of the continuum that was either the Regiment or Delta Force.

The SSM, Tommy Baker, was a card fanatic. 'Doctor Who' was the son of a Kent miner and he'd introduced a game called Yucca to those who liked to play with him – basically the arse crawlers who thought being close to the warrant officer would enhance their career. It was one of those games that was a mystery to those who didn't play – combining a card deck and Cribbage board with its own exclusive language. It intrigued the poker-playing Yanks, though they didn't stay long to watch, returning confused to their own schools of Stud or Draw.

One or two guys wrote poetry, though they kept a low profile to avoid the others taking the piss out of their flowery verse. At least half the SAS troopers mentally sketched out the lines of that book they were going to write, and dreamed of penning the million pound best seller that would see them, like some previous members, hit easy street.

Up front sat the Ruperts, Americans and Brits, chatting away to each other in an atmosphere of almost total mutual incomprehension. It was a truth barely alluded to that, all the way back to the First World War trenches, neither army understood the other. The Americans were slightly boastful, loud of speech, patriotic to a huge degree and technology mad. They were sober and committed officers who, when they addressed their men by their Christian names, did so out of a genuine feeling of equality. Their troopers returned that in equal measure, with sometimes to a British mind, an excessive air of respect.

The Brits were just as loud, but were self-deprecating and traditional with regimental rivalries never far below the surface. Then there was class, which manifested itself in an endless number of ways, discernible only to those either giving or receiving the slights. They too used Christian names with their troopers, though for some it sat uneasily, emerging as a strangulated glottal stop rather than the genuine article.

Respect was gifted to a few Ruperts of clear ability and few hang-ups. Most were tolerated rather than loved, and all were guarded with the men, aware that the troopers they technically commanded could take the piss out of them without leaving them much room to respond.

Whatever the internal tensions in both groups, there was an overwhelming air of optimism. There was hardly a man on the plane who was not a strong individualist, Rupert or trooper of either nationality. You couldn't do the job, given the amount of mental strength it required, without acres of self-confidence and a real faith in your own ability.

The oddity was not that there were frictions, but that there were so few.

158

The helo maintenance crews had a nightmare of a job reassembling and preparing the craft that had been flown to Bahrain, forced to work through the night in sealed hangers to avoid the presence of the Special Forces craft being spotted. The Fast Rope Masters – like Winston – had to examine their equipment thoroughly. The miniguns had to be checked, followed by the laying out of the ropes for inspection. They had to ensure there were no cracks or defects in the anchor points of the retaining pins, then rig the helos so they were ready to go. The Night Stalkers lifted off before dawn and headed out to sea.

The USS *Essex*, the deck from which they would depart, used the docking facilities at the Saudi port of Al Jubayl. It was easy for the Marine Amphibious Landing Ship to clear some of its own choppers out of the holds to accommodate those from the 160th SOAR. Then *Essex* headed out into the Persian Gulf, away from eyes close enough to pry, even those of its own pilots whose space the SOAR had occupied.

The captain of the ship had no idea for what task these Special Operations helos had been put aboard. He was simply ordered by his admiral to proceed at flank speed to a staging position off the Pakistani coast opposite the small port of Pasni and await further orders.

Aboard the USS *Carl Vinson*, Rear Admiral Brandon Teitmayer when he stood on the bridge, looked over a deck 1092 feet long. The flight deck was 252 feet wide and his ship displaced 97,000 tons. The *Nimitz* class carrier was powered by two, four-shaft nuclear reactors. She was capable of a speed of 30 plus knots and carried a total of 85 aircraft, and Teitmayer had to pinch himself every time he remembered that the ship cost about $4.5 billion.

The carrier was simply one of the most formidable fighting ships afloat; at the sharp end of American policy, its mission to provide a credible, sustainable, independent, forward presence and conventional deterrent in peacetime. *Vinson* and the other American carriers had to act as the cornerstone of allied maritime expeditionary forces in times of crisis. *Carl Vinson* was designed to operate and support aircraft attacks on enemies, protect friendly forces, and engage in sustained independent operations in wartime; indeed to threaten and destroy anything, land or water-based that denied free use of the sea. Teitmayer had under his feet more power than the whole US Navy had deployed in World War Two. The ship's company totalled 3200, the Air Wing accounting for 2480 of those. It was, as the Admiral liked to say, 'big potatoes'.

From the bridge he controlled the activities of his Carrier Battle Group, which had just received orders to put in place certain elements for the JSOC plan. Teitmayer assembled the necessary personnel to oversee the launch of the Tomahawk Land Attack Missiles – the captains and weapons control officers of the *Aegis* class cruisers. He knew the number of missiles to be deployed, and the target, but the men he addressed had no idea of any element of the plan that did not impact on their personal contribution.

He had to be more forthcoming with his air staff officers and the flight commanders, tasked to fly the Close Air Protection mission with F14 Tomcats and F18 Hornets. They had to know what it was they were protecting, so they were made aware of the ground operation, the possible locations of the TLS, as well as the target. The flyers of his fighter wing were on immediate standby rotated round the clock. Teitmayer put a dedicated team of pilots, the best and most experienced he had, on to the task of providing the CAP, this to take precedence over all other operational flights from the carrier's deck, regardless of whether that interfered with standard operations in Iraqi airspace or not.

Only he knew that the *Essex*, also under his operational command, had been despatched at full speed to the Pakistan coast carrying Special Forces helicopters. That was why he and his senior staff played things close to their chests. It didn't take a genius to add the Special Forces helicopters to Tomahawks and two standby fighter wings flying a CAP mission for that number of helos and C-130s to come up with a mission scenario.

CHAPTER SEVENTEEN

Diego Garcia, part of the Chagos Archipelago, lies halfway between Africa and Asia, so remote from either that its atlas reference is world. It is a place of zeros: no arable land, no forests or woodland, no permanent crops and no people. Part of the British Indian Ocean Territory the archipelago consists of 2300 islands. Not even the officials who adminster the place lived there. Diego Garcia is flat and dry too; at no point is there an elevation of more than sixteen feet. The original inhabitants having been moved to Mauritius for 'humanitarian reasons', it was seen as an ideal spot for a Cold War air base.

Everybody knew all the stats of the place by the time they arrived, thanks to Mike Hutton; and the view, as the Starlifter made its approach, confirmed the picture. The whole aerial appreciation was of just enough land to support one long runway. Even the long breakwaters stretching out from the shore were designed solely to prevent any erosion of the reef on which it was built. The beaches were endless white sand, but apart from clumps of deep green gorse, a few palm trees and the huts and building of the US command, the island was featureless. It had been one of those places the British had snapped up as a maritime power more to stop anyone else than because they wanted it. It had slept on until the US, insecure in the regions to the north but knowing their strategic value, had decided to lease it as a base.

After a long boring flight, and knowing the time window for departure was hours away, everybody on the plane just wanted to get into the water and have a swim. But there was one more thing to do, and that was to listen to their final battle orders, given separately to each group. This last briefing was given by the man who would lead them into battle – Johnny Lancing, B Squadron commander – and consisted of the confirmatory orders for the operation. He was a tall man with delicate facial features enhanced by so keen a manner that you could almost see the schoolboy he'd once been. His voice had that clipped public school quality that exuded enthusiasm for whatever he was engaged in, be it war, or a village cricket match.

'Summary of the op,' he snapped.

The image on the screen, which had held the words he'd just used, skipped to the two targets.

'This is a joint US and UK strike on the terrorist Osama bin Laden's HQ and specialist training camp overlooking the lake at Zu ol Faqar. US Delta Force will destroy the HQ and arrest bin Laden. SAS will destroy the training camp.'

The image changed to show a long shot view from across the Zu ol Faqar lake.

'You will be delivered on to target by Black Hawk and Chinook Helos, with gunships in support. They will launch from the Amphibious Ready Group at present in position off the coast of Pakistan. The operation will be supported by Cruise missiles and MC-130 Spectres. Tomahawk Land Attack Missiles will be fired from the USS *Carl Vinson* Battle Group to impact on the target just after first light. That will be followed by a Spectre gunship sweep over the target area. When they are satisfied that the area has been suppressed they will call us in. Black Hawk gunships will precede the troop helos.

'The USS *Carl Vinson* will already have launched an air wing to assist, most notably F-14s and 18s providing Close Air Protection. They will ascend to their CAP stations as soon as the Tomahawks impact, with a Hawkeye to overview the airspace. We can therefore be reasonably certain that we will not be disturbed. The operation will involve a FARP at a TLS set up by our incountry agents, and air refuelling on the return leg, which will be to the USS *Essex*.'

Lancing paused for a couple of seconds to let that sink in. The image changed again, to a close appreciation of the SAS target.

'Ground!

'Gentlemen, enough has been said about the ground, and you have all carried out in-depth ground studies from the digital video provided by our agents and from the satellite photography. Our target is north east of Kandahar, a substantial conurbation and the second largest city in the country. Kandahar has a military airport, as well as a Taliban garrison, but only one road that leads into the region of Afghanistan's southern plateau. That plateau is at an altitude of three thousand five hundred feet. The actual location of our target is in the foothills of the mountain range to the east of the River Helmand, by the small village of Zu ol Faqar, and a lake of the same name. That is eighty-five Ks from Kandahar.

'Situation, enemy forces,' Lancing continued, briskly. 'The enemy comprises a permanent cadre of instructors, a guard force and a senior officer planning group. This totals three hundred men with about one hundred students being put through a variety of specialist skills training at any given time. So the total strength on target is three to four hundred. The HQ and training camp are linked to each other by a single approach road and they are in an isolated area. They are separated by about six hundred metres of open ground, with the nearest main ground and air support coming from the Taliban garrison eighty-five Ks away at Kandahar. Dedicated air support is provided by one Hip helo on target, which is used for bin Laden's own private movement. Neither represents a credible threat to what we will employ over the target.'

The picture disappeared to be replaced by a written list, headed **Weapons**. Lancing's staccato voice read them off.

'They nearly all carry Makarov pistols. They have a full range of AK weapon systems and that includes the new AK-100 series, AK-74s, AKMs and the old AK-47s. They also have the latest AN-94 Abakan assault rifle; Dragunov sniper rifles; RPK light and PKM general purpose machine guns; 12.7mm heavy machine guns with a ground and air role; RPG-7 rocket launchers and some triple-A in the shape of two pairs of 14.5mm ZPU 2s. They may also have some Stingers left over from our own endeavours in that theatre. This is quite a comprehensive list of weapon systems and, gentlemen, they have a lot of experience using them.'

Mike Hutton was nodding. The others, if they were curious, knew they could ask about them later. Old Egghead would know the lot; rate of fire, calibre, everything. *Jane's Weapon Systems* catalogue was the Bible of everybody interested in international weaponry. Mike was a walking talking edition of that book.

Now it was air power. 'The Taliban airbase at Kandahar. They will be warned to stay on the ground. It is unlikely they will be able to intervene but should they try they will be picked up by the Hawkeye before they are airborne and be intercepted by our CAP. That will be no contest. Their air power is old and poorly maintained. It comprises of 8 Mig-21 Fishbeds, 3 Mig-23 Floggers, 7 Mig-19s and 7 F-5E/F Tiger II's. Their helo force is 6 Hip, 2 Hind and 8 Pumas.'

The screen went blank, and then came up with the heading, '**Friendly Forces. Outline of Plan**.

In essence it was a repeat of what they'd already been told, but that was standard. You do not make assumptions when planning an op for Special Forces. You cover everything and if that involves saying something two, three or more times, so be it.

'To avoid confusion on the net and to keep traffic to a minimum as per a counter terrorist op, we will adopt the two team system. Delta Force are designated Red Team, B Squadron are designated Blue Team.

'The simultaneous attacks will commence immediately following a heavy TLAM and Spectre gunship strike on both targets. Each group will have one Spectre gunship to suppress and two Black Hawk gunships on call providing close air support during the action. The Spectres will ensure that the target area is secure.

'Mission! Our mission is to destroy bin Laden's terrorist training camp at Zu ol Faqar. I say again, our mission is to destroy bin Laden's terrorist training camp at Zu ol Faqar.'

Again a pause, and the staccato acknowledgement of the heading to change the subject. **Execution: general outline**.

'This will be a five-phase operation. Phase one, infil to FARP/TLS. Phase two, action at FARP/TLS. Phase three, approach to target. Phase four, action on target. Phase five, exfil.'

The screen showed, in big bold letters, the words that Lancing read out, using his laser pointer to identify each troop.

Organization and Tasks.

6 Troop.   Callsign: Blue Two

'Your task is to destroy the triple A position located in the north-west turret. You will then concentrate your fire on to the barrack complex and take on opportunity targets. You will fast-rope on to target from a Black Hawk.'

7 Troop.   Callsign: Blue Three

'Your task is to destroy the sentry position located in the east turret. You will then concentrate your fire on to the barrack complex and take on opportunity targets. You will fast-rope onto target from a Black Hawk.'

8 Troop.   Callsign: Blue Four

'Your task is to destroy the sentry position located at the rear of the camp. You will then concentrate your fire on to the barrack complex and take on opportunity targets. You will fast-rope on to target from a Black Hawk.

9 Troop.   Callsign: Blue Five

'You will have elements of Seven and Eight troops attached to you. Your task is to destroy the sentry position located at the entrance to the base. You will also be responsible for the triple A position located just outside the entrance to the base on the north-east. You will then secure the entrance, concentrate your fire on the barrack complex plus take on any opportunity targets. You will fast-rope from a Chinook.'

Lancing flicked through a series of different headings.

Phase 1. Infil to FARP/TLS.

'This will be by MC-130 Combat Talon.

Phase 2. Action at FARP/TLS.

'When we land at the TLS we will immediately disembark and provide close protection and await the arrival of the helos. Once the helos arrive they will refuel. We will then load up on to our respective helos and await the final order to attack. A small protection party that will remain at the FARP. They will lift off with all the remaining aircraft once we have been given the final order to attack and set off on the mission.'

Phase 3. Approach to target.

'The entire strike force will fly low level along the flight path already studied. The helo packet, Delta and SAS, will split at the end of the approach corridor and line up on their respective targets.'

Phase 4. Action on Target.

'At H-hour the TLAMs will strike the target. This will immediately be followed up by an attack from the Spectre gunships. The firepower from the Spectres will destroy anything that moves on target. The Spectres will then pull off target to provide air cover on demand. Once the Spectre has done its task the helo strike force will begin its final approach to target. The Black Hawk gunships will lead and provide close air support and will stay in close support throughout the mission. The remainder of the callsigns will follow in behind the gunships and attack their respective targets.'

The sandstone castle came up again, by now looking quite forbidding.

'Once all callsigns have completed their primary tasks you will concentrate your firepower on the barrack complex and engage any opportunity targets. Once all tasks are complete you will carry out a quick search of the area to collect any information that can be used for intelligence analysis. I will then call for pick up.'

The screen showed, **Phase 5. Exfil.**

'I will give the command to the helos for pick up. All callsigns will be picked up at their infil points. The entire air packet will exfil immediately after and return back via the infil air corridor with the helos air refuelling. Close Air Protection will continue to be provided by US F-14s and F-18s.

'Co-ordinating instructions and timings. Gentlemen, due to the nature of the operation I am unable to give you timings. All timings will be confirmed as and when the mission is given a go. However, the following timings are for the final assault. At FARP/TLS, load onto helos as soon as we are given a go.

'Approach to target. H-hour will be just prior to first light. TLAMs strike target, followed at H + 2 by Spectre gunships attack. All timings from here on will depend on the success of the Spectre Gunships. The helos will be called in by the Spectres on completion of their attack. The F-14s and F-18s will be in the air and will move to provide CAP as soon as the TLAMs have impacted. H plus thirty or on completion of tasks I will call for pick up.

'Summary of execution. We will move from base on board a C-130 to a FARP/TLS site just inside the Afghanistan boder. The helos will then arrive flying in from the USS *Essex*. They will then refuel and we will transfer to the helos and await the final order to attack. Once the order to attack has been given, the TLAMs will be launched from the USS *Carl Vinson* Battle Group and we will begin our final approach. The CAP will take up station outside hostile air space out of any radar window.

'At H hour the TLAMs will strike the targets, followed up by the Spectre gunships who will commence a heavy concentration of fire on the target.

'Once the Spectres are happy that they have suppressed any potential threat, the helos will make their final approach to target being fired in by the helo gunships. All callsigns will fast rope on to their targets and carry out their tasks. Once all tasks are complete I will call for pick up. We will all return to the USS *Essex*, air refuelling *en route* with the F-14s and 18s providing continuous CAP even when we are out of hostile airspace.

'Service Support. Dress is desert fatigue, equipment, light order. Day sack for ammo and medical equipment. Night vision goggles to be carried and used at your own discretion. Weapons: M4 Carbines with M203s, Minimis, M72 LAWs, L2 grenades, explosive entry charges. Ammunition! Minimum of six mags per man, 1000 rounds per gun, as many M72s and grenades as you can carry.

'Feeding,' Lancing said, with a hard look at Tony Parsons. 'As per normal arrangements.'

'Task an extra C-130,' whispered Jake Steel, digging Parsnips in the ribs.

'Medical,' Lancing continued. 'On the assault each team will provide its own medical cover. There will be a full medical support team on call aboard the Osprey Tiltrotor for fast casevac. Callsign will be Angel One. All casualties will be removed from the scene. We will not leave anybody. I repeat, we will not leave anybody. Those that require fast hospitalization are to be loaded on to the Osprey, which will exfil ahead of the assault force for a direct and fast flight back to a base facility.'

'POWs! We will only take prisoners of an extremely high rank. All other survivors will be disarmed and left on target.'

That was just another one for the record. No one in the room was expecting any survivors.

'Command and signal! My command group callsign Blue One, will be onboard the first Black Hawk gunship callsign Bluebird One, and will remain onboard throughout the attack.

'Signals! Each callsign will have SMT radios. All individuals will have PRM bodysets. Each team will have its own dedicated channel; if necessary you will be able to switch between channels. Codewords. The Codeword for exfil is Lion's Roar. The company signals rep will give a thorough signals brief after these orders. Time check!'

Everyone synchronised their watch before Lancing invited questions.

After hours of planning, several briefing sessions and rehearsals there was nothing left to ask so Lancing handed over to the signallers, who in turn commenced their own briefing.

Before anyone could relax each man had to make sure their kit was ready, and go through his individual battle orders. As soon as the signallers were finished the squadron broke up into its callsigns – teams of eight and twenty-four – and began final preparations.

The Rupert commanding Blue Five, Captain Ben Forsyth, was one of the few officers the men respected. He had a great brain, lots of common sense, could run faster and longer than most of the men he commanded, and was a right hard case at unarmed combat. The best thing about him though was his lack of the usual Rupert snobbery. He didn't pretend to be one of the boys, he just was.

The general opinion was that his career in the British Army was doomed. Soon he'd run into that glass ceiling, the class barrier mounted by the run of the mill or truly thick, an obstacle that kept good officers from high command positions. Wisely he broke his twenty four man callsign down into two smaller groups to carry out their final briefing, one taken by himself, the other passed over to the SSM, Dr Who.

Lance Price was the patrol commander of callsign Blue Two, the only team without a Rupert to annoy them, a bonus, since they were all 6 Troop and used to each other. Magazines were filled and checked, each man deciding for himself how many to take – or they would have done if Chemo hadn't nagged them all into adding an extra pair. Each man primed his grenades, then assisted the demolition experts in making up small explosive charges, big enough to blast open a heavy door – should that be required when they reached their secondary target. All optics were checked and so were the super powerful Yank Sure-Fire combat flashlights they'd been issued with. Weapons were cleaned, checked, and the laser signs zeroed at 300 metres.

Radio equipment and the batteries that powered it had to be checked, especially the personal radio mikes worn by each trooper. More fuck-ups occur through malfunctioning comms on operations than for any other reason. In addition the troop commanders had to ensure that their minicams were operating properly, pinned to their ops waistcoats in such a way that they presented a forward visual view to the tactical commanders. The troopers fitted the night vission goggles with new batteries and loaded both them and a spare set into their day sacks.

Medical equipment was checked, the prime responsibility of one man per fire team, who had the added task of ensuring that each member of the callsign was equipped with a trauma pack to provide emergency first aid both to himself and any of his mates. The Camelback hydration kits were emptied and refilled with fresh clean water, something that would happen every day until they took off. That was important kit, a regimental mantra being 'hydrate or die'. Water was fuel for the body, without it a fighting man soon lost his effectiveness. The great thing about the Camelback was that it not only re-hydrated but kept the trooper effective while it did so.

Lance, even though they'd only just left the main briefing ran through the mission, forcing his troopers to answer questions so that the orders were fixed in all their minds: reference points, situation of enemy and friendly forces, command and signals, in fact everything that was needed for execution of their mission.

This he did, not once, but several times, making sure that everyone was up to speed. If they weren't, this was the place to find out, not once they were on the target.

'Is there any chance of me getting some scoff?' said Parsnips, after the fifth run through. 'I'm fucking famished.'

'One more time,' Lance replied.

Jake Steel threw Parsnips a Hershey bar.

'Thanks mate,' Tony said. 'It's hard to think when you're hungry.'

General Aaron Bronowski was not physically or mentally equipped for the finer flights of diplomacy. A short, beetle-browed man he had risen through the ranks of the US Army by sheer application. He had no connections, no sponsors and was not a man to make friends easily. But nobody worked as hard, nor trained his units more ferociously than this son of a pre-war Polish immigrant. He had been brought up on the Chicago West Side and still had the accent to prove it.

He smoked short cheap cigars, had been married to the same woman for thirty years and went to church every Sunday in the company of his seven children and countless grandchildren. A paragon of whatever community he resided in, he had only one known defect: impatience.

As Vice chairman of the Joint Chiefs of Staff he had ample opportunity to display that trait, exposed as he was to the seemingly endless excuses of better educated but lazier subordinates. To Bronowski, the army he served in was riddled with a spend, spend, spend mentality. It was computerized this and laser-guided that. He had no personal down on technology but carped on endlessly that, when push came to shove the grunt with the gun was the main man. And, having served in action himself, he knew that the toughness required came from an inner discipline that had nothing to do with computer chips. Ready to state that opinion at each and every opportunity, he was not popular among the grandees of the American armed forces.

Tasked to be polite to the generals of the Pakistani army, he existed in a constant state of pent-up rage. With their linear descent from the old army of the British Raj, the senior officers in this part of the world prided themselves on a degree of sophistication that rankled even with professional diplomats. Casually dressed or in full uniform they exuded panache. Their manners were impeccable, their conversation calculated to be flattering and delightful, but all that did was mask their greed and ambition. In politics they wanted power without responsibility, for their forces they wanted the very latest America could provide without paying for it, emphasizing the need for regional stability while at the same time, with their bellicose attitude to India and their utter indifference to the deeds of the Taliban, actively encouraging the opposite.

170

The nuclear tests they'd carried out, in response to the Indian government's programme, had opened a rift of monumental proportions between Pakistan and the United States. Orders placed for F-16 fighter aircraft had been cancelled and the deposits returned. The three Orions needed for electronic intelligence gathering were embargoed. So, being an American military representative in this country was, right at this moment, a mite uncomfortable.

Bronowski knew he had a message to deliver at some point on his trip. He didn't know what it was, but since he rather than the Ambassador, had been tasked to give it, he guessed it wouldn't make for pleasant listening. So, as he sat through long-winded conferences, at which each general present sang his own praises at the expense of his peers, the Vice chairman of the Joint Chiefs drew hard on his cigar and kept his temper in check. And he prayed that the message would come soon so that he could wipe the smiles off the faces of these smug bastards.

CHAPTER EIGHTEEN

A fghanistan is not blessed with many roads, but it is riddled with routes that were originally created by men with donkeys, then slowly widened, sometimes deliberately, to take vehicles. These were the arteries by which the Mujahideen had kept up their fight against the Russians, the commanders moving troops and supplies, often on the backs of their fighters, over terrain that the Ivans could never control, except from the air.

They'd crossed the Helmand River at a point where it was wide, slow and fordable, manoeuvring round rocks the size of several houses. Then they climbed into what were no more than foothills compared to what existed further north and east. Yet it was bad. For a conventional army, Afghanistan is an appalling place in which to fight. High hills or mountains overlook every plain or plateau. Venture into those mountains, with their deep valleys, sheer cliffs and endless escarpments, and you'd find a fighter behind every rock.

Blue, as they bounced along on the loose shale of the route, couldn't help looking at the place from the viewpoint of 'Basic Boris'. The Russian conscript soldiers must have hated this place. He wasn't too keen himself, though the sector they were crossing was tame. You only had to look back to their escort and observe how tense they were – AKs waving to cover the surrounding hills – to realize that there was little or no security. That tension would stretch to breaking point each time they came across a knot of armed tribesmen, groups that appeared from nowhere in what looked like a deserted landscape. Each stop involved Gino Manganelli in lengthy negotiations. While Abdul and his nephews stroked their weapons, Blue Harding, AKSU-74 short barrelled submachine gun resting an inch from his hand just out of sight, tried to look like an innocent.

Inevitably, after much haggling, a sum of money would change hands; dollar bills in a country ravaged with hyperinflation had the status of gold dust. It was a trade off. The tribesmen knew that these Westerners had a lot more cash and they would have robbed the party in an instant without the presence of two factors. Firstly their potential victims were armed and numerous enough to put up a fight; secondly such a robbery might draw unwelcome attention on to themselves. That could lead to a raid by the Taliban, who would kill everyone – men women and children – just to show what happened to those who flouted their authority.

There was little cursing when they came to the rockslide that had washed the road away. Both men reckoned that in a country like this they'd been lucky to get this far without having to pull over. And the only way to solve the problem, to get round the obstruction, was a recce on foot. Pluggers were good, but they could only give you your position and the direction to your next RV. You still had to navigate the terrain, and only a fool would take a vehicle up a succession of blind valleys. Gino and Blue studied the maps spread out on the bonnet, searching for possible routes. There wouldn't be a road as such, but there might be a way through that would bring them back to the same road on the other side of the slip.

'We'll have to reverse up to this bearing, whatever happens,' said Blue, pointing to a map reference that showed a small area of flat ground running north. 'I spotted it when we came through.' His finger continued, showing where the flat ground ceased there appeared to be a series of defiles, several of which ran in the right direction. 'We'll probably have to move some rocks but I reckon it's worth a look.'

'Affirmative,' Gino replied.

'I'll take old Abdul with me. You get the Patrols back and we'll RV there when I've finished the recce.'

'OK. You take the Plugger, then you can feed in the route you've chosen.'

Blue grinned. 'Are you telling me you don't trust my map reading?'

'Just insurance, Blue,' Gino replied, entering the co-ordinates.

Blue checked his sub-machine gun and his Makarov pistol, taking with him spare mags for both. He still had his own GPS in his pocket as well as his compass, so the chances of getting lost, never high, were zero. Abdul had filled two water bottles, one of which he clipped on to the belt kit he'd borrowed from Gino. Matching Blue's, it had a knife, a compact medical kit and a pouch for spare magazines.

They moved out to the sound of high pitched reversing engines, clambering up the slope to the rim of the escarpment that overlooked the road. Before them lay an undulating, seemingly endless series of grey-brown rocky ridges. Blue felt uncomfortable up here. The SAS never worked the high ground; that was for idiots who desired a bullet. They always moved below the skyline, out of sight, and that ingrained habit was still there. Abdul signalled a route that Blue had already worked out on the map, a gorge that would take them across the angle between their present position and that flat ground he'd identified. That impressed the ex-trooper. The old bastard could read terrain and direction from merely examining the ground. Abdul Siygas didn't need maps.

Below the skyline, out of the wind, the sun was hot, and with humans passing and what little wildlife existed in hiding, totally silent. Blue tried to stay away from the loose shale that would make a noise, keeping to the slightly elevated edges of the track to minimize noise. Abdul did likewise, but with a seemingly better grip on the surface than Blue. Any communication tended to be monosyllabic. The old Mujahideen fighter was not, it seemed, much of a talker. There was grey in his beard, but the alert eyes stood out prominently on his dark face. He gave the impression that his slightly hooked nose was always twitching, as if smelling for a threat, and the lips moved often and silently as he carried on an internal dialogue, probably with Allah.

On high ground again they could trace the routes of the various defiles. Their first choice was a no-no, being blocked by a landslide of rocks too large to move. The second was more promising, ninety per cent navigable by the Nissans, with the odd rock that needed shifting, which given they had ropes and powerful vehicles, would present little difficulty. Eventually they emerged back on to the road on the other side of the rockslide hot, covered in dust, but successful.

They could have gone straight back down the road but Blue wanted to retrace the route, on the grounds that time spent on reconnaissance is seldom wasted. They were halfway back to the RV when that twitching nose of Abdul's picked up something that merited a loud sniff. It was several yards later that Blue detected what had excited the Afghan: the slightly sickly sweet smell of fresh dung. It lay at a point where two of the defiles crossed, surrounded by a mass of flies and already drying out in the heat of the sun. Abdul knelt to touch it and pronounced it still very warm.

There was, as yet, no cause for alarm; these trails would be criss-crossed by any number of people – milk and butter carriers, small traders who went from household to household repairing metal utensils or even making shoes. It was a fact that the seemingly empty landscape that Blue had observed from the high ground was anything but. It was far from over-populated, but there were people there, going about the kind of business that had gone on, unchanging, for centuries.

Both men had stopped to drink from their water bottles when the sound of the single shot split the air, rapidly succeeded by another, that followed a second later by a four-shot burst, all coming from the spot where they were due to RV with Gino and Abdul's nephews. Without a word, Blue and Abdul started to jog down the defile, with the ex-Mujahideen fighter grunting and pointing every time he saw the evidence of recent traffic-displaced loose shale, exposing the darker grey of another piece only recently exposed to the elements.

They stopped before the crest of the hill that overlooked the position, creeping forward to observe. The clearing was no more than fifty feet across, dotted with scrub bushes and the occasional rock. Gino and two of Abdul's nephews were standing weapons trained on a group of four tribesmen in the same pose. The third of the nephews was slouched against a Nissan holding his arm, from which blood was streaming. One of the Afghani group, still holding the lead rope of a donkey, was crouched over the recumbent figure of a tribesman, flat out on the ground, writhing and moaning. Another donkey stood braying at the point where the small stretch of flat ground ran round to join with the roadway, a tribesman trying to calm him by rubbing his neck and talking incessantly.

It was a Mexican stand-off and, given the tension, one that could see a mass of casualties if anyone got too twitchy. Gino was talking, his voice barely reaching them. But he'd be trying to calm the situation, Blue was sure, by an offer of money.

He tapped Abdul and drew back from the crest. The ex-Mujahideen fighter had an AK-47 with the standard 413mm barrel length, longer, more accurate than his over a greater range. Blue indicated that he wanted him to take the high ground to the right of the RV and establish a fire support position to dominate the area. The elevation should give him a clear shot if he needed one. Should the opposition fire then Abdul's job was to suppress them and sow confusion, giving the rest of their party a chance to slot them. Blue would move from the spot he was in to give support.

Blue used his hands to tell Abdul that he was going to edge round to the left, in order to get to a point where he would outflank those facing Gino and also be much closer to them. He had the decision to make. If he opened fire, so must Abdul. If the enemy opened fire, they would both do so anyway. There was a hard look in the older man's eyes as they exchanged a confirmatory nod, an expression that hinted at something dangerous, like the notion that having shot one of his family, these people had to die.

'We have to get out of this, Abdul, in one piece. There's a job to do.'

He wanted to say he had a family too, that he shared the Afghan's feelings, that he thought his own son's life was going to depend on the success of their mission. But there was no time and too few words of communication for that.

He wasn't sure if Abdul understood every word, but he must have got hold of the sentiment because he nodded sharply and moved away. Blue went in the opposite direction, now doubly careful to minimize any noise of movement. He tallied off about 135 seconds, the time it took him to get to where he wanted to be: a position between two large rocks, split by a stunted bush, that gave him a clear view of the situation from a side on position. That was three more than the two minutes he'd calculated for Abdul, so he assumed when he took stock that the opposition were already under threat.

Gino was still talking, his own sub-machine gun up and ready, but it was in the local lingo which Blue didn't understand. The tone wasn't calm and that worried him, given that the American was a good negotiator, very experienced, something he'd already proved on the way here. The shots had occurred over five minutes ago and he was still pleading. Judging by the faces of the men facing him he'd be doing that for a long time to come, especially since the tribesman on the ground had stopped writhing and was now still. The one who'd been leaning over him had moved away, with the donkey, to a position closer to the second Nissan, which he was now touching in an envious way.

Blue would have let him carry on. After all money was scarcely a problem and another ten or twenty minutes would make no difference. There was only one problem. The tribesman who'd been trying to calm the second donkey by the roadside was no longer anywhere near it. A quick look at the angles established that elevation was the only reason Blue had seen him in the first place. He'd been out of sight of those by the Nissans. Now he was out of sight of everybody and that could only mean one thing: he was moving, just as Blue was moving, to take up a position which could dominate the area.

The shift in attention was immediate, eyes lifting to scan the higher ground on the other side of the flat area. The location of that guy became a priority, because even if Blue and Abdul slotted the others before they could harm the rest of their party, the four of them would still be exposed to fire from a concealed position. The 'shit' was mouthed but not said, as Blue examined the opposite rock faces, searching out the points which would give the guy what he needed. Luckily, there weren't a million of them and whatever position he took up had to be similar to Blue's, giving him a clear shot at the opposition without endangering his own.

Had the Afghan kept as still as the man looking for him, he wouldn't have been spotted. But he moved just enough to ease aside a bush and make the way he was cradling his weapon more comfortable. And now that he had him, Blue could separate his dirty garment from the grey of the rocks and the burnt colour of the vegetation. He was leaning forward, looking down the barrel of his weapon, clearly about to fire.

177

Blue immediately slid into a firing position, instinctively employing the four marksmanship principles that are indoctrinated into all British soldiers: position and hold must be firm enough to support the weapon; the weapon must point naturally towards the target without any physical effort; sight alignment aiming must be correct; the shot must be released and followed through without any disturbance of the position.

Those principles applied, Blue put a double tap right into his target.

He didn't look to see the result. The muzzle dropped and he got the guy nearest his position, a split second after Abdul opened fire, taking out the one furthest away from Blue. The tribesmen might be good fighters, but they were untrained, unable to cope with fire coming from three angles. Three because Gino had let fly with his AKSU-74 rapid controlled bursts of fire that ripped through the confused opposition, men in the process of dying, if they were not already dead.

When the firing ceased, Blue was surprised to hear the sound of an engine, even more amazed to see the second Nissan begin to move. It had been facing away from the road and the guy holding the donkey had jumped in to try and escape. The animal, loose and scared, was careering around, bucking and rearing, preventing anyone from stopping the Patrol. Abdul had only a brief chance at a shot before the angle of fire was cut off by the height of his position.

Blue didn't wait. He was already moving to cut across the angle the driver had to take, discarding the mag he had in the AK and slotting in another on the move. The Nissan contained some of their kit, he couldn't remember what, but the loss of it would jeopardise the mission so the guy had to be stopped. Blue was rushing over the ridges to get to a point where he knew the Patrol would have to slow down, a point where several rocks they would have had to clear blocked the route. He only just made it, cresting the final knoll as the sound of metal on rock floated up to his ears.

Coming over the crest, he had a half view of the wild-eyed driver crunching the bull bars into the boulders to move them out of the way. He only failed with one and so slammed the Nissan into reverse, shot back and came at the last rock at speed. The bull bar gave way under the impact, and so did half the wing, but the rock moved enough to clear a passage and Blue heard the engine noise increase as he tried to push on through.

Dropping the AK and taking out his Makarov pistol was all one movement, accomplished as Blue slithered down the slope on to the moving Patrol. Thinking is not an option in such a situation, reacting is, and even though it was potentially fatal he took a furious leap to land on the bonnet, catching hold of the roof rack to stop himself from going right over. His knees gave way and he dropped down to look through the windscreen at a terrified face. It wasn't that for long. It fell apart as Blue put a 9mm bullet right through the glass and into the forehead. The Nissan slewed round until one wheel running up the bank killed the forward momentum.

Blue jumped down and opened the door, dragging the guy out on to the ground. He didn't doubt he was dead, he just didn't want too much blood on the seats. The Patrol had to be reversed back to a point where he could turn. By the time he got back to the open ground, Gullam, the one who'd been wounded, had been seen to medically, and the bodies of those who had died had been jammed into a small defile in the rocks. There was no sign of the donkeys, though their loads were on the ground, one pack split open.

'Take a taste,' said Gino, holding out a packet full of brown paste.

'Heroin?' said Blue, guessing, even though it was in its raw state.

'Yup. Which explains why my offer of money didn't take. They probably thought we were Drug Enforcement.'

'The bodies?'

'Will have to rot, Blue. But we'll scatter this stuff around them so it will look like a fight between smugglers.'

'A million dollars?'

'Not here, Blue. That's unrefined. In this part of the world it's cheaper than beer.'

'Time to be out of here, Gino.'

Blue got the story, of how they hadn't been bounced, just believing the guys coming out of the gully were ordinary traders. The shot had been because one of them had opened the door of a Nissan while Gino was talking. Gullam fired a shot in the air to warn him off, which was followed by him getting a slug in the arm. Gino downed the first man to die, then they were as Blue and Abdul had found them.

'How long before somebody finds them?' asked Blue.

'Not long,' Gino replied. 'But they'll steal the heroin base and leave the carcasses to the vultures.'

'No impact on us?'

'Can't see it. People round here don't go phoning the cops.'

'Good!'

Before twilight they were out of the hills, on to the flat plain of the Dash-I-Margo, able to keep up a good speed along straight avenues bounded by endless irrigation ditches. To their right, when night had fallen, they could often see the silver ribbon of the Helmand gleaming in the moonlight, and up ahead, after a couple of hours, they saw the dark mass of the range of hills that was their destination. Off to their left, rising in tiers, were the higher mountains of Afghanistan, running all the way to the heights of the Hindu Kush.

They had to pull over when they reached the first of the rising ground: it was time to eat and drink. They took turns at sleeping and, while awake, speculated on whether they would find what both maps and satellite photography had told them should be there.

America had been in these parts long before, engineers from the army on an aid mission to help one of the poorest regions in the world. The country had been at peace then with tribal rivalries less fraught and fewer bloodbaths than now occurred. There were just so many damned guns in the country, left over from twenty years of conflict. Back in the fifties the teams could work in peace, building a small dam on a tributary of the Helmand, diverting its course so that water flowed on to the Dash-I-Margo plain to irrigate the soil. In doing so they had also created a salt lake on the small plateau through which the river used to run. That was the destination of Gino Manganelli and Blue Harding, one they set off for as soon as there was sufficient light to see.

The maps they had were good, but this was not civilization. Roads got washed away and were not repaired; and diversions led the party up several blind alleys that were bad enough going forward, ten times worse in reverse. Blue kept an eye on his watch, as aware as his partner that time counted; that if they could not find a way through on wheels in a certain time, then it was Bergens on and a hot, heavy tab.

'Leaving the Nissans will not please Abdul,' said Gino, as they were confronted by another impasse where rocks had fallen to block the route. The merest suggestion that it was time to take to walking had Abdul haranguing his nephews, with all four Afghans, even Gullam with only one arm, setting to work to clear the rocks while Gino and Blue stood stag.

'Why not?'

'Don't ask me how he's figured it out, because I don't know, but I reckon he thinks there's a very good chance we're not going to be driving out again.'

'He can't know.'

'I make you right, ol' buddy. But have you noticed the way he's reacted to that damage to his vehicle?'

'No,' Blue replied.

'Normally, if these guys drive anything we provide, they couldn't give a shit what they hit, as long as they can keep going. Not old Abdul Siygas. He crossed the Helmand as if he was carrying eggs. I don't think he went over any rock more than a foot high since.'

'Some doing on these tracks,' said Blue, looking at the fifty-foot sheer fall to his left.

'I got eyes in the back of my head. Abdul's been taking so much care not to scratch his car any further, I wouldn't be surprised to see him wash and polish the mother if we find more water.'

'If we airlift out . . .' said Blue nodding.

'That's right, buddy. Abdul's got two new Patrols, one slightly bent, and all the kit we leave.'

'And he won't bring them back.'

'Only in my dreams. The next time I see the old bastard he'll be telling me a tale of how a group of bandits robbed him, stole his vehicles and made him return to Pakistan on foot.'

'I'd like to see the guy that could rob that old bastard.'

'You can't, Blue old buddy. He ain't been born.'

With half an eye on the surrounding hills, both men watched as an endless stream of rocks were slung into the valley, their four escorts sweating and panting, until there was only one huge boulder left. It took all six of them to shift that, very satisfying as it went over the edge, bouncing noisily off the cliff until it landed with a deep thud.

'The Plugger puts us within one kilometre of the salt lake.'

'I like the look of the rest of the place,' Blue replied, with a grimace.

It was barren rock all around them, the odd stunted tree bent by the wind but no discernible pasture or terraced cultivation. There would have been no point in even eyeballing the site if there had been any kind of serious habitation, but lots of pasture would have meant lots of shepherds, with their flocks of fat tailed sheep. Such a detail would have been taken into the Headshed calculations. The whole area would be under saturation satellite coverage, every movement logged, to ensure that the TLS, if it was going to be here, couldn't be compromised.

'There's our baby,' said Gino, as they crested the rise.

Both men climbed out to have a good look, shading their eyes against a sun now high in the sky. The salt lake – flat, long and narrow – gleamed in the morning sunlight, running north to south, a white, near empty expanse of hard packed ground that, from this distance, looked perfect for a Tactical Landing Strip. Blue went back to the Patrol and pulled out his machine pistol.

'You wait here.'

'What for?'

'I'm going to do a recce.'

'Are you kidding me,' said Gino, poking a finger at the clear blue sky. 'Do you know how many guys are probably looking at this place right now?'

'Dozens,' Blue replied. 'If the orbit timings are on us.'

'That's right. There are times of the day when we can't even take a piss without they'll be checking our blood sugar.'

'Not all the time. I'll be happier if I have a look around.' Gino still wasn't convinced, forcing Blue to insist. 'Never take anything for granted. Never assume because that's a good way to get slotted. We could have the Father, the Son and the Holy Ghost eyeballing this place twenty-four hours a day and I'd still want to do a recce. And I don't want we should get bounced again.'

'Time?'

'An hour won't kill us.'

'Suit yourself. Do you want Abdul and the boys with you?'

'Abdul. You keep the boys.'

Blue moved off, going at right angles to the parked Nissans, his eyes examining the small rocky defiles and the patches of scrub, especially those with low stunted trees, looking for any sign of habitation, wondering if he was, in fact, being paranoid. Gino was right about the satellites, but there were places into which they couldn't see, and times when they were not overhead. And there were other considerations. If the watchers were looking for anything it would be a force large enough to threaten the use of the salt lake as a TLS, but two ragheads with decent rifles, if they caught Gino and his party out on the flats away from the rocks, could take them out well before they could get to cover. They didn't have to be Taliban or anything else. They could just be bandits.

If this place was designated as the TLS, it would, for a certain period be occupied by a force strong enough to defend it against anything the locals could throw at it. But that wasn't a threat to which Blue gave much credence. It would take a minimum of twenty-four hours to even get such a force on the road. There was no reason for the Afghans to suspect what was coming, no reason for them to mount an operation to compromise an unknown military threat.

But that didn't make it secure. A small group with any kind of rocket-propelled weapon – anti-aircraft or anti-tank – could render the whole site untenable. A C-130, taxiing, would be a sitting duck. Catch it in the right spot, like the central area that would provide the runway and the whole TLS became useless. Satellites or not, Blue knew he could get an SAS patrol in here. They would lie up, and time their attack to trap any air assets on the ground. If he could do it, so could other people. So, if paranoia was a possibility in his present state of mind, he was glad to have it.

There were signs of human presence; sheep droppings and the odd trace of a shepherd's charcoal fire, but it was all long dead stuff. He and Abdul moved easily around the rocks, eyes casting left, right and ahead, Blue noting the places from which he, if he'd been an enemy, would operate. Each one was looked over until he was totally satisfied that no threat existed. In his mind he logged each point. Gino would no doubt scoff again, but while they were here these places would be recced every morning and every night, examined to see if anything had changed.

He wondered if there were, at this precise moment, guys back in the USA, watching his efforts. If there were, some, no doubt, would be laughing at him and calling him an asshole, while others would be cursing at the time he was using up. But they weren't soldiers. Any one who was, especially from Special Forces, would approve. They would have the same attitude as him: never take anything for granted, never assume, always check and then check again. It's the only way to stay alive.

As they came back to the point where Gino was waiting with Abdul's trio of nephews, Blue suddenly stopped, looked skywards and gave the satellites the finger.

'Are you OK now?' asked Gino.

'Happy as a pig in shit. The place is clean.'

'Can we go to work'

'That's what we came for.'

Even in his cell like room, with its thick walls, Aidan McGurk heard the heavy beat of the helicopter blades. The embrasure that acted as his only source of daylight gave him a fleeting view as the helo swung over the clear blue water of the lake on its final approach. That brief glance wasn't very reassuring. As it came in he could see that it was heavily laden, seeming to struggle slightly as it slowed. He could also see the peeling paint, the dents in the fuselage, the loose rivets and the bits of plating that seemed less than firmly secured. Then it was out of view, hovering in to land on the helipad.

But both ground and air view were still on the screens at Langley, in the command centre on Diego Garcia, and in the warfare control room aboard the USS *Carl Vinson*. The entire JSOC command had flown in to the carrier, which would act as the headquarters for the forthcoming operation.

'We appear to have quite a load,' said the voice from Langley.

He went on to identify bin Laden, Sheikh Tassir Abdullah, as well as several other men, leaders of various proscribed Islamic terrorist groups from around the world. Each had his bodyguards along, which put some strain on the lift capacity of the old Hip.

'Maybe they're planning a conference.'

'As long as we're invited,' said Lucius Morton. 'How much longer do we have on overhead?'

'One hour and fifty minutes, general.'

Morton didn't ask about the gap between the departure of the daylight satellite and the arrival of the one re-routed to overfly at night. That, he knew, was six hours. It was a minor problem as long as the digital ground camera kept operating, cutting down the time when the site would be out of observation to no more than an hour.

CHAPTER NINETEEN

Gino drove down on to the surface of the lake bed and stopped, got out with Blue and looked round. Both men knew the rules for what they were about to do and were ruminating on them.

A TLS had to be related to the limitations of the aircraft that were going to use it, as well as the parameters of the mission. Dimensions in this case were vital, since the lake had to accommodate a sizeable helo force in an area that would not impede any of the C-130s from making an emergency take off. With such big planes, the size and terrain features were of paramount importance.

Recognition from the air was always a plus, regardless of how much electronic kit the pilots had at their disposal. A flat surface was less important than a clear one since a rock the size of a man's hand could wreck a plane's undercarriage. And Blue and Gino were responsible. They would set up their digital video and send back pictures, but when it came right down to it the pilots put their lives in the hands of the men on the ground. Fuck the technology, the guys coming in wanted common sense.

They were in an area without triple A defences – very necessary given the vulnerability of planes to ground fire when landing and taking off. The surrounding hills didn't rise much above the surface of the plateau so the site was reasonably easy to defend. Although the salt lake narrowed in the middle it was broad enough at both ends to allow the C-130s to make a 360-degree turn. Right now the wind was blowing from the south, which meant that both approach and landing could be made from the north, over the crest of the rise they'd just surmounted. The C-130s would have to taxi back up to this end to prepare for take off if the wind stayed true.

The chance of fog in such an arid spot was zero, and the salt was so compacted that little of it would blow off in a wind, certainly not enough to cause a hazard. Low cloud was a potential problem, but at this altitude the weather could change in seconds. They had taken a Plugger reading to establish that altitude, one which would be co-ordinated with the ground reading to give the height of the hills so that the pilots could feed into their computers the correct angle of approach.

Once on the salt lake surface Gino drove his vehicle to the edge by the rocks, entered a waypoint into the GPS, then set the trip on the speedometer to zero and drove straight down the centre of the site. Every so often he stopped so that Blue could climb out and jam into the surface a long sharp spike with a white mark 600 millimetres up the shaft. The C-130 is a heavy plane; land it on ground with no depth to hold it and it would be there forever.

'I used to do this with paracord,' said Blue.

'I think you're bucking for a old age pension, pal,' Gino replied, laughing.

But it was true, and he still had it. He fished it out now and dangled it in front of his companion: knotted parachute cord he'd used for pacing in every job he'd ever done. Years ago he'd measured his own pace to the millimetre. He knew just how many steps it took to make up a hundred metres. He would count them up in his head, slip one knot through his fingers and start on the next. Using that, he reckoned he could be as accurate as Gino.

'I'll even back the speedo,' said Blue.

'No way, buddy,' Gino scoffed, stroking the Plugger.

The TLS, for C-130s, had to be a minimum of 750 metres long, plus an addition of ten per cent at each end for safety, and since they must allow for a night landing the width had to be thirty-six metres. As they drove slowly along they looked out for any indentations. At least on this surface there were no ditches, logs, fences or hedges but there were rocks that would have to be cleared. There was a slight gradient but it was a lot less than the three degrees that would render the site untenable.

'What you got caveman?' asked Gino, grinning, when they reached the point at which the salt lake gave way to a mixture of rocks and scrub.

'One thousand two hundred and four metres,' Blue replied, having examined the speedometer.

'You're dead, buddy,' said Gino, holding up the Plugger. 'You're out by a whole five metres. Time to get into the twentieth century.'

They measured across, they measured every indentation in the layout. The lake was long enough and had the dimensions, which Gino outlined, to provide a secure area for helos to park up. There should be no danger of the kind of collision with a fixed wing either taxiing or taking off which had marred Operation Rice Bowl. The Plugger had given them an exact measurement of the area, and that information was passed back, at the end of their supposed office number, to JSOC.

Blue set up the TACSAT, aiming it forty-eight degrees in elevation and 170 degrees north, called in on voice then linked up the digital camera that would beam back the images. Lucius B. Morton, along with his fellow committee members, sat in the briefing room seven thousand miles away, watching in near real time while Blue Harding and Gino Manganelli filmed every aspect of the site. The information was recorded and, within minutes, sent on to Diego Garcia and the USS *Essex*, along with the graphics that had emerged when the information had been put into the computers. Thus the pilots had a three dimensional package that could be fed into their simulators, allowing them to practise the approach and landing. All possible weather conditions and wind speeds had already been loaded, so that they could test out the variations.

'OK,' said Gino, once the transmission was complete and the TACSAT was set to receive. Abdul had got the gas burner going, and was busy cooking a big part of the fresh rations. 'Let's eat.'

'Sounds good to me,' said Blue.

He looked around the barren, grey-brown hills, his mind once more on Jake and the operation of which they were both a part. Except he wasn't really part of it. He was just back up. The days had long gone when he would have been at the sharp end of that very rare thing, a squadron operation. And he missed it, was saddened by the idea that he and the boy he'd only recently discovered he had, couldn't go into battle together.

'Probably just as well,' he said to himself. 'I'd probably get us both wasted trying to take care of him.'

188

'You talking to yourself again, Blue?' asked Gino.

'Nope,' he replied, gazing up at the clear blue sky, the emotion he felt stinging the corners of his eyes. 'Just praying to the patron saint of soldiers.'

'Do they have one?'

'You're the Catholic, Gino. You tell me.'

The message was received in Diego Garcia less than an hour after it was transmitted from the proposed TLS. There was another team in, eyeballing an alternative site, and they had yet to report. But JSOC was happy with the salt lake, which had always been the favourite. They would let the other team go ahead, just in case, but Lucius Morton felt in a position to pass up a signal to the President that everything they needed was in place, except the personal target.

The same group of people assembled in the White House briefing room as had attended the initial conference four days previously. Before each lay a numbered copy of the plan of attack, detailed in every respect, with a summary for those who lacked the technical know how to read the battle orders. The President's first remark, made direct to Lucius Morton on the whole wall video screen, was to congratulate him on the speed with which he had assembled and trained the forces to be employed.

'I read here,' said the National Security Advisor, 'that you are staging out of Diego Garcia.'

'We intend to use Marisah as a forwarding base to actually launch the operation. But we would not land there if our target has flown, and we will not remain there if a late stand down is called.'

'You would return to base.'

'That is correct. Though, after a study of bin Laden's habits we feel that any stand down will occur before we lift off from here. He has habits; in particular most of his visits are made in the morning and he's gone before noon. If he's there after that he is probably staying put for the night.'

'That still leaves you with a high risk of having to signal a last minute recall. Does that not put an extra strain on the personnel?'

'Again, the answer is yes. It's a matter of three elements: time, distance and security.'

'Please explain, general,' asked the President.

'Well, sir, we looked at various other locations. The most obvious are our bases in Bahrain and Saudia Arabia. They have the advantage of being closer, yet they are neither of them as secure. Nearly all the civilian labour force at the bases emanates from the Indian sub-continent. There is no way of guaranteeing their loyalty, and if I was bin Laden, I would certainly have people in place in the US bases nearest to Afghanistan.'

'A valid point,' said the President.

'The arrival and presence, possibly for several days, of such a force as Delta and the SAS, along with the 16th Special Forces Air Group would not pass unnoticed, and could lead to the mission being compromised. Diego Garcia has a small population that depends on us entirely for its existence. Then there is the political angle to consider.'

'I thought that was our job, General Morton,' said the NSA. The remark was made jokingly, but Jensen's voice failed to convey any humour.

'It is, sir, and you have the power to overrule. But our Target Panel at JSOC looked at the problem, and came to a very fast conclusion: that neither the Saudi royal family or the rulers of Bahrain would want it known that an assault on a fellow Muslim, however much they personally detest the man, was launched from their soil. They would be more concerned with the views of their co-religionists than the success of the operation.'

'I think that analysis is correct,' said the President.

'What I have in Diego Garcia, sir, is just over one hundred guys chomping at the bit. But we have no indication that bin Laden is present, sir, and we have only just received confirmation of our Tactical Landing Strip. It will do no harm to give our aircrew more time on their simulators, so that they get to know the terrain, as well as the approach to the TLS.'

'You've done a good job, General Morton.'

'JSOC has, sir. I'm only one of the cogs.'

'Please tell the men my thoughts are with them,' the President said.

'I will, sir.'

'Thank you general.'

The team was a good one to have when there was nothing to do. Some guys found that aspect of the job hard, but fate had thrown together in 6 Troop people who knew how to use spare time. The beach, which ran very close to the air-conditioned barrack block got great use when the sun was out. Parsnips liked to be as black as possible since it saved on cam cream, and was out in the sun as much as he could, reminded by all and sundry that it was a court martial offence to get sunburn. The water was a different thing; there were sharks around and no nets to keep them away, so they used the pool.

If they were going, take off time was between 11.00 and 14.00 hours, and once a certain point had passed with no sign of the air crews getting ready, they knew they were there for the night. Equatorial, the sun went down fast, leaving a mass of stars that Mike Hutton liked to sit outside and study. Astronomy was just one of his subjects for the endless quizzes that Bull Bisset started.

Gaz Mowlem, it turned out was an expert on Oliver Cromwell, so good that he could quote his speeches verbatim. Jake Steel was the music man, who seemed to know every pop record ever composed, right the way back to before he was born. Everybody had a favourite – with Bull it was sport – and once he'd kicked off with some bone question about a distant Five Nations Rugby Grand Slam they were away.

Parsnips was the general knowledge guru. It was well known that he went to pub quizzes back in the UK. Inevitably, after hours of questions getting steadily more obscure, things would either get silly or get heated. That's when Trivial Pursuits became trivial disputes. But it passed the time, and stopped the troop from thinking about what was coming next.

There was fear but it manifested itself in a way that made good sense: it made them sharp. Every member of 6 was happy to be here. They knew that back home, when the other squadrons found out, they'd be as sick as parrots at having to miss out. It was what you wanted when you

191

passed selection into the SAS. The highest priority on your wish-list was one day to be involved in an op like this.

Left to his own devices, with no sign that bin Laden was planning to see him, Aidan McGurk wandered around the old castle which seemed nothing more than one great dormitory. Brick structures had been added on to the old walls in a haphazard way, taking little or no account of the architecture. But, considering what al Kadar had hinted went on here, the place was deserted. Occasionally someone would cross his path giving him an odd look, but he never saw enough inhabitants to justify the number of cell-like rooms that lined the corridors.

He had just stepped into a large lofty-ceilinged chamber when the high-pitched voice rent the air. Coming from the top of the battlements, it was by now a familiar sound, one he'd heard many times since arriving in the country. The call, from a mullah, was to bring the faithful to prayer.

The number of people who emerged from a series of doorways amazed him for a moment, and they arrived in such a rush that he had to press himself against the standstone wall to let them pass. Every one wore a full beard, some were in turbans and black uniforms, others wore the red and white checked keffiyehs. Each carried in his hand the highly decorated mats that they knelt on to pray.

Not wishing to intrude, McGurk slipped through a doorway that led to the outside, staying close to the wall and in the deep shade. The rock on which the castle stood being higher than the flat topped house, he had a view of that too, and could see dozens of the faithful, lined up under the heavy cover of the trees, answering the call to say their midday prayers.

They knelt in serried ranks, facing Mecca, listening to the calls from the battlements and chanting quietly their own submissions to Allah, unaware of the Irishman counting them, first the ones behind him and still inside, then those under the trees close to the house. The numbers, given the sleepy nature of the place, genuinely surprised him. He stopped when he got to 250, adding another fifty to account for the sentries who had joined in the prayers but had not left their posts. Somewhere down there, bin Laden was among them, but in that crowd he was invisible.

Aidan McGurk hadn't been in a church since the requiem mass that had been held for the twins. He was not a religious man. Yet he could not help but admire these men. They could kill as easily as they could pray. There was no need for conscience, since they were obeying the tenets of the faith. How much more advanced would the cause of a united Ireland have been with that kind of conviction!

Prayers over, they filed back whence they'd come, straggling through doorways that McGurk now realised led below, to basement rooms under the castle. There had to be a bunker under the flat-topped house as well, since there was never enough room for the numbers who'd emerged from there either.

'You should have stayed in your cell, Mister McGurk.'

Al Kadar was standing behind him, prayer mat in hand.

'I lost that habit a long time ago, son. If you'd ever been banged up in jail, you'd know why.'

'Please return there now! These things are not for you to see.'

'If that's what you want.'

'It is.'

Al Kadar watched him go, then went through a door and descended some stairs. As soon as he was out of sight McGurk retraced his steps, back to the top of the now silent stairway. The steps were stone, well worn and steep, the smell of damp and the coolness of the air increasing as he descended. And they went down a long way, some thirty feet, lit only by a small lamp that gave out a low glimmer. The Irishman pushed a heavy door and emerged into a circular chamber, well lit with white painted walls. There was a well in the middle, with a low wall and a metal arch holding a pulley and a rope. Doors led off, and, still being open, they revealed rooms that could have fitted into the central chamber like the slices of a cake. Each had what looked like a group of students working at desks. Presumably, out of sight, someone was teaching them.

'I see you are not an obedient man, Mister McGurk.'

'Rebels rarely are,' he replied. His finger moved in a circular fashion. 'What are they?'

193

For a moment, McGurk thought he was going to refuse to reply. But the Muslim obviously realized that there was no point, as the Irishman had seen them.

'What they look like: our classrooms. These were the grain stores when the castle was in use.'

'I hope you don't teach bomb making down here, Mohammed. This deep in rock, if someone gets it wrong they'd mash everyone inside the walls.'

'What we teach down here is our business.'

'I had a good look when we came in to this place. Sentry positions yes, but no ranges, and all of them prayers said indoors or under the trees. It would have to be about satellites, would it not.'

Pride got the better of caution, and al Kadar started to tell McGurk things he really didn't need to know. It wasn't a mistake the Irishman would have made. Rule one for him was tell no one anything that is not directly related to any action you are about to undertake. It's the only way to stay secure.

'Precisely that, Mister McGurk. We do a few things above ground during certain hours of daylight. We take care to try and fool their satellites, even those that fly at night. What our enemies see is a lazy place where not much happens.'

'Anti-aircraft guns?'

'They are hidden, and the sentry positions are immune even to thermal imaging. Even if they wonder at the defences, they never see the activities. Over there they see a faint outline of a house. The satellite communications dishes are well hidden by the trees, as are the faithful when they come out to pray.'

'This is where it's really at, isn't it? That camp I was in at Kandahar is just for show.'

The youngster must have realized he'd opened up too much. Suddenly he looked angry, as much with himself as with the questioner McGurk surmised. 'You are too inquisitive. You ask questions the answers to which are not yours, by right.'

'I don't have to be asking,' said McGurk, tapping his skull. 'I have eyes to see and a brain to think it through. It'll be here you train your fighters, for certain. What will it be now: recruitment techniques, intelligence gathering, target analysis? Making, planting and detonating bombs at some other spot. I've taught them all in my time.'

'We also teach other things.'

'Like?'

'Reading and writing, how to add and subtract.'

He saw the look in McGurk's eye, the one that said: are you having me on?

'The people who come to us are uneducated. Few, if any, have even seen a school, let alone attended one.'

'The Taliban have.'

'We do not recruit from the Taliban. That is something you should learn, Mister McGurk. Mullah Omar and his followers we admire. But they have a country to win, we have a world.'

'It wouldn't be that you don't trust them?'

'We are not like you.'

'And what's that like?'

'So steeped in treachery that you see it everywhere you look.'

'Take a tip from me, son. It's the only way to be if you want to live. Now how long am I going to be here?'

'I told you. I don't know.'

'You don't agree with him, do you, about me?'

'No, Mister McGurk, I do not.'

The Irishman grinned then, because Mohammed al Kadar, by pulling a stiff face, had just told him that bin Laden was going to back him. He felt a surge of excitement, the like of which he hadn't had for a while. He'd fooled the bastard after all!

Gino Manganelli and Blue Harding knew within twenty-four hours that the site they had eyeballed had been selected for the TLS, that they, along with Abdul and his nephews, would be sponsoring the landing. They were also told what to expect in the way of fixed wing, helo and rotor planes. Guidance on sponsoring called for more bodies than they had available, but Gino had brought with him enough sets of the Litton infra-red marker kits. Stood upright, these would do the job normally done by men holding up torches to mark out the runway parameters, pointing them at the aircraft on approach and turning to keep the beam in pilot view as they sped past. Invisible to the naked eye, from the air, with the right goggles, it would look like a proper strip.

Four more IRM kits would be used to mark out the helo landing zone, safe in an indentation off to the south side of the salt lake. Apart from an infra red strobe, these would be the only markers the helo packet would see in an otherwise pitch dark landscape. Anyone without night vision gear would see nothing at all.

There was always a moment when you imagine things going pear-shaped; when you think that because of some bone action of yours the whole operation is compromised. Blue had had that feeling and he was sure that Gino would too. Abdul, who only knew very vaguely what was actually happening wasn't phased. Why should he be when he had Allah to blame?

CHAPTER TWENTY

JSOC had a frustrating half-hour when they went completely blind. Between satellites there was nothing they could do. The in country agent was uncontactable, since his comms equipment was linked up to the digital camera that was no longer sending pictures. It was the old problem with rechargeable batteries: unless they were completely discharged they only took on the amount of power missing, then failed to run for their maximum time.

'He'll be back on stream immediately after dark. That's when he changed his batteries last night. We've asked the listening stations to beef up the electronic sweeps, but they are fully committed to that already.'

'Thank you, Langley,' Lucius Morton replied.

He was calm on the exterior, though suffering from inner turmoil. The fog of war is something a commander prepares for, but can never quite be happy with when it occurs. How much more must his predecessors have suffered from, not having a clear sight of the enemy and in a position where a decision might have to be made. How had people like Pershing, Bradley and Patton felt?

He made a mental note for his next staff college lecture. You might have the best and most sophisticated equipment the world has ever seen, but if it goes down you could be plunged into mental darkness in the world's worst terrain, of the same kind that has faced generals all the way back to Alexander the Great.

Aidan McGurk, sitting on the narrow bed, was thinking he might as well lie down. With the last of the light going and no kind of illumination in his cell, there wasn't really much to do except sit and think about the things that bothered him: like how he'd got here; what he was going to do if the whole idea of getting money out of bin Laden fell flat; not least, how he was going to find and kill the man he was after.

Blue Harding tended to fill a lot of the Irishman's sedentary thoughts. In his Belfast cell and this one, it was little different. The face from that wedding photograph was etched into his mind, made more cruel and murderous than it was in real life. Every conceivable way of capturing and killing him had been researched and played out a thousand times in imaginary scenes of retribution. Some were bloody and bullet-filled as they stalked each other; others took the form of the calm interrogation of a frightened individual strapped to a chair, pleading that he'd only been doing his job.

Whatever fantasy he was replaying, Aidan McGurk was always in control, the man on top of the situation, deadly with a gun, or so superior in wit and intelligence to his captive that the man was forced to act like a trapped rat. Yet underneath all that, repressed for the sake of sanity, was the reality. The bastard had had him over once. If Aidan McGurk wasn't at the very top of his game, he might just do so again.

Very little in the way of noise disturbed these wavering ruminations – the odd footfall, an echoing shout, faint in the distance. He assumed that was how the place functioned: early to bed, early to rise, sleep timed to fit in with the ritual of prayer. So deep was he sunk in his thoughts that when the door opened he nearly jumped out of his skin.

'Our leader wishes to see you,' said Mohammed al Kadar, holding up a fluorescent light.

It was then that McGurk realized he'd been sweating, in fact he could smell himself, his thoughts of death so passionate that they'd made his blood pound round his body. The edge of his hair, all the way round from forehead to neck, was wet. He didn't want to appear before bin Laden like that, or even to let al Kadar see something he would surely report back to his master, so he leapt off the bed and dived for the towel at the top of his grip.

'I'll be right with you. Just wait outside a minute while I change my shirt.'

Al Kadar withdrew as McGurk dragged his towel out, ignoring the bits of paper that flew out to cover the floor, the product of previous musings on targets and arguments to put to bin Laden. He whipped off the damp shirt and threw it aside. A quick, vigorous rub with the towel, aided by the cool stream of air coming through the narrow embrasure made him feel much better. He searched for and found his deodorant spray, applying it liberally to kill the musky smell of his drying sweat. Cool shirt on he felt much better, and after a few deep and calming breaths he opened the door, indicating with smug confidence that al Kadar should lead on.

The interior of the castle was in darkness, but there was the faintests hint of a glow left from the sinking sun as they emerged through the small arched gate. There was also a din, as a line of black four-wheel drive Land Cruisers ground their way up the slope towards the gate. They were exactly the same type of vehicle as the ones McGurk had seen outside bin Laden's airport compound. Blacked out windows prevented him from seeing what was inside, but there was no doubting they were fully loaded, judging by the way the heavy square bodies pushed down on the springs.

Walking down the slope, listening to the increasing shouts as the Land Cruisers disgorged their contents, the Irishman wanted to look back. But al Kadar was beside him, so he kept his eyes firmly fixed forward, not even looking when they turned on to the path to the house. There were two black clad guards outside the door, armed with state of the art weapons. One had the new AN-94 Abakan assault rifle, the other the latest AK-104 small size assault rifle, both butts were folded back in the close quarters battle role and both fighters had the latest MP-443 9mm Grach Makarov pistol protruding from their well designed ops waistcoats. One of them stood back to open the door for al Kadar. Neither man looked at McGurk.

They went through two doors, one being shut before the other was opened. The room they entered was huge, rectangular, brightly lit and expensively furnished in that overblown Arabic way – too much colour and too much gold – which made the artefacts look cheap instead of what they were, very costly. The floor was tiled marble, which reflected the lights that lined the pale walls between several sets of doors. Adjusting his eyes, McGurk looked in vain for bin Laden. The only door to open was the one he had just come through, to admit two young Arabs dressed in black combat suits, both of whom greeted al Kadar warmly.

He talked to them as though McGurk wasn't there, a mistake given his improved grasp of Arabic. The words 'your father' followed by a brief explanation identified them as bin Laden's sons, somewhat taken aback that they'd have to wait to see their parent because he needed to talk with this Irishman. They looked at McGurk with their soft brown eyes, slight smiles on their full lips, never letting on with either what they were eager to say with their mouths; that he was a Mushrikeen, a non-believer and deserved, like the rest of his kind, a painful death.

Al Kadar looked at his watch, then spoke. 'It is time.'

He headed for a set of double doors, followed by McGurk, who heard the television come on, and caught the first words of an English speaking satellite broadcast just as the doors closed behind him. They descended a set of shallow marble-tiled steps, the plain walls softly lit by filigree lamps. Two turns changed that. Passing another door, they carried on down, this time on steep steps hacked out of the rock, that spiralled out of sight. This time McGurk counted as he descended, calculating that sixty-six steps, at some nine inches each, had taken him to a spot some fifty feet below ground level.

The room he was shown into made him think he was taking part in a Bond film, with stone cave-like walls, dark passages leading off at each corner, and dozens of computers on desks in between. A pair of black clad guards sat in one corner, their weapons leaning against the rock wall, their eyes alert, assessing him as a potential threat. That's where the fantasy stopped though: what furniture there was tended towards the functional rather than the exotic; and he was sure, with these fanatical Muslims, there'd be no half-clad women around. Osama bin Laden was at one screen, reading e-mails and occasionally making remarks to other operators that set them typing messages of their own.

He knew a bit about computers, did Aidan McGurk. His studies in the Maze, which the Prod screws had thought were a preparation for a proper career outside, had been more to do with keeping up to speed on the technology. There was strict limit on what you could and could not do inside: no sending e-mails or downloading stuff without strict supervision. But they never seemed to realize that the computer magazines were what McGurk was after. Reading those, he knew what the latest equipment was and how to operate it long before he ever saw freedom.

It was very necessary to keep up with the techniques of surveillance, including the electronic kind, a subject of constant conjecture for men who had spent years avoiding being caught. If anyone was being monitored it was this guy, probably by both the Yanks and the Brits. McGurk could guess how he got round that and got his messages out and in. Landlines were more secure than satellite, so there had to be one run in here. Multiple domain names and codes, plus the avoidance of key words would provide decent security.

With millions of messages filling the airwaves nowadays, the watchers had trouble keeping up. And only one message in a hundred would have anything worthwhile to say, sent to a passive e-mail recipient whose sole job was to re-code it and send it on through a different server, using a different domain name to the one used to receive. It was the same with satellite phones. As long as you avoided certain words, the mainframe computers, of awesome power, were unlikely to pick up a trace.

Again, that smattering of Arabic came in handy; words were exchanged as if he wasn't present or could not understand. There was some kind of alarm on; perhaps not panic, but certainly an air of haste. McGurk could sense it as well as hear the odd hint. It was something he'd experienced himself, when time was never going to be long enough to allow you to extricate yourself from a difficult situation.

Osama bin Laden didn't keep him waiting, even though the list of e-mails on his screen seemed endless. He stood up, taking hold of his stick, calling for another to take his place and issuing an instruction. Aidan McGurk wasn't sure he understood, but it sounded like an order to filter out those that were important from the mass that were less significant.

McGurk bowed his head to acknowledge the Arab greeting then followed bin Laden when the Muslim gestured that he should do so. Immediately the two guards grabbed their AN-94 assault rifles, leapt to their feet and followed. Bin Laden took McGurk down one of the tunnels, turning into an antechamber laid out as a sitting room cum bedroom. Sitting down, he indicated that his visitor should do likewise.

Al Kadar, who'd followed in their footsteps, was given a peremptory order before he got through the doorway, one that judging by the look on his face didn't please him. He in turn snapped at the two guards, who, after a nod from their master, disappeared in his wake.

'Mister McGurk,' Osama bin Laden said slowly as he pulled a printed sheet of paper from the pocket of his flowing white garment. He read part of the document before he carried on. 'You have come to me with a request for help.'

'I have that. I . . .'

Bin Laden held his hand up, the paper between thumb and forefinger to stop the Irishman from continuing.

'Please do not plead your case again. You did that eloquently enough on our last meeting. Instead, tell me what it is you need.'

Bin Laden's gaze returned to that single sheet of paper, while McGurk took his time to reply. It was right that he should think before replying imbuing what he was about to say with the proper gravity. But McGurk's mind wasn't on the offer of help, it was on the reasons why it was being made. That in turn had an impact on what he could request. Something serious was going on. The atmosphere that had existed at the first meeting had changed, and that was only underlined by the staged way bin Laden was reading something he must already have pored over. It was as if bin Laden was in trouble, and a man in that condition was likely to be a damned sight more amenable than one who was secure.

'Money to buy arms and mount a campaign,' he replied, allowing himself a little more time to think. 'Plus access to a training facility.'

'That I already know. I wish you to be more specific.'

'We need handguns, the make less important than a common nine millimetre calibre. When it comes to rifles, AK-47s are more than good enough, and now they're easier to access than Armalites. Rocket propelled grenades will give us the capacity to mount major attacks on well-defended targets. But, most of all, we need explosives, preferably Semtex, and the detonators to set them off. That will allow us to select and destroy prime sites both in Ulster and on the mainland.'

'How many people do you seek to equip?'

That was a tricky one to answer. Right now it wasn't too many, but if things went well it could run into the hundreds. On top of that, you always had to have a multiple of what you would ever use because arms and explosives needed to be smuggled in, and that was dangerous. Those weapons that got through had to be hidden, and it was for certain that some of them would be found. What to ask for? Too much and he'd sound like a fool, too little and there was no point. How much clout did he have here? Was the impression that al Kadar gave him the right one; that bin Laden was eager to use his services? Or was he reading the signs in the wrong way?

Not normally an indecisive man, McGurk was made aware that he'd lingered too long. Bin Laden held up the paper again, his eyes fixed on those of his visitor.

'Before you reply, Mister McGurk, I have here an e-mail sent to me from Ireland.'

'Have you now?'

There was a slight smile on the Muslim leader's lips, indicating that he found his own words amusing. 'Allah, in his wisdom, has seen fit to spread his sons around the globe. Where you observe only a dark-skinned stranger selling you strange and exotic foods, I behold a believer; and, what is more, one who has the means to tell me what he sees and hears.'

'So?' McGurk asked, guardedly.

'So I know more than you think of what you might possibly be able to achieve.'

McGurk's temper got the better of him for a moment, which was silly, given that he would have done the same thing – investigated his supplicant – if the positions had been reversed. In truth, he was more angry with himself than bin Laden.

'So how bloody big were you when you started?'

'Small, I grant you,' bin Laden replied, refusing to respond to the Irishman's outburst, thus rendering it even more absurd. 'But then I had ample funds. If you think I seek to trap you, then you are mistaken. I just wish to ensure that when you ask for my help, you do so in a way that will help convince me that it might be a proper course of action. Neither of our needs would be served if you were to exaggerate or tell me a lie.'

'Before I left, there were five full four-man cells.'

'Twenty in all.'

'But not all trained in the proper use of arms. That increases the requirements.' Bin Laden nodded. 'Then there will be losses: through accident, counter activities by the British . . .'

'And perhaps some of your fellow countrymen?' bin Laden interrupted.

It wasn't a jibe, just an observation, so McGurk ignored it.

'Smuggling arms into Ireland is a high-risk business. Any shipments have to be split up so that, if compromised, everything isn't lost at once. And each time you undertake a contraband operation the risk increases. Best to mount one large transaction than to do it in dribs and drabs but split the arms up and bring them in before the watchers are alert to the danger.'

'In short, you would like to have on your Irish soil the means to equip recruits as and when they return from whatever training base in which they can be accommodated?'

'I do.'

'Where would you seek such supplies?'

'Eastern European countries. Romania or Bulgaria.'

'And how much would you wish to spend?'

McGurk didn't hesitate this time, he practically snapped out the response. 'A quarter of a million dollars, with the same sum to finance operations. As long as we are free to pursue our own goals, we will undertake to do the same for you. In many ways they might coincide.'

Bin Laden nodded slowly, but didn't respond, his eyes still fixed on the Irishman. McGurk held the gaze, knowing he had to act confidently. He couldn't believe that it was the money. Half a million dollars was chicken feed to a man like his host.

'I wonder what you would do if the positions were reversed,' the Muslim said finally.

'That would depend on an awful lot of things.'

'For instance?'

McGurk took a chance then. 'If I was under pressure, that would make a difference.'

That produced another of bin Laden's soft smiles. 'Would you not, perhaps, ask for some sign of good faith? Some indication that the person asking meant what they said.'

'I might.'

'Only might, Mister McGurk? I doubt that to be true. You strike me as a man who would insist.'

'Is that what you're asking for?'

Bin Laden indicated towards the doorway that someone should enter. McGurk looked round to see al Kadar standing in the doorway, a metal box a couple of feet square, in his hands. Responding to his leader's orders, he came forward and put it on the table between them, flicked the catches and opened the lid. That was padded, and so was the inside of the case. Four small silver coloured flasks nestled in the black padding, one of which bin Laden picked up and handed to McGurk. Only when he took hold of it did he realize that it was actually plastic.

'I believe you once studied to be a chemist?'

'A lifetime ago,' McGurk replied, weighing the flask in his hand. It wasn't heavy, but it certainly wasn't empty.

'But you will surely know of what I speak when I say these flasks contain elements of a suffonated organophosphate compound.'

McGurk laid the flask gently back in the niche cut out of the padding. He couldn't be sure what was inside, but no great genius was required to guess, given the past warnings bin Laden had given about the use of nerve agents. Organophosphates formed the basis for any number of things, from harmless fertilizer through to lethal gases like Sarin and VX.

'You wouldn't encourage me to take off the lid and have a sniff?'

'No. Truly that would be unwise.'

'Do all these flasks contain the same?'

'No. They are in pairs.'

'If they were combined?'

'Very effective.'

There wasn't a freedom fighter born who hadn't at some time or other, considered using poisons and nerve gases. Relatively cheap, lightweight and easy to transport, they could cause massively more damage than any bomb. The IRA had thought about it, engaging Aidan

McGurk in the dialogue because of his background. They'd then discarded it just as quickly, not least because the propaganda effect would be disastrous.

'I require these to be delivered to a group of my followers in London.'

Fuck! McGurk thought.

Bin Laden continued. 'If you undertake to do this for me, then I will undertake to finance the needs you have outlined.'

'Tell me what is in the flasks?'

'These are binary nerve gas agents, Mister McGurk, safe as long as the two elements are not combined. I break no secrets when I tell you that they were made for me by a good son of Allah, a former biochemist who worked for the Soviets. He is at present in America, where he has created more of that which he made here.'

'Why didn't he take these?' asked McGurk, pointing at the flasks.

'That is no concern of yours.'

Bin Laden could still only hope that he was speaking the truth about America, since the codes continued to confuse rather than reassure. Perhaps this Irishman was right. Perhaps Luchayadev should have taken his flasks. It was his own notion that it was not safe to do so, US customs being among the most rigorous in the world. He had insisted that if he got through the border, and was unmolested for a few days, he would know it was safe to proceed with manufacture of another set of agents.

'If that combination is achieved by an explosion,' bin Laden continued, suppressing his anxieties, 'I believe the expression is that the mix goes aerosol. Then the effects would be devastating. I would, of course, never countenance such a thing. Too many innocent people would die, and that would not serve my cause. My disputes are with governments not populations.'

'Then what's the point?'

'I merely wish to have these flasks in place, so that I can say to the two governments that any attempt to use force against me will result in retaliation of the kind they will understand. No more cruise missiles.'

'If they don't believe you?'

'Steps will be taken to ensure that they do.'

The Irishman looked at the roof of the anteroom, solid rock that went up for fifty feet. 'You're safe enough here.'

'It would be better to be able to move about more freely. And I know that not even this place would be safe from the kind of response that might follow the use of a compound like VX. It is, in short, mutual deterrence.'

McGurk was in a bind. Could he truly believe bin Laden would never deploy the nerve gas? But that was a secondary consideration. What would happen to him if he refused to be the carrier? A bullet in the back of the head, that's what!

'You could ask any number of people to do this.'

Bin Laden had always known that McGurk would get to the flaw in his request. It was not in his nature to underestimate people, and that applied to this Irishman. He had a brain and a good one. Perhaps he might even deduce the tripartite nature of the deterrence that bin Laden had in mind. The threat of use would scare Mullah Omar just as much as it would terrify Western governments. It ought to. The old Muslim scholar would be sitting under the retaliation. McGurk was just the safest way to get it out.

'I am asking you, as a trade off for those favours and that assistance you seek from me. Deliver these, and I will give you the help you need.'

'This is not a decision that I should make on my own.'

'If you wish to keep it from your compatriots, that is your affair.'

McGurk wore his best poker face as he replied, but in his head he was saying to himself, insistently, 'You've got to get out of here, Aidan. You've got to get out.'

'Half a million dollars?' he said, prevaricating again.

'Will be released to a place of your choosing once I know these flasks have been delivered. Two hundred thousand dollars has already been placed in a bank account in Dublin, to which you will have access. I will undertake to finance the trips necessary to accomplish your mission. You will be given contact procedures to the people in receipt and the means of contacting me after that. I also must tell you, Mister McGurk, that I require a swift decision.'

'OK,' he said suddenly, since there was really no choice. 'When do I leave?'

'Mohammed here will wake you at around four o'clock. There is a gap in the satellite coverage then.'

'You know when the satellites are overhead?'

The pause was natural to a man like bin Laden, who would rarely answer a question without considering the implications. Really, he'd slipped up in mentioning that such knowledge was available.

'We have friends everywhere Mister McGurk. This I have told you. Some of those friends live in countries with advanced technologies, and have access to the equipment necessary for such a task. Rest assured it is a good time to go.'

'So soon!' McGurk, said, determined to be sarcastic.

'You are right,' bin Laden replied, the irony going right over his head. 'It is little enough time to learn how we must communicate.'

CHAPTER TWENTY-ONE

All the trooper's day sacks were packed with emergency rations and ammo, the only state of unreadiness resting with the few people who didn't have their boots on. For the pilots, on ship and shore, it was different. They needed time to carry out pre-flight checks, to talk to and receive from their maintenance crews the assurance that all was A-OK. Once those checks were completed they had to sit in their ships until they were stood down.

The minutes ticked by towards the moment when they'd get a stand-down. But that didn't happen. Instead the comms went haywire as the orders came through to enplane the assault teams. Aircraft engines were fired up, the roar sending the frigate birds screeching into the air. The loading was done slowly and methodically, each unit filing aboard their designated craft, troopers swapping jokes, easing tensions.

It would be the same aboard the *Essex*. The Bald brothers would have had a signal that a go was likely. They would be crawling, with their mechanics and their flight crew, all over Grover, checking every piece of that machine. The carrier-based pilots would soon receive their final briefs from the flight controllers. The Hawkeye and the AWACS would be readied for take off. And in the bowels of the *Aegis* class cruisers, the men responsible for targeting and controlling the cruise missiles would be checking their computers.

On the flight from Diego Garcia to Masirah the troopers worked hard to stay calm, caught in their own private thoughts. In subdued lighting it was easy to talk, but just as easy to get lost in vivid imaginings. Every man knew that, even at this stage, there might still be an abort, and that helped them to avoid the kind of adrenaline rush they would experience when it came to a real go. It was necessary to stay level, too easy to allow the tension to build to the pitch essential for going into action. Anybody stupid enough to subject themselves to that state of hyped up stress would be in shit order by the time they got to the TLS.

Jake made himself think of Blue Harding, the man he'd wanted to emulate ever since he'd found out the veteran trooper was his real father. Blue had been here, in this very situation, perhaps even a worse one, keyed up ready to go into action. What had been his thoughts? Though Jake didn't realize it, pursuing that train of speculation stopped him from worrying about how he himself would perform.

He replayed their last moments together, Jake's pager going off: Blue's phone call taking him away from that football match: Blue squeezing Yan Yan, who was close to tears.

'Jesus Christ, Jake Steel. You're a fucking berk!'

'I hope you're not looking for an argument,' said Parsnips.

Jake couldn't respond, couldn't tell him why he'd said that, because others would hear, people he didn't want to talk to about Blue Harding. He'd grown up never believing in coincidence, and when he put what had happened in Blue's apartment back into his mind's eye, it only made sense if Blue was somehow involved in the same fastball that had got Jake back to Hereford. Grozny was a blind, he knew that. So what was so urgent for a guy who did black ops? Could it be true? Could Blue be involved in this op, out preparing the ground for the regiment?

'God,' he whispered to himself, so quietly that no one could hear. 'Don't let me fuck up. Don't make me let him down.'

The man least concerned about that, contrary to what should have been the case, was Gaz Mowlem. Being the youngest trooper had its advantages. The buzz of being badged only recently was so great that it tended to insulate the new arrival from doubts. He had none of the older guys' cynicism and had not yet realized that the SAS, though the best, was a far from perfect organization. He believed in the regiment with all his being, and having made his fuck ups during the rehearsals was sure that, on the day, everything for him would go right.

Parsnips was hungry. But then he always was on the way into a job. It was the way his nerves operated, acting through his stomach in a way that kept him on edge, not in a nervous way, but in a state of readiness. Those pangs, he knew, would disappear as soon as they got the final go.

Chemo Harris was cursing the song that kept playing in his head, the Colonel Bogey march. It was a tune he hated passionately, because it made him think of Ruperts and what cunts they were. That invariably led him on to the kind of prats who blew smoke up their arses, the guys who did more to harm regimental morale than anybody else. You saw it all the time, the stripes and the gongs going to wankers who were never going to be any good in a real tight scenario. Even worse, to his mind, were fucking woodentop guardsmen.

Chemo was neither a big-head, nor was he overly modest. He thought of himself as adequate or just a bit better. But he was actually a very good soldier, trusted by his mates because he was very cool under pressure, the kind of man who rarely made mistakes. But if anybody else fucked up, fellow trooper or Rupert, he was inclined to give them the good news big style and immediately, which didn't endear him to those classed as his superiors.

Lance Price counted it a blessing that Chemo was in his troop. Lance had been in combat in the Gulf. That was a place where a lot of tosspots had found out the difference between talking a good fight and having one. He'd seen major balls ups by both Ruperts and squadron NCOs. What was gnawing at him now was that he might do the same. He was the troop commander, and even if he had been a patrol commander more times than he cared to remember, it didn't feel the same as this. He didn't want to drop a bollock, to get either killed or wounded, nobody does. But what kept coming up in his mind was worse: that by some bone action of his own he would get the members of his patrol into deep shit.

He wasn't in love with them all; in fact he was sure that the kid, Gaz Mowlem, was a flash young bastard who needed a good kick in the bollocks. Mike Hutton got on his nerves as well by the way he looked every time Lance was giving orders – like he was a fucking idiot and Mike knew better. But it made no odds whether he liked them or loathed them. They were his responsibility and they were all coming home unscathed.

Mike Hutton was thinking about his kitchen, which had taken on the character of a nightmare, the rubble of the battle he was about to be heading towards intermingled with the mess he'd left at home. He forced himself to imagine it finished, gleaming, new and tidy. Then he realized how long that would last. Mike loved his wife, even if she did drive him mad and he knew that she would mess the fucking place up before the paint was dry.

Bull Bisset was the only one on permanent hype, chewing Hershey bars he'd bought in the PX, running constantly over in his mind the subject which the others were trying to force to the back of their minds: the op.

'Rope down,' he was mumbling to himself. 'Break right and cover the arc three o'clock to six, kneel to fire, watch those either side for hand signs. Don't wait for a shout, there'll be too much noise.'

'For fuck's sake Bull,' hissed Jake, sitting next to him, still thinking about Blue – a mindset not helped by Bisset's monologue. 'Calm down.'

'I can't mate. I fucking can't.'

'Think about shagging. That will take your mind off it.'

'How can I think about shagging at a time like this?'

It was Chemo who answered. 'How can you have a time when you don't.'

It worked for about two minutes, then Bull was off again. It was a state of mind the rest wandered in and out of, their concentration on the op increasing as the time passed. The time would come when it would be pushed right to the front of their minds, but that was not now. It was the same when they landed at Masirah, where they were allowed to debus and stretch their legs.

Aboard the USS *Carl Vinson* all eyes were on the faint green outlines on the screen, the result of the thermal imager on the satellite coming in to range of Zu ol Faqar. It took time and some camera adjustment to get a fix on the target. But when they did, Langley confirmed that the Hip was still there.

Within two hours, with the C-130s fully refuelled, the whole Masirah air packet was airborne again, only this time the helos were going up as well. The aircraft headed for the coast of Pakistan, well below the ability of radar to pick them out.

Gino and Blue were on the TACSAT, very aware of the estimated time to wheels down since it was being given to them as a constant update from the Hawkeye. Abdul and his nephews were waiting, ready to run down the line of infra-red lights to turn them on. Gino and Blue were at either side of the line of approach on the infra red strobes that would bring the aircraft in. The C-130 pilots had their terrain guidance systems pre-programmed to put them right onto those lights.

On the aircraft it was horrible. Few things are worse for men going into combat than low-level flying, and the long duration of this flight made it so much worse. There was practically no time at which the planes were in level flight, and at low altitude every air pocket had an effect. So the swooping, dropping and banking needed to follow the course was added to by the sudden gut wrenching falls and lifts of thermals in the night air. Some of the guys would have spewed up anyway, as a release to tension. More did so during the flight due to plain ordinary air-sickness.

They'd flown the pre-planned safe corridor as low as a hundred feet in a tight packet, weaving in and out of river valleys, crossing the most barren parts of Pakistan, staying as far away as possible from habitations of any kind with each plane following precisely the same route. Close to the TLS each adjusted his air speed to open up the tight entry formation so that they would arrive on the strip at the correct intervals. They made a noise certainly, that couldn't be avoided. But they were black ships in a black sky, flying at a ground speed of 300 miles an hour, making their identity and their destination a mystery.

The helos, flying even lower, were on a different route, crossing friendly and hostile airspace at less than a hundred feet. Flying at maximum speed, they likewise were making a lot of noise, though it would take a real genius to figure out on sound recognition the difference between the Hips the Taliban used, and the Black Hawks and Chinooks.

Blue was thinking about Jake again, gnawing at the contradiction in his hopes. One part of his brain didn't want him anywhere near this place which had to be the stopping off location for a forward battle. His mind went back to the briefing papers Bowers had given him, part of which outlined the kind of opposition any assault might face. God forbid it should be the Taliban. That he doubted, but he couldn't help imagining the kind of shit his boy could get into against those bastards.

Bin Laden, a more likely target, wasn't rosy either. The info on him had told Blue of large well manned camps stuffed full of fanatics happy to die for Allah, of flat open landscapes which were intrinsically bad for Special Forces, plains where the enemy could deploy long range weaponry. Yet there was another part of his mind that said, 'Think what you would want.' If he'd still been serving and there was a big operation going down, he would have wanted to be on it. He had no reason to suppose that Jake would be any different. He had to admit he would be disappointed if his boy ducked out.

The sound was faint at first, enough to clear Blue's thoughts and make him concentrate, the whirr of the blades on the lead plane growing steadily as it flew in at a slightly higher altitude to clear the rocky hills that surrounded the TLS.

'Let's get them fired up, Blue,' said Gino, 'they're beginning their approach.'

The tribesmen set off at Blue's signal, running down the line. At the same time he and Gino turned on their infra-red strobes aiming their powerful intermittent beams into the inky sky. At first, in the cockpit of the lead Talon the strobes were the only thing they could see. Then, as Abdul and his nephews switched on each light in turn, to those able to see it, the landing strip was lit up like a real airport.

'JFK, man,' the pilot said as he eased the stick forward to make his descent.

Years of training meant that all the cockpit crew were relaxed. They'd done this dozens of times, and prided themselves on their ability to come down on a TLS and make the kind of landing that would please the captain of a passenger jet. Blue listened as the props on the C-130s changed their pitch, sometimes rising more often falling as the pilot dealt with the vagaries of the wind. The overall noise increased, deafening to someone who had been in near silence for several hours, until right on the landing point, the C-130 came in, directly over his head, the down draught pushing him towards the ground. He heard the wheels screech as they made contact with the salt and listened, heart in mouth to the engine note, his tension easing as the pilot threw the props into reverse to slow the plane. That meant the landing was A-OK, a message he sent immediately over the still connected TACSAT.

Back in Langley they whooped and cheered, as if it was some kind of successful space mission. In the Warfare Control Room aboard *Carl Vinson*, where they had the landing plotted by the Hawkeye, the reaction was more subdued. It was more a case of one move down, ten to go – quite natural to military men who knew that there was still a lot that could go wrong.

The C-130 didn't actually stop. The number one rule was to get into a take off position as fast as possible. You do not take chances on a Tactical Landing Strip. You always assume you are going to be bounced. The Combat Talon swung round 360 degrees and taxied as quickly as it could to the head of the runway. Then it spun again so that it was facing into the wind ready to hit the throttle and lift off.

The tailgate dropped and the A squadron Delta Force deplaned at speed, rushing to take up their defensive positions. Only when they were in place, and had come in on all callsigns to say that the area was secure, would the pilot shut his engines.

Talon Two, with the SAS on board, was beginning its approach, timed to coincide with the message that the TLS was secure. Gino and Blue were on their strobes again. Both were subjected to the increasing scream of prop engines, to the sound of the plane yawing around in the wind. Aboard the Hawkeye they received from callsign Red One that all Delta callsigns had reported the all clear. This was time to give Talon Two the chance to abort on approach. No abort was signalled and the C-130 screamed in to land, the crunch of wheels on the salt just as evident.

Talon Two, after reversing props to brake, reached the end of the TLS, the point where Abdul and his nephews were standing. There was no swing round this time. With the touchdown end secured, Talon Two deplaned B Squadron at this end of the field, the SAS fanning out to take up a defensive position, weapons up and covering the arcs. Only when they were clear did the C-130 begin to taxi to its take-off point swinging round to take up position in front of its brother ship.

The Combat Shadow was making its approach. Before it landed, Abdul set out the infra-red lights at the right edge of the strip to show it the point to which it should taxi, adjacent to the site of the helo landing zone. That put it off the runway at the point where the helo packet could hot refuel and out of the way of the last planes in, the two Spectre gunships and callsign Angel One, the Medivac Osprey Tiltrotor.

Their landing was as smooth as the planes that had come before, and they taxied to their take off positions in front of the Combat Talons. To the guys on stag occupying the perimeter defences, the silence when they killed their engines was welcome. The night was suddenly quiet and the air chill. Vision adjusted to the darkness, over a hundred pairs of eyes gazed out from the TLS.

There was nobody out there, certainly not the kind of force that could interdict such an operation. The nearest large military base was at Kandahar itself, enough Taliban with armour and artillery to take them on. But that wasn't a worry. Even alerted to the possibility of a hostile force they'd never move towards a threat they hadn't assessed. That would take a day on its own, by which time the whole op would be over. But it was a good way to keep the guys occupied.

The distinctive rhythmic thud of helo rotor blades, faint at first, grew to a deafening roar. The whole packet came in over the landing zone together, dropping down to the ground in staggered formation close to the Combat Shadow. The crew members were on the ground before the wheels, rushing to carry out the procedure for hot refuelling. Only when they were gassed up did the order come through for the troopers to enplane.

This too had been rehearsed, so that each callsign knew exactly where to go. They snaked through the airframes, under slowly revolving blades, and filed into the cabins in the reverse order to that they would use to fast rope out. No longer vulnerable, with their full loads aboard, the helos killed the engines.

'All callsigns this is Blue One. Radio check,' said Johnny Lancing. He was in his command Black Hawk, Bluebird One, sitting behind the two signallers with access to both comms nets. One was listening to Red One calling in the Delta callsigns, while the other had his set rigged for the SAS comms. Lancing had the option of listening to either. One side of his headset was tuned to his own net, the other to Delta's, with his signallers primed to keep him informed of anything important on whichever net he wasn't using. Once the comms were checked, the patrol commanders' minicams were switched on. On the screen above his head, the SAS ground commander could look at the ghostly green faces of the troops he was to take into battle. Those images, along with the sounds of the checks, was being beamed all the way back to the Warfare Control Room on the USS *Carl Vinson*.

Lucius Morton had a direct line to the White House, to the man who would personally have to give the go order, and there was a comms link to Whitehall so that the Prime Minister could listen in. There was no idle chatter on any net now. Everyone, apart from the air commanders quietly communicating with the fighter cover, was silent, waiting for the decision. The voice that broke the hush, a few minutes before the appointed Tomahawk launch time, was calm and even.

'Well, General?'

Morton was aware of telling the President what he already knew. But it was the right way to report.

'Bin Laden came in on the Hip at thirteen hundred hours and it is in place, sir. NSA will have told you that the signal traffic is heavy, and nothing has come in from the CIA agent to indicate bin Laden's departure either by air or surface vehicle. All our ground forces are in position at the TLS with no indication of any problems. Our monitoring of the radio traffic around Kandahar shows that it is a touch livelier than normal, but that is taken into account in the battle plan. We know we can't make that much noise on entry without someone alerting their military command. The Close Air Protection is in place, flying below the radar window outside hostile airspace so that is not a threat.'

'Weather?'

'Slight mist on target at ground level, clear skies overhead. In short, conditions as good as they're going to get. First light is at zero six o seven, sir.'

Lucius Morton would never know if the President paused for effect, or because he thought the decision he had to take so portentous as to

217

require further consideration. Whatever it ratcheted up the tension in the Warfare Control Room.

'Commence Operation Joint Strike, General, and may God go with you.'

The fax machine whirred at the same time, spitting out the written orders to proceed: a numbered set of command signals to all units deployed, air, naval and ground troops, signed by the President.

'Admiral,' said Morton.

Teitmayer nodded to his chief of staff, who immediately relayed his orders into the microphone on his headset. On the glass board in front of him every element employed was plotted, the position of each ship and aircraft tracked by computer, even the USS *Essex*, now steaming at flank speed away from the Pakistan coast.

'Two minutes to launch,' Teitmayer's chief of staff intoned.

Fumbling around in the dark, Aidan McGurk had cleaned up his bits of paper, shoving them into his sweaty shirt and throwing that on top of his bag to cover the money and papers which al Kadar had given him. He now had ten thousand crisp dollars and a brand new portable computer. He'd spent two hours on that, discovering the software was brilliant, set to scan for key words and erase them before automatically encoding whatever text he wrote next. He had a list of e-mail addresses all over the world, each one innocent enough to withstand scrutiny, plus a contact in Switzerland who would, on instructions from bin Laden, release agreed sums of money when he'd completed his side of the bargain. He'd succeeded, but he was far from happy.

With only an hour to go before he left, McGurk lay down and tried to think, his mind in a whirl. Why was this Muslim bastard asking him to help?

'There's a bit of trouble with the old Taliban,' he whispered to himself, closing his eyes. 'That's for certain.'

The next thing he knew, Mohamed al Kadar was shaking him awake. He grabbed his grip and followed the Muslim outside to the waiting Hi-Line.

The sweep of the dimmed headlights made Ahmal look up from his labours. The new batteries were in place and he was about to switch the digital camera on again. He decided the lights were unimportant. What was important was that the helicopter was still there, the helipad covered in a thin mist, the light from the stars enough to show the faint outline of the rotor blades.

The noise of the vehicle faded as it crested the rise and took the road to Kandahar. Now nothing stirred. The landscape was utterly silent.

CHAPTER TWENTY-TWO

General Aaron Bronowski had a very fair hand, and the pot in the middle of the table was rising to a goodly sum. The air was thick with cigar smoke and the odour of whiskey. He'd been alerted by a signal to stand by at 0600 hours. Rather than stay in his room and make a phone call, he'd invited the people that mattered to the embassy for dinner and kept them there for a game of cards. And did they ever love to play? Happy to stay all night as long as there was a chance to take American money. He had round the green baize table the Pakistani Foreign Minister, the Chief of the Air Staff and the commanding general of the Air Defence System.

Seven hundred miles away from Bronowski's flush the two *Aegis* class cruisers had swung on to their firing course. Deep in the bowels of each ship the programmers looked at the plotted course they'd fed into the Tomahawk guidance systems. The Fire Control Officer stood silently, his finger over an array of red buttons, listening into his headset for the order. As that came, he spoke and pressed down.

'Fire number one.'

No one was allowed on the after deck during firing, and as usual at such a time the ship was closed up for action stations. Those on the bridge heard a rumble as the missile engines ignited, imagined they saw the two dark noses rise out of their tubes to reach for the sky. Twin fire trails, as the missiles lifted away from the ship, were very real – slow uneven looking flares of yellowy-white that seemed to wobble slightly until the thrust increased enough to take the rockets clear. Over the water, a mile away, they could see the TLAMs leaving their sister ship.

The programmers watched their screens intently: checking on thrust and the trajectory, confirming to the Fire Control Officer that the short wings had deployed successfully, so that the missiles could sustain flight and establishing that the gyroscopes were fully operational and that all computer links aboard the Tomahawks were functioning. As soon as the first salvo reached the top of their firing trajectory and began to dip towards their cruising height just above sea level, the Fire Control Officer launched the next pair.

That was repeated a further four times, so that on completion of their task twenty Tomahawks were on their way to Zu ol Faqar, skimming across the Indian Ocean, speeds adjusted so that they would impact within seconds of each other. The estimated time of arrival over Pakistani airspace was calculated and added to the pre-prepared signal for Aaron Bronowski which was immediately sent off to the US Embassy in Karachi.

'There's an increase of signal traffic at Kandahar,' said the voice from the NSA listening post.

'What do you read?' asked Lucius Morton.

The NSA had Pushtu speakers and knew all the Afghan callsigns and codes. They had hacked into the air control system so comprehensively they could read the flight plans and orders of aircraft that hadn't even left the ground.

'They are about to launch an air reconnaissance: two MIGs to fly a low radar and visual towards the Pakistani border, then sweep north and return on a heading from the Iranian border to base. We're putting up a probable scenario on your plotting table now.'

It came up as a red route, a line from the military airfield at Kandahar running south-west to a point which, when they reached it, would have been long passed by the cruise missiles. The sweep to the north, speculative at this stage, showed their potential route was well away from either the target or the exfil route.

'Any notification of rules of engagement?'

'None, which will mean pilot discretion.'

That was commonplace in a war zone. The Taliban air assets, like the Russian aircraft before them, fought a low-level war in the valleys of Afghanistan, much of the time relying on visual contact rather than signals intelligence or radar to identify their targets. That meant they had a wide degree of latitude when it came to engaging an enemy.

'Where does that put them at H-hour?'

The best estimate came up as a cross on the red route. 'Nowhere near the target, sir. Although their position will depend on their speed and actual course.'

That would be tracked by the Hawkeye, their relative position shown on the plotting table as a deviation from their proposed flight plan. The planners had always known this was possible. Lucius Morton had the command decision to make, because you can't plan for everything and just programme a computer to issue orders. There were variables and this was one of them – what looked like a routine air patrol that had nothing to do with air packet incursions. And, since they represented no threat to the security of the operation he was happy to ignore them. What he did once the Tomahawks impacted would depend on their reaction.

The voice came over the net to every man in B Squadron, listening on his own earpiece. 'Hello all callsigns, this is Blue One. The mission is go, go, go. I repeat the mission is go.'

Every swear word in the lexicon passed someone's lips at that point. Few, Delta or SAS, were still and silent. Fists were bunched, stomach muscles tensed as each man worked on his own method of self-motivation. If the fear was less about fighting than making a fuck up, it didn't matter. It was a positive emotion not a negative one, sharpening every sense and activating every nerve that would be needed in the coming contact. The helos and fixed wings fired up their engines, filling the TLS with a sudden cacophony of sound that helped to release some of the internal tensions. Moving is so much easier than sitting still.

On the USS *Carl Vinson* the computers were doing their job, running through the battle plan stage by stage, showing on the plotting screen every facet of Operation Joint Strike, alerting the commanders to the time to initiate each stage. In the end though, it wasn't technology that controlled the battle, it was men – in this case those aboard the two command helos at the Tactical Landing Site.

The voice of Lucius Morton came through giving them the order to begin the approach: 'Red One and Blue One. Proceed with approach to target.'

'Affirmative. Let's go kick ass,' from Stan the Man Fuller was quickly succeeded by the crisp, 'Blue One. Roger, commencing approach to target,' from Johnny Lancing. That was followed by the voice of the air controller giving his 'go' order to the Night Stalkers.

The Tomahawks were now well into Pakistani airspace, programmed with a flight plan that would bring them in on the target bearing from the south, using a route that would keep them well away from the air assault packet. Flying at one hundred feet they'd crossed the coast at H-hour minus one-hr 55 minutes. The helos, with the lowest flight speed, would depart the TLS first. Once airborne, the Hawkeye would calculate their locations and actual flying speeds so that the much faster Spectre gunships would arrive on target and be in position to commence their attack at H-hour plus two minutes.

6 Troop's ship, Grover, was airborne and flying itself. The avionics read the ground below and up ahead, and kept the ship in the right place in the formation by reading the distances to the other helos. Tucked in behind the lead helo, the Bald Brothers could look out through their NVGs and see the valley they were flying through. The river would have been visible anyway, picking up the light from the sliver of moon, but to the naked eye the hills were non-existent. There was no way through this valley in such a moon-state without the use of the most sophisticated navigational aids.

The technology allowed the Bald Brothers to act as if they were relaxed. The truth was very different. Each was keyed up in his own way, a combination of exhilaration and fear that led to a lot of surreptitious touching of the controls. It was all done easy, no haste, but it would have been much better if they could have talked to relieve the tension. Instead, they were locked into the head up displays. They might have been back in the simulator, except for the involuntary tensing of various muscles.

In the back, the dispatcher, Winston, constantly touched the headset through which he communicated with the pilots as though he was convinced it was going to malfunction. Alternatively he fiddled with the coils of rope, as if they would tangle themselves as soon as he took his eyes off them, like every other member of the crew concentrating on his part of the task to keep the ship functioning at peak.

The troopers, sitting with weapons between their knees, were now hyped up to the eyeballs, the sound of spat curses and statements, 'Fuck! Shit! We're going to do it, man, do it!' vying with the noise of the rotors. Their concentration was total, all other thoughts pushed right out of their minds as the helo packet approached the end of the Zu ol Faqar Lake. There were no more quizzes, no more maddening tunes. Every trooper had in his mind the same mantra as Bull Bisset had mouthed on the way to the TLS, only adjusted to his own role. Mind on, breath easy, think it through, remember what you rehearsed.

'You're going to fucking do it! You're going to do it right!'

The Spectre gunships had taxied to the far end of the TLS, the pilots keyed up with impatience for the signal from the air controller in the Hawkeye. Up there, way out of radar range, they were tracking the Tomahawks as they snaked across the terrain at a ground speed of 550 miles per hour, never more than a hundred feet off the surface, using valleys to stay low as they sashayed through the mountains. They would be seen by those rising for early morning prayers, probably by the afterglow from their engines. But they came and went at a rate that invited disbelief, or even fear in superstitious minds.

The signal pinged up on the Spectre's display. The release of tension as the pilot opened his throttle to increase engine power was felt throughout the ship, every member of the fourteen-man crew just glad the waiting was over. Blue, standing close to the lowered tailgate that led up into the interior of one of the Combat Talons felt rather than saw the way the Spectre strained against its brakes. As they were released the engine noise increased to a scream. The ambient light was strong enough for him to feel again that impression, as the aircraft took off, of a duck turning into a swan. They always seemed so lumbering for the first ten seconds, then, as they gathered speed the front wheel lifted and the nose sought the sky, so elegant.

'Fuck me, Blue,' he said to himself. 'You're turning into a poet.'

The second Spectre took off almost in the wake of the first. It was not an easy task to lift off without being able to give maximum boost to the engines and adopt a high climbing rate. The Spectres had a very low ceiling under which they had to operate in order to avoid radar recognition. The slight gradient of the TLS and the steady wind during take-off helped, but it was not a manoeuvre even the most experienced commercial flyer would try. That was what made the pilots of the Special Operations Wing so unique.

Gino and Blue had already said their goodbyes to Abdul and his nephews, an occasion of many ritual blessings from the tribesmen tempered with a careful examination of all the equipment the two Western agents removed. Everything left behind would be for sale, and that included the Litton infra-red marker kits and the unused batteries. Abdul's eyes had a sad air as he watched the rest of the technology disappear. The TACSAT, the Plugger, the digital camera, the Iridium satellite phone and the notebook computer – in fact he looked as pissed off as a man burying his children.

'Let's go Blue,' said Gino, from the top of the tailgate.

'I didn't say this to you before, Gino, but I've got a son serving in Special Forces.'

'No kidding,' Gino replied warily.

'And I think he might be on this op.'

'Do you ever pray, old buddy?'

'Haven't done for years.'

'This might be a good time to revive the practice.'

The request to the God he wasn't sure he believed in to look out for Jake, was silent.

'Now let's go,' urged Gino.

It was time to get aboard. The Combat Talons needed to get into position for lift off, which would happen as soon as the Tomahawks impacted. They could then take off normally, climbing steeply and safely to their cruising height, the need for secrecy gone.

Bronowski's aide entered in that discreet way so common to his breed that it had to be part of his course at West Point. Having collected the last pot, Aaron Bronowski was shuffling to deal as the aide bent to

225

whisper in his ear and the signal was passed to him. It was lengthy, telling him the nature of the action without going into compromising details. In essence it informed him that the TLAMs would be entering Pakistani airspace, and that would be followed by the complete air packet exfilling through the same air corridor over the following two hours.

Casually, Bronowski dealt another hand. He kept playing, an occasional eye on his watch which he had taken off and laid by the folded signal. The game flowed back and forth, both in money and polite conversation, until the hands on the timepiece were near to being totally perpendicular. It was his deal again, just before he was about to deliver the message, so a pause was in order. He shuffled slowly until another minute had passed.

'Gentlemen,' he said, placing the pack of cards carefully on the table. 'I have here a signal from Washington. It informs me that a joint strike force from the United States and Great Britain is about to mount a police action within the confines of the state of Afghanistan. In order to facilitate this, it will be necessary for the following elements to pass through your airspace.'

Bronowski read out the list of air assets slowly, with their entry and exfill routes looking up to see what reaction this was causing in his guests. The civilian minister was visibly agitated, but the soldiers reacted with studied calm, no doubt calculating from what the Vice-chief was saying where such a force was headed, and trying to discern the target.

'Had it been possible to request permission for this incursion the US and UK governments would certainly have done so. But the security of the police action was, and is, paramount. We hope that you will oblige us with a free passage as befits a nation friendly to our governments.'

Bronowski paused to let his visitors take a deep breath. Ever since the nuclear tests relations had been very strained. He wanted them to have air in their lungs because the next bit was even less pleasant.

'Naturally we have put up a Close Air Protection flight of F14s and F18s. Our need to jam radars inside the target area will overspill on to your Air Defence System, causing severe disruption to that facility. My government assures you that our own systems will ensure that no outside agency will be able to take advantage of this.'

Translated, that meant India.

'It is also necessary for me to advise you that our CAP has instructions to engage any force, air or ground, that shows the least intention of interfering with our air packet. In order that there should be no misunderstanding, I am obliged to request that you keep your airforce on the ground for the duration of this police action, and that all your air defence missile batteries remain inactive.'

'This is outrageous,' the Foreign Minister protested.

That earned him a look of total contempt from the soldiers, men who prided themselves on demonstrating a stoical response to any emergency. And it was beneath their carefully cultivated dignity to react to the implied threat to blast out of the sky any aircraft they launched, let alone to destroy any air missile site that even locked on to investigate the incursion.

The Chief of the Air Staff stood up and went over to the telephone, picking it up and requesting that the switchboard put him through to the Prime Minister's residence. There was a sharp exchange with someone, no doubt a command to wake his boss, then a more measured explanation, interrupted several times, with angry undertones. The American general waited until that call was complete.

'My Prime Minister,' the Chief of the Air Staff barked, 'has ordered me to protest in the most forceful way at this unfriendly act.'

'My government regrets the necessity,' Aaron Bronowski replied. Then he paused for five seconds, counting them off in his head. 'I am also ordered to inform you that after long and hard deliberations, the President has agreed to sign the executive order necessary to release to the Pakistan armed forces the Orion AWACs you ordered. This will come as a package to include training both in the United States and here in Pakistan.'

That meant the Pakistani generals could mount, from the air, a continuous electronic watch on their more powerful Indian neighbour, especially the nuclear test and launch facilities in Rajistan. The air defence commander looked at his boss, who nodded. He then signalled to his own aide, who'd been dozing by the door, and whispered in his ear. Aaron Bronowski didn't have to hear the words since he knew their content. The man was standing down his entire capacity to engage an enemy, ensuring that no overzealous officer sent up anything, manned or unmanned, to engage an American plane. Just as well, since it would, given the advanced US weaponry, result in their utter destruction.

'I think you should complete your deal, General Bronowski, don't you?'

The Chief of Staff spoke with all the urbanity and *sang-froid* that he could muster, easing himself back into his chair and following his words with a slow and lengthy draw on the cigarette jammed into the long ivory holder he used to smoke.

Bronowski couldn't stop himself from grinning as he replied, 'I'm sorry, General. I thought I already had.'

CHAPTER TWENTY-THREE

It was hard to imagine that outside the air packet, away from the noise the aircraft were making, all was silence. This was a land without clocks, where the rising and setting of the sun had more to do with the cycle of life than arbitrary commitments to time. The odd pre-dawn lamp shone in the sprawling village of Zu ol Faqar, single pinpricks of light that were surrounded by halos of low, thin mist. But that changed as the helos dropped their air speed to hover at the end of the lake, the noise they made enough to wake the whole community. But they could not be heard on the target, the assault group standing off at a predetermined distance out of auditory range.

Watching the white glowing exhaust trails of the first Tomahawks as they came round from the eastern end of the lake was a strange experience, even for the well-trained pilots of the Night Stalkers. Turning slowly and elegantly in the first hint of grey morning light, the missiles climbed preparatory to slamming into the target. The computers had been set to allow the whole cruise barrage to close up, so two quickly became four, then six, and by the time it was eight the first missiles had impacted right on H-hour, their target the flat topped residence.

The flash of the first explosion, followed by the faint rocking caused by the blast, was simultaneous with the order from the command helo to gain altitude. The whole flight of a dozen Black Hawks and two Chinooks lifted at once, rising to a height that put both the castle and the single storey residence and comms centre beneath them.

That would have been true if they had still been there. But by the time – what seemed like a matter of seconds – the helos had lifted, their target, in terms of recognizable buildings, had disappeared. The effect of blast, as Tomahawk after Tomahawk homed in, was now almost continuous, and more noticeable at height, as the flight split into its two component forces, hovering some 600 metres apart, black noses, rocket pods and air armament aimed at the exploding mountainside.

The castle walls, the gatehouse and the turrets seemed to disappear, the dry sandstone suffering devastating damage from the almost constant blast. The trees that had provided cover for bin Laden's satellite dishes were shredded like so many matchsticks, one reception disc ballooning up into the air like some giant Frisbee, then landing to roll down the slope towards the lake. The Hip Helo was a wreck, on its side and on fire, the concrete of the helipad cracked and broken up.

If the first Tomahawk had hit where it was supposed to, the flat topped residence, it might have removed the thinking head of bin Laden's organization. But a miss of only one hundred metres was enough to nullify its tactical impact and to alarm the garrison. Everyone in the place was awake waiting to say their morning prayers, there was in place a well-rehearsed drill regarding what to do if attacked by cruise missiles. It wasn't difficult, it was to get below ground to safety.

With only a ten-second gap between impacts there was little time, and the second land attack missile took out the south-western triple A battery, the weapons ammo adding to the fireworks. Number three hit one of the castle turrets and reduced it to dust, but by that time those inside were rushing down the staircase, just as they were doing at bin Laden's house. He, naturally, was the first one through the door, hobbling along aided by his sons, his slow pace responsible for several deaths; though they went unnoticed among the hundred or so casualties that fell to Tomahawk five. Number four, aimed at 6 Troop's target, the north-western triple A had also missed in terms of pinpoint accuracy, exploding on impact with the rock face fifty metres to the left rather than right on target.

To those that made it below, the earth seemed to offer little protection. The ground shook as if there was an earthquake. Above their heads those caught out and confused by the blasts who had lost any hope of finding a way to safety were dying. But even as it shook, the rock of the mountain held, and provided security for the hundred or so who had managed to get below.

One of the first things to do was to get a signal off to Kandahar, informing them of the attack.

Aboard the USS *Carl Vinson* the air controllers had acknowledged the lift off of the Combat Talons and the Shadow from the TLS. Now, through the Air Controller, they were directing the F18s and F14s to climb to their CAP height, handing them over to the EC-2 Hawkeye for command and control. The EA-6 Prowlers flying with the Hawkeye were alongside to provide the electronic counter measures necessary to ensure that the CAP was safe from surface to air missiles.

The message to the Taliban air command at Kandahar was sent by fax, telex and in plain voice – Pushtu, Arabic and English. It was essentially the same as had been delivered by Aaron Bronowski in Karachi.

This is a police action directed at a specific target. It will not cause any collateral damage either to your citizens or their property. You are advised, we repeat advised, not to interfere.

This is not an unfriendly act towards the Taliban Government of Afghanistan.

We have a substantial air presence in the area and any counter measures will be treated as hostile and dealt with accordingly. Our aircraft will interdict and destroy any air or ground asset that in any way threatens the security of our police action.

This message will be repeated at five-minute intervals until all our forces have exited your airspace.

'Try and open a direct line of communication,' said Lucius Morton. 'We've got to make sure they keep those two MIGs out of the way. And arrange to have someone on the line who can talk to them in their own damned lingo.'

At the lake the light was now strong enough to see the Spectre gunships swooping in, their bulbous, seemingly unwieldy shapes suddenly taking on the characteristics of Chinese firecrackers as the weapons that protruded from their fuselages simultaneously opened up. The firing was patterned to make sure that nothing could live; two 20mm Vulcan cannons discharged 3000 rounds in minutes, each shell landing less than a foot from that which preceded it. Backing the Vulcans up for a heavier punch came the 40mm Bofors cannon and a 105mm howitzer. These were reserved for the hard assets: used to pound buildings, sandbagged positions and the triple A sites.

Ahmal had come out of his home at the sound of the first explosion, rushing to a vantage point that gave him a distant view of the collapsing castle. Not that he could see much now, just a great billow of dust with two huge planes swooping slowly over the area, impervious to the mushroom cloud they were skimming through, blasting the ground apart. He was above the helo packet, which looked from where he was standing like a flight of angry insects.

Aboard Grover, Winston had given the hand signal for two minutes, alerting the Bald Brothers and the men of 6 troop. They knelt in two lines, facing the cargo doors of the aircraft, going through their final equipment checks making sure the slings on the Carbines were secure, that nothing on their belt kit could snag. They were still spitting the curses to themselves that would keep their adrenaline pumping, punching one free hand into the other, the impact taken by the thick working gloves.

The Spectre pilots had two options for clearing the call that would alert the Special Forces, telling them it was time to come in: thermal imagery which showed them all ground activity, if there had been any, had ceased to register any threat. That was backed by the pilots' and air-gunners' visual appreciation, which could locate no movement. Each gunship was on one net, dedicated to either Delta or the SAS. The Bald Brothers, hovering in the SAS pattern, heard the transmission sent to Johnny Lancing quickly followed by his own order to deploy, sent to the flight commanders.

'Blue One to Blue Flight. Commence approach, I repeat commence approach.'

The sudden forward thrust as the helos dipped their noses and put on speed rocked every man on board, forcing them to use their elbows and a good handhold to keep in position. Winston was on an intercom link to the pilot and was using visual signals to inform the eight-man 'chalk' kneeling in two four man teams, facing the open cargo doors ready to go of what the pilots were saying. In the cockpit Biryani and Dirty Dick Dandeneau watched as the two Black Hawk gunships, well ahead of the pack, blasted the ground in front of them – first with rocket fire, then with their 30mm cannon – designed to keep any curious heads that were still attached to bodies well down. The Bald Brothers were waiting for the moment when the gunships would peel away to make it possible for the troop carriers to initiate the final approach to target. Brian saw them begin to fade right and left, and eased his stick forward to increase speed.

With continuously increasing light the Bald Brothers could faintly make out the rock that overhung their primary target, the triple A position. Behind them, other troops were already fast roping out of the Chinook and the Black Hawks on to the shattered remains of the old castle. Brian and Dirty Dick were unaware that they were actually whooping with excitement, but that died in their throats as they saw the trail of smoke emerge from the ground, telling them that they had incoming ordnance heading right for the nose of their helo.

Brian Bewley threw Grover sharply to the left, an action that would have sent the Fast Rope Master out into thin air if he hadn't been wearing his safety harness.

'RPG, for fuck's sake.'

The rocket-propelled grenade was past their eyes before Bewley got the expletive out, leaving a light trail of smoke. Both pilots had a hard time holding on to their shit until they heard the grenade explode well to their rear. But Dandeneau had kept his cool. He'd given the go, telling Winston to get the guys out. They'd been lucky the missile had not hit the helo. A second time they might not be so lucky, and if the ship went down very likely everyone aboard would go with it.

Winston heard the order to go on his headset and signalled to the two four man sticks in the chalk to kick the ropes out through the cargo doors. Looking out Winston saw that the RPG had, in fact hit another Black Hawk. It was pulling away, having successfully dropped 8 Troop on its target, but the effect of the missile slamming into the rotor gear on the main blade was enough to make control impossible. As he leant out to check the ropes were touching the ground, the first man was up and ready to go on his signal. From that signal to the entire eight-man chalk exfilling was a matter of seconds.

Too busy seeing his charges out the door Winston didn't see the crippled helo begin to lose altitude, though he could hear the screaming of the changed engine note. It skewed to one side with its nose in the air, the pilot fighting to get back on an even plane, using what power he could muster to slow the inexorable descent. One rotor end hit a rock and the struggle was over. Bits of blade began to detach from the helo and the airframe crunched into the rocky ground.

That was happening behind 6 Troop, who had hit the deck and deployed in their rehearsed pattern. The problem was they were fifty metres from the target, not on top of it but below it; and they saw the first flashes of small arms fire begin to emerge from a triple A site that was supposed to be totally destroyed.

Lance Price shouted 'How the fuck?' But that didn't stop him from reacting.

'Blue One, Blue One. This is Blue Two. Triple A site not destroyed, repeat not destroyed. We are in a firefight.'

It is an SAS maxim always to attack, laying down so much shit that the enemy will wonder what's hit them. The first thing to go in were the pre-loaded 40mm grenades, spewing out of their underslung launchers to mullah the target. Even as he was firing Lance Price was up, moving and screaming, with Mike Hutton to his left, Jake Steel and Chemo to his right, while the other four laid down covering fire – short aimed and controlled bursts. The rate of fire determined the length of the run. The front four dropped to one knee and opened up as Gaz Mowlem, Tony Parsons, Bull Bisset and Whacker Simpson stormed forward.

'Coming through, coming through.' Four screams, four charging figures, two fellow troopers emptying their weapons in the same short bursts while the other pair reloaded their grenade launchers, the firing of which coincided with the front runners going to ground. The HEs exploded under the overhang, every trooper taking cover until the blast was past. Then they were up and moving again, four and four, pepper-potting towards the battery position, employing classic fire and manoeuvre, each bound repeated twice against a steadily diminishing and finally non-existent response.

In the command ship, Johnny Lancing had listened to that exchange along with all the other actions taking place. It was clear from his own net, and from the Delta comms, that resistance was greater than anticipated. He could see in the increasing light that the Tomahawks had done their job, and so had the Spectres. The castle was just a shell mixed with piles of rubble; and the Delta net told him the flat topped building had been razed to the ground. But there was still a battle going on in both places.

The minicams worn by the patrol commanders jerked around end-lessly. But they stopped enough to show Lancing just how much of a battle B Squadron had on its hands, as the main body of his troopers fought their way into the rubble of the castle. The same images were being beamed via the Hawkeye to the USS *Carl Vinson* where they induced a sobering silence among the force commanders. That silence was explained by the certain knowledge that there was nothing they could do. The battle was in the hands of the men in the field, control vested in the ground commanders, not them.

But everyone shared the same thought: the air bombardment had been designed to kill practically every living thing before the troopers even hit the ground. Delta and SAS had been tasked for what should have been no more than a mopping up operation, taking out any dazed and disorientated remnants of bin Laden's men. That was not the job now.

'Blue One. This is Blue Three.' The voice came from inside the ruins of the castle. 'We have a lot of tangled metal as well as rubble.'

There was enough left to identify them as four wheel drives, and the odd radiator badge indicated that they were the remains of several Toyota Land Cruisers. Getting past them under fire was proving to be a real bastard. The opposition, if it had been dazed, wasn't now; they were laying down defensive fire in a very professional way from positions that indicated the underground areas had protected them from annihilation.

The lines back to the US, to Langley and the NSA, were suddenly full of conversation, until the 'good news' came through from Lucius

Morton to the ground commanders. They in turn passed it on to their callsigns.

'Hello, all callsigns. This is Blue One. Be advised that enemy resistance may be greater than expected. Blue Three has identified the transport elements of Raghead One's bodyguards.'

That made the two signallers sitting next to Johnny Lancing look round. Theirs was one of only two helos still above the battle, the rest having withdrawn to a holding area out of the hot contact zone. If incoming was going anywhere, it was going right up their arse.

'Fucking charming,' said Lance Price.

He, Jake, Mike Hutton and Chemo had reached the lip under the overhang, while the other four stood off with their weapons up and ready to mullah the target, which was that area a foot above the damaged sandbags that had formed the parapet where a head might appear. Chemo and Jake rolled on to their backs, then on to one elbow in preparation for throwing grenades. Jake went first, pulling the pin and half-rising and rolling to get maximum force into his throw. Chemo did likewise one second later, then everybody hunkered down for the blast.

Every man in 6 Troop had thrown a lot of grenades in his time, either in the open air or inside buildings and other confined spaces. They knew what to expect, but what they got didn't quite make sense. The blast, which should have been coming off a solid rock face, was nothing like as heavy as it should have been. Even the sound was muted, more like an echo than a crack. Not that there was time to articulate that. Each trooper had stood up and was pouring a magazine of ammo on to the target; dropping to reload while the four behind rushed forward to continue the fusillade.

'Coming through,' they yelled as they vaulted the ruined parapet, rushing to the sides to take up positions, laying down a curtain of fire so that the first team could follow them over.

'Cease fire,' shouted Lance Price, as he hauled a grenade from his bandolier, loading it into the M203. 'Everybody down.'

The other members of 6 Troop obliged as Lance levelled the weapon and fired. Then he threw himself to the floor, slamming hard into Bull

Bisset who called him a cunt. The explosion sounded more like rolling thunder than a grenade crack.

'This fucker goes back a long way,' said Lance, before lifting his wrist to report to Blue One.

'Are you clear to proceed to secondary target?' asked Lancing.

'Blue Two. Negative. We have a deep cave and cannot confirm that it is clear.'

Lancing made his decision in a second, with no certainty that it was the right one. But war is like that. Better to do something than prevaricate.

'Blue One. Roger. Clear that target.'

'NVGs' Lance shouted.

Four men stayed weapons up in the alert position covering the entrance to the cave while the others kitted up with night vision goggles. The headgear the goggles fitted to they were already wearing, so it was just a matter of quickly clipping them on. As soon as they were ready the positions were reversed. Not that they could see much until they switched on the infra-red torches that washed the area with a light that only a man wearing NVGs could see. The grenades had created a lot of debris, and dust was still floating in the trapped air. Lance tapped Jake Steel and pointed to his reloaded M203. He put up five fingers, receiving an affirmative hand signal. Five seconds later both men plunged into the gloom of the cave, the light from outside fading to be replaced by the ghostly green images of the NVGs. Touch revealed that the walls of the cave were clean, smooth and dry.

'Man made,' said Jake.

'Yep,' Lance replied, before radioing that back to Blue One.

The twin cracks as a pair of rounds shot past their ears had them both hitting the deck and rolling to slam into the side walls. They didn't fuck about looking for a target, but blasted off their grenades without much in the way of aim, relying on the smooth cave walls to carry the projectiles on. As soon as they exploded the troopers were up and moving, laying down fire ahead of them, searching through the ghostly gloom for a target. It was Jake who saw him first, a green shape pulling away to his left, but when he pulled the trigger on his M4 carbine nothing happened.

'Stoppage!' he screamed, dropping to one knee and going through the immediate action drills for clearing his weapon.

Lance didn't hear him above the sound of his own echoing weapon. He had seen the moving figure a second after Jake and raised his weapon, using the red dot on the laser sight to zero in on the target. The guy was dead as soon as he opened up, as soon as that red dot connected to his body.

Both men rushed forward, reloading on the move, calling for the rest of 6 Troop to follow. Before the others arrived, they'd found three bodies plus the still-twitching frame of the guy Lance had just slotted, the blood from his shattered ear drums running down his head. One by one the troopers went to white light, and established that they were in a small cavern which had acted as the billet for the crew manning the triple A. There were smashed bunks, a table, chairs and the remnants of food. As well as the route by which they'd entered there was another passage, dropping slightly away from the cavern, the blast of cool air coming up it evidence that it went somewhere.

'Somebody has fucked up big style here,' said Chemo, his chest heaving from running up the tunnel.

'Blue One. This is Blue Two.'

It was another voice that came back, one of the signallers. 'Blue One is on the other net. Wait out.'

The signaller who was monitoring the Red Team had alerted Johnny Lancing that the traffic on the Delta Force net was important enough to switch over. He knew they'd taken the remains of the house and fought their way down to the bunker underneath. From now, from what he was hearing, instead of trapping their enemy there and slotting them Delta was taking casualties as they sought to pursue bin Laden's men down a twisting narrow tunnel which led off from the bunker. He switched back to his own net.

'Blue Two. This is Blue One. Reference your last send. Over.'

Lance gave a quick sitrep, and requested instructions. Only the Headshed would know what was important, how the other guys were doing at their tasks and whether they needed support. He heard Lancing go through the callsigns, heard that the other triple A site was secure and that Blue Four were on their way to their secondary objective, ready to back up the guys who'd fought their way through the rubble and tangled metal of the destroyed Land Cruisers. They were now in the underground chambers involved in a heavy firefight. Then Lancing asked Blue Two to hold firm.

'Chemo, Whacker, cover the rear. Remainder cover down that fucking tunnel. We're going to go firm here and wait for further instructions. Make sure we're not fucking bounced.'

CHAPTER TWENTY-FOUR

There was no time for bin Laden's commanders to count the men who had survived. They themselves were too dazed to think clearly, but they knew that the bombardment had failed in its primary purpose. Their leader was still alive, and thanks to the depth of the bunkers, and the composition of the rock, so were they. The missiles would stop eventually, and then they could go back up and assess the damage.

The helos coming in, spotted by one brave soul who'd stayed at ground level and somehow managed to survive the Spectre sweep, shocked them back into life. They had no idea of the numbers they would face. All they could do was take to the tunnels and try to mount a rearguard action, holding off the enemy till they were sure Osama bin Laden was clear. The first thing to do was to hold the bunker, then, if that fell retreat to the maze of tunnels. But in order to cover their backs, sections had to be dispatched early, to secure the route and prevent the enemy from manoeuvring to cut their leader off.

Everyone was grabbing weapons: assault rifles, machine guns, grenades and RPGs. They might die here, but if they did, it would not be cheaply. It was the same in the castle, as those who lived took up their weapons and prepared to put the rubble the Tomahawks had created to their advantage. Every man shouted, 'Allah u Akbar!' before going into battle.

'Those MIGs, General.'

Lucius Morton turned away from the image from the digital camera to look at the plotting screen. The red track of the Afghani jets was sweeping round in a tight arc. He watched it until it settled on a new course which left no doubt of the intended destination. One of the men tasked with monitoring that part of the operation turned up the volume so that the general could hear the exchange of talk between Kandahar and the fighters.

'How long?' he asked the air commander.

It was a seaman who answered, the man whose computer screen told him exactly how long. 'Eleven minutes and falling.'

'Get on to Kandahar,' he said to the translator. 'Tell them they have four minutes to prove to us that their aircraft have changed course.'

The translator went to work, insistent, speaking in staccato Pushtu. Then he looked at Morton. 'They say they've recalled them, sir.'

That was plainly bullshit, since the red streak of the course was still as straight as an arrow towards the target. Morton could hear, close beside him, the air commander getting his fighters into position. 'Tell them we can see they have not changed course.'

Another exchange, and the same result.

'Listen to their radio traffic,' Morton asked. 'Does it sound like a recall?'

'No sir,' the translator replied.

'I hate to spoil his day if he's an idiot.' A nod had the translator talking again. That was followed by another even more excited radio exchange. The course of the MIGs never wavered. He nodded again, this time to the air commander. 'They're all yours, Tom.'

The first question went to the Hawkeye, code name Cajun.

'Cajun, who's on TARCAP?'

'Bison flight. Fokker and Indian on TAD Two.'

'Shit. Two jarhead eighteens,' said the air controller. 'OK. Have them take out the trash.'

'Bison. Cajun. Bandits sixty-two north-west bullseye, nose on.'

'Bison. Copy. Fokker TAC Port. GO!'

The two marine F/A18 fighters were on the TAD 2 fighter control frequency, and they also had a secondary tactical frequency for plane to plane comm. Bison was the mission callsign while Fokker and Indian were the pilots' personal callsigns. Radio chatter was on both frequencies, every word audible in the command centre, full of the particular vernacular so beloved by airmen, as the Hawkeye and the two fighters combined to take out the two enemy MIGs.

'Cajun. Bison. Picture?' asked the flight leader.

'Two bandits, north-west, angels twenty-eight trail, nose on,' replied the Hawkeye, reading from the radar-scope in front of him which showed the two targets flying in line as distinct blips.

'Indian. Check the trailer.'

'Wilco,' Indian replied, concentrating on the second MIG.

'Cajun. Bison has a hit at fifty-four angels, twenty-eight.'

'Roger, Bison. Confirmed bandit, cleared hot.'

'Hey Fokker, I'm shackle high,' said Indian, manoeuvring his plane into a position above his leader, giving himself a clear shot without interference from the other guy's radar.

'OK.'

'Indian, I can't believe these gappers are in trail.'

'No shit, must be old fucks like us.'

'Better watch for the lead-around.'

'Yup.'

The lead-around is a MIG tactic. The leader in a two on two combat will turn away inside 20 miles in an attempt to draw the fighters after him while the trail bandit sneaks up for a shot at both fighters.

'Cajun. Bison. Picture?'

'Bandits steady, forty-six trail, nose on, clear.'

'Indian, you got the trailer?'

'Ya, tied on sweet, he's two low.'

'Cajun. Bison. Picture?'

'Only two nose on at thirty-eight, Bison.'

'OK.'

'Indian, I'm gonna sweeten up and take him down the throat.'

To sweeten up and take a guy down the throat meant to manoeuvre as close as possible to a head-on shot, increasing effective range and shortening missile time of flight to the target.

'Good idea, pony soldier.'

'This is too fucking easy.'

The F/A18s had lined the two MIGs up like rats in a barrel. The equipment they carried meant that once locked on the computers did the rest. In the MIG cockpits the warnings started to flash, red lights

242

that said they were in a missile lock. Both pilots started their evasive manoeuvres as the two American fighters closed on them. But the AIM 120 AMRAAM is a MACH 3+ missile that has an active seeker in the heart of the envelope and there is no escape manoeuvre.

'Well now, looks like lead's turning left.'

'It's the old lead-around.'

'No shit. I'll take him at thirty off.'

'Don't wait too long, pardner.'

'Bison One. Fox away!'

The air to air missile streaked out from under the wing.

'Bison Two. Fox away!' The pilot watched his missile depart, then spiral earthwards. 'Shit, a mud seeker. Trailers jinking left.'

'Stay on the fucker. I got lead.'

And he had. Once a missile is launched within the launch acceptable range, it is in the heart of the envelope and the enemy can kiss his ass goodbye. The jargon called it 'putting the dick-head in the basket'.

'Shit, what a fucking fireball, Bison one. Slash the lead bandit.'

One of the red blips disappeared off the plotting screen. They could see the trail as the MIGs turned, as well as the F18 cutting the angle to fire a second missile.

'Bison Two. Fox again.'

'Indian. I'm visual right three low.'

'OK.'

'Oh, real fucking nice, Bison Two,' the voice said, as the second red blip disappeared. 'Splash the trailer.'

'Indian, come hard right. I'm at your right three low.'

'Aay, OK. Visual. I'm Joker.'

'Cajun. Bison. Splash two Vectors.'

'Nice work Bison,' said the voice from the Hawkeye, before adding a new position to which they should vector. 'Make it one four eight.'

'Shit, Fokker,' whooped Indian. 'That was easy, now we gotta get aboard the fucking boat.'

'No shit,' was the reply.

This was said in a deliberately calm voice, meant to convey that what they'd done, as well as what they were about to do, was an everyday event.

'Call Kandahar again,' Lucius Morton said. 'And tell those dumb bastards not to warm another goddamned engine. Anything military moves we will hit it before it's airborne.'

'Red One. This is Blue One. Over?'

It was a long thirty seconds before Stan the Man answered, and meanwhile Johnny Lancing could hear quite clearly why. Traffic on the Red Team net was furious and not more encouraging than on his own. All the callsigns were reporting in that they faced strong resistance. Fighting in confined spaces is the hardest form of combat going. Leadership counts for little: training and sheer raw courage are what matters.

Delta, like B Squadron had hit serious resistance. Lancing's men were making progress, fighting their way down to what seemed to be a series of underground chambers in the castle. Clearing the staircase was taking time. The tight confines of the battle meant that the SAS commander couldn't deploy his full strength. Callsigns coming on to this, their secondary target, were merely backing up those at the sharp end.

Osama bin Laden had learnt from the Kabul raid and had occupied a position with more natural strength. More than that, he had clearly added to the natural features and created a facility that was prepared for resistance to a ground attack.

Lucius Morton shared that thirty second wait. He felt helpless, but that was a situation any officer of high rank could experience. He did have time to ruminate on the reasons for what he was hearing. One was a failure of intelligence, but not one that he could lay at the door of any of the spook organizations. They had given JSOC all the information they had in good faith.

Time on target would be lengthened, but that only complicated matters regarding the occupation of neutral airspace. With no mere mopping up operation in progress, casualties must inevitably be higher. The consequences of that weren't hard to imagine and there was a point at which the game wasn't worth the candle. Nothing, so far, gave even the slightest indication that there was any risk of defeat. But could they complete the task? He had the authority to pull his troops out, but that was an even less appealing prospect.

'Blue One. This is Red One. Over.'

Jay Fuller's voice was as calm as Lancing's own, more like the host at a good party than an under pressure commander.

'Blue One. Send. Over. Red One, we are experiencing strong resistance in a tunnel system but have some callsigns who are not getting a piece of the action. Do you require assistance? Over.'

'Blue One. That's a negative, I repeat negative. Our situation is the same.'

'Blue Two is firm in a tunnel system behind the triple A position. Initial resistance has been dealt with. I am about to commit them further. Inform your callsigns to avoid a blue on blue. Over.'

With no idea where the tunnels led, Lancing couldn't send a patrol in without letting the Delta commander know of their presence.

'Red One. Roger that. Give those mothers a serious dose of lead poisoning. Out.'

Lancing switched nets to talk to 6 Troop. 'Blue Two. This is Blue One. Over.'

'Blue Two. Send.'

'Blue One. You are to continue with your task and clear that tunnel. Roger so far, Over.'

'Blue Two. Roger.'

'Blue One. Callsign Blue Four will provide back up. Red Team have been informed. Beware blue on blue. Over.'

'Blue Two. Roger that. Continuing with task. Out.'

Everybody was on the net and had heard the exchange of traffic. It was Jake who articulated the common thought while Lancing was giving his orders to Blue Four. 'Does that bastard know where these fuckers lead to?'

'Not our business, Jake. Let's just get on with it,' Lance replied. 'NVGs.'

They were clipped back on and he then called softly down to Chemo and Whacker to tell them they were coming through. Once by Chemo's shoulder, he tapped him and made the sign for 'Anything seen?'

Chemo gave him the silent response that meant, 'Jack shit.'

Lance gave a hand signal followed by a tap on the arm of the nearest trooper. Immediately they split into pairs, instructions were passed and they divided into two fire teams adopting file formation, the teams hugging either wall. The rest of the hand signals told them to keep the bounds short. One team to move then go firm, before calling the other team through. Any obstacle, split in direction, or anything unsure of, go firm until the situation is assessed.

Pull back ten metres then go firm, indicated Mike Hutton.

Lance nearly put him down out of habit, but he held his hand. What Mike Hutton was doing made sense. He tapped Mike to acknowledge, then repeated the instructions. Pull back ten metres then go firm until we've assessed the situation.

Jake and Bull led the first team off, weapons held with the butt in the shoulder at the alert position, their arms brushing the now rough hewn sides of the tunnel. The first thing Jake spotted was a trail of dust falling from the tunnel roof. He stopped and indicated with a hand gesture for Lance, in the next pair, to come forward. Lance got in front of Bull Bisset and edged down the wall, peering up with Jake providing cover.

Close to the thin trail of dust they could see how the rocks had been cut away to provide an air shaft. The ground attack had blocked the shaft with rubble, but loose stuff was filtering through. Lance was just about to indicate to Jake that it was no problem when his cover man opened up, filling the confined space with the deafening racket of gunfire. Lance felt his guts turn over as he dropped to one knee, knowing that Bull was behind him and also in a better position to shoot.

Jake had got off two aimed rounds at the outline that appeared, seemingly from the tunnel wall, about twenty metres ahead. He'd seen the muzzle flash first but the guy came out too fast to provide a hard target. The shots, a wild burst from a machine gun, hit the tunnel walls and ricocheted, lethally. Bull, firing over Price's kneeling body, sussed the positive effects of rapid fire and gave half a mag in return. There was no way of knowing whose rounds downed the guy, and it didn't matter. He went over like a sack of wet shit, as Bull and Jake ran forward to secure the position, a bend in the tunnel, before any of the enemy could make further use of it.

Lance carried out a quick casualty check and found that Gaz Mowlem had a surface wound on his left thigh where a round had sliced through his combat trousers leaving a deep gash. Whacker, the patrol medic was already strapping it up, tight to slow the blood flow. It wasn't pretty, but it was effective.

Down at the bend, Jake and Bull had decided that, to make the position secure, they needed to dominate the area right in front of them. They didn't wait for Lance, they just took the responsibility themselves. Two grenades were followed by two controlled bursts into the smoke and debris, with the troopers edging forward all the time trying to ignore the aching in their eardrums caused by the blast in a confined space. Bull kicked the one body that their action had taken out. Lance, behind them, had dragged the first kill back slightly then put a torch over him to see what he could find. Number one conclusion was that he was not bin Laden.

The dead eyes stared back at him, brown and glinting as they reflected the light. The guy was dressed all in black with good boots, as well as an ops waistcoat with the kind of kit in it a Special Forces trooper would carry. As well as the latest AK-104 assault rifle with folding butt, he had a Makarov MP-443 9mm automatic pistol in his belt and a knife strapped to his thigh; all of which Lance removed. The guy looked the part, but the way he'd come out into the line of fire was real bone, a man asking to be slotted. Properly trained, he would have waited, then used a grenade when one pair were closing in on the corner. They would certainly have gone down and he might then, with luck, have got a couple more with his AK.

'Silly cunt,' hissed Lance as he searched the man's pockets for some form of ID. All he got was a set of worry beads.

Jake and Bull had moved forward out of the dust, and had taken up positions to dominate the tunnel. They waited patiently until the rest joined them, then they went back to the previous formation, edging forward, eyes swivelling to look at everything – including the tunnel floor, which would be a great place to leave the kind of charge that could blow 6 Troop to buggery.

Without the NVGs, they would have walked straight into the guys behind the rock fall a hundred metres further on. Mike Hutton and Chemo were point, and they both saw the slight movement of the head at the same time. The reaction was swift but controlled. The victim didn't see the dot on his head from Chemo's laser sight, but he felt the bullet in the split second before it killed him. Mike was sweeping the area above the rocks waiting for a target to appear. It did in spades, four heads coming up together.

'Down!' he yelled, firing a quick burst as he dropped to one knee. The guys behind didn't ask why, they just did as they were told, also dropping to the one knee firing position which presented a smaller target.

'Get some fucking grenades in there!'

Gaz Mowlem and Whacker had their M203s up and aimed forward. In front of them, Chemo and Mike Hutton were flat on the ground so they had a clear field of fire; and they could see for themselves the heads popping up and down behind the rock barrier trying to find a way to respond through the shit that the two point men were laying down.

The ragheads must have known what was coming, because those heads disappeared. They couldn't get up to run without getting slotted, they had to be crawling. It didn't do them much good. The two grenades impacted on the roof and dropped to the floor behind the rock barrier. Everybody on the 6 Troop side hit the deck for protection as they went off. The noise was horrendous, close to eardrum splitting, but brief. The screaming was worse and went on. There was another noise, a heavy cracking sound, but they ignored that.

Mike Hutton and Chemo were up and over the barrier, using double taps to ensure the dead stayed dead and the wounded were given the third eye and joined them. There was no time for sentiment. These cunts were trying to kill them and the best way to ensure they didn't was to slot them first. There was no time for prisoners, and no inclination to take any.

'Blue One, this is Blue Two. Radio check. Over.' Lance repeated the call when there was a garbled response.

Blue One knew they were in a fight. Blue Four had reached the entrance to the cave system and could hear the battle noise, information that they had passed back to the command helo. But the mass of rock was playing havoc with the comms, cutting off those deep underground from tactical control. Lancing had another command decision to make, one he had to share with Jay Fuller.

Delta Force, according to Red One, were breaking into a tunnel system too. Behind them, in the bunker area, the Delta teams tasked to raise intelligence had gathered up anything written, as well as CDs, books, Zip disks and piles of 3½-inch floppies; while others stripped out the hard disks from the wrecked mess of the computers.

Behind the guys still fighting under the castle, one of Lancing's callsigns, Blue Three, had completed their task. They were now searching the classrooms and cells, filling up bags with everything they could find: clothes, radios even some scraps of paper and a dirty shirt found on the floor of a cell that had stayed undamaged. The only thing the Joint Strike force hadn't done was confirm the kill on bin Laden. But they'd been on target twenty minutes, and the exfil would take at least another five. Did the two commanders let their men carry on, or was it time to pull them out?

'Get me bin Laden,' whispered Lucius Morton, even though neither of the two squadron commanders could hear him.

Time on target, up to a point, had always been at their discretion. Thirty minutes was a guideline only. They could stay on to complete the task provided no one further up the chain of command ordered them out.

The casualty count, considering the nature of the fighting, was low; mostly flesh wounds easily treatable, though Delta had two dead and four serious casualties, while B Squadron had lost one trooper and had already pulled out six others with various incapacitating wounds. Each force now had a callsign acting solely as medics, transporting the wounded back to the Osprey which had landed on the remains of the helipad.

The discussion was brief, private and positive between two commanders who saw dead and wounded not as a reason to withdraw, but as a reason to go on. There was nothing worse, to their minds, than the notion that whatever sacrifices had been made should be in vain.

'Blue Four. This is Blue One. Move to assist Blue Two. Roger so far. Over.'

'Blue Four. Roger. Over.'

'Blue One. Comms at Blue Two's location are difficult to unworkable. Be prepared to use runners to keep me informed. Roger so far. Over.'

'Blue Four. Roger over.'

'Blue One. Inform Blue Two that Red and Blue Teams are still engaged. We will stay on target until the mission is complete. Over.'

'Blue Four. Roger that. Out.'

Lance Price swore hard, having only picked up one word in ten of that last exchange. He wanted desperately to be told what to do. All he knew was that up ahead he could hear, very faintly, gunfire and explosions. This was the Gulf War situation he'd dreaded; where he would have to make a command decision that might get the whole lot of them killed. Price was no gung ho arsehole, who would go on just for the sake of it, a flag waving army barmy cunt who thought bravery was charging the guns. He had the balls to pull back when it was the right thing to do. At this moment that was his problem. He didn't know.

'O Group,' he croaked, indicating that the guys should gather round. They did so, each one following his example by sucking on the tube from his Camelback water container.

'Right, we're off the net, with no fucking idea where these tunnels lead to. But somebody up ahead has a contact, and that might be our mates in the castle.'

'We go on,' said Chemo, without hesitation. He had his back to Price with his weapon aimed down the tunnel. As he spoke another dull thud erupted. 'The sound of the guns, old chap.'

'Don't take the piss.'

'I'm not,' Chemo replied angrily.

'I think we should re-establish comms,' argued Mike Hutton.

That alone made up Lance's mind. If Mike Hutton wanted to go back, he wanted to go on. As usual, few had an opinion worth a shit. Only Jake Steel spoke up, backing Chemo.

'Right, we go on. Same as before.'

A quiet hundred metres settled any doubts in those that had them, which was every patrol member. The tunnel floor had levelled out, but now it was strewn with rocks that had to be picked over carefully. Another one dropped from the roof, catching Mike Hutton on the shoulder. It didn't break anything but, judging by the string of swear words it hurt like fuck. Everybody stopped, which meant that when they heard the phut of the RPG they were static. Not for long. It was choose your way to go time, with no real idea if, by diving right or left, you were putting yourself into or out of danger.

As it was, the rocket propelled grenade missed everyone in 6 Troop. Miraculously, it even missed the tunnel walls for a while, exploding well behind them, the blast throwing everyone forward on to their bellies as a shower of deadly rock splinters swathed past them. Jake Steel could feel them slamming into the soles of his boots, a few whacking into his legs and back. But that wasn't what took his attention.

The loud crack and rumble filled their brains not their ears, as to their rear, the roof of the tunnel, weakened by the explosions from the Tomahawks and the Spectres, collapsed. The rumbling went on for what seemed like an age, and when it ended the tunnel seemed, as far as retreat was concerned, totally sealed.

There was no time to examine the rockfall, to see if there was a way of shifting it, because at that point powerful torches started to weave around. That was followed immediately by rapid gunfire, from the AK assault rifles the lights were attached to.

It was Chemo who reacted first. He knew that to stay still was to die. They might take some shit, he might even get wasted, but they had to attack. His screams had them all up and moving, short sharp rushes of five to six paces at a time, firing through the thick dust that was the only thing keeping them alive. They weren't dead yet, only because their enemy couldn't really see them.

'No grenades, for fuck's sake,' shouted Lance Price, as one from an M203 fired off right beside his ear. He wasn't sure anyone could hear him but he was going to tell them anyway: firing grenades could turn this place into a tomb. 'You'll just bring more shit down.'

It was the last thing Lance Price ever said. The first bullet hit him in the chest, stopping his forward motion. The second, from the rapid firing assault rifle, took out his larynx, while the third lifted off the top of his head. No one saw him drop because they were all too busy, expending ammo they couldn't spare, laying down a curtain of concentrated fire that nothing could live through.

Whoever they were up against either died, or didn't like the odds, because the incoming stopped. So did 6 Troop.

CHAPTER TWENTY-FIVE

The firing seemed, to Osama bin Laden, to be coming from all around him. But that was just an illusion, quickly confirmed by his two sons, who, despite their youth were trained fighters, and knew more about guns and gunfire than he did. Hailed as a great leader, he knew just how false were the pictures distributed of him holding a rifle. Bin Laden was a thinker and an organizer, who could create the conditions in which others could fight. He was not himself a man of action, though he had the ability to fire weapons and his deep faith precluded any fear of death. But that self-knowledge didn't answer the most pressing question: which way to go? He was at a crossroads. One set of tunnels led up to each of the anti-aircraft positions, but Abdullah vetoed that idea, insisting that they would be primary targets. Any hope of getting out past the men fighting was impossible, which only left the water system that fed the castle.

The Emir who'd built the castle had never intended that he should be forced out by thirst. He had cut a reservoir below the level of the nearby lake and opened a channel to let the water in. Once in that reservoir they could float out well away from the action, but that begged another question: how much did those attacking know about the place? They might well understand the water system and be waiting for anyone trying to use it as an escape route.

Neither bin Laden nor his children had any illusions about what would happen if they were caught. The attackers would not take them prisoner. They'd be shot on sight, since they possessed little in the way of weaponry to make a fight of it: only two hastily acquired sub-machine guns. To get to the water they had to get to one of the openings to the well. Clearly the one in the castle keep was out of the question. The only other one was the access from the underground chambers.

The youngest boy, Ali, did a rapid recce and discovered that the men who'd fallen back from the ground floor were still holding; that the access point, though exposed to a degree of fire, was accessible. Limping, his stick long gone, bin Laden followed his boys, the sound of battle increasing till it was deafening in the confined space.

The sight of their leader cheered the young men fighting to hold the SAS at bay. In truth it was the building itself, including the wrecked vehicles and the piles of rubble that had aided them. Exposure of any kind generally got them killed by men who were all marksmen. Bin Laden's son Abdullah hastily explained what they were trying to do, while his brother hauled up on the rope that was used to bring up the water bucket.

To his impressionable disciples, to die for Allah was to enter the gates of paradise. Yet they also understood that their leader must live to carry on the fight. Ten of them charged the staircase, sending up such a hail of bullets that they forced the men above to keep their heads down. As the fire slackened, as it had to do, the martyrs were picked off one by one. Bin Laden got one foot in the bucket and his two sons let him down, too fast for comfort but this was no time to be gentle.

Above his head, Captain Ben Forsyth, the SSM and the patrol commanders were discussing tactics, re-discovering that 'tactics are like arseholes, everybody has one'. In other words, everyone had an opinion as to how the base of the staircase should be cleared. They'd used up their 66mm LAWs getting this far, though Forsyth had requested via the Headshed to be resupplied from the other callsigns. The senior NCO wasn't being much help. Battle seemed to have slowed him down rather than made him sharp. It was one of the troopers who solved the problem, and he didn't ask for permission. He just gathered as many grenades as he could, threw them into his day sack, pulled the pin from one and chucked them down into the chamber where the base of the stairs met the central chamber.

The rope had gone tense, proof that it was at full stretch. Ali first, then Abdullah, threw themsleves on to it, sliding down, ignoring the pain. Abdullah saw the sack drop into the chamber just as his head went below the parapet of the well. The blast, as the grenades went off, blew half the side of the well in, several large stones dropping past his body to the deep water below. The fighters who had been holding off the SAS took the same blast. The screams of the dying now replaced that of gunfire, as bodies writhed on the cold stone floor.

Abadullah had to let go – his hands were burning. Below, he heard a splash and hoped his brother was clear. He felt himself dropping, his weapon clattering against the curved stone wall. He struggled to stay head up, well aware that if he did not he would smash out his brains. It was pitch dark and the water, when he hit it, felt like rock. He opened his mouth to scream in agony and swallowed several pints before he could close it again.

'Back up the tunnel!' said Jonathan Burroughs, the Rupert in charge of Blue Four. His voice sounded even plummier in the confined space than normal – if that was possible. He was a real number Captain Jonathan, a Rupert to his socks; not John or Johnny, but the full moniker. 'Jonathan laddie, and don't you bloody forget it.'

'I just hope the poor bastards aren't under that lot,' said his Staff Sergeant.

'If they are, they're staying there. Let's back up and inform Blue One.

'That was a big fucker,' said Chemo.

The dull thud of the sack of grenades exploding seemed to come through the walls. Then they heard a short sharp scream, cut off as though someone had died, mingled with the occasional burst of gunfire from further up the tunnel.

'Let's move, slowly. Jake, pair up with me.'

The rest sorted themselves out and nobody questioned Chemo's right to command. He was the senior guy and best soldier in the group, and in the SAS that was enough. Jake did as he was asked, taking up a position on Chemo's right, moving forward slowly. That's when they heard the voices, distorted, as though they were coming out of a box. Thirty seconds later they saw the shaft of light.

NVGs off and looking up they could see that it was a smooth almost glassy watercourse where a small river had run into the tunnel. It was too narrow to climb. There was a larger hole at their feet where it had poured down into the ground.

'What is it?' asked Gaz Mowlem.

'Water storage,' said Mike Hutton. 'Must have been built up in case they were besieged.'

'Which is what we are,' said Parsnips. 'Talk about fucking Hampton Court Maze!'

There was another, much softer voice from below, carried up by an echo.

'There's some fucker down there,' hissed Chemo.

'Take cover,' said Bull Bisset, softly. He didn't shout, that only alerts the enemy. Neither did his mates rush to obey, and that was nothing to do with the fact that there was no cover. They moved slowly, each taking up a position that gave them a forward arc of fire and as much protection as they could manage.

'What we got?' asked Chemo.

'Movement,' answered Bull. 'More than one.'

The sudden burst of fire had them all trying to crawl into the rock, arses twitching, but nothing came their way, and it was a moment before they realized that the fire was directed away from them.

Chemo's hand signal indicated 'Jake, with me'.

He signalled the others to follow at intervals of ten paces. The fire slackened as they began to move, one foot placed slowly in front of the other. In the renewed darkness they replaced their NVGs and flooded the place with light from the infra-red torches. Both troopers saw the outlines of the men crouching, backs to 6 Troop. The fire intensified, and this time it was coming this way, single controlled shots that ricocheted off the walls, whistling past their ears. Curses were coming from all sides.

'We've got a fucking blue on blue,' said Bull. 'That's either Delta or our guys shooting at us.'

Chemo was talking on his comms, trying and failing to get a response.

'Switch comms to the red net,' said Jake.

That got him a big nod but what they got wasn't clear. The signal varied in strength making understanding difficult. Chemo had to assume it was the same the other way round. He identified their callsign, repeated it and informed whoever was on the other end of their intentions.

'The ragheads. Let's take them out, Jake.'

They had infra-red sights on their weapons, so aiming was no big deal. They both fired at once, M203s low so that the grenades wouldn't travel too far. When they exploded the flesh seemed to melt into the bright flash of the kill to form one mass. In the silence that followed, Chemo started shouting at the top of his voice, giving their callsign.

An American voice came back. 'Red Five. Identify yourself.'

'We just have you dozy cunt.'

'That's a good ID,' the voice replied. 'I don't reckon any of these guys to blaspheme.'

'Blue Two coming through. Seven up.'

'OK.'

They went forward slowly, until identification was confirmed.

'How are your comms to the Headshed?' asked Parsnips.

'Holy shit, they ain't no fucking good in here.'

'What's behind you?'

'Fresh air and Delta Force.'

'Sounds good.'

'The route out is easy. Just follow the bodies.'

'Anybody slotted bin Laden yet?'

'Haven't heard any confirmation.'

'What about those voices we heard?' asked Chemo.

'We should check in and let the Headshed know we're still active,' said Parsnips.

'Gaz, you go,' Chemo said. 'You've got that leg wound. Send a sitrep to Blue One. If he wants us out he can send a runner.'

'We're forty minutes on target.'

'Look, Tony, if Lancing wants us out he'll say so. Now let's get back there to that shaft and see what's happening.'

It was silent now, that was until Mike Hutton threw an empty mag down. It rattled from side to side, then audibly hit water.

'Rig up a line,' Chemo said. 'I'm going down.'

'What about a grenade first?' asked Bull.

'Don't let me stop you.'

They all had loop lines and karabiners. Two were quickly attached to form one long line. Only Bull didn't reach for his. Instead he pulled the pin on a HE grenade and dropped it down the shaft, everyone automatically stepping back.

The boom sounded worse in bin Laden's ears than it did to those above. And it got them to their feet, all three dripping wet, Abdullah with a broken arm and Ali with more bruises on his body than he could count. Only their father seemed to be in one piece; his voice insistent but falling on deaf ears that they should leave him behind and save themselves. They'd covered half the distance to the lake three stumbling figures splashing through the water, before Chemo emerged from the shaft, hanging on to the assembled line.

Firing a weapon while swinging on a rope isn't easy, but he tried; then he splashed down into the freezing cold water, which came up to his chest. The arch that led out to the lake was a distant crescent that silhouetted the staggering trio. Jake Steel was down behind him, going straight into the water, gasping. Then he and Chemo began to push forward, only to hear Mike Hutton call down, 'Stop, stop, stop. Lions Roar, Lions Roar', giving the code word for all callsigns to cease action and move to pick up now. That was an instruction you just did not disobey.

'Fuck,' said Jake, as he took hold of the rope to haul himself up. 'I'm soaked.'

The tunnels were as Delta said, full of bodies, each one thrown on its back to be checked for identity. 6 Troop went back for Lance, conducting their own search as they went. They had it easy compared to the guys on the surface who had to check bodies mangled by the missile and Spectre attacks. Pockets were emptied, papers and photographs removed, the whole complex scoured for anything that might just possibly tell the guys in intelligence what to look out for.

They carried Lance Price out through the ruined bunker, trying not to look into those glassy staring eyes. You never get used to death especially one of your own. Lance had failed to beat the clock. There was a big brass plaque on the clock at Stirling Lines. Soon his name would be added to all the others killed in action. Not much good to a wife and two kids.

Lucius Morton wanted to ask if they had got bin Laden, but there was no point. They would say on the ground if they had a positive ID. And so many of the terrorists had been vaporised by the Tomahawks or deracinated by the Spectres that he could be anywhere. Morton had to be satisfied when told that they had found a storage area with chemicals, all non-toxic in their present state.

The raiders had their own casualties, enough in bad shape to make the Osprey take off well before the rest of the packet, to get back to the carrier as fast as possible. Delta and SAS, every man now weary and hurting somewhere, climbed aboard their helos, giving high fives and cool greetings to the men who got them in.

The comms buzzed as numbers were checked to make sure that everybody breathing or not was in some airframe. 6 Troop could hear the commands over the radios and felt a surge of elation as the helos lifted in a tight group, climbing this time to a proper flying height, then pointing their noses east to the USS *Essex*.

Behind them barely a stone was standing. Already the carrion birds were circling, waiting to feed on bits of flesh so small they could swallow them whole. Beneath them six dark eyes looked up from three filthy faces, the curses silent but forcibly felt.

Osama bin Laden put his arms round his sons, pulling them to him, and hissed, 'We have the means to make them pay for this. We have the means and we shall employ them.'

There would be no more bluff, either with the West or with Mullah Omar and his acolytes. If that binary nerve gas got to where it was intended to go bin Laden was now determined to use it.

Aidan McGurk heard the first news as he waited for his transfer flight at Karachi. The whole place was wild with rumour and speculation: bin

Laden was dead; he was alive and spitting revenge; the Americans had shot at him and the bullets had failed to penetrate his flesh.

What was obvious was just how close he must have been to being blown away himself. And, not for the first time in his life, the question was posed: what now? He couldn't see any alternative to just taking his flight. No good would be served by hanging about; better to get to Amsterdam, then contact Keegan and Boyle in London. He had always been damned sure he was never going to accept bin Laden's proposition on his own. Let the collective leadership do that.

His bag had gone through three X-ray machines now, but the plastic flasks hadn't been picked up. They were now safely stored in the hold of the Air Pakistan flight to Rome and London. He'd get off at Rome, then take a flight to Amsterdam. But with $10,000 in his pocket, he might just stop off for a day. That would sort out what had happened at Zu ol Faqar. Maybe he'd find that bin Laden was alive. He would pick a good hotel, have a proper bath and a decent meal, and then he'd have a woman.

There was no way of getting away from the story. The television was full of images of Special Forces fast roping from helicopters. The film of the siege at Princes Gate was dug out and shown time and time again. Aidan McGurk nearly screamed at the TV; to stop treating them like fucking heroes when all they were was murdering bastards.

Why the news shifted to a cabin in a snow covered landscape he didn't understand. He heard the name bin Laden, but not speaking any Italian he had no idea why they were showing it. That was until they showed the fractured plastic flask, very like the ones he was carrying.

'Holy shite!' he swore.

Then he phoned the concierge; he wanted his laundry done. That's when he discovered that his shirt was missing.

CHAPTER TWENTY-SIX

It was a top priority getting everything back to the USA for analysis. And this time, with the security code cracked, they could get straight into bin Laden's files. They found codes, e-mail addresses; purchase orders for arms, ammunition and food. The accounts showed just how much money bin Laden had coming in and from where. Several outgoing items also caught the eye, not least the bribes to Middle Eastern potentates who claimed friendship with the West. Then there was the recently opened Irish account, showing an initial deposit of $200,000.

Also, there was the shirt. That itself yielded nothing except a strong odour of use. But the bits of paper in the pocket were different. They listed targets from Buckingham Palace through the Channel Tunnel to the new Millennium Dome. Oddly, everything was written in English, not Arabic. The make of the shirt was traced to Ireland, and that led the FBI to access the UK fingerprint bank and identify Aidan McGurk.

Contact was a two-way affair. MI5 had coded access to all the paramilitary groups in Northern Ireland, including the Provisional IRA. The discussions on this occasion were long and detailed, not curt at all. The whole peace process would be endangered if this cell was allowed to go active. The idea to curtail their activities, cobbled together by the two interested parties, was clever. It went all the way up to the Provos Army Council and came back as approved.

'What in the name of Jesus are you two doin' here?'

'We got bounced, Aidan,' said Keegan, 'and had to leg it. Christ knows how they picked us up, but I wouldn't be surprised if it was some of our old friends grassing us up.'

McGurk gently twitched the curtain. 'Is this place sound?'

'Of course it is!' exclaimed Gilhooley. 'Christ it took me weeks to pick it.'

'Arrived less than ten minutes ago, sir,' said one of the watchers. 'The good news is they have no idea we're on to them.'

'Fine,' said Bowers. 'Keep me informed.' Then he pressed his intercom and asked his secretary to get him Blue Harding.

'Got another little job for you, Harding.'

'What's happened? Have I become flavour of the month?'

'Let's just call it your reward for the splendid job you did on your last engagement.'

'When.'

'This one's top priority.'

'On my way,' Blue replied, his back to Yan Yan. But he didn't have to be looking at her to know she was unhappy.

'I don't like this, Aidan,' said Connor Boyle, pointing at the two flasks under the café table. 'I don't like it at all.'

'All we're doing with it is delivering.'

'To what? A bunch of mad Muslim bastards.'

'They're just as sane as us.'

'My arse.'

'Look,' McGurk said, spreading his hands. 'I said I would put it to you. I said I would not go making a decision myself. If you say "Aidan, get rid of it", I can do that. But we kiss goodbye to the backing we need to get the Provos where they belong. There's two hundred thousand dollars just waiting for us to access. It's up to you all.'

'A vote's the best bet,' said Keegan.

'Right,' McGurk said. 'I'm in favour.'

'So am I,' said Keegan.

'Me too,' Gilhooley added. 'I had fuck all to cheer about here. I want to do something instead of sitting on my arse.'

Aidan McGurk gave Boyle a heavy slap. 'Look, youse have been banged up here too long sipping *cappuccinos*. Let's go out and have a jar tonight, and get serious tomorrow.'

'Jesus,' Boyle replied. 'I could fair murder a pint of stout.'

'What are we going to do with those?' asked Keegan.

'The flasks? We'll take the fucking things with us; they're harmless.'

'No fear,' Gilhooley replied.

Tailed to the railway station, it was easy to deduce that they'd put something in a locker. But what and in which one, was a mystery that required the place to have its own team of watchers.

'Ingenious, don't you think, Harding?' said Bowers, looking as smug as Blue had ever seen him.

'It might not be possible to do what you want.'

'A man of your ability . . .'

'Don't overrate me. I've got to get that into either their flat or Gilhooley's car, without being seen and hidden in a place where they won't spot it. All you have to do is pick up the phone. Muggins, as usual, gets the dirty work.'

'You should have studied at school, Harding. Then you might be where I am today.' He picked up the bomb from his desk, turned it over in his hand and examined it. 'Pure IRA, this little beauty, even down to one or two of McGurk's own little signatures. When they are apprehended, there will be no doubt about their intentions. And they won't be able to claim it's been planted.'

Every bomb maker has a signature in the way he constructs a bomb; one that can be recognized by forensic experts.

'Where did you get it?'

'Need to know, Harding. Do you like tulips?'

'Why?'

'We're off to Holland, that's why.'

'They picked up their parcel from the station around eight, sir, then headed off straight down the A26 to Rotterdam. We have two cars on them now, and three back up vehicles.'

'Four if you include ours,' said Bower. 'We'll be up with you in half an hour.'

They tailed the four Irishmen across Holland, no easy matter on such flat open roads, never getting close enough to be compromised. Blue and Bowers were a mile behind, well out of sight. It was a pure opportunity job. HMG wanted, if possible, to have them nicked outside the UK, so as not to wind up the Unionists too much. Failing that, they'd settle for planting the device on the terrorists in England, which they guessed was their destination.

'They're pulling off, sir. At a service area. Our back up car will go in after them.'

'Right!' Then he glanced at Blue. 'What do you want to do, Harding?'

It was very much Blue's call. For him, the sooner the better. Sitting with a bomb on your lap, even a safe one, was no fun.

'All four are mobile. The car is unattended.'

'I'll go for it.'

Bowers cruised in to the parking lot and slid his vehicle in beside Gilhooley's. Then he waited while he learned that three had gone for a piss, while McGurk had gone to the food counter.

'Looks like they might be staying a while.'

Blue got out of Bowers' car, shoved the thin piece of metal down the window of the Irishman's vehicle and jerked open the lock. He opened the back door, then reached back into Bowers' car and pulled out the bomb. Getting the back seat up wasn't easy, but he managed, placing the device where it couldn't be seen, but where it would be found easily by whichever police force Bowers alerted. Everything was back in place, the car re-locked and he and Bowers re-parked on the other side of the car park before the three from the toilets had got served.

The surveillance teams left before the Irishmen did: one far enough ahead to double back from the next junction and get behind Gilhooley, the other just as they stood up, to get ahead of them. The second team was several miles down the motorway when Gilhooley overtook them. Bowers was still well back out of sight, weighing up which jurisdiction would be the most severe for an Irish terrorist caught with a bomb in their car.

You don't look at the cars passing you on a three-lane AutoRoute unless they are exceptional. The big Mercedes, Dutch registered, with the blacked-out windows was just that, and out of habit both Bowers and Blue looked at the boot to see the engine size, normally there in silver figures. There was nothing, which meant it was a big bastard engine. As if to underline that, it began to accelerate away even more.

'There'll be at least one other car between us and them,' said the gentle Irish voice, as he turned and looked out of the black windows at the car they'd just passed.

The driver was also Irish, with one of those heavy Belfast accents that had come to bore the people of mainland Britain. 'We're going past them, right?'

'Well, you wouldn't want to be behind the gobshites would you? Put your bloody foot down.'

The Mercedes shot passed the second surveillance car doing a hundred and ten. By the time they caught up with Gilhooley it was one twenty. Even with the blacked out windows, neither passenger nor driver looked right. In fact, the passenger, as an extra precaution, put up a hand to cover the side of his face, even though these men he knew so well could not see it. They were a hundred yards past when he picked up the radio device, two hundred when he flicked the switch.

The boom of the explosion sent a shock wave back that nearly stopped the car. Bowers put his foot down, seeing the flaming fireball right ahead.

'Was that your idea?' asked Blue, not trying to hide his disgust.

'No, Harding, it was not.'

'Why don't I believe you?'

Bowers wasn't listening, he was calling to make sure his operatives were all right, his shoulders heaving with relief as the occupants of the closest car acknowledged they were, but that the vehicle was not.

'I'm coming to get you. Dark blue Passat.'

'Right, sir.'

Gilhooley's car was a total burning wreck, spread across the highway. One body had been blown right out and was hanging over the barrier on the central reservation. Several other vehicles were slewed about, all damaged in some way. The surveillance team car had been just far enough away to have suffered no more than the loss of its windscreen.

265

Bowers barely slowed as the men who had been using it ran towards his car. As soon as their arses touched the seats, the car was off, weaving through wreckage and bodies before screaming down the now deserted motorway.

Bowers sensed that Blue Harding was still seething. For all his hard exterior it bothered Bowers to be thought of as a cold blooded murderer. He'd order, and even carry out a death sentence if it was required, but what had happened here was not his doing.

'If it's any consolation, Harding, I have to tell you that I have been comprehensively had over.'

'The bomb was genuine Irish?'

'It was.'

'The Provos?'

'Must be,' Bowers replied angrily. 'For them a very clean solution. They took direct action against a threat to their own organization, and we bloody well did it for them.'

The small group that travelled through Zu ol Faqar excited less attention than their appearance demanded. Osama bin Laden bent in defeat, face and clothes filthy, eyes hollow and sad, was a picture of such dejection that no one recognized him for who he was.

If he looked like a beaten man he didn't feel that way. His forlorn look came only from his deep thoughts as he calculated his strengths and weaknesses. A glance behind would have shown the still smoking ruins of his specialist training centre on the hillside above the lake, a pile of rubble full of the bodies of his best fighters, the ruins of his equipment and the death of a great part of his hopes.

But not all of them. The Americans would wonder if he was dead or alive. They would not hear the truth from him. He had other houses, and communications could be re-established. The world was full of the followers of the faith, and his head lifted as he mouthed softly the words which lifted his spirits.

'Allah will prevail.'